Two things happened at once. Kallow punched his palm in Kali's direction, letting fly, and at the very same time the runic pattern completed, the door it surrounded sliding open with a hiss. Kali coughed and gagged as a noxious cloud – the product of the plants and gods knew what other strange materials that had rotted inside the room for years – erupted into the air outside.

Gas. And a lot of it.

The fireball never reached her. It ignited the cloud as soon as it left Kallow's hand and the space between them was engulfed in a sheet of flame that blew her pursuers off their feet, turning them into fireballs themselves. Only Munch escaped the worst of the blast, but even he was slammed across the chamber floor some fifty feet, bouncing and rolling, smoking and charred, even further beyond that.

"I told you you were making a mistake," Kali said.

An Abaddon Books™ Publication
www.abaddonbooks.com
abaddon@rebellion.co.uk

First published in 2008 by Abaddon Books™, Rebellion Intellectual
Property Limited, Riverside House, Osney Mead, Oxford, OX2 OES, UK.

Distributed in the US by National Book Network, 4501 Forbes
Boulevard, Suite 200, Lanham, MD, 20706, USA.

10 9 8 7 6 5 4 3 2 1

Editor: Jonathan Oliver
Cover: Mark Harrison
Design: Simon Parr & Luke Preece
Marketing and PR: Keith Richardson
Creative Director and CEO: Jason Kingsley
Chief Technical Officer: Chris Kingsley
Twilight of Kerberos™ created by Matthew Sprange
and Jonathan Oliver

ISBN: 978-1-905437-75-7

Printed in Denmark by Norhaven A/S

TWILIGHT of KERBEROS

THE CLOCKWORK KING OF ORL

Mike Wild

WWW.ABADDONBOOKS.COM

For Doreen – My Wife and Life

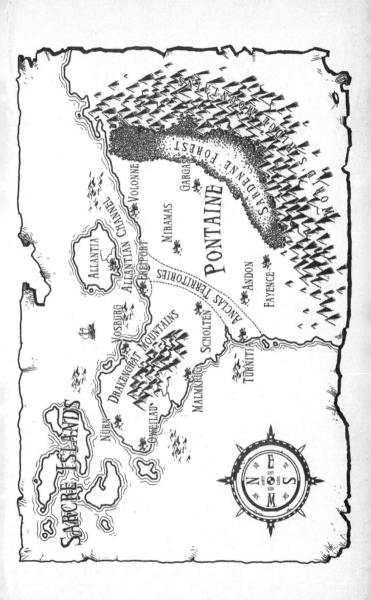

CHAPTER 1

The beast craved flesh.

There, within the dark depths of the Sardenne Forest, that primal place curving like a great black bow beneath the frozen and fiery peaks of the World's Ridge Mountains, at the eastern edge of the peninsula, where civilisation stopped, the beast rolled insane and bulbous eyes, ground together huge and slavering jaws, and with a ravenous snort slowly advanced on the human it knew to be helpless before it.

The dark-maned young woman stood with her hands on the waist of her billowing squallcoat, head cocked to the side, weighing up the heavy creature as it came. She stood her ground, boots planted firmly against the foetid night winds of the forest, feeling her soles tremble as the ponderous beast thudded closer, unflinching despite the fact she was unarmed and facing it alone. There was no one nearby to help her. No one, in fact, anywhere within leagues of her, for this was a place humans rarely trod, and where the ones who had come before the humans had not trodden for countless aeons, since their civilisations had gone. She had long ago left behind what settlements dotted the edge of this dark expanse, long ago passed the silent stares and downed tools of their inhabitants as she moved between their homes and on into the darkness. Even those hardened woodcutters only ventured into the forest's outlying regions, and only then under the guard of their best fighting men, men who kept watchful eyes – and readied weapons – trained on the shadows that gathered about them. Beyond, the forest was considered impenetrable, and those who sought to prove otherwise – those who invariably never returned – to be foolhardy in the extreme. So it was the Sardenne had remained all but unexplored. The oldest of evils were said to lurk within its dark depths, and tales were told – in hushed tones, behind bolted doors – of creatures fantastic and terrifying that wandered there, waiting to corrupt or devour any intruder who entered their lair.

The young woman was not foolhardy but she was determined. By now, she had been travelling for three days, ever inwards, and so by all measures of the forest's dangers should be dead – or worse. With stealth, forestcraft and some alchemical guile, however, she had managed to evade the attentions of its darker denizens, though she had lost count of the times roars, rattles, whispers or blood-curdling screeches had alerted her to their presence, close by, in the darkness around her.

The darkness. What passed for night on the rest of Twilight – the haunting, azure halflight filtered through the gas giant Kerberos – was here more akin to longnight, the greater darkness that only occurred when, four times a year, the world's distant sun passed behind Kerberos and the eclipses came. It was worse than longnight, in truth, because while then the grey and silver-streaked surface of the looming giant could still be discerned above her, here the forest's canopy was almost total, as smothering and as dark as an oubliette.

Dark, that was, apart from the moist whiteness of the eyes of the beast, glittering, demanding saucers that had grown ever closer and loomed before her now. Yes, she might have made it this far but this was a confrontation she could not avoid. This particular beast would not allow her to progress until it had taken everything she had, its unnatural hunger sated.

She let it come, one hand slipping into a pocket of her squallcoat and wrapping itself in readiness around a small round object hidden within. Seeing her movement, and perhaps suspecting something, the beast reared its head and snorted steam from dark and expansive nostrils, and on the end of a thick, anvilled snout a pair of huge and fleshy lips curled back to reveal an array of tombstone teeth that, exposed in this way, appeared to grin as insanely as the bulbous eyes had rolled. The young woman steeled herself, her hand ready, but then without warning the beast lurched forwards and a slimy tongue the size of a rowing boat paddle slapped across her face. She batted it away, gagging and recoiling from a blast of foetid breath, took a step back and, with a groan of disgust, wiped a sliding patch of viscous slobber from her cheek and the lapel of her squallcoat. She flicked it to the ground with a grimace, shaking her hand until all of it was gone. *Gods, that was disgusting!*

Kali Hooper sighed.

"I taught you to wait," she said, exasperated. "All right, fine, okay. But this is the last, you hear me?"

The beast whinnied, nodding its head rapidly, and Kali

produced the round object from her pocket, a lardon of bacon she tossed towards it. The meat hit the beast's snout, from where, its party trick, it was deliberately bounced back into the air before being caught in the huge mouth then manoeuvred beneath it. The beast rolled its insane eyes again and chomped down gratefully, drooling copiously as it ate.

"Those things will make you fat, Horse, you know that?" Kali said. "*Eff – ay – tee.*" She punctuated the letters with hearty slaps to the shire's thick neck, prompting a head-butting that almost pushed her over. "What use will you be then, you obese lump? Going to be you riding me to the Spiral, is it?"

The Spiral, Kali thought, and sighed again. The truth was, she'd be happy lugging Horse there if only she could find the damned thing. She slapped his neck a final time and slumped herself down at the base of a tree, once again unfolding the map she'd paid fifty full silver for from a contact in Turnitia some weeks before. Focusing on it in the dimness, she made a tired, brubbing sound with her lips. Acquired from a collection whose legal ownership she wasn't privy to, the old and hand-drawn map purported to show the whereabouts of an Old Race site whose name she'd translated as the Spiral of Kos. She'd had her doubts about the map's provenance at the time but had handed over her money not because of what the Spiral of Kos was – frankly, she hadn't a clue – but rather its location here in the deeps of the Sardenne. Its very inaccessibility meant the site was likely untouched, and potentially that made it – and what it might contain – her most interesting find yet. Trouble was, authentic or not, the map was not to scale, and having found nothing so far she now had to decide whether to venture deeper into the forest, knowing that there lay Bellagon's

Rip, reputed to be the stomping ground of the Pale Lord himself. While she didn't have any problem with that wayward necromancer – as long as he left her alone – she had to admit the vast army of undead under his command gave her pause for thought. If she wanted to spend the rest of her existence staggering around gibbering, she'd rather just be permanently betwattled, thank you very much.

Kali wished she could have a drink right there. Her chosen lifestyle – what she liked to think of as athletic archaeology – was one hells of a way to make a living.

She started. She had been so absorbed in her thoughts she had almost missed the fact that some thing had moved in the nearby undergrowth just then, something that alerted her with a crack of wood and a flash of something... *chitinous* at the edge of her vision. She instantly tensed, hunched to make herself small, and her eyes darted from left to right in her otherwise frozen form. *Dammit,* she thought – she'd broken her own golden rule, grown too complacent, stayed in one place too long. What was worse, she'd only just noticed that in wiping off some of Horse's drool she'd also smeared away some of the floprat render with which she'd been coating her squallcoat to deceive curious noses, and in doing so had released a whiff of her own human scent.

Humans were a delicacy here, and a whiff was enough. Whatever was in the bushes had found her because of it. And whatever it was, it wasn't friendly.

Kali didn't hang around, springing gymnastically onto Horse's back. Behind her, heralded by a sudden flight of panicked shrikes, she saw not one but maybe three predators – it was difficult to tell – glistening, angular carapaced things that reared out of the undergrowth on stickwood legs, and then in total silence, bar a sound like baby bones snapping, folded themselves around the trees towards her. Kali had no idea what the things were, and didn't want to know – and neither did Horse.

Her entreaty of "Go, go, go!" was entirely redundant as the great beast had also spotted the monstrosities and, with a panicked bray, was off, not at anything that could be described as a gallop but building his own hulking momentum, designed to get him and Kali the hells out of there, whether there were trees in the way or not. The pair ploughed ahead, gaining a few seconds as their predators sniffed at what Horse had involuntarily left behind, but then they could be heard behind them once more, folding and snapping themselves through the forest in a determined and slowly accelerating pursuit.

Accelerating some himself now, Horse thudded blindly on, neither he nor Kali caring where they headed. But then the pair of them broke through, suddenly, into an unexpectedly treeless area of the forest, a large glade where the canopy opened to the sky. Despite the openness the place was almost unnaturally still, thick with lazily hovering insects and bestrewn with strange vines that covered the ground and crawled in a tangle over a central low but sweeping hill. Kali urged Horse on towards the rise, reasoning that if they could make it to the top she might be able to make a stand against their pursuers. But just before they began to climb, she threw a glance backwards and saw that though they had emerged into the glade they had ceased their chase, having come to a sudden stop at the edge of the trees. A nervous twisting and cracking of their chitinous forms suggested that for some reason they were wary of going on, and then they actually skulked away, back into the forest. Kali was so distracted by the development that it took her a moment to realise that Horse had stopped just as suddenly as they had.

Horse? she thought, but that was all, as the direct consequence of him halting so abruptly was that she was thrown out of her saddle and over his head. Kali's world turned upside down, and for a moment all she could see was the dizzyingly swooping sky, and then she landed hard on the slope of the hill, flat on her back, with an *ooff* and a crack that sounded like her spine had snapped in two. She lay where she was, stunned, while her brain tried to reorientate itself inside her skull. Rather ominously, she was dimly aware that Horse had begun to bray and snort and back away behind her.

Surprisingly, she found she could move – but when she did, stopped doing so immediately. There had been another crack beneath her, sounding this time not like her spine but the fracturing of ice on a frozen lake. It happened again – *kuuchruuck!* – and Kali hissed in a sharp breath as the slope shifted beneath her, a drop of perhaps only half an inch but one that felt so vertiginous it made her heart lurch. She didn't think twice, somersaulting from where she crouched, feeling the ground give again as she rolled to where Horse circled nervously below her.

What in all the pits of Kerberos – ?

Panting, Kali picked herself up and turned to look where she had fallen. The hill before her had looked solid enough but evidently wasn't, and had to be why both Horse and their chitinous friends had refused to go on. That, or they sensed something else. She had to admit the glade had a strange feel to it, a sense of something dormant and waiting, undisturbed for lifetimes. Something old.

Something old!

Kali felt a buzz of excitement – maybe, at last, she'd found something. Maybe. She calmed Horse then took off her squallcoat and tossed it over his saddle, revealing beneath the shnarl-hide working gear she'd had made in Freiport a couple of years earlier. The figure-hugging outfit, bespoke-tailored with artefact pockets on its arms and legs, was showing its age as well as some of her it shouldn't, but Kali didn't care, the kinds of places she wore it being well away from public gaze. She was rather fond of it, actually, as every tear or gash and every blood-stained hole brought its own memory. Around its waist she strapped a leather toolbelt she took from a saddlebag, and then to that a rope she took from another, securing the opposite end to the nub of the saddle itself. In the absence of trees in the glade, Horse would serve as an anchor for her safety rope. It wasn't the first time she had used his bulk in such a way.

Kali returned near to the spot where she'd been thrown, then knelt and swept her hand back and forth to brush away tiny plants and topsoil, creating an arc of investigation. The surface was thin and came away with surprising ease, and she realised this was because there was nowhere for roots to take hold. There was metal beneath. Riveted metal. By the look of it, some kind of supporting rib.

She sat back, surprised and confused. Not only because of the incongruous presence of the rib but the fact that metal would not have cracked beneath her the way she had felt the ground do. It was doubly odd. Checking the tightness of the rope, she inched her way up the rib until she overlooked the exact point where she had fallen, and again swept her hand back and forth. This time the topsoil offered absolutely no resistance at all, sliding away and trickling down to form a heap at the base of the hill. What lay beneath made her breath catch – a shiny, dark material as smooth as glass other than where hairline fractures marred it, fresh fractures that wouldn't be there except for her own ignominious crash-landing. She stroked the surface with her palm, realising two things. The material itself wasn't dark, it just had darkness beneath it. And it wasn't glass – it was crystal.

Kali stood, puzzling over what she'd found when she heard a shifting above her, and suddenly the trickle of soil about her feet became a small flood. She looked up and saw that where she'd wiped away the topsoil she had, in turn, disturbed the soil above it, and it, too, had begun to slip towards her. And with it gone, everything above had become unstable.

Horse brayed, hung his head and looked at her with chastising eyes. She'd caused a landslide. The entire bloody hill was coming down.

"Ohhh, bugger!" Kali said.

She staggered back along the metal, trying to get out of the way as the mass of soil and roots came crashing past her to the forest floor, almost dragging her off her feet and choking her in a dense, fibrous fog. She waded against the thick tide for what seemed like an eternity, and when, finally, it ceased, and its cloud had dispersed, found herself staring up at what remained.

Her mouth dropped open.

The hill hadn't collapsed, only the detritus with which nature had hidden what it really was over the course of long, long years. And now, rising away from her and sweeping off to her left and right, was a dome.

A vast, ornately ribbed, crystal dome.

Kali's heart thudded. Steaming pits of Kerberos, she had never seen anything like this!

There was no question about what to do next. She had to find out what was inside. Unlacing a pouch on her toolbelt, Kali dug through various odds and ends, took out a small hammer and clambered back up the rib to where she had knelt earlier, intending to tap the fractured crystal to create an exploratory hole. But as she raised the hammer to strike she felt tugs on the rope about her waist, minor at first but then hard enough to actually jerk her off balance. Unusually for Horse, it seemed he was getting skittish. But turning to see what the matter was, Kali realised Horse was more than skittish, he was clopping about in considerable agitation.

She looked past him and saw why. Something was coming at them out of the trees – *fast*. They must have worked up some courage because their friends were back with a vengeance.

There was no time to act, no time to hide, no time to dodge – Kali didn't even have time to brace herself. The chitinous things came swooping around Horse and straight at her, folding and flapping and then slamming into her with a speed that knocked the wind from her lungs. Their intent was presumably to pin her to the ground where they could rip her apart but, of course, there was no ground and, with a sound like a shocked and sibilant hiss, Kali and her three assailants crashed into and through the surface of the dome.

All four plummeted into blackness – Kali backwards with the things clinging on to her front – falling helplessly amidst countless shards of the partly shattered dome. Under different circumstances Kali might have found the susurrating crystal rain surrounding her mesmerising, but she was too busy bracing herself to hit the ground beneath the dome to pay much attention. No impact came, however, and she realised the dome must enclose something more than the forest floor itself – but what? For a moment she forgot the rope, imagined herself plunging ever downwards into some unknown abyss, but then the rope reached maximum length and she came to a halt with a whiplash jerk that made her internal organs collide and winded her worse than the folding bastards had moments before. Those same things, which until that moment still clung tenaciously to her front, triangular maws trying to snap at her face, were wrenched from her and tumbled away screeching, down and down into the dark. Seconds passed and then she heard the sound of three impacts from somewhere far below.

Kali groaned and hung where she'd halted, limp as a discarded doll, rotating slightly, the rope creaking above her in the silence that followed the fall. A dot in darkness, her head flopped backwards, she stared down into a vast and circular subterranean chamber lit vaguely by the half-light penetrating the broken dome. Whatever the place was, it seemed deserted and utterly still – the only movement motes agitated by her intrusion bouncing in the air – and the centre of it was dominated by a strange, shadowy mass that the whole structure seemed to have been built around. Also circular and broad at the base, but tapering gradually with greater and greater height, it rose towards her from the chamber floor like some huge ant hill – a hill within a hill – ever upwards, almost as far as the lip of the dome itself. It was a dizzying sight, especially when viewed upside down, and while Kali hadn't the faintest idea what it was, she did know she wanted a closer look.

The air in the chamber – *old air*, the kind she liked – acted on her like smelling salts and she snapped to, realising she had to find a way down from where she hung. But that was going to be easier said than done. Even if she whistled Horse to the edge of the dome, the rope on which she dangled was nowhere near long enough to reach the top of the mass, let alone the chamber floor, and unless she was going to be happy taking home memories of a bird's eye view of... wherever she was, she was going to have to find another way to descend. She pulled herself upright and turned on the rope, eyeing her surroundings, and had gone almost full circle before her gaze lit upon what looked like a platform, metal and ornately railed, running like a stretched-out horseshoe along the curving upper chamber wall. Some fifty feet away and below her, it would do as a start. It looked like one hells of a jump, however, and in taking it Kali knew she'd be committing herself to a descent with no return, because there was no way she'd be able to reach the rope again.

But she hadn't come all this way for nothing, and as Horse was probably getting a little disgruntled holding her dead weight, why not do him a favour and lighten his load? Besides, whoever had built this place must have built it with a front door, and in her experience of these old sites front doors were always easier to find from the inside than from the out.

Decided, Kali detached the rope from her belt and began to swing back and forth, building up an arc of momentum that would allow her to make the jump. She continued to swing until she had reached her desired speed and apex, and then with a determined cry let go of the rope. She flew, arcing through the air and then dropping, and landed hard on the platform, rolling to lessen her impact. Lessened or not, there was an eruption of dust and a loud metallic clang that echoed around the ancient chamber, quieting only after Kali thought she might go deaf. She very much doubted anyone was home but, if they were, they now sure as hells knew she'd come to visit.

All remained still and Kali stood, cautiously at first, but then, realising what she stood upon, throwing caution to the wind and instead grabbing the ornate railing to stare down, amazed. Still high above the chamber floor, the platform was clearly built for observation, and what it observed was the strange mass that dominated the place – the hill within a hill. Only it was no hill, she could see now, but a huge and vertiginous, winding metal stairway.

Kali swallowed because it really couldn't be anything else.

She was looking at the Spiral of Kos.

It was as incredible as it was mystifying. Overlooking its summit – still impossible to reach from where she stood – the dizzying structure was constructed in the same ornate fashion as the railing on which she leant, the steps of the stairway itself spiralling up inside a superstructure composed of flowing and curving ironwork the likes and artistry of which she had never seen. What drew her attention more than anything, however, was where the stairway led. Because there, at its top, completely isolated from the rest of the chamber, was another railed platform, and on it a large metal plinth.

And resting on the plinth was a giant key.

A key! Oh, she loved keys. Kali had no idea why it was there, where it had come from or what it unlocked, but she was certain of one thing – she wasn't leaving until she had it in her hands.

She turned, meaning to find a way off the platform and down to the first of those stairs, but as she did she caught a hint of movement from the Spiral itself. She turned back and squinted. Her eyes more adapted to the gloom, she noticed for the first time that the superstructure had apparently once housed some kind of hanging garden, for the dry and neglected remains of plants – thick tendrils and a number of presumably once-corpulent pods – still draped it now. That explained things. Perhaps one of those had shifted slightly in a draught from above – or then again, perhaps it had been nothing. A trick of the light.

Kali moved off the rail, searching for the way down that had to be there. Oddly, though, she found no connecting walkways, no ladders, no obvious way off the platform at all other than a small gate that led to... well, she wasn't sure what it led to. But as she walked closer, she felt a glimmer of recognition. The gate led to a cage, large enough that she could, if she so wished, step inside and which had a single entrance-cum-exit. Though it was different in many respects – more ornate, more complex, more *mechanical*-looking – it was clearly a version of the devices in use in the more industrialised areas of Vos – hoists and pulleys that had once lifted warehouse materials but now lifted men. Was that what this was, then? A... *lift* that could transport her off this platform? If so, where was the rope or chain suspending it? Curious, she leant around the edge of the cage, examining it more closely, and saw that though there was nothing to suspend it from above, the rear of the cage was secured to a thick metal arm that rested in the upper of two wide recesses in the chamber wall, recesses that swept away and down the wall in a reverse spiral to that of the Spiral itself, vanishing into the shadows below.

It had to be the way down. But after ages of disuse, could she trust it? Would the thing even *work?*

There was only one way to find out. Kali opened the gate and stepped warily into the cage, feeling for any kind of shift beneath her feet, all too aware that under the suspended floor there was nothing but a long, long drop. But she found it solid enough and so turned and closed the gate.

Kali waited. Nothing happened.

She waited more, and still nothing, and she frowned.

Then she spotted a dust-shrouded lever on the wall of the cage next to where she had entered. Some kind of switch? Swallowing, she laid her hand on the lever and pulled it down. There was an empty clank.

Again, nothing happened – for a moment. Then, from somewhere inside the walls of the vast chamber, machinery that Kali knew to be older than her civilisation groaned as it stirred into life, filling the place with a bass cacophony as if it were haunted suddenly by its builders' ghosts. The noise resounded around the chamber, growing in volume until Kali felt the walls themselves rumble, and then silence descended abruptly and unexpectedly once more. *Dammit*, Kali thought.

And then the cage lurched.

Nothing could have prepared her for what happened next, and for a few exhilarating seconds she knew fully why she pursued the things she did. This was Old Race technology she was using, the first living being to have done so in perhaps a thousand years or more, and it was working.

Oh gods, was it working!

Kali laughed out loud.

The cage in which she stood released itself from the platform and swept majestically down along the chamber wall as if it floated freely in the air, the movements of the mechanisms that propelled it barely discernible at all. The passage down the spiralling recess afforded her a constantly rotating view of the Spiral of Kos, travelling so smoothly she could have been flying around it. Down and down and round and round she went, ducking involuntarily as, at what she guessed must have been the halfway point, a vast counterweight swept up the lower recess and beneath the cage with a heavy *whooooshh* that seemed to take the air away.

Kali watched the counterweight rise away and whooped, the magnitude of what was happening – what she'd found – hitting home. Her biggest find yet, *all* of this was hers to explore, and hers alone, the first person to tread within these walls since its Old Race occupants had gone. *All* of this – and that mysterious key.

Gods!

She looked down, almost clapping in anticipation of the cage berthing into a lower platform, and then she saw the light.

Her heart thudded.

It was hardly anything, a flare of whiteness perhaps two hundred feet below, but it was what the flare illuminated that was important.

People.

There were people below.

It couldn't be.

Kali stared at the shadowed figures, unable to distinguish who or what they were, only that a small group were crossing the chamber floor towards the base of the Spiral of Kos, their way lit by the raised hand of one of them. A glowing hand. Were they Old Race? Was it possible that some of them were still alive? Was it possible she was looking down at the builders? *It couldn't be. It just couldn't.*

One thing was clear. The cage in which she stood was going to deliver her right into their midst. And she couldn't chance that, having no idea if they were friend or foe.

Kali did the only thing she could. She rammed the lever back into its original position and, with a protesting groan, the cage lurched to a sudden halt, throwing her hard against its side. The groan caused the figures below to look up, and Kali threw herself to the cage floor, crawled to its edge and peered down, relieved as she saw them turn away. She'd been lucky – it seemed the figures had dismissed the noise as unexplained.

Nevertheless, she was too exposed where she was. All it would take to reveal her presence above them was another curious glance at the lift, a whim. She had to get out of there and down – and quickly. Keeping her eyes on the unknown group, she crouched and then swung herself quietly out of the front of the cage, twisting so that she could grab onto its side, and from there swung herself onto the metal arm on which it rode. Then she worked her way into the recess, wide and deep enough to accommodate her crouching form. Using it to get down would still leave her exposed but if she kept in its shadows, and her luck held, she would make it unseen.

She began to inch her way down towards the chamber floor. She had perhaps a hundred, a hundred and thirty feet to go.

And it was then that the vision hit her.

Searing agony cut through her mind, as if someone had embedded an axe in her forehead, and suddenly her world was yellow and red and white, everything the colour of raging fire. What had been a shadowy, abandoned chamber a moment before was now consumed by a blaze apocalyptic in intensity, the Spiral of Kos being destroyed in a conflagration beyond imagining. Things lashed and writhed within the flames – strange things that she had no time to identify before agonised screams swept them away. For a second she was outside the dome, staring as a pillar of fire rose high above the darkness of the Sardenne, and then she was back once more, in the fire's raging heart, in its midst. It couldn't be real but it was. She didn't just see it, she could *feel* it, the heat from the fire strong enough to sear and bubble her skin and to blind her with its bright, bright heat. *What the hells am I seeing?* she wondered. *What the hells am I feeling?*

Instinctively she flailed against it, and in that second realised where she was. Where she *really* was.

But it was too late. Her flailing had taken her too far towards the edge of the recess, beyond balance.

She tumbled out, and fell.

And when she landed, the fire faded to blackness.

And, as shadows loomed over her, so, too, did she.

CHAPTER 2

Kali felt something thudding again and again into her side and, with slowly growing awareness and annoyance, realised that it was a boot. Her eyes snapped open just in time to see the offending article coming at her again, and she instinctively grabbed and twisted it, flipping its wearer heel-over-head to the accompaniment of a startled cry.

"Don't do that!" she growled, without even thinking who it was she might be talking to.

Great, she thought, reprimanding herself. Possible first contact with an Old Race and what does she do? Fling one of them on its arse.

She sat quickly up, bruised, throbbing and disorientated, and looked around. There was no more fire – no more vision – but neither any time to think about where it had come from or where it had gone as the wearer of the boot, a cloaked and hooded figure, had also risen and, snarling, loomed over her again, boot swinging back for another strike.

Kali was about to kick his legs from under him and punch his lights out when a hand moved across the figure's chest and pushed him back to where others stood silently looking down at her.

"Enough, brother," a gruff voice said. "Do you not see that our visitor from on high is awake?"

"My apologies... *brother.*"

The speaker, becloaked and hooded like the rest, knelt by Kali, sighing as if somehow inconvenienced by her presence. The man was short, more accurately squat, and thickly muscled, his powerful bulk evident even beneath the loose folds of his cloak. Pulling back his hood he revealed a mane of grey hair flaring back from a face that was gnarled and scarred, inset with the coldest, grey-tinted eyes she had ever seen. Whoever he was, Kali thought, if he didn't have some Old Race blood in him – and she knew *which* Old Race – then her name was Fundinblundin Hammerhead.

"Who are you?" the man asked slowly. His tone, civilised, patient and polite, was totally at odds with his appearance. "And what is it you are doing here?"

Old Race blood, but not Old Race, Kali decided, ignoring his question for a moment. The thought that had struck her before her fall – that some of the builders might still be alive – had never really been likely – next to impossible, actually – and now that she'd had chance to see these people close to, it only confirmed the fact. But though their origin was far more prosaic, who these people were came as only slightly less of a surprise than the alternative. Six of them in all, their garb, speech and, most of all, the crossed-circle talismans they wore pinned to their sleeves, left no doubt as to their identity. This bunch were Final Faith, members of the most pervasive, most consuming and most intolerant religion to blight the peninsula, zealots to every woman and every man.

They were not her favourite people.

That, however, was immaterial right now.

What *was* material was the obvious question. What the hells were the Final Faith doing in the Spiral of Kos?

The key. It seemed to be the only thing in the place so it had to be the key.

Well, if that was the case... Sorry, but she'd got here first.

"I asked you a question, girl," the apparent leader reminded her. His tone had already hardened somewhat.

Girl? Kali thought, and stared at him. "Oh, you know," she said innocently, "went for walk in the woods, got lost, fell down a sodding great hole..."

The man nodded then abruptly tugged her toolbelt from her waist, tipping out the contents of some of its pockets. Kali shrugged as he picked through a selection of pitons, hammers, clamps and other excavation gear, regarding her questioningly when he also came upon some marbles, a sock and a mouldy, half-eaten pie. Okay, so maybe she should have a clearout once in a while.

"Impressive tools for a walk in the woods," Mister Nosey nevertheless concluded. He glanced over at the broken, shard-covered bodies of the stickthings, which coincidentally she seemed to have landed on or nearby. "You managed to survive three brackan, too. Equally impressive."

Brackan, eh? Kali thought. *Have to remember that.* "Yeah, well, I –"

"You are intruding here!"

The statement came so suddenly and so forcefully that it threw her off guard.

"Excuse me?"

"Intruding. This... *reliquary* is under the jurisdiction of the Final Faith."

"Oh, really?" Kali said, bristling. "And since when did your little glee-club extend to the Sardenne?"

The man smiled coldly. "Since my arrival here."

Kali stared. She was only just getting over the shock that she had survived that fall – and its cause – let alone finding she had company, but one thing was already abundantly clear to her – this man was serious. And despite his superficial civility, he was dangerous. She could feel it exuding from his every pore.

The fact didn't stop her speaking up, though. That was her trouble, people kept telling her, though it never did any good.

"Well, then – you're a little off the beaten path, aren't you, *priest?*"

The man's hand – leather-gloved – shot out without warning and clenched itself about her neck. Kali gasped and fumbled to release its grip, but it was strong. Very strong.

The man stood, and, her throat constricting, she actually found herself being lifted from the floor.

"My name," he told her, "is Konstantin Munch, and despite your disdain I am not one of the Enlightened Ones." He used the phrase that described the Final Faith's priesthood with a degree of disdain of his own, which she found peculiar. "I am, however, an agent of that church, acting on its behalf and that of the Anointed Lord, and so I ask you again – *what are you doing here?*"

"Actually, I... bought the place," Kali rasped, choking. She hung a hand vaguely in the direction of the Spiral and its dead plants, twitched it. "Thought I'd open a herbalist's emporium but... was never very... green-fingered."

Munch's hand tightened, the leather squeaking. "Ah, I see."

"And you?" Kali ventured. "Mind... telling me what... you're... *kaa-hurr*... doing here?"

"Actually, yes. Why don't we just say that my friends and I were led here by the Lord of All."

No surprise, there, Kali thought. These people did everything in his – *god's, her? Its?* – name, including all the sacking, raping and pillaging, by some accounts. But Lord of All or not, something had led Munch and his mates to the Spiral's front door, when even her map hadn't been specific about its location. And though she found it difficult to believe, she thought she knew what.

She flicked a pained gaze – already flaring and soon to blink out, if she wasn't careful – to the side, examining Munch's companions again. Sure enough, the clenched fists of one of them still pulsated ever so slightly with the aftermath of energy release – the same release, presumably, that had lit up the floor of the chamber earlier. She couldn't see much of his face beneath its hood, only that it seemed harsh, thin and sallow, but there was an overly intense penetration about the shadowed eyes that Kali had seen once before, and cared not to remember. They were the eyes of someone who would normally be denounced by the Final Faith. Eyes that stared out not only at this world but beyond, into another layer of being. Eyes that saw the threads of the universe, used them and followed them. The eyes of a –

"Shadowmage?" Munch said, sensing her recognition and puzzlement. He smiled, bobbing her dangling and struggling form almost playfully towards the mage in question. "The young lady wonders not only why we are here but why one such as I is in league with one such as you, Kallow," he said. "Are you offended?" Turning his attention back to Kali, he added, "Unusual, I grant you, but let's just say the Anointed Lord allows me some... latitude in my choice of companions, depending on the task she has set for me."

"Tashk?" Kali enquired, the one word all she could manage now. She could feel her eyes bulging painfully and her tongue thick between her lips.

Munch shrugged modestly, making her bob again. "Certain errands of import – troubleshooting, damage-control, the *elimination* of various problems." He smiled as he stressed the word before tossing Kali to the floor, where she scrambled back. "Whatever it is, in fact, the Anointed Lord wishes me do."

Kali hacked rawly, rubbing her throat, trying to ignore the pounding in her skull as blood rushed back into her brain. The man had almost killed her just then, and she had little doubt that was his ultimate intent, especially as he had just brushed back his cloak to reveal a particularly vicious-looking gutting knife.

"Last chance, girl, as I have no time for inconveniences. What is it that you are doing here?"

Kali thought fast. After that little ordeal, she was still too dizzy to run and too weak to defend herself, and so the only possible way out of this was to bluff. The question was, with what? It would have helped if Munch had given her a clue as to why he and his people were here, because without that juicy tidbit it would be so easy to say the wrong thing.

But then it struck her. Why was Munch so interested in what *she* was doing here? Surely that was obvious? Given that he hadn't just stumbled across the place, could it be that he'd come to the Spiral for the key without knowing what he'd find when he arrived? That he thought she knew something about the Spiral that might help? If that was the case, maybe he didn't know everything about the key itself.

It was something she could work with. A gamble, but worth the ante. If nothing else, it would buy her time.

"All right, all right!" she coughed. "The truth is, I came here for the... romfiffelypop."

Munch's eyes narrowed. "The romfiffelypop?"

Kali looked at him in a way that suggested everyone knew what the romfiffelypop was, then pointed towards the Spiral. "The *key*, dammit! I've been searching for it for years."

One of Munch's people – a woman by the sound of it – made a *pishing* sound, but Munch ignored her.

"The key?" he said, evenly. "Forgive me, I have never heard it called by that name."

Kali just knew she had him on the hook and shook her head wearily. "You wouldn't. It's an ancient Varondian dialect – a tribe in the Drakengrat Mountains – long extinct." *Oh, good one*, she thought.

"Is it, now? I see. And you are something of an expert in these matters?"

Kali nodded. "I've been around a bit, seen some things." She thought of others who did what she did, mainly blundering vandals – *tomb raiders* – in it solely for the money from the artefact trade. "The name's Orlana Dawn."

Munch pursed his lips, nodding. "Tell me, *Orlana* – have you experience of whirling blades, shooting spikes, rolling boulders, lava tiles and other lethal, death-dealing traps, triggers and devices?"

What? Kali thought. *Was that meant to be some kind of joke?* Sure, she'd come upon one or two 'protective measures' in her time but, for the most part, she'd had more problems with animals around the sites than anything inside them. Truth was, most contained nothing worth trapping at all.

"Why?" she asked, suspiciously. "Should I be?"

"We have encountered some such hazards recently. There is a possibility we may encounter some today."

Kali realised he was being serious, and couldn't help but be intrigued – where the hells had these people been? "Well, then," she said, "I'm your man."

Once again, the woman made a noise, but Munch silenced her with a slice of his hand. For the first time he looked Kali – openly and unashamedly – up and down. "Now," he said, "I know you are lying."

A lech as well as a psychopath, Kali concluded. But at least her gamble seemed to have paid off. For the moment, she would live – an extra member of Munch's team. The fact was, she resented that immensely – the Spiral should have been *hers* – but, on the other hand, she'd bought herself chance to examine it properly for the first time – and maybe when she knew more she could make it hers again. It had to be better than being sliced like a rack of shnarlmeat on the floor.

Munch, his people and Kali moved off across the vast chamber floor, their way lit by a fresh flare of light from the shadowmage. As her feet crunched on crystal shards, Kali looked up at the Spiral, noting the circular runics inscribed on massive plates that ran in a ring beneath the dome, wondering for what mysterious reason the builders had put them there. The sheer scale of what the Old Races had achieved never failed to leave her in awe, and now, with the advantage of this lower perspective, she found herself staring open-mouthed and more awed than ever before. Walking through the Spiral was like walking through a cathedral, a construction of staggering proportions, but however impressive it was, its actual purpose left her puzzled – and a little troubled. Her first thought – that it was some kind of museum – didn't really work, as what kind of museum contained only one exhibit? What, then? Some kind of memorial – but to a *key*? No, it had to be something else. A huge key perhaps suggested some accompanying huge vault, but then she had seen nothing here that a key such as the one atop the Spiral might open, and besides, what kind of vault, whatever its size, left the means to open it on public display?

Okay, so the place was hardly public. The point was, *it didn't make sense.*

The party reached the base of the Spiral and Munch and the others stared up the towering structure, assessing it. But left feeling uneasy by her inability to pin anything down, Kali's gaze was drawn instead to the grey remains of the plantlife that wrapped it, the nagging doubt about what she thought she'd seen earlier returning. As she watched, a tiny triangle of light – *natural light* – lit a patch of the lifeless tendrils and pods.

Kali looked up, blinked. The still-mottled but otherwise soil-free dome had begun to glow, the planet's distant sun rising and shining into that one patch of the Sardenne not obscured by its dark canopy – the clearing above.

Daylight was coming to Twilight.

And with it – in tenuous shafts that must have been intruding here for the first time in long and unknown ages – to the Spiral.

Kali looked down. She couldn't be absolutely sure but it seemed to her that the plants had stirred, as she thought they had earlier.

"*Uurrmm...?*" she said to the others.

Munch had apparently noticed something, too, as he had stepped back. He addressed her directly. "Did you see that, Miss Dawn?"

"I'm not sure," Kali responded. To her eyes, the plants seemed more... *fleshy*, too. "It could be –"

"It's nothing," the woman who'd protested earlier interrupted. "A trick of the light, that's all."

Munch looked again, but the plants – if they *had* moved – were now still once more.

"You are certain?"

"Of course I'm certain," the woman said, stripping off her hood and cloak, "or my name's not Orlana Dawn."

What? Kali thought. *What?* The woman had announced herself so casually that for a moment the name hadn't really registered. But nonetheless Orlana Dawn stood before her now, arms folded and smiling daggers, a buxom blonde putting all the right curves into a dark silk bodysuit. It was of a kind favoured by certain members of Vos and Pontaine's thieves guilds, which she had clearly adopted as her working gear. Kind of appropriate, really.

Still, it had a certain something. What Kali thought was: *I have to get me one of those.* What she said was: "Okay outfit, shame about the ass."

She looked at Munch. He had clearly been playing games from the start, probably even knew fully what the Spiral and the key were.

"If you knew – ?"

"Why didn't I kill you?" Munch answered. He inclined his head to the Spiral. "Frankly, because I do not know what hazards I face here, and I have lost too many people in recent months to waste an extra resource." He sighed lengthily. "The question, therefore, is which one of you goes first?"

"Konstantin!" Orlana Dawn objected.

Another sigh. "It's simple, Orlana. The two of you obviously share a passion for this kind of thing, but

34

I have no idea which of you is the most competent at handling it. If I send you first, and you die, I send her in with the knowledge gained of what killed you. Or, I send her first and –"

"I get the picture," Orlana said. She looked suspicious of him, suddenly. "If she goes first – and succeeds – do I still get paid?"

Munch shrugged. "Sadly, the funds allocated to me are limited."

"Farking poxes from the pits! You're a bastard, Munch, you know that?"

"This I have been told before," Munch rumbled, unconcerned.

Their exchange faded in Kali's ears as her gaze flicked from the tower to the dome, the dome to the tower and back again, already ahead of them and working out what she needed to know. Then it struck her. The Spiral of Kos was no museum, no memorial and no vault, it was a greenhouse – a greenhouse specifically designed around its centrepiece, not the tower but the plants. In reaching that conclusion, however, she was still left puzzled. Because in the middle of the Sardenne Forest, what possible need could there be for *more plants?*

Unless...

"I'll go first," she said, suddenly, and what she hoped was decisively. She had no interest in the money but, as much as she disapproved of Orlana Dawn's motives for doing what she did, if her theory was right, she couldn't let her take the risk.

"Go to hells!" Orlana Dawn hissed at her. "She's a greenhorn, Munch."

"Hey, who are you calling a greenhorn?" Kali objected, despite herself. "The Maze of Moans," she cited, pointing proudly at her chest. "Me."

Orlana Dawn stared at her, momentarily nonplussed.

"Oh, really. How about the Lost Plateau of Thurst?" she retorted, with a snort.

Kali *piffed*. "Couldn't have been that lost. The Booming Room. The Booming Room, eh?"

"Quinking's Depths."

"Quinking's Depths."

"I already said that."

"Third level."

"Impossible. Look, this is my job, you interfering bitch. Konstantin, this is nothing I can't handle –"

"Miss Dawn goes first," Munch declared, putting an end to it. "The real one, that is." He gestured two of his people towards Kali. "In case she is tempted to help, hold the other one."

Kali was grabbed by both arms and struggled as Orlana Dawn sighed with satisfaction. "Munch, this is a mistake," she protested. "Orlana, don't –"

Munch hushed her. "Bring me that key, Miss Dawn," he ordered.

Orlana nodded, and Kali watched helplessly as her rival took one, two, then three tentative steps up the first turn of the Spiral. Even Dawn couldn't fail to notice that the plants *had* filled out somewhat now beneath the strengthening rays of the sun, but other than giving them a cautionary frown she continued slowly upwards, too inexperienced, too stubborn or simply too greedy to back down. As she did, one or two of the pods that Kali could now see formed the hearts of the various sets of tendrils belched something foul-smelling into the air, and Dawn stared down at them, curling her mouth in distaste. She was now past the fifth turn of the Spiral, and halfway round the sixth, and as she concentrated on putting her foot on the next step she failed to notice that some of the tendrils were, with a sound of sucking mud, slithering slowly onto those beneath her.

Kali pulled against her captors, but even if she had been able to break free, knew now that there was nothing she could do. What had become increasingly obvious to her – that the plants weren't dead but long dormant, untended since the demise of the Old Race and deprived of light as nature had reclaimed the dome – was, in truth, academic. What mattered was, reinvigorated, these things had a purpose, a purpose that answered the question of why the Old Race had needed more plants in the Sardenne. Because they weren't plants at all – not *just* plants. They had been grown here as guardians. Guardians of the key.

The Spiral of Kos hadn't been designed as a greenhouse – it had been designed to be a deathtrap.

"Orlana!" she shouted. *"Get down off there – now!"*

But it was too late – had been too late the moment Orlana Dawn had taken her first step onto the Spiral. Too late the moment the sun had begun to rise. And now, as it became fully bathed in light, the plants that covered it thrashed suddenly, shedding the accumulated dust of ages to reveal a horrible glistening green beneath – and the Spiral of Kos exploded into flailing, carnivorous life. Munch stepped back, raising an eyebrow, and motioned to one of his men, who pulled a crossbow from beneath his cloak and began to fire off bolts. Kallow the shadowmage, meanwhile, quickly rewove his threads to produce not light but thrumming balls of flame, pummelling the plants with a barrage of fire. Unfortunately, neither type of missile seemed to have any effect at all.

Orlana Dawn had no chance. Her way down the Spiral was now completely blocked, her way up – and it was still a *long* way up – filled with countless more of the plants that had manoeuvred themselves insidiously beneath her. While those above her snapped downwards like some deadly curtain, lashing themselves tightly about parts of the metalwork before whipping off in search of meatier prey, those below writhed graspingly upwards, slapping, probing and feeling their way around the Spiral like the tentacles of some inverted giant squid. There was nothing Dawn could do, and though she pulled a knife from her bodysuit to defend herself, spinning around and around in panicked circles, it was clearly going to be useless against the thick feelers that surrounded her, seeking out the intruder in their midst. Suddenly one of the tendrils darted at her neck, and though she dodged it, yelling, another darted from behind her to wrap itself quickly and tightly around her waist. Dawn doubled over, not only because she was struggling against its grip but because of the needles that even those below could see spring from it, puncturing both her bodysuit and her flesh. Dawn's mouth opened in surprise, some unknown toxin flooding her body, and as it did the second tendril struck at her neck once more, wrapping itself about her gulping throat as constrictingly as a slave's collar. Dawn jolted, her eyes widening in alarm as needles pierced again. Held in place by the two tendrils, others within reach sought her, found her and gripped by her ankles and wrists as well, and the struggling Dawn was lifted from the Spiral steps like a helpless marionette, tugged in every direction as each tendril sought to claim her for its own. She didn't scream, because she couldn't, whatever toxin had entered her system tainting her veins a pulsing shade of green, sending her into spasm as they poisoned every drop of her blood. It was, in a way, a mercy, because a second later other tendrils whipped in at her, their needles no longer piercing but tearing, ripping away first her bodysuit and, when that was gone, her flesh. Unable to move, unable to utter anything but the merest whimper, only Dawn's eyes reflected the agony of her paralysed and corrupted form as it was taken apart shred by shred. Her body jerked for a while longer but her eyes stared blindly now from a cadaverous skull, and soon after that she was nothing but a bloody skeleton, and then not even that. The pods opened, and, piece by piece, deposited inside by their tendrils, the skeleton, everything that had been Orlana Dawn, was gone.

The plants calmed, and then they were still once again.

A second passed, the remainder of the party staring up at the Spiral in shocked silence. Then Munch coughed and wiped a lump of cheek from his cheek, leaving a bright red smear.

"Well," he said, "that was a new one."

"Orlana was right, you are a bastard," Kali said without emotion. "You *knew* there was something, threw her life away –"

"There is always something," Munch said, wearily. "You just have to find out what. Which is why I am glad of your company today, because it enabled me to send the *stupid* one first. It seems that you are now in the employ of the Final Faith, Miss – ?"

"Kali Hooper. *Remember* it."

"Kali Hooper, good. So, Kali Hooper – explain to me how it is you mean to tackle the little problem that presents itself before us." Konstantin said, throwing her tool belt back to her.

"I don't mean to tackle it at all," Kali responded. "At least, not for you." The truth was, she had already worked out how she might beat this thing, not only for the key but now, also, for the memory of Orlana Dawn, but when she did, it would be on her terms, not those of a certain Konstantin Munch. She'd learned what she needed to know and – it was time to go.

Munch swept back his cloak, revealing the gutting knife once more. Almost friendly in his tone, he sighed and said: "Kali, if I have let you live for nothing, I *will* kill you."

"Stan," Kali replied, going with his familiar name, "you won't get the chance." Her adrenalin built during Dawn's death – the grips of her captors having weakened in shock, anyway – she knew this was her moment, and took it. Slamming her elbow into the stomach of the brother on her right, she doubled him over and flung him round so that his head rammed into the stomach of the one on the left, then booted the first up the backside so the two of them sprawled to the floor in a heap. That done, she ran like hells.

Munch growled, and Kali heard the unsheathing of his knife echo sharply. She also heard him bark orders to Kallow, and suspecting what might come began to weave to the left and right. Sure enough, a second later, fireballs impacted with the ground on either side of her, detonating bits of the floor and following her as she ran. Kali kept weaving and moving, heading for the shadows at the edge of the Spiral's chamber, where the light from the dome did not reach. Crouching and moving as quickly and silently as she could, she began to manoeuvre herself around the rim, searching for the way in that Munch and his cronies must have used. Not that she had any intention of abandoning the place – hells, no, the key was far too interesting for that – but she needed to reach the surface, and Horse, to get more equipment from the saddlebag before she could even attempt to go for it. The fact that the plants' sap made them impervious to flame did not necessarily mean that they were invulnerable to it, and she figured that if she could create a heat that was intense enough she might be able to burn away some of the plants at the summit of the Spiral and lower herself to the key from above. All she needed was the magnifying mirrors she used to illuminate corridors in the darker sites, then using the sun and the crystal of the dome itself...

Kali stopped dead, realising she had just scrambled by a door – not the exit she sought but another door – an arched door, made of crystal like the dome. She rose slowly, the hairs on her neck rising, thrilled not only by the door itself but what she could see through it, shrouded in gloom – workbenches, strange tools, shelves filled with belljars containing the dried remains of plants.

She spun around, flattening her back against the crystal, a thought striking her. And peering along the vast curve of the Spiral's edge she saw what she suspected she might. More doors like this one, that she supposed led to more rooms like the one she had already seen. Yes, it made sense. The plants that protected the Spiral were no natural species, that was certain, so they had to have been cultivated, engineered, maintained. And it was here that that had been done. These rooms were what made the Spiral tick.

It was incredible. She hadn't come across *anything* like this before. This vast place, these rooms, *all* of this effort to protect that key – *why*?

It was possible the room contained a clue. Kali turned back to examine the door, but there seemed no visible way of opening it. It was thicker than the crystal of the dome, too – too thick to smash. Then she noticed that the frame of the door was traced with a faint runic pattern – not a circle like beneath the dome but a squiggle that surrounded it like a vine – and she brushed her fingertips across it experimentally. There was a sound like a long intake of breath, and on the lower left the curls and strokes lit with a brilliant blue light that began to work its way around the frame as if it were somehow loading it with energy.

Kali staggered back, falling onto her rear, staring at the pattern, so stunned that for a second she didn't realise the light of it was illuminating her as if she were experiencing a visitation from the gods. She would have sat there still were it not for the sound of footsteps approaching. She scrambled up and away from the door but it was too late – drawn by the strange spotlight, Munch and his cronies had found her.

Munch stared at the glowing pattern and sighed.

"Miss Hooper, my job is hazardous enough, and I really cannot afford loose cannons," he said matter-of-factly. "Regrettably, then, I must find my own way to the key." He turned to the shadowmage. "Burn her!"

Kallow raised a hand that still flickered from the volley he'd launched earlier, flexing his fingers to combust it anew. Kali stared at the ball of flame that appeared hovering in his palm and backed away, swallowing. This time, there was nowhere to hide.

"No, wait," she said. "You're making a mistake."

"No," Munch said, already walking back towards the Spiral, "meeting me was *your* mistake."

Two things happened at once. Kallow punched his palm in Kali's direction, letting fly, and at the very same time the runic pattern completed, the door it surrounded sliding open with a hiss. Kali coughed and gagged as a noxious cloud – the product of the plants and gods knew what other strange materials that had rotted inside the room for years – erupted into the air outside.

Gas. And a lot of it.

The fireball never reached her. It ignited the cloud as soon as it left Kallow's hand and the space between them was engulfed in a sheet of flame that blew her pursuers off their feet, turning them into fireballs themselves. Only Munch escaped the worst of the blast, but even he was slammed across the chamber floor some fifty feet, bouncing and rolling, smoking and charred, even further beyond that.

"I told you you were making a mistake," Kali said.

She ran – because there was nothing else she could do. Behind her, the open room boomed as the gas remaining within ignited, and Kali felt the floor quake not once but thrice, the explosion starting a chain reaction that was beginning to work its way around each room on the rim of the chamber. As she ducked and weaved, the arched crystal doors blew out of their frames one after the other, shattering around her. Great plumes of flame erupted from where they'd been, carrying inside them vials and bottles that then also shattered, spreading who knew what upon the floor, but something flammable that added to and combined with the plumes to create a ring of fire in the heart of the Spiral – a ring of fire that was rapidly turning into an inferno. Kali looked for the exit, and with relief spotted it, but she did not run towards it yet, instead veering towards Munch, and aiming beyond him. The recovering psychopath loomed before her, and, without even thinking, Kali leapt upwards and somersaulted over his surprised form, twisting in mid-air and plucking his gutting knife from its sheath as she went. It was a move that rather surprised her, too. *Whoahh*, she thought, *you're getting good!*

But she was going to need to be. Because she wasn't leaving without the key.

Okay, it wasn't exactly the plan she'd had in mind,

but the imminent destruction of the Spiral *had* forced a rethink. The sea of flame wasn't killing the plants at the base of the Spiral – not yet – but it wasn't sparing them, either. Already burning furiously beneath the lower steps – and refusing to go away – it had sent them into a sweating, writhing paroxysm that Kali hoped would keep them distracted while she did what she needed to do. Suicide, she knew, but since when had that ever stopped her? And unless she wanted the key to disappear forever in this conflagration, what choice did she have?

She sprinted straight for the Spiral and up, her footfalls clanging rapidly on its steps, gaining as much height as quickly as she could. All around her the lethal vegetation lashed and snapped as though it had a hundred victims in its malignant grip, tendrils twisting and twining with each other all about her, their needles locking and causing sudden, frantic struggles between them. Kali didn't wait around to see which won, the fire hot on her heels, spreading now not only with its own momentum but flicked ever higher by the panicked whiplashing of those plants it had already consumed. It was actually starting to damage them, the tendrils' outer flesh splitting in the intensifying heat, spurting their sap until they became slick with their own green juices. The resultant friction between them made them sound as if they were screaming – and perhaps they were.

Disgusting as it was, the sap was exactly what Kali needed. The acrid smoke that poured now from the plants she could just about cope with, but the heat was another thing, and the sap was as welcome as a mountain waterfall, enabling her to keep going. And keep going she did, using Munch's gutting knife to slice at any tendril that flopped in her path, not so much harming them as batting them out of the way to die. And the Spiral *was* dying, from the bottom up.

Still, it seemed neverending and Kali was starting to think that it would make one hells of a morning workout when, at last, she reached the top.

The key sat on its plinth before her, bigger than it had seemed from above, a peculiar thing – an oddly *disturbing* thing – carved in the style of gristle and bone. But far too unwieldy to carry, especially in current circumstances. Thinking quickly, Kali loosened her toolbelt, slung it over one shoulder, then hefted the key and stuffed it behind the strap.

Hells, it was heavy. But whatever it was, it was hers. She had done it. All she had to do now was get back down.

Kali took in two deep lungfuls of air and was about to begin her descent when the Spiral shifted beneath her. She stumbled and picked herself up. Then the thing shifted again, and she realised what she had been afraid would happen was happening. The heat of the fire was weakening – perhaps even melting – some of the Spiral's lower superstructure, and the whole thing was starting to collapse beneath her.

She looked down. The lower levels were folding in on themselves to create one mass of red-hot metal and superheated mulch. It was a giant furnace in the making.

There was no way down. Unless she got out of there now, the Spiral of Kos would become her funeral pyre.

Kali spun, searching for an alternative route. She could barely see anything, the explosions beneath her growing in their intensity and height. But then above the roar of the flames and the intensity of the heat haze she heard a peculiar clanking, looked down and saw the lift she had abandoned a seeming eternity ago bucking against its brake. But why? Another explosion drew her attention and, looking up, she saw it had reached almost as high as the observation platform – but obviously hadn't been the first explosion to do so – because the lift's counterweight was bucking against its own brake, the rail in which it sat mangled beneath it. And as she watched, the counterweight broke free.

It was coming down.

And as it did, the lift began coming up. *Fast.*

Once again, Kali didn't even think. Acting instinctively, surrounded by fire, the summit of the Spiral ringed by the thrashing tendrils of the last plants to die, she leapt into space, allowing one of the tendrils to smack her away through the air.

And she flew, in exactly the direction she wished. Her trajectory and timing must have been perfect because she slammed onto the lift's roof as it passed her by, falling heavily so as not to slide over the edge.

She stood, legs apart, riding it upwards, the wind of acceleration blowing back her hair.

The counterweight hurtled by like some heavenly hammer.

Kali looked down. In the light of the conflagration, the last thing she saw was the counterweight smashing through the buffers of the lower platform and screeing across the Spiral's floor towards a pursuing and furiously roaring Munch.

And then the lift impacted with the buffers of the upper platform, and she flew again.

Out, through the dome.

Out of the frying pan and into the fire.

CHAPTER 3

Kali had to give Horse his due – the old boy could move when he needed to. When he *really, really, really* needed to. And Hells, did he need to now!

Her explosive departure from the Spiral of Kos had not been quite the relief it should have been. Sure, she had escaped relatively unscathed and, sure, she had been glad to see Horse waiting faithfully where she had left him, but as she had flailed through the air, crash-landed and rolled to what she thought would be safety, what she had not been glad to see was the dome erupting with fire behind her. A great, roiling mass of it, the biggest fire she had ever seen, every second punching explosively higher and higher into the air.

It wasn't the explosions, or the fire, that was the problem – it was what they did. They shook that part of the Sardenne Forest to its core, and lit it up for leagues around. As a result, it seemed that every crawling, slithering, squelching, squawking, flying or ground-pounding denizen that lurked in that vast expanse was coming to see what was going on.

Coming towards *them*.

There was nowhere to hide, the billowing flames casting their light deep under the canopy and making it as clear as day. Kali and Horse were therefore not only able to see what horrors came, they could be seen by the horrors in return.

They were *exposed*. Which meant that if they didn't get out of the forest right away, they would be dead.

"Hyyyah!" Kali shouted, totally unnecessarily, to Horse, as he once again thundered through the trees. He was not so much mount any more as a battering ram, his bulk crashing through wood and foliage, crushing small rocks and undergrowth, uprooting smaller trees. Kali squeezed her calves hard into his flanks and Horse responded without protest, but she could see the sweat breaking out on him and hear how heavily he breathed. She slapped his neck proudly. There'd be one of his favourite bacon stews in this for him – if they made it out alive. *"Hyyyah!"* she shouted again. *"Hyyyah!"*

Kali rode, covering in minutes a distance that, on their way in, had taken half a day. She considered it wise not to look at the creatures they passed, but those she glimpsed out of the corner of her eye were dark, rotting or slimy things, things of bone and things of glowing hide. Those of them that dared an assault, Horse barged through or she booted swiftly away, their tumbling, misshapen forms crashing into their counterparts and torn apart in an instant, for food or for fun. The two of them had to swerve in their flight once as what appeared to be a black puddle oozed up from the forest floor – and then again, narrowly avoiding instant death as a giant fist came swinging down at them from behind the trees.

At last the glow from the conflagration began to fade, and the horrors that surrounded them retreated once more into the dark. Instinctively, Horse slowed, but Kali rode him on for another ten minutes or so before she felt safe enough to rein him around and look back on what they had left behind.

In the distance, visible even through its canopy, a giant pillar of fire still rose above the Sardenne, identical to the one she had seen in the vision that had caused her fall. The moments she spent staring at it were the first chance she'd had time to think about what had happened to her, and she frowned. There was no doubt now that the conflagration she had witnessed was that of the Spiral itself, and that meant she had seen the future – how could that possibly be explained? *Gods*, she thought, *how could the whole bloody day be explained?* Death traps, the Final Faith, the giant key still slung across her back – *everything* about it posed a question.

Thankfully, she knew someone who could help her find the answers. She reined Horse around again, and together the two of them began the long trek back out of the forest. When they emerged from it, she knew, they would be taking the road to Gargas.

Their exit from the Sardenne – and subsequent trek across the eastern plains of Pontaine – took four days, and while it was a relief to be amongst such dramatically different scenery, the endless fields dotted by the occasional hamlet that comprised this far eastern part of the peninsula made for a wearisome journey. But at least Kali was able to make camp each night relieved that she did not have to watch the movements of every shadow, and by the final night's rest she had visibly relaxed.

"You ever wonder, Horse," she mused as she lay by her

campfire nursing her sixth bottle of flummox, "if your ancestors are trotting around, looking down on you from up there?" She was gazing at the azure mass of Kerberos, where, common belief had it, souls went when the body died. There, they were meant to soar in endless majesty through the gas giant's clouds – but only if they'd been good, gods-fearing boys and girls – condemned to its pits, the hells, if they had not. Kali suspected *she* knew where she was going. She took a swig from her bottle and waved it around. "I'm asking only because then they'd have to have been *believers*, wouldn't they? You a believer, Horse? Is there some horsey church you go to when I'm not looking? Where you go clip-clopping up the *neeiigghhve?*" She giggled and yawned, stared at the distant sun. There was an eclipse coming. "No, I'm serious – wouldn't it be nice to just drift around as light as a feather?"

Horse chomped his bacon stew, ignoring her.

"Speaking of light as a feather. You're not listening, are you?"

Chomp, chomp, chomp.

"Thought not," Kali said, and promptly fell asleep.

The next morning they resumed their journey, the final leg, and reached the outskirts of Gargas by late afternoon. As they passed the sign to the market town, Horse perked up considerably, his trot breaking spontaneously into a canter without any prompting at all. Kali smiled and patted him on the neck. She was looking forward to seeing the old man too.

Kali had known Merrit Moon almost all her adult life, since the day he had introduced himself in the Warty Witch in Freiport. What had always stuck in her mind – become part of what drove her, in many ways – were the words he had imparted to her at the time. She had just

returned from one of her first expeditions, only slightly
less naïve than the day she'd been born, and had been
sitting in the tavern bruised, battered and exhausted
with a much-needed jug of ale and the artefact she had
managed to extract from a ruined site some miles outside
that town. As she sat there examining her prize, turning
it in her hands, caressing it with a great deal of curiosity
and no small sense of wonder, she'd been oblivious to the
stares that the small, scintillating sphere was attracting
from the Witch's other clientele. They, too, were curious
about it, though their curiosity had little to do with the
archaeology that motivated her and everything to do
with lining their empty purses with gold. Two of what
were presumably the more desperate among them,
licking their lips, had begun to move over to her table
when a hand had swept slowly across her own, pressing
it down and hiding the object it held from view. At the
same time, another hand waved the curious back towards
the bar. The owner of both obviously possessed sufficient
gravitas because the men left without question.

"What you are holding in your hand," a voice had said,
"belongs to those who came before us, and is not a bauble
to be toyed with. More importantly, it is not a bauble to
be displayed in a place such as this."

A man had slipped then into the seat beside her, and
she had looked over at a face of perhaps sixty years of
age, weatherbeaten but at the same time gentle, with
grey eyes that suggested a wealth of experience and a
core of steel. Though a little portly, she'd suspected he
hadn't always been so, much as she'd suspected that the
shoulder-length silvery hair that now looked suspiciously
like a bad wig, but wasn't, had once been more kempt.
He was dressed, as she herself had favoured back then,
in loose leathers but, rather startlingly, had slung about

them a cloak of thick wool that looked and stank as if it belonged on a horse. And it was pink.

The stranger introduced himself as Merrit Moon. She had been sure she had seen him somewhere before, but he assured her she had not.

"Thanks for the advice but I can look after myself," she had answered.

Merrit Moon had smiled. "Oh, of that, I have no doubt. But as much as that might be the case, don't you think it a little foolish to provoke the need to do so?"

He signalled for a drink and, as it came, continued, quietening only as the tankard was set down. "Ours is a rich world," he said, "but most of those who live upon it do not even begin to realise where its true richness lies. Nor do most of them wish to. They have closed minds, and to those minds all there is around them is Vos, Pontaine, the Anclas Territories, places busy with petty dealings and squabblings, trade agreements, embargoes and hostilities. They are, of course, aware, somewhere in their closed minds, that we all live with the legacy of older races who came before us, but they choose to ignore that legacy because their minds are too full of the mundane day-to-day struggles it takes to survive in this blighted land."

He'd gestured to the object she'd held. "Such objects might stir greed in some, as happened with those... gentlemen, but in others they stir fear – fear of the unknown, fear of instability, fear that their own lives and existences could as easily be snuffed as were the lives and existences of those who once crafted such things."

She had stared at him. Merrit Moon had the air of a man who had made his own way on Twilight, much as she had herself, and she instinctively trusted him.

"You sound as if you have knowledge of the Old

Races."

"Enough to know when to keep that knowledge to myself, for fear of a knife in my back."

She had glanced up at the men and kept the sphere low, but had not been able to resist stroking it with her thumbs, wondering at its smoothness of manufacture. Smoothness, that was, apart from one intriguing dimple...

"This thing," she had asked. "What is it?"

Unexpectedly, Moon had laughed. "Do you know how many times I have asked myself that same question? Not, of course, with what you hold – I *know* that – but with many a hundred other objects – perhaps a thousand, I have found? And perhaps with one object in each hundred I have actually come up with answers." He'd smiled. "Though not necessarily the right ones."

"What kind of answers? I mean, what things have you found and what do they do?"

Moon had leaned in eagerly, almost conspiratorially, and his eyes had twinkled as he spoke. "Narrow cylinders of light that, unlike candles, never dim. A ring that when spun speaks with the voices of beings long gone, in a language long dead. A gauntlet that generates a field of force *nothing* to do with the threads of any mage, shadow or otherwise."

She had looked at him in wonder. In all her ventures up to that time, she'd found nothing so exciting. Except, perhaps, what she held then. Whatever it was. "And this one?"

"That one?" Moon had said, as if it were nothing. "That one's a bomb."

"Bomb," she'd repeated, thumbs frozen where they were.

"Icebomb, in actual fact. Quite ingenious but quite common, and I'd advise you not to touch the dimple."

He'd sighed heavily. "I touched the dimple..."

"You did? What happened?"

"Froze my dog solid. Tried to fetch it when I threw it away."

She'd looked at him to see if he was joking but there was a definite tear in his eye. "*Pits*! Hey, wait, I wasn't going –"

"Don't lie. Yes, you were."

"Okay, I was." She'd quickly put the sphere down and changed the subject. "So what are you telling me – these objects you found, they harness magic?"

"Not magic, young lady. *Science*. Old Race science."

"They were that advanced?"

"That – and less, and more. The truth is, they dominated this land for a long time – through three ages – but tales from the Final Age tell of them actually preparing to send ships to the heavens. To explore Kerberos itself."

"Kerberos," she'd whispered. "But I don't understand. Other than this thing, I've never –"

"Found such things?" Moon had finished, chortling. "Perhaps that's because you haven't been looking as long as I have. Or perhaps because you haven't been looking in the right places."

Without a word, he'd slid a map across the table in front of her.

"What's this?"

A shrug. "The location of an Old Race city. Only three streets remaining, but interesting nonetheless. I'm giving it to you because I'd like to help you in your pursuits, if I may."

She'd gawped at the map. "Why? Why would you help me?"

And he'd smiled. "Because of your very first question to me. 'What is this?' you asked. Not 'What is this worth?'

but 'What is this?' because you are interested in its *history*."

"That doesn't mean I mightn't still want to sell it."

"But you won't, will you? Because you now know what it is. You have a great deal to learn before the things you see and find begin to make sense, but you have already learned the first lesson – that Twilight is not ready for its own past. Hide the sphere and keep it safe, because perhaps one day you will need it."

"Hey, old man – a girl's got to live."

"And you *will*. Oh, how you will! The true baubles you find? Sell them, as I have done over the years. Sell them so you can go to greater depths, in search of greater secrets. Sell them to finance the life you'll lead."

"The life I'll lead?"

"Finding out what happened to the elves and dwarves, of course!" Moon had declared with sudden passion. He'd squinted at her, a smile playing on his lips. "That is what you want to do, isn't it?"

"All I ever wanted," she'd breathed.

"Hah! Barkeep, two more drinks," he'd shouted, then, thumping the table in glee before turning to her. "Then join me, Kali Hooper. There's a whole world out there, and it *isn't* ours."

There's a whole world out there, and it isn't ours, Kali thought. The old man had spoken those words five years earlier, and in that time Merrit Moon and Kali had shared adventures and expeditions, the old man teaching her tricks and techniques that had proved invaluable since – but also in that he'd become less physically capable and had eventually begun to act as advisor rather than active participant in their finds. And then, there had come a time when he had retired from the field altogether. He could not shed himself of his interest in the subject, of course, and on moving to Gargas had opened a shop whose income allowed him to maintain that interest, particularly when it came to acting as a sounding board for her more *intriguing* discoveries.

The smallest population centre in Pontaine, Gargas was a market town that sat alone amidst the eastern plains' northern farmlands. Merrit had chosen it as his home because, unlike Andon or Miramas or Volonne, it enjoyed a tolerably low level of interference from Pontaine's governing bodies and, latterly, from what he considered to be the scourge that was the Final Faith. For a large portion of the year its wide cobbled streets were empty, its inhabitants dots in a desolate community, but twice a year, when the harvests came in, it was transformed into a bustling centre of trade and commerce as farmers and merchants distributed their produce from all over Pontaine and beyond. Then, the city's population more than tripled in size, its streets thronged not only with legitimate salesmen but wheelers and dealers of every kind, the shops that lined them enjoying a week or so of frenetic prosperity that sustained them throughout the rest of the year.

It happened to be market time now, and as Horse trotted in through Gargas's southern gate Kali was almost overwhelmed by the riot of colour, noise and smell that greeted her. Garlanded and festooned stalls crowded every open space, their equally colourful owners selling cloths and spices, ales and trinkets, meats and fruits, and everything in between. Kali dismounted Horse and led him by his reins through the bustling throng, dodging hawkers who regaled her with tales of products that would change her life and worgles that rolled hopefully along the ground in search of scraps, and avoiding by as much of a margin she could the foul breath of traders' mools, the black and white patched ruminants they used to ferry their goods. More than once she had to swerve swiftly off course, hurrying along as Horse nosebagged a sausage or a pie from its seller's stall, the baskets they sat in and all. With all this going on, it took her a good half-hour to wind her way through to her destination but there, at last, it was.

Merrit Moon's shop was hidden away down a side alley behind a flummox still run by brother and sister Hannah and Arthur Greenwood, and Kali winked to them as she passed. But though hidden, Wonders of the World was no less patronised for it – in fact, it was one of the most popular destinations for the punters filling Gargas's streets. The old man had certainly tapped a vein when he'd decided to market souvenirs of Twilight's more inaccessible areas, and it had become quite the thing in the cities to own a rock from the foothills of the Drakengrat Mountains or a walking stick carved from wood chopped on the edge of the Sardenne. It was all junk, of course, but it was profitable junk and it was genuine and it allowed Merrit to rid himself of some of the more useless items he had accumulated over the years. Not that he didn't still collect – in fact he paid good bonuses to the would-be adventurers he employed to gather his sticks and stones if they ever returned with something more interesting.

Few, of course, provided him with the kinds of finds she did. Spotting her as soon as the bell jangled above the door, Merrit tried to conceal his pleasure at seeing her by merely raising a finger to acknowledge her presence. Kali smiled – it was rare these days that her visits were for purely social reasons, and she could see the eagerness in his eyes to discover what she'd brought him this time. His interest in selling a throbsnake's shedded skin to some Vossian noble waned instantly, offering the man the supposed aphrodisiac at a significant discount just to get him out of the door. The rest, timewasters by the look of them, he shooed away with a Drakengrat death-rattle, flicking the sign on the door to 'closed' as soon as they had gone.

"Hello, old man," Kali said. She moved to embrace him but Merrit, as always, scuttled away, pretending some nonexistent business. Again, Kali smiled. She'd get him one day.

"You have the smell of the deep Sardenne about you," Moon said brusquely, sniffing the air in the room with distaste. "Have you been taking my faithful old friend somewhere less than healthy, young lady?"

My faithful old friend, Kali thought. The old man was referring to Horse. Sometimes she wondered whether Moon cared more about Horse than he did her – knowing that, if not, it would be one hells of a close-run thing. For the fact was, when he had stopped adventuring, she had stepped not only into Moon's metaphorical shoes but into his metaphorical stirrups as well, Horse having been his companion before hers, and for a good deal longer. They had been through a lot together, those two, but, when it had come time for Merrit's retirement, it was clear Horse would not be happy wandering in circles in some field all day, and had actually twice run away, lurking on the edge of town staring dolefully into the distance, where such adventures – and perhaps some exotic variant of bacon stew – lay. So Moon had offered him to her. She'd had her reservations at first, because Horse had seen a lot of miles in his time. But then in a sudden moment of insight it had occurred to her that time was precisely the point. All of the places she wished to go had already waited so many hundreds of years, so what difference would an extra couple of days – okay, in some cases a week – in getting there on a slower steed actually make? And, as it turned out, it even gave her time to prepare, to think. It was an arrangement that kept everyone happy.

Speaking of which, Moon was circling her, prodding and sniffing at the key she had bundled up on her back, eager to unwrap her latest find. Kali nodded to a trapdoor in the floor of the shop, indicating that what she had might be a little too important to reveal here. Even more intrigued now, Moon rubbed his hands together and lifted the trap.

A ladder led down to a cellar and Merrit and Kali descended, the old man waving his hand over light cylinders to illuminate the subterranean room where he kept his – and her – more unusual finds.

Kali stripped off her backpack and waited as eagerly as he had above as Moon unwrapped the key from the oiled cloth in which she'd wrapped it. She had lost count of the number of times she had brought artefacts here for him to examine, and had witnessed a gamut of reaction, ranging from vague disappointment to child-like excitement to awed reverence. But the way he reacted now she had not seen before, and it made her feel momentarily cold inside. The old man's face had darkened.

"Gods of the Great Pits," Merrit Moon said, slowly. His voice was filled with dread and he actually backed away from the key slightly, staring at it from the greater distance as if he could not believe what lay before him. When he spoke again, which was not for a few moments, his voice came out almost as a whisper. "Kali, where did you find this?"

Kali hesitated. *Merrit?* she wondered. *What the hells is the matter? Is there a problem here?*

"Tell me!" he barked, suddenly and totally uncharacteristically.

"All right, old man!" Kali shouted. She was surprised to feel her heart thudding. She had never seen him, never heard him like this. "In the Sardenne. A subterranean site called the Spiral of Kos."

"How old?"

"What?"

"This Spiral of Kos, girl – how *old* was it?"

Kali frowned, wondering where this was leading. "I don't know exactly, but from the architecture possibly Mid Age. The vegetation inside was of unknown genus, but I doubt that it was indigenous. I think it may even have been cultured. Oh, and by the way, it ate people."

"Yes, yes, yes," Moon hissed, impatiently. He was nodding vigorously, as if the information he had asked for was causing him pain and he was trying to shake it out of his head. "Oh, gods of the Great Pits," he said again.

"Merrit, what is it? What's wrong?"

The old man stared her in the eyes and said: "Kali, this... artefact has to be returned where it came from – right away – *right now!*"

"I don't understand."

"Returned *immediately*, Kali."

Kali could not hold his gaze. "Yes, well," she said, slowly. "That could prove to be a little difficult."

Merrit Moon paused. "Oh, gods, tell me you didn't –"

"I did."

"Gods!"

"Merrit, it wasn't my fault."

The old man flung his hands up in the air. "For Kerberos' sake, child, when will you learn to curb this... this *destructive* streak of yours. 'Thanks for the advice but I can look after myself'," he muttered.

Kali actually felt herself becoming annoyed with the

old man. "I don't know, Merrit! Maybe when people or things stop trying to kill me." Her mind flashed back to the last time something like this had happened, and she felt a twinge of guilt remembering how in escaping the Temple of Rahoon she'd brought down its plinths like ninepins as she'd raced down the steps with the Rock of Ages rolling hot on her heels.

But at least Moon had *liked* that artefact.

The old man sighed. "Sorry. I'm sorry. Are you all right? What were you up against this time?"

"I'm fine. And it was Final Faith. But not normal God Squad. More like some special –"

"*Final Faith?*" Moon repeated, incredulous. He seemed more staggered by this revelation than by the appearance of the key itself. "It can't be," he said. "Tell me, Kali, did these people seem specifically interested in the key, or were they, do you think, there only by chance?"

Kali shrugged. "I can't really imagine any scenario where anyone would find themselves in the heart of the Sardenne Forest *by chance*. No, from what Munch said I'd say they were specifically interested in the key."

"Munch..." Moon said. He rewrapped the key in its shroud of oiled cloth and laid it carefully on the shelf behind him.

"This... *thing* needs to disappear, Kali. I need you to understand that. To be hidden again, this time once and for all. And its resting place needs to be far from prying eyes, scheming brains and grasping hands." Moon sighed again. "Which is why, the first thing in the morning, it and I will be heading for the World's Ridge Mountains."

Kali stared at him, speechless. It wasn't that he was taking the key from her, because in that decision she trusted him without question – it was just where he was talking about *going*.

"I'll be taking the southern road," Moon continued, aware of her reaction and expecting fireworks any time soon. "But even so I expect to be gone for some weeks."

"Then I'm coming with you."

Moon shook his head. "No, Kali. The fewer people who know the key's location, the safer the peninsula will be in the future. And you cannot get fewer than one."

"Are you saying you don't trust me? Tell me what the key is, Merrit!"

"No. And you know that I trust you. It is other forces out there that I do not. If the Final Faith are indeed aware of what this key is and knew that you were privy to its whereabouts, then their pursuit of your knowledge of its location would be... zealous indeed."

"But the World's Ridge Mountains – it's suicide, old man!"

Moon grabbed her suddenly by the shoulders. "I will be fine," he insisted, giving her a reassuring squeeze, "*Fine.*"

Kali told Moon about her vision, then, but the old man had no idea where it had come from, or what it meant, and she pursued it no further. Their business done, Moon prepared a hot supper of pot-roasted rufoon, redbread and dripping, which Kali devoured eagerly, sending the food on its way with a bottle of black wine that the old man swore was part of a batch he had found in an Old Race cellar years before, and which he reckoned was a still-palatable and particularly fine vintage. It was his theory that its owners had been saving the bottles for some celebration that ultimately had never come. Kali made the right appreciative noises, but the fact was the old man had never been very good on the booze front, and the reason it had remained in the Old Race cellar was more likely that it wasn't fit to be served to the rufoon they were eating – or perhaps was even what had killed it. She forced it down, though, trying her best to turn her grimaces into smiles, as Moon questioned her about what she was going to do next.

"Ar dunnof, really," Kali shrugged, her mouth filled with redbread. She spat sizzling crumbs and waved the half-torn loaf in the air, forming little spirals that burned into her retina. "Back to the Flagons for a few dayf reft and then one of the loft canals, mayfee. Had a tip there'f an entranfe to be found somfwhere near Turnifia."

"An entrance to one of the lost canals near Turnitia?" Moon repeated, intrigued. He stroked his chin. "Yes... yes, that would make a lot of sense."

Kali dunked her redbread in the dripping and took another bite, nodding. "Mmmmf, I'fe fought so, toof."

As they finished, the noises from the street outside diminished to the last clatters of carts leaving the market, a few scattered farewells and goodnights, and then to the kind of solid silence that could only descend on a remote and rural town such as this. Moon, of course, had an early start, and so wanting to retire, offered her a bed for the night, but Kali declined, ready for some fresh air after the heat from his fire and preferring, anyway, to travel by night. It was a preference that worried Moon – the isolated and winding country lanes that were the only way out of there had, because of their isolation, a reputation of being dangerous enough by day, let alone night – but Kali held to the logic that anyone who willingly travelled in the darkness would be perceived by whichever grabcoins lay in wait as probably too dangerous to be approached in the first place. So it was that she gathered together her things and stepped out onto the cobbles, slinging and securing her saddlebags onto a snoring and slightly startled Horse as she readied him for the journey. She stared at Moon as he stood watching in the doorway, lit by the warm glow from inside, and then over his shoulder to the door to the shop, and the hatch to the hidden reliquary that lay beyond. An image of the key, wrapped in its protective shroud in readiness for its journey, flashed into her mind.

"Merrit," she said, "be careful, up there, please."

The old man smiled, reassuringly. "I am never anything else, young lady. Believe me, you do not get to my age in a world as surprising as ours without constantly being so." As Kali mounted Horse, Moon tossed his one-time steed a bacon lardon, and Horse bounced it off his nose into his mouth and munched down gratefully, eyeballs spinning. "Besides," the old man added, "it will not be the first time that the World's Ridge Mountains have welcomed these old bones into their cold embrace."

Kali raised her eyebrows and then nodded. She should have known.

"Another tale, Merrit?"

"For another time."

Kali smiled and squeezed her heels into Horse's flanks, then reined him in the direction of the road out of Gargas. "I'll be in touch, old man," she said, and urged Horse forwards. The old mount swung its head in the direction of Moon, whinnied a goodbye, and then began to clop slowly forwards.

"Safe journeys, Kali Hooper... and you, too, my faithful old friend," Merrit Moon said, smiling to himself. "Safe journeys."

The relic-monger watched Kali and Horse until they had fully crossed the market square and begun to descend the slope to the town gate, then turned inside to his parlour. The fire crackled, as welcoming as ever, but as he closed the solid wooden door behind him, the old man's smile faded. It was indeed not the first time that he had had cause to journey to the World's Ridge Mountains, but he did not regard the coming prospect quite as casually as he had led Kali to believe. The mountains were a wild and rugged place, as untamed as the Sardenne and as anywhere on the peninsula, and their dangers were not to be underestimated. To travel there alone, as Kali had reminded him, would be considered suicide by most.

Luckily, he was not most.

But he would need to prepare.

Merrit Moon bolted the outside door behind him, took a last swig of his remaining wine and then headed through to the shop and back down the ladder into the reliquary, this time bolting its hatch above him. As far as the reliquary went, he had never been wholly truthful with Kali about it – it was indeed where he stored his rarer items, but what Kali did not know was these items were neither the rarest, nor the sum total of them. Waving another light cylinder into life, Moon took a small key from his pocket and inserted it into the lock of a display cabinet against the far wall, turning the key not clockwise as might be normal but anti-clockwise, twice, until there was a dull click that did not come from the lock but from the wall behind it.

With the slightest touch of his hand the wooden cabinet swung away from the wall on iron hinges, revealing yet another room – a round chamber – beyond.

A small collection of objects glistened on stone shelves in the light of the cylinder outside.

Sighing, his heart heavy, Merrit Moon stepped towards them.

CHAPTER 4

Killiam Slowhand had become used to every kind of reaction to his performances, from laughter and tears to boos and hisses, showers of flowers and hails of rotten fruit. He'd had standing ovations and he'd had people who'd stood up and walked out. He'd been welcomed in towns, run out of towns, almost lynched in towns and had, in some, been called names which even he had not heard before. Most hurtful of all, he'd had women who'd cackled at his tights.

But before tonight he'd never felt the tip of a dagger pressed coldly and threateningly against his spine.

A tad overcritical, he thought.

The performance had gone well, and the sound of the audience's laughter and applause still ringing in his ears, Slowhand had exited backstage, it being divided from the front stage by a curtain slung over a rope – a method of construction which, in fact, made up his makeshift theatre, wherever he went. Once there, he had quickly begun to wipe off his greasepaint with a damp cloth, attempting at the same time to strip his torso and legs of his spotted tunic and stripy tights, the colourful costume he wore on stage. The ritual would normally have been a far more leisurely affair, done with a good stiff drink or three, but the night's show *had* been a good one, loud and raucous, and not only in terms of the numbers in the crowd but the number of them he had seen react to his little vignettes. Quite a few more seeds had been planted, this night, and if Slowhand didn't miss his guess there was a good chance he was going to be paid a visit because of it.

Sure enough, though a little too soon for his modesty, visitors had arrived, and he had heard the other curtain – the one behind him, the one leading to the outside world –suddenly ripping open, and in a flurry of activity had found himself cornered and grabbed by both arms while the cold, pointed metal was rammed into his flesh, almost but not quite piercing the skin.

Critics, he thought again.

He coughed and turned slowly, the dagger tracing a thin red line around his waist until it settled in his navel, and he found himself – wearing his tights around his ankles – facing three robed figures.

The three were strangers to him, but he knew exactly who they were. One was female – and cute. Or at least would have been had she not been the one sticking the dagger into him – or represented what she did.

Slowhand played it casual, ignoring the crossed circles on their sleeves. "Sorry but I never do autographs after a show. It's making the fluffy animals out of the balloons, you know... makes the wrists ache."

"We have no interest in your autograph, Mister

Slowhand, or your fluffy animals. We are here regarding a different matter. That of your growing reputation."

"My, er, growing reputation?" Slowhand said. He couldn't help himself – he looked down then back up with a smile, winking at the girl. Rather disappointingly, her gaze remained impassively and steadfastly fixed on his face and didn't drop an inch. Not that an inch would have done the job, he reflected. Nope, not even close.

"It has come to our attention that certain... subject matter may not be serving the best interests of our church."

"Certain subject matter?" Killiam repeated. He adopted the same dramatic pause as the man who had spoken. "Are you talking about my... little play?"

"Your little play. The Final Faith does not take kindly to being portrayed as the Final Filth."

"Oh," Slowhand said, "dear."

"As a result, the Anointed Lord wishes to converse with you. Now."

"The Anointed Lord?" Slowhand said, feigning shock. Bingo, he thought. "Right... well. How can I resist? May I dress first?"

"We wish you would."

"Thank you."

Killiam turned to his wardrobe – a pile of clothes strewn on the floor – then turned back, indicating with a toss of his head that he'd like his visitors to turn their backs. In actual fact, despite what he was slipping on, he wasn't remotely concerned whether they turned or not – he just wanted to see if the girl had problems doing so. And yep, she was lingering, lingering...

Ha! Got 'em every time!

Satisfied and dressed, Slowhand found himself escorted from his makeshift theatre, noting as he was led outside that others in the robes of the Faith were already tearing it down, folding and packing the cloth into sacks for removal, probably to be taken away for burning. Some members of his audience who still remained milling about in Ramblas Square made discomforted noises but, of course, none of them said anything to the demolition team. None of them dared.

Slowhand didn't mind. The Faith was doing itself no favours with this kind of behaviour, and it was something else that would hopefully lodge in his audience's minds.

It was a measure of the Faith's sensitivity that his little play had attracted such attention, but then by bringing it here to Scholten he had rather hoped that it would.

The Final Faith, he reflected. As churches went, Twilight had never known anything like it, or those that ran it. Appearing out of nowhere not so many years before, and rapidly growing to become the largest organised religion on the peninsula, the Faith preached belief in a single god named the Lord of All, said to be the creator of all things. Slowhand wasn't a religious man but he did know that before the Faith's arrival there had at least been a *choice* of gods, and to his mind this single deity must have made for much rubbing of hands in the church because its followers knew exactly who to give their money to. Oh, yes, the Faith had got quite a little business going on that front.

It wasn't, of course, the first church that had supported itself by means of its followers' donations, but what disturbed Slowhand was that with the Faith there was a price to be paid for everything. Its followers prayed to the Lord of All for little other than for what followers had always prayed – a good harvest, prosperity, or the simple wellbeing of their loved ones – but in each case there was a price – *a price for prayer* – that was all too eagerly levied by the Faith, more often than not on those who had little or nothing to spare in the first place. He had actually seen people reduced to ruin in their desperation to please the Lord of All, but the Final Faith's answer to these tragic turns of events? Prayer.

As he was led through the city, Slowhand scowled. Would that that was the all of it. He had travelled far and travelled wide, and in those travels had seen or heard examples of the Final Faith's influence in spheres where churches should really have no business – influence in spheres that made him feel at best uneasy and at worst actually fearful of their ultimate aim. The priesthood of the Faith – from the Enlightened Ones at the bottom of the hierarchy to the Eminences at the top – were taught that the Lord of All did not simply desire but demand unity for humankind, a distinction that made the heavenly helper seem less benevolent father figure and more malevolent dictator. Only through such unity, it was said, could humanity achieve ultimate and complete ascendance as a divine creation, but one only had to look at events in Turnitia and other cities in recent years to realise that *unity* sometimes came about by means of the rod, and was merely a euphemism for their true objective – nothing less than the complete and utter control of the peninsula, under the law of the Faith and the Faith alone.

And here, looming in front of him, was the heart of it. The base of Final Faith operations. The multi-spired monstrosity that was Scholten Cathedral.

Slowhand, dagger still held at his back, was ushered along Enlightenment Avenue towards it, the broad approach lined with red-tabarded cathedral guard and thronged with cathedral-goers and the officially sanctioned hawkers of religious tat who preyed upon them. The most blatant misuse of donated funds he could imagine, the structure towered over and dominated the city, serving not only as head office for the Faith but as a place of pilgrimage for those faithful who had clearly been sufficiently indoctrinated not to share his opinion of the place. They came from every region on the peninsula to bask in its magnificence, to worship in its endless banks of pews, or, if they arrived at the right time and were selected by the guard, to attend the weekly audience of the Anointed Lord – one of which, by the incessant clanging of the cathedral's bells, was happening now. Each of them would go home happy – if lighter in the pocket – because the pomp and the ceremony that was trowelled on to blind them to the truth made the experience seem like a little bit of Kerberos on Twilight.

Slowhand was spared the pomp and the ceremony. He had to settle for being shoved roughly along side corridors, any pretence of being a group of mates out for a stroll gone now that he was away from the public eye.

Again, he didn't mind. Being backstage, as it were, gave him chance to see with his own eyes the operation at work. All down the side of the corridor along which he was shoved, one after another until he was in danger of losing count, he could see into booths where the faithful were in consultation with priests. Alone or in groups, they passed over coin to the superficially sympathetic and nodding clergy, they in turn passing on benedictions in response to requests for divine favour ranging from fertility for their mool to a cure for a village's collective pox. And hells, they were good – so good they could have gone on stage themselves the way they made the money disappear, surreptitiously slipping it into tubes behind them and benedicting ever more loudly as it clattered down some central shaft into a communal coffer in the basement. It was a treasure trove that ever grew and never stopped, and one thing was certain – if for whatever reason the Final Faith didn't eventually subjugate the peninsula by rod, then they'd have no problem buying it outright. Even he hadn't realised just how massive a business it was.

Slowhand was shoved on, and his surroundings, other than for the sound of a distant choir, grew quieter. He was brought to a halt in a large chamber designed in such a way that anyone entering was channelled immediately and directly towards a raised dais in its centre, the path by which they entered unobstructed so that they might depart without turning, stepping backwards all the way. He knew the reason for this was that, as the Lord of All's supposed representative on Twilight, no one was allowed to turn their back on the Anointed Lord, the ruling no mere fancy of power but written – apparently – in the holy scriptures and enforced by its hard men – the Order of Dawn – as a crime punishable by death. Handy, that, he'd always thought, because if the Anointed Lord wished someone gone, then presumably all the Anointed Lord had to do was order them to turn around.

Speaking of which witch, here she was now. The head of the Final Faith swept into the chamber fresh from her audience with her flock, flinging off her holy vestments with a theatrical sigh of annoyance that suggested she was more than glad to see the back of them – in a manner of speaking.

Slowhand studied her, stimulated despite who she was. That the Anointed Lord was striking was undeniable, being tall and statuesque in build with a face that was handsome, if somewhat stern, this topped by a long, flowing mane of fiery red hair reaching down to her buttocks. Her eyes a bright green, they would have been attractive were it not for the way she used them, looking upon her underlings with some degree of disdain. They made him think that the term striking could also be applied to her in the way it was applied to a cobreel, fangs bared and about to lunge for your throat, and in that respect she certainly had the sinuous curves.

They had never met face-to-face, but Slowhand knew her.

Her name was Katherine Makennon. And the last time he had seen her, she had been a Five Flame General in the Army of Vos.

Makennon mounted her dais and flicked a glance at him, noting his presence, and he was about to step forwards, say 'Hi', when his escorts pulled him firmly back by his arms. It appeared that it wasn't yet his turn.

A man slammed through the main doorway and strode towards her, iron-capped boots thumping on the polished floor, though there was nothing polished about the man himself. A squat, barrel of a thing, he struck Slowhand even from a distance as being distinctly ugly and unlikeable, and his dishevelled appearance hinted he had just this second returned from some assignment in the outside world. Wherever it was he had come from, it had to have been somewhere hot. The man was charred and blackened as if he had been caught up in some great fire, and Slowhand swore that parts of his clothing still seemed to smoke.

He was announced as Munch, and Makennon's expression darkened as he approached her – he had obviously not brought good news. There was an altercation. Words were exchanged. At one point, the Anointed Lord slapped him across the face. Slowhand wondered why he took it – statuesque or not, Anointed Lord or not, he could have snapped Makennon like a dry twig.

The exchange ended and she dismissed him, holding out the back of her hand in a clear sign that his audience with her was over. Munch kissed it, not once, twice, but three times, and Slowhand could almost hear the mantra that would have accompanied each contact of his lips – the very same mantra he heard almost everywhere he went.

The One Faith. The Only Faith. The Final Faith.

It should have been over, but the small brute of a man lingered still, his lips hovering over her flesh. He actually looked likely to go in again. *Ah, that was it,* Slowhand thought. *The little bastard has the hots for her.* Okay, that was understandable – he might, too, given a moment of flung-about-the-bedroom masochism. But really...

He sighed, loudly. "Look, I hate to interrupt, but have you done with the tonguing yet?"

The pair shot him a fiery glare, then Makennon ordered Munch to the sidelines with a flick of her finger. Another flick followed, this time commanding the lapdogs who held Slowhand to bring him closer.

He and Munch passed midway, and Slowhand bent to whisper in his ear. "Little tip, pal. If you wanna get your hands on the boss's bazooms, try to grow higher than her knees."

Munch roared and spun towards him with a balled fist, but Killiam caught it readily and solidly, stopping it dead and holding it, unwavering, six inches from his face. He held Munch's stare, veins pulsing in his temples, an unexpected steeliness in his eyes matching that in his grip.

"I wouldn't do that," he said.

Munch considered, a gamut of emotions crossing his face, not least surprise. Then a cough from Makennon reminded him that he had just turned his back on her. Growling, he snatched his hand from Slowhand's grip, turned, and continued to shuffle backwards.

"Quite a show of strength," Makennon observed, "for a common street player."

As the Anointed Lord spoke, Slowhand was jostled into position before her, where he bowed with theatrical exaggeration, sweeping his hand under his stomach and then up into the air.

"Actually, I prefer to think of myself more as an artiste. Troubadour, bard and all-round entertainer, in fact."

"Really."

"Absolutely." Killiam pulled a balloon from a pocket, blew into it and, with a series of tortuous squeaks, twisted it into the semblance of a fluffy animal. "I even do balloons."

Makennon slapped the shape from his hand, ignoring it as it bounced away across the floor.

"Why is it that you are doing what you are, Mister Killiam Slowhand?" she asked without preamble.

"Ah. So you know my name."

Makennon gestured with a flyer in her hand. "'Killiam Slowhand's Final Filth – Every Hour, On The Hour'," she read. "It wasn't hard."

Slowhand smiled. "No. Suppose not."

"And why is it that you have so little respect for our church?"

"I don't know," Killiam said, though, in truth, he had every reason in the world. "Why does your church have so little respect for the other ones out there? How does that little ditty go again? The One Faith, the – ?"

"Ours is the *true* faith."

"Right, of course. True as well. You consulted the Brotherhood of the Divine Path about that, lately?

The Azure Dawn? Or the rest of them your mob have squeezed out or shut down or *disappeared* since you began annexing the whole damn peninsula?"

Makennon smiled grimly and stared him in the eyes. "Killiam Slowhand. That really is the most ridiculous name..."

"Hells. You should hear my real one."

"Those churches are irrelevant," Makennon declared, answering his question. "Misguided fancies, the beliefs of fools. They – and others like them – will come to understand the way of things."

"When you've knocked it into them, I suppose. If you really want to know why I have so little respect for your church, Anointed Lord, then I'll tell you." Slowhand remembered her as she had been. "This isn't Andon and the peninsula's no longer at war – but most importantly, you're not a general any more. Stop running your religion as if you're still trying to build an empire and maybe, just maybe, people will *voluntarily* listen to what you have to say."

Makennon laughed out loud, as if the whole idea were ludicrous, then stopped suddenly and leant forwards until she was staring Slowhand directly in the eyes. "I'm not the only one no longer serving my country as a soldier, am I, Mister Slowhand?" Her eyes grew curious and her tone deepened as she drew in almost seductively close to him and he could feel her hot breath on his cheek. "Oh yes, I know you just as you know me. So tell me, *Lieutenant* – what makes you do this? Just why is it that you are donning the garb of a fool and attempting to undermine us in this ridiculous, seditious way?"

Slowhand's eyes narrowed. "I have my reasons. And one of them is I just don't like people running other people's lives."

"Hmm. But surely someone has to do just that, don't you think? Otherwise the whole of society would simply degenerate into an unruly and unruled rabble."

"Rabble, eh? Why do I get the impression that as far as your opinion of your flock goes it rather neatly sums things up?"

"We provide them with guidance."

"They didn't *ask* for guidance."

Makennon sighed, then gestured around her audience chamber with her hand, sweeping it to indicate what lay beyond as well. "You think this all a sham, don't you?"

"A sham *and* a scam, actually."

"That we have no destiny? That our only concern is with our own material gain?"

"*Bang*! Nail on the head."

"That we do, in fact, lust solely after power?"

"Woohooh, you're good. No wonder they made you the boss."

Again, Makennon leaned in close. "What if I could prove to you that it was otherwise? That our future is plain. Would you then cease your public mockery of our church?"

"That would be something of a tall order."

"Then allow me to fulfil it."

Slowhand stared at her, unsure of where this was going. "What's this about, Katherine?" he asked with intended familiarity. "I'm far from the only seditionary out there, so why the special treatment – this personal touch? Why didn't your lackey's dagger go all the way in? After all, it's happened before, so I hear."

"Because I want you to join us."

"What?"

"The Final Faith needs people such as you. People possessing *certain skills*." She turned and walked to the wall of the chamber, where she opened a compartment and Slowhand found himself staring at something he thought he'd never see again. "Where did you – ?"

"Does it matter? The point is, it's yours if you join us. Yours to use again, in our cause."

Again, Slowhand stared, but this time at Makennon – getting the woman's measure. It was clear her style of running the Final Faith was unorthodox, but it was also clear that she *believed* in what it did, at least to a degree. But despite the incentive she'd just offered, he had no interest in joining her, though, he had to admit, she'd got him curious.

"Okay, Katherine – what do you have to show me?"

Makennon led him out of her audience chamber and along another seemingly endless corridor, to the furthest reaches of the cathedral, the threesome who'd brought him to her trailing behind. There, she showed him into a library whose shelves were filled not with books but rolled-up scrolls. Other scrolls were unfurled on the walls, images daubed on them in red and black ink – images of hellsfire and damnation, praying and weeping souls, vast marching hordes. Before them knelt figures he didn't recognise – stylised, twisting forms that somehow didn't look quite human – and symbols splashed here and there, some of which reminded him of the crossed circles of the Faith, others vaguely of keys. He had no idea what any of them meant. But he knew who was responsible for them.

Hunched and twitching over long tables down the centre of the library, Final Faith brothers scratched away at scrolls with quills, creating more of the strange images. Hollow-faced and exhausted, the worst aspect of them was that they were not looking at what they were doing – their eyeballs, to a man, rolled up into the backs of their sockets, completely white.

"Hey, fella, are you all ri –?" Slowhand asked, touching one, and then found himself somewhere else entirely, where other hands moved across another scroll, in another room he sensed was far away – *gods, was it the League, in Andon?* He spasmed suddenly, totally disorientated, and then felt his own eyes begin to roll upwards in his –

Makennon slapped his hand away and he gasped. He knew now who these people were – telescryers, remote-receivers, weavers of the threads whose particular use of magic wrecked their bodies and burned their brains away.

And Makennon had them working some kind of... production line.

"What *is* this?" he said.

Makennon smiled. "The future. The scattered pieces of a jigsaw held in a hundred sealed collections and forbidden libraries across Twilight, being brought together, here, for the first time, so that the path of the Final Faith might be fully divined. Prophecies, Mister Slowhand – prophecies as old as time. Prophecies that show the *destiny* of the Final Faith."

"Let me get this straight. You've got these poor bastards telepathically purloining a bunch of dangerous-looking old doodles because you think they are relevant to you?"

"Yes." She swept her hand across the walls. "Don't you see?"

Slowhand saw nothing – except maybe that Makennon had got a bump on the head on one battlefield too many. But he reminded himself it made her no less dangerous – if anything, more so.

"Join us," Makennon urged. "There are *many* things to be achieved."

"Erm, no thanks. I'll come back when your god's got his head screwed on."

Makennon's expression darkened. She summoned the escorts.

"Oh, let me guess," Slowhand said. "This is the part where you lock me up and throw away the key?"

"You are a nuisance to me, and I cannot afford to have a nuisance... *spoil* things at this time. I would have preferred to convert you to our cause because the removal of someone who has made himself so obvious on our streets is itself obvious, but then what choice do I have?" She directed her attention to the escorts and said: "He's a tricky one. Have him stripped and searched thoroughly. Take *everything* from his person."

"Everything? Katherine... not my balloons?"

"*Including* his balloons. When you're done, take Mister Slowhand to the Deep Cells. He'll be staying in our most prestigious quarters for a while."

The escorts grabbed Killiam by the armpits and began to shuffle him off, noticeably turning his back into which the knife dug once more towards the Anointed Lord. This breach of etiquette wasn't a privilege, he guessed, but a sign he was considered already dead. Nevertheless, he let them take him. Actually smiled. Because this was the other thing that the Final Faith excelled in – they made people *disappear*. And in forcing Makennon to make him disappear he'd got her exactly where she wanted him.

No, wait. Exactly where *he* wanted *her*.

At any rate, they had each other where...

"How long a while?" he called back.

"Until you come around to our way of thinking, or until you die."

"Right. In that case, about those balloons..."

Makennon watched him go and then returned to the

audience chamber, summoning Munch back before her.

"I've considered your report," she said. "This Kali Hooper. I want her found."

Munch nodded. "Yes, Ma'am."

"Take whoever you need for the task and locate her. Quickly. Bring me that key."

"Just the key, Ma'am?"

Makennon stared at him, then laughed. "Has your pride been injured, Konstantin? Is that it?" She waited a moment. "Very well, Munch, just the key. The girl is unimportant. Feel free to do with her what you will."

There was a pause, and Munch smiled in anticipation.

"The One faith."

"The Only faith."

"The Final Faith."

CHAPTER 5

You win some, you lose some, Kali mused. It was a week later and she was halfway down her third tankard of ale, draped at the table by the captain's chest in the upper nook of the tavern, the affair of the Spiral – despite a lingering nag about her vision – fading from her mind. Time to think about what to do and where to go next – there was, after all, enough choice out there. The Lost Canals, as she'd mentioned to Merrit? *Uummm*, maybe – she didn't yet know. But it was something that she intended to plan out, here, at this very table, over the next few days.

While at the same time getting some serious drinking done.

She quaffed the rest of her ale in one and signalled Aldrededor for another – no, make that two. The swarthy, grey-haired and ear-ringed Sarcrean winked and blew her a kiss as he set the golden brews down, pleased to have her back where she belonged. Behind him, down a small flight of bowed, skewing steps, business in the Here There Be Flagons was busy and lively, the air thick with laughter and banter, and a cloying mix of pipe, rolly smoke and sweat whose strength could still not mask the heady aroma of Dolorosa's Surprise Stew. The stew had been on the menu – was the menu, in fact – for as long as Aldrededor and his wife had been at the Flagons, and the surprise about it was the reaction anyone got if they were stupid enough to enquire what was in it. "*Why* you wanna know?" the tall, thin and equally swarthy woman would demand loudly. "You think Dolorosa trying to poison you, ah? You think maybe she cook witha the weebleworm anda the flopparatta poo? Well, Dolorosa tell you, iffa Dolorosa wanna you dead she would sticka the cutlass inna your belly and she woulda laugh! Like-a this – ha-ha-ha-ha-haaar! Now go! Getta outta theees taverno! Go away, go, shoo, go, go, go..."

Kali smiled. Dolorasa's more... unusual approach to business was, along with the captain's chest in a tavern landbound for leagues in every direction, a clue to the fact that before the elderly couple had fetched up here, they had pursued their own, long career on Twilight's roiling seas. Exactly what that career had been she had never felt the need to ask, because as far as she was concerned the ear-ring and the cutlass and the hearty laugh said it all.

It was what she loved – had *always* loved – about this place – the mixed bunch all of them were. Looking down towards the bar, she could see Fester Grimlock and Jurgen Pike engaged in a game of quagmire, the merchant and the thief staring daggers at each other as usual. There was Ronin Larson, the local ironweaver, and Hetty Scrubb, the herbalist. Between them weaved Peter Two-Ties, who had prepared the render for her expedition to the Sardenne. And then there, perched on his groaning and perpetually buckling stool, as he was perched every day – but only during the day – was Red Deadnettle, the flame-haired giant of a man who was the reason she was here in the first place.

All of them had made her welcome over the years, and all of them were friends, but to Red she owed it all. Kali knew nothing of her parents or her origin, only that she had been found, twenty-two years before, abandoned and naked as the babe she was, by an unknown adventurer exploring an Old Race site – a site she had never since been able to find. The becloaked adventurer had rescued her and walked the roads on a storm-lashed night, looking for somewhere or someone to take her in. That someone had been Red, who, seeing dawn coming, had brought her here. The rest, as they said, was history – and the adventurer had never been seen again.

A number of shadows darkened the outside of the small, whorled-glass windows of the tavern, before continuing on towards the door. Kali would not normally have given them a second thought – more customers – but their bulk and the way they had skulked for a second outside gave her cause to suspect something might be amiss. Sure enough, a second later, five half-uniformed thugs entered the tavern and headed straight for Red. They were heavies for hire, guards in the employ of local landowners to protect their interests on their estates, and while they had every right – at least in the eyes of the law as it had conveniently been written by their employers – to apprehend people on their land, they had no right to do so in a public place such as this.

"Mister Deadnettle?" their somewhat obese leader enquired. "Mister Red Deadnettle?"

Still hunched at the bar, his back to the man, Red did not move or respond to the question in any way. The thug swallowed and thumped him on the shoulder.

"Deadnettle, I know it's you. I insist you –"

There were sharp intakes of breath – warning hisses, really – from the others seated along the bar, and then a slow and universal shaking of their heads. The hubbub of the tavern quietened as Red rose from his seat, dwarfing the hulks before him as his fists balled.

Kali sighed. She was tempted to let Red continue but if she didn't want her relaxation – and indeed the Flagons itself – ruined by the earthquake that would suddenly and inevitably come, she knew she had better intervene. She leaned down and opened the captain's chest Aldrededor let her use, pulling a small blackjack from beneath a pile of maps, diagrams, schematics and other Old Race paraphernalia, just in case. Then she picked up her ale, descended the steps, and with a slow lowering of her hand bade Red sit down. That done, she tapped the guard on the shoulder.

"Is there a problem, officer?"

"No problem," the guard said tiredly, without even looking at her. "This gentleman and I needs a little chat, that's all. A matter of a small misdemeanour."

"He was taking a short cut across your boss's fields, unless I miss my guess," Kali said, though she knew full well that Red had been poaching again – it was in his blood. "Don't you think *misdemeanour* is a little strong?"

"It's the law of our lands, Miss. Or do you think that folk should just be allowed to wander wherever they want, eh?"

"I do, actually, yes. To wander... and explore." She gestured outside, beyond where the ramshackle tavern was slumped like a knackered cat beside Badlands Brook. "To see what's out there."

The guard turned and looked Kali up and down. She'd only got back to the place an hour before and, having spent a chunk of that time stabling Horse and reassuring him that Dolorosa's stew did have bacon in it, as yet hadn't changed, and the guard took in her sap-stained and torn clothing, the general dishevelment of her appearance. He sniffed as he saw the toolbelt at her waist.

"Oh, you're one of *those*. Take my advice and stay out of this, adventurer," he said with undisguised disdain. "Our business with Deadnettle is no flight of fancy – and no concern of yours."

Kali immediately railed at his attitude. She had never understood how people such as him could live on a world such as theirs and not be curious about it. As Merrit had said, their lives were mired in the mundane, obsessed with petty issues and their own selfish concerns. When all they had to do was look up at Kerberos and wonder –

Hells. She would have given him a lecture but he wasn't worth the bother. "Red is a friend of mine," she said.

"Yeah, he looks like he would be. Now off with you before I have the innkeeper eject you from the premises."

Red said something for the first time, then, leaning down to whisper quietly in the guard's ear. It was still a rumble. "That might be difficult, Mister Policeman. 'Cause Miss Hooper, she owns the place."

The guard guffawed and looked Kali up and down again. "Don't make me laugh. A strip of a girl like her owning a grub's den like this in the back of beyond. Why would she want to do that?"

Kali took a sip of her ale and stared at the guard measuredly. What Red said was true – the tavern had hit hard times a few years ago, and so, when she'd had the funds, she'd bought it, simple as that. But she hadn't changed anything. Except the name. You just didn't with this place. The year before one of the local gentry had objected to the fuggy atmosphere and had suggested it became a non-smoking tavern. After the laughter had died down – *a non-smoking tavern?* – Red had dragged the man to Bottomless Pit and thrown him in. *After* setting him on fire.

"It relaxes me."

Fatso guffawed again. "Bet that don't take much, either. Size of you, it'd only take a thimbleful before you was off your bloody head!"

"And ready for a good time, eh?" Kali said, calculatedly.

The guard's eyes narrowed, and he smacked his lips. "Tell you what – why don't we put that to the test?"

"I'm sure I don't know what you mean."

"A little competition. You, me, a few drinks. And if you're the one that remains standing, I let Deadnettle off the hook. Whaddya say?"

Kali slipped the blackjack back into a pocket, relieved she hadn't needed to use it. "You've got yourself a deal."

"Whoa, careful, little lady," another of the guards interjected. "At the Dead Duck in Miramas they call Sarge the Ale Whale."

Kali stared at the Ale Whale, hardly surprised. "*Phoo.* Well, it won't be a problem, then, will it?"

"'Ere, Sarge," another said. "You're supposed to be on duty."

Kali smiled her most girlish smile. "Surely he can hold his own against me? A thimbleful and I'm gone, remember?"

"Go orrrn, Sarge," one of the other guards snickered

dirtily. "'Old your own against 'er, eh?"

"Why not, eh?" the sergeant cackled. "Why not indeed."

Kali looked at the bar but Dolorosa was ahead of her, having the first drinks lined up in readiness – four flummoxes with ale chasers. She dipped her head towards Kali as she swept them up.

"Poor bastardo," she whispered.

"Hush, woman."

Kali and the Sarge retired to the nook, and it began. One drink. Two drinks. Three drinks, four. An hour later, the Sarge's mates had lost count.

"'Ere, jush 'ang on a mo'," the Sarge said at last, slurring and straightening himself none too successfully in his chair. He made circles with his tankard, spilling great slops of ale over the side. "If thish is your hosteryl... your hotslery... your hoslerurry..." He hiccupped and frowned, determined to get something out. "If this is your pub, how am I to know your shour-faced wench ain't sherving you shome speshal watered-down muck?"

Kali looked down at her own ale, a thwack, triple the strength of his own. She'd tired of flummox and, besides, liked a challenge.

"Taste it for yourself," she said, smiling and proffering her tankard, which he took and quaffed greedily. All that was left, just to be sure.

"Okay?" she asked.

"Ish very nishe, yesh. *Blup. Orf.*"

Nodding, Kali motioned to Dolorosa to bring two more of the same. None too keen on being referred to as a sour-faced wench – or, indeed, any kind of wench at all – the concavity of the tall woman's cheeks clearly signalled she was sucking up to deposit a small present into the guard's beer, until Kali shook her head subtly. Dolorosa shrugged – *okay, maybe the man was suffering enough* – and instead slammed his tankard down hard, soaking his lap with beer. The guard looked down vaguely, his head bobbing, as the ale penetrated the cloth of his pants.

"Gawds, ah fink arve gone un me pished meself."

"No need to waste time going, then, is there?" Kali observed as he giggled. She raised her refreshed tankard to show she was still willing and able. "Come on, Sarge, drink up."

"Wha – ?" the guard said, startled. "Oh, yeah. *Cheershh!*"

The Sarge raised his tankard to his lips and stared hard at Kali. Or at least as hard as he could when he had finally managed to pull her into focus. Almost got her now, he thought to himself. *Ah mean, look at the state of the bloody woman... so betwattled she's blurred and swaying all over the place. Ey up, she was bringing on a reserve now, and all – another one who looked just like her. Nah, stood to reason that, as a gentleman, like, he was gonna have to say something for her own good, or she'd be off the bleedin' chair.*

"Wimmin," he bemoaned to himself. "They jush can't take their drinksh."

"Dolorosa!" Kali called. "Another!"

"Dolorosha," the sergeant repeated. "Godsh, sheesh uggle... uggloo..." He gave up and jabbed a finger across the table – jabbed it everywhere, really, including into his eye. "But you, Mish," he warned, "youse pretty an' oughts to givvup before youse lose your looksh... *ow, bloody 'ell.*" He looked stunned, suddenly, and then added, "Oh gawds... oh, *bluurrrffff!*"

Kali's tankard froze in mid-air as the sergeant's head hit the table with a thud. She sat back with a smile then motioned to his men to take him away, which they did, bundling him out of the door while their heads shook in disbelief.

Another triumph for the Tavern Tot, Kali thought.

She bounced down the steps and slapped the now reseated Red on his back. "Next time," she advised, "wait 'til longnight, eh? Dolorosa, get this man another ale. Me, too, while you're at it. Please."

"You musta be hungry? You wanna some Surprise Stew?"

"Don't know. What's in it?"

"Oh, the beer hassa made the bossgirl funny, now! Hey, why not washa that outfit of yours because you steeeenk. Anda while you at it, sew uppa the pants because your bum it sticka out! Hoh, she smiles! Aldrededor, where issa my sharpeeest knife?"

Kali was halfway back up the steps when shadows darkened the windows again. Another group of men entered, clothed in common travellers' garb, but she recognised the leader of them immediately.

New recruits but same old story. The Munch Bunch.

But something was different. From the shapes that were barely concealed beneath his and his men's cloaks it was clear that they were more heavily armed this time. It wasn't the weapons themselves that worried Kali but the fact that their Final Faith talismans were absent from their sleeves, too. Munch and his cronies had obviously gone to lengths to distance themselves from looking like agents of the Final Faith, and that could mean only one thing. The gloves were off.

"Miss Hooper," Munch said. "You have been really quite difficult to track down."

"I like it that way. How's tricks, Stan?"

"They will be better when I have recovered what belongs to me. The key, Miss Hooper? Please?"

"The key? Oh, that key. Little difficult – I don't have it any more."

"You... don't... have it." Munch repeated, slowly.

"That's right. I threw it away."

Munch laughed out loud, spun to face the watching locals in the tavern. "Did you hear that?" he shouted. "She doesn't have it! She threw it away! Oh, well that's all right, then – we'll all just leave and go home to –"

Go on, Kali thought. *Say it. Say Scholten and give yourself away. Let all these people know who you thugs really represent.* But instead of continuing Munch slammed his fist down on the bar and with a roar swept away the drinks standing there. "Hey, watch out there," Red said, and made to move on him, but in under a second Munch had whipped a shiny new gutting knife from under his cloak and held it to the big man's throat. He pressed the point into Red's flesh until he was forced to sit back down.

Munch turned back to Kali. "Go home?" he said again, as if pondering. "No, I don't think so."

"I already told you, I don't have the key," Kali said. "Now, why don't you just leave before I tell everyone here who you are?"

"That would not be wise," Munch said. "Because then we would have to kill them all." As one, his cronies took crossbows from beneath their cloaks and trained them on the regulars.

"Miss Hooper, if you really do not have the key then I fear I have no choice but to change my plans again. This involves causing you great pain. Do you understand? Oh, and if you are thinking of fleeing from us as you did from the Sardenne Forest, I'm afraid that without the means that might prove a little problematic." Munch smiled coldly. "But if you doubt me, why don't you take a look outside?"

What the hells is he talking about? Kali wondered. Automatically her mind flicked back to her flight from the Spiral, the escape from its conflagration, the gallop away on Horse. *No*, she thought suddenly. *No!*

Surely even this bastard...

Kali pushed past Munch and his cronies and burst out of the door of the tavern into the stable-lined courtyard beyond. There she stopped dead. Horse was being led towards her by another of Munch's men. But something was wrong. Very wrong. Horse stumbled as he came, sweating, whinnying sadly, his eyes rolling as they always did, but this time in pain. As Kali fought to take in what it was that was wrong with him her eyes were drawn to the reason for Horse's weak and unsteady gait. The fetlocks on both of his hind legs had been cut almost through. Sinew and cartilage dangled from raw and sliced wounds that bled freely and left a trail behind them, like red ribbons on the ground. The trails, Kali saw, led back to his stable, where this vicious deed had obviously been done, for there a puddle of blood the size of a small pond had already begun to soak into the straw. With that much blood gone and the wounds that he had, it was a wonder that Horse could walk at all. Kali already felt sick enough but then the true cruelty of what had been done to him – and to her – became clear. Horse's fetlocks had been sliced with an almost surgical precision, to the degree where they were held together only by the finest threads of gristle and tissue, and the fact that he was being forced to walk towards her now was providing the strain that would finish them off. As Kali watched in horror, the remaining threads of the fetlocks snapped away and, with a loud whinny of pain, Horse collapsed, dropping onto his rear, the blood beginning to run from him more freely than ever.

Kali roared and attempted to run to him, but Munch had stationed two more of his men on either side of the tavern door and they each grabbed one of her arms, holding her back. At the same time, more of Munch's men appeared on the roofs of the stables, aiming crossbows down. Munch stepped casually through the door behind her and said, "The nag was old. If the strain of fleeing once again hadn't killed it, the knacker's yard would have finished it soon enough." He stepped around to Kali's front, and smiled. "Trust me, Miss Hooper, I was doing you a favour."

Kali spat in his face, and struggled anew in the hands of her captors. Over Munch's shoulder she saw Horse fold down onto his front legs and then, with a winded and tremulous expulsion of breath, collapse heavily onto his side, his legs kicking spasmodically. Blood began to pool there, too, and he began to shake, soaked in his cold sweat. His dazed large eyes – as innocent as a child's eyes – rolled in confusion, for there was no way he could understand what was happening to him.

But Kali knew what was happening, and she couldn't believe it.

Horse was dying right in front of her.

"Let me go to him," Kali said. "*Please.*"

Munch laughed. "The interfering adventurer shows her softer side. A compassion for all living things, all... *creatures* great and small. What a wonderfully pious attitude." He chuckled and, leaning in, whispered, "Perhaps you should consider joining our church?"

"*Damn you!*"

"The Lord of All knows my cause is righteous."

Behind her, the others were bundled out of the Flagons. Munch signalled his men on the rooftops to train their weapons on them.

Red and Aldrededor and Dolorosa stared grimly out at the scene before them, the woman raising her hand to her mouth. "Oh, no, no, no... oh, all the gods," Dolorosa said.

"'Ere, wosh goin' on out here?" another voice enquired, and the Sarge, his head looking as though it had been dunked in a bucket of water, strode from a stable, his men following behind. Munch scowled, and with a flick of his head ordered his men to lower their weapons. Idiots these men might be, but they still represented what passed for officialdom in these parts and, obviously, it was Munch's intention – perhaps *his* orders – to keep the situation as unofficial as he possibly could.

Unfortunately for him, it seemed to have already gone too far. The sergeant squinted at the dying Horse, then the restrained Kali, his brow furrowing. "'Ere..." he said again.

"There is nothing here to concern you," Munch said. "A tragic accident, that's all."

The sergeant pulled down his tunic, hiccupped and stared at him. "Looksh a bit more than that to me," he said. He gestured to his own men, who laid their hands on their weapons. "I'm afraid, sir, I'm going to have to ashk you for your provincial papers."

Munch scowled, considering the situation, and then actually smiled. But he made no move for papers of any kind. The poor fool confronting him had no idea how far he had just stepped out of his depth.

"Sarge, don't," Kali called to him. "Stay away."

But it was too late. Munch signalled his men and a rain of bolts took the sergeant's men down. Only the sergeant himself was left unscathed. For him, Munch had reserved something special.

It was over in seconds. Munch grunted as he forcefully levered his gutting knife from the chest of the sergeant fallen before him, and Kali could see him fighting the dull tugs on his bones as the roughened edge of his vicious blade grated and snagged between the dead man's ribs. Pulling it free of the corpse, he took a breath – a very satisfied breath – and then slowly turned and plunged the still-dripping blade into one of the gasping, weeping men who had survived his men's bolts. He did not go for a quick kill, instead impaling the man's guts and then twisting the hilt with both hands so that the end of the wide blade began to gouge a hole the size of an infant's head in the stomach of his screaming and helpless victim. The bucking man tried to grab the blade with his own hands, as if this would somehow ease his agony, but Munch pressed the sole of his boot onto them, slicing the grasping palms down the blade and, fingerless stumps now, into the gaping wound itself. As the man spasmed and uttered a final, guttural sob, Munch swiftly withdrew the blade, spewing a rain of intestinal matter onto his face and ending him.

Munch turned away from the corpses, wiping his knife on a patch of grass, but not replacing it in its sheath. It was clear to Kali that he hadn't murdered these man the way that he had just for fun. He had been *performing* for her – showing her how good he was.

How much of a challenge she was about to face.

Across the courtyard, Aldrededor knelt by the fallen Horse and trembled in helpless fury. Kali could see in his eyes how much he wanted to help her, to launch himself at Munch and his men for what they had done, and to kill them. But after his years of travelling the world Aldrededor was no fool – he knew the realities of life, of greater numbers, and of age. Instead, the old man stroked the neck of Kali's quickly fading companion, doing what he could to make the last minutes of Horse's life comfortable amidst the carnage. For his part, Horse's eyes were trained on Kali, perhaps wondering why it was she did not come. Wanting her badly to come.

"Arrrrgh!" Kali screamed, straining against the grips of her captors.

"She's mine," Munch shouted to his men. "Let her go."

Her captors released her, and Munch beckoned her to him, the courtyard having become his arena. Kali's first instinct was to charge at the bastard, to rip him limb from limb, empowered by the rage that had built – was still building – inside her like a volcano. But that would be foolish, she knew. She was no fighter, she just threw the punches she had to and, unless she was careful, Munch would likely skewer her before she could land a blow. Instead, she went halfway, starting to circle Munch in a half-crouch, ready, when her opening came, to spring. The trouble was, Munch was far too good a fighter to give her an opening, and as he too circled, expertly swinging his knife in a criss-cross defensive pattern, she knew that any such opening would likely be a feint, designed to draw her in. She had to play him at his own game, let him come to her.

"Something the matter, girl? Don't you hunger for my blood?"

"I'd prefer to just watch it leak away."

"Well, here's your chance," Munch said.

He raced at her, roaring loudly, swinging his knife diagonally right and left. The blackjack in her pocket useless to counter him, Kali knew she would have to rely on agility and speed to survive, and allowed herself to fall backwards to the ground. As his knife sliced above her, she rolled neatly out of his way and let his momentum crash him into a stock of barrels behind. Munch righted himself with another roar, and she quickly flipped back to her feet, beckoning to him, their positions reversed.

Munch came again, this time slicing his knife out in a wide arc before him, a manoeuvre that caused the air through which it passed to thrum.

Kali jumped back, jack-knifing herself at the waist so the tip of Munch's blade swept by her abdomen a few inches away and then, as it completed its arc, somersaulted forwards beneath Munch's plane of attack, slamming her soles into his gut. Munch buckled, winded, and, as he staggered back, Kali came upright again, grabbed him by the arm and, by sheer momentum alone, managed to spin him around. Once again Munch careered into barrels and, dizzied, collapsed to one knee. It was obvious he needed a second to recover but Kali had no intention of giving him the chance, and booted him in the face, knocking him onto his back.

Munch struggled to get back up. If his roar had been loud before, then now it was deafening, and purposefully not pressing her advantage – knowing Munch would use every dirty trick in the book and try impaling her from his prone position – Kali smiled. This was exactly what she wanted – to get the bastard angry, because if he was angry then he would start to make mistakes. Panting, she bounced on the balls of her feet like a pugilist, her fists clenched, waiting for him to come again.

Munch did, but quickly and with surprising agility, and Kali felt a surge of panic. She had known this was never going to be easy, but it was only at this moment she realised how hard her survival was going to be. Caught off guard, she flung herself desperately to the left as Munch's knife pierced the air in the spot she had stood a half-second earlier. That she had avoided, but unexpectedly Munch also rammed his elbow into the side of her head as he moved. Stunned, her head ringing, Kali felt herself weaving away and supporting herself on one of the beams holding up the stables, without a clue as to where her assailant would come from next.

The knife slammed into the beam hard, sending a chunk of wood and splinters flying into the air, and Kali felt the whole structure vibrate. Had the wood not been in the way, she would have been missing half her skull. With a gasp, she stumbled back into the stable proper, Munch wrenching his blade from the timber and following.

"Where's the key, girl? Tell me before I slice you in two!"

"Go to hells, you bastard!"

A distraction, she thought. She needed a distraction. Then, on the stable floor, she spotted the patch of straw into which Horse had first bled and, swallowing at its warmth, plunged her hand into it, flinging it in Munch's direction. Under normal circumstances it might have bought her a second before it was batted away, but with Horse's blood causing the straw to stick to Munch's face, it bought her two. Kali used the time to reorientate herself and ran back towards the yard.

"Come here, girl," Munch called from behind. No longer playing by his own rules, he signalled to two of his men to block her path. She spun to face two more, blocking the way she had come. And Munch came relentlessly on between them.

Kali spun where she stood, double-taking on any possible escape route, anywhere she could run to buy more time, but there was none. But then something clicked in her head. Whether it was her rage or the booze coursing inside her, she couldn't say, but she was seized suddenly by a rush of... well, she didn't know what it was, only what it made her do.

Surprising herself as she had at the Spiral, Kali ran straight for the nearest of Munch's men, and as he raised a sword to stop her she leapt upwards, using his sword arm as a platform to leap onto his shoulder, and from there onto the stable roof, the recoil from her heel sending the man staggering forwards onto his face. One of the men on the roof came at her and Kali spun, bringing her leg up and around, impacting with the side of his head and sending him flying from the roof, crashing into another of Munch's men on the ground. Another came and she ran straight at him, clutching his chest and flipping herself over and above him, maintaining her grip so that as a result he himself was flipped as she landed, slammed down, dazed. Working her way around the roof – kicking, throwing and punching any man who stood in her way, despatching them into the air until none were left above – she manoeuvred herself until Munch was directly below, staring up at her in some amazement amidst the chaos she'd caused. Kali panted and stared back, and she hoped her message was clear. *Get ready, you little bastard. Because I'm coming.*

She only wished she knew how, because she was making this up as she went along.

But so too now was Munch. Snarling, he flicked an arm at those men still standing, ordering them towards a stack of barrels that reached to the lip of the roof, and they began to clamber up towards her. Kali didn't give them a chance, booting the highest barrel down at them, scattering them aside. She booted another, and then another, and as they arced through the air, leapt out between them, landing and rolling in the midst of those who meant to do her harm. The first of the barrels had already crushed a man to the ground, and the second, come to a stop on its side, she booted again, rolling it into the legs of her nearest assailant, buckling the man over it, onto his back, where she leapt and knocked him cold. As another came at her, she dropped to her haunches, curled her fingers under the rim of the third, upright barrel and, with strength she hadn't known she possessed, spun it end over end, sending it smashing into his chest where he instinctively caught it, dropped it, and screamed. Kali didn't let it go to waste. Seeing another of the men coming straight at her from behind his broken-footed comrade, she ran forwards, heaved the barrel up and then kept going, using it as a battering ram to crush him up against the stable wall. The barrel shattered and, with a groan, the man slumped to the ground, unconscious.

Kali spun, panting and sweating, ready for the next.

But that was it – other than the men guarding Aldrededor and the others, she'd done it.

Now it was just her and Munch.

He stood there, his knife held in readiness by his side, smiling, waiting. Why the bastard hadn't attacked alongside his men, she didn't know. Maybe he wanted to use them to tire her out. Maybe he just wanted to see what she'd suddenly become capable of. It didn't matter, because all she could see, behind him, was a weeping Aldrededor and her now dead Horse.

Kali roared, and disregarding the caution she had felt when the fight had begun – knowing somehow that whatever move he made now she'd cope with – ran straight for Munch.

He raised his knife. But she didn't give him the chance to use it.

Kali used her speed to leap upwards, pirouetting in the air and sweeping her leg around to catch Munch with a sickening kick to his jaw that knocked him sideways.

She landed, rolled and rose, spinning up from a crouch to bring her other leg around and deliver an equally numbing blow to his opposite side. *Turn the other cheek, you bastard,* she thought – *they teach you that in church?* Munch spat and grunted, as much with surprise as with pain, and, double-whammied, staggered about like the drunks he had slaughtered. Kali gave him no time to get his bearings, racing in at him and grabbing his knife hand by the wrist, at the same time bringing up her knee so that it impacted with his underarm, numbing his nerves and forcing him to release his grip. The gutting knife clattered to the ground and Munch stared at her, mumbling something incoherent. Kali didn't care what it was, using her leverage on his arm to twist him towards her and then ramming her elbow, hard and again and again and again, into his face. Munch grunted with each blow, blood spouting from his nose, and weaved backwards, totally stunned. As he did, Kali booted him first in the crotch and then the chest, and finally under his chin, sending him crashing backwards to the ground. She bent over him, panting, hot with rage, and pulled back her fist.

She was about to deliver the first of what she intended to be a volley of blows when it happened again. A vision. Only one much more painful than before. She suddenly couldn't punch anything, and all she could do was slam her hands to the sides of her head.

The last thing she saw of her home and her friends was Munch rising, snarling, and reaching for his knife.

And then agonising pain plunged her into blackness again.

CHAPTER 6

Boots, again. Thudding this time not into her side but hard onto the ground. Many, many boots, thudding down one after the other, in militaristic rhythm.

The sound of marching.

But Kali saw nothing, saw no one. Only a sea the colour of blood. No, not just the colour of blood, for blood it seemed to be. Viscous and slow, it spread languidly across a flat and desolate landscape beneath a sky the colour of fog. A sea of blood that flowed ever outwards, seemingly without shore, until it covered all there was to see.

There was screaming, too. A distant and tortured screaming of many mouths that, though it seemed far away, was nevertheless all around her. But again, she saw no one – in the midst of the blood and the screaming, she stood all alone.

Kali stared down at the sea and wondered – was this the hells? Had she, despite everything she believed, been taken by Kerberos? Was she there? Would she see Horse?

There was movement on the horizon and she looked slowly up. Something was coming towards her. No, not something – *many* things whose bootfalls were in time with the marching she heard. Huge, looming figures that were somehow familiar in shape and somehow not, a dozen at first, and then a dozen behind, and then a dozen more still, marching towards her, advancing in rank after rank after rank.

Marching through the blood.

The ground trembled, and the blood flowed away in sluggish banks, revealing layer upon layer of bones – human bones – whose flesh had rotted where they lay. And the skulls and ribcages and femurs were crushed beneath the boots of the advancing horde as it came ever on. Kali could see now that the figures had looked familiar because they were human-shaped, but human they most definitely were not. There were no boots on those heavy, crunching feet. And it was not armour that clanked. And the sky of fog made their metal skins shine.

She turned slowly, struggled to run from the things, but her legs moved as if mired in sludge. The marching came closer and closer until it was right behind her, and her heart thudded. And then a great shadow loomed over her.

She turned again, looked up. Red and evil eyes stared at her and then a vast hammer came down hard.

"*Aarrgh!*" Kali said, awakening bolt upright. That she awoke in such a position came as a bit of a surprise, but then awakening in any position would have been a surprise, considering she hadn't expected to wake at all.

Where? she thought. *What?* And then she remembered. She wasn't dead, then – she hadn't been finished by Munch. What she had seen had been another vision. But why the hells couldn't she move?

Ah. Kali realised she was restrained on a solid chair made of wood that could once have been butchers' blocks, on a raised platform in the middle of a cold, stone room. Thick iron collars integral to the chair circled her ankles, wrists and neck, holding her almost immovably in place. Her first instinct was to jerk against them, which she duly did, regretting the move when she found the insides of the collars had been inlaid with small sharp pins that stabbed immediately into her skin. Kali yelped, winced and stayed still. This chair had been designed by someone who liked inflicting pain, and she had a horrible suspicion who that might be.

All kinds of things went through her mind, not the least of them that she had been stripped of her working gear and was clothed only in her vest and pants. The goose pimples on her arms and legs were, however, the least of her discomforts, the greatest being the bloody great thumping headache she was not sure was the result of the second vision she had suffered or what must have been a knockout blow from Munch. Obviously the bastard had never intended to kill her – only make her think so – after all, he'd never find the key if she were dead.

The key. What was so important – and so *disturbing* to Merrit Moon – about that key that had driven Munch and his cronies first to the Spiral and then to the Flagons in its pursuit? Bloody images from the tavern that she did not want flashed into her mind, and she pushed them away.

Just what the hells was going on? And, more importantly,

where the hells had she been brought?

Headache subsiding slightly, Kali looked around her place of captivity – as much as her iron collars would allow. There wasn't much to see – torches mounted on the walls illuminated a circular chamber accessed by a single heavy door, featureless other than the chair in which she sat, rather troublingly the obvious centre of attention. There were no windows, so it was likely a cellar, and by the absence of outside noise a cellar somewhere isolated and deep. But where exactly? She had no idea how long she had been unconscious and therefore no idea how far she had travelled. She could literally be anywhere on the peninsula.

Kali strained to listen, hoping perhaps to hear some noises from the outside world – perhaps a clatter of cartwheels on mud, cobbles or stone – an indicator of which town or city she was in, or snatched voices speaking in some regional accent. But there was only silence except for the vaguest hint of something in the distance.

It took her a few seconds to place what it was because it seemed so far out of context to the predicament she was in. But then she had it.

It was singing.

Somewhere above her, people were singing.

What sounded like a mix between a battle hymn and a song of praise.

The Final Faith, she thought. Munch must have brought her to one of their churches, and she was sitting beneath one of their congregations. But which congregation, in which church, where? She strained to listen and, beyond the singing, caught the sound of bells.

Twelve bells to be precise, each of them pealing in turn. Kali felt her heart thump as recognition dawned.

There was only one place she knew of that had such bell towers. Pits of Kerberos, the little bastard had brought her to Scholten – abducted her halfway across the peninsula, to the cathedral itself.

The realisation – and its implications – sinking in, Kali began to struggle anew against her bonds, but as she felt blood start to trickle, she let out a cry of frustration.

At the same time she heard footsteps approaching on the other side of the door.

A key turned in its lock and the door opened.

Three people walked into the room, studying her but staying silent. The first of them was Munch, the second a disturbingly tall, thin man she didn't recognise, and the third a woman she did – but only because she looked a bit like her statues.

It was Caroline MacDonald. The Anointed Lady.

No, hang on, that didn't sound right, Kali thought. *MacDonald, maybe but... Christine? Katarina? Katherine.* She was sure it was Katherine.

Yes, that was it. Katherine MacDonald, the Anointed Lady.

Hells, she really ought to get to church more often.

"We do seem to be plagued by pests of late," the woman sighed. She strode towards Kali and looked directly at her. "Kali Hooper," she intoned. "Age twenty-two, sex, sometimes, current occupation proprietor of the tavern formerly known as the Retching Weasel and now the Here There Be Flagons, situated in the hamlet of Stopford, in the western county of Tarn."

Kali smiled. "Thanks for reminding me. Now I'll be able to find my own way home. Whenever you're ready, that is."

"I'm not. Oh, and if you're thinking of shouting for help, don't bother." She pointed up. "The Eternal Choir never stops."

"That must get on your tits."

Makennon ignored her. "Not much to go on at all, Kali. And that is all the information in our records – tell me, don't you find that strange?"

Kali stared at her. "No, what I find strange is you have records about me at all. Tell me, Katherine, it is just a church you're running here, isn't it – not a dictatorship? And hey, I could have done without the crack about the sex."

"Proprietor of the aforementioned tavern and sometime tomb raider, I am led to believe."

Kali's eyes narrowed.

"Actually, I prefer to think of them more as repositories, or reliquaries – museums of the past. To be honest, I'd be pretty much gobsmacked if I found anyone dead in them, their owners having been gone for quite some time. But seriously, Katherine, you are really going to have to go to interrogation classes if you're going to ask me questions and then ignore everything I say." She smiled sweetly. "Kind of defeats the object, doesn't it?"

Makennon slapped her suddenly and unexpectedly on the cheek, hard.

"This isn't a damned game, tomb raider!"

Her head involuntarily snapped to the side, Kali worked her jaw and spat out a small glob of blood. Then she snapped her head back and glared at her captor, hair mussed over eyebrows that were deeply veed, her expression thunderous. But she spoke steadily.

"I'd kind of worked that out when your hired psychopath here slaughtered my horse."

Makennon smiled. "What can I say? Konstantin has a... passion for his work."

"Burn in the hells!"

Makennon cocked her head, almost curiously. "I hardly think that's likely, Kali, do you? I am Katherine Makennon, the Anointed Lord, head of the largest faith – the largest church – on Twilight. Hundreds of thousands of people see me as the Lord of All's representative on this world of His, and they revere me as much as they do Him. Each of these people pray for my well-being on a daily basis, and each of them will solicit my passage to the heavens when my time eventually comes. Think about it. With that kind of support, how could I possibly burn?"

"Oh, I'm sure there's a big enough match somewhere," Kali said. *Makennon, right.* "Why have you brought me here?"

"You know why, Kali. I want the key."

"I thought it was Munch who wanted the key?" Kali retorted. It was a weak retort but the best she could do in an attempt to halt the growing unease in her gut. "What are you going to do – fight amongst yourselves?"

"My desires are Munch's desires, and our desires are those of the Faith. The key belongs to no one individual but to the Church itself – it has been written."

"Oh, really? By whom?"

"The Old Races. The forefathers of we, the Divine Race."

"Oh right, them," Kali responded casually. Makennon was obviously referring to the elves and the dwarves, but other than that she didn't have a clue what she was on about. She just wished someone would tell her why the key was in so much demand or what it was that the damn thing actually *did*.

Makennon studied her, a smile playing on her lips. "You don't know what it is, do you? You haven't a clue. The key was just some... *bauble* you saw your chance to steal from us."

"Why don't you tell me what it is?"

"When you tell me *where* it is."

"You know, I am getting heartily sick of that question. As I told your flunky here – *I don't know.*"

"That we shall have to see, won't we?" Makennon said. She turned to Munch and the tall man. "Get on with it," she ordered. "Report to me below when you're done."

Below? Kali thought. *But weren't they already in the cellars?* She thought no more of it, though, as she realised Makennon was about to leave, and in her current circumstances being left with Munch and his mate as they got on with it made her feel more than a little concerned.

"Makennon, wait," she said. "You're the head of the Final Faith – a church – how can you countenance this?"

The Anointed Lord smiled. "I don't. I just ignore it."

With Makennon gone, Kali stared at Munch and he stared back, saying nothing but slowly rubbing his hand over large black bruises on his face, what looked like a broken nose, a stitched gash above his eye. He breathed shallowly and Kali noticed that bandages wrapped his ribs. She'd given him a good drubbing, all right, but right now it didn't make her feel much better. The bloody mouth Makennon had given her was nothing compared to the damage Munch could inflict while she was as helpless as she was.

But she was not going to let it matter what he did to her. She couldn't. Because if she told him about the key then she would have to tell him about Merrit Moon, and there was no way she was dragging the old man into this.

All she could hope for was that she blacked out quick.

Unfortunately, it seemed that oblivion was not going

to be. As Kali swallowed in expectation of what was to come, it wasn't Munch who made the first move but the tall, thin man. With no expression showing on his sunken, sallow face he walked behind her, cupped her skull in his hands and then tipped it from side to side, fingers rubbing gently. The incongruity of what he was doing made her swallow harder still, her unease made all the worse by the fact that she couldn't see a thing. "What's with the massage, Munch?" she asked, sounding calmer than she felt. "You think maybe I need to relax?"

Munch spoke for the first time. He sounded calm and in control but Kali caught a flash of bloodlust in his eyes that belied his manner – the little bastard was looking forward to this. "This gentleman's name is Querilous Fitch," he said. "Mister Fitch is here to ensure our session lasts as long as is necessary. It is his job to ensure that you remain attentive and do not lapse into unconsciousness, a technique at which he is particularly adept."

"Then I'd better warn you I drop like a stone at the sight of blood," Kali said. "I don't think Fitch's massage is going to help very much."

Munch smiled. "His technique is a little more than a mere massage."

"Oh? What's he going to – " Kali began, and then stopped suddenly, gasping. It seemed to her that the fingers that a moment before had been caressing the back of her skull had somehow just slipped *inside* it, and while she was pretty sure the sensation couldn't actually be physical, it sure as hells felt like it. She felt cold and woozy and sick at the same time, and the really creepy thing was that she could feel different parts of her brain throb one after the other, as if the fingers were feeling their way around.

Thread magic, it had to be. Fitch was *weaving* inside

her head.

Kali groaned loudly, and as she did Munch wheeled a small iron trolley into the room and locked it into place by the side of her chair. She flicked her eyes towards it. It looked innocuous enough but she somehow doubted it was there to provide her with a manicure to go with the massage. Too disorientated for a wisecrack, she found Munch speaking for her.

"I imagine you're expecting a selection of instruments crafted to cause you physical injury," he said slowly. "Branding irons? Pincers? Thumbscrews?" He lifted the lid. "Unfortunately, the Anointed Lord has decreed that such tools are only to be used should there be a failure in our more advanced techniques. I find these techniques rather *uninspiring* personally, but who am I to argue? The Anointed Lord has, after all, engaged some of our best alchemical minds to develop both these and their effects."

Kali looked numbly at what Munch had revealed. The trolley held a number of vials of coloured liquids, greens and oranges and reds, some of which looked more viscous than others, and each of which was marked with a strange symbol she did not recognise. They could have been reptile venoms or plant toxins or some other kind of poison and, though some bubbled of their own accord, what worried her most was that each sat next to a strip of needlereed, the hard, strawlike growth that, filled with a dart and the right ingredients, was a favourite tool of the assassins guilds.

But they were not going to poison her, surely.

So what?

Munch picked up a strip of needlereed and dipped it into one of the vials, the green, and then again, into the red. He tapped the end so that the viscous fluids mingled and slipped down inside, then raised and examined the reed, smiling in satisfaction.

"The dosage and combinations of these distillations have to be quite specific," he explained, "or can prove instantly lethal. But used correctly their effect is wondrously telling – though I'm told quite unpleasant – making your mind as pliant and as loose as I wish it to be. They do, however, cause some dizziness and lack of muscular control."

Kali swallowed. "Hey, then why don't you just give me a bottle of flummox? No, make that a case." She eyed the needlereed. "Is this going to hurt?"

Munch smiled. "This... no. But you may still feel some little pricks."

He flicked a lever on the side of the chair and the iron collars holding her clamped tighter, the pins piercing her ankles, wrists and neck. She bucked in her seat but found she could now barely move at all. Her limbs stung and blood flowed into the nape of her neck.

"Uuurngh!"

"As I said, they may cause some dizziness or delirium," Munch reiterated, "and it is essential for Mister Fitch's work that you remain absolutely still."

He dug the needlereed into the bend in her elbow, shoving it hard into her flesh, and Kali felt sick to the stomach as she saw the vein on her arm pulse and tinge green, the colour spreading up.

The noxious substance coursed quickly through her bloodstream, and there was nothing she could do to stop it, no way she could even try. Whatever it was Munch had given her, she felt instantly as if she had been on a week-long bender in the Flagons, the room about her tipping and swaying like a ship on the Sarcrean Sea. Sweat broke from every pore, her skin began to tingle, and as her stomach cramped agonisingly she vomited foam onto her chin. But however bad what was happening to her body was, it was nothing compared to what was happening to her mind. Her vision exploded suddenly with great bomb-blasts of orange and yellow and red that detonated and then spread like spilled paint, coating the inside of her eyes with a vibrant, cloying sea. Her head tipped back deliriously, and that part of her neck that thrust out as a result was pierced more deeply by the pins, making her blood run ever more freely. But she didn't care – the red of her blood was simply part of a rainbow that wrapped itself now around the inside of her skull, dizzying and disorientating, swooping and sick. As the colours swam, so too did her thoughts, and images of anything and everything began to flood her inner eye. Lost inside her own head, aware that she was dribbling and moaning, there was nothing she could do now but listen to the voice.

"The key, Miss Hooper – where is the key?"

"Told you... don't know..."

"Of course you know. The key, girl, where is the key?"

Kali tried to fight, to pull her thoughts into some kind of order, but the awareness of what the voice wanted produced precisely the opposite effect. An image of Merrit Moon flashed unbidden amongst a kaleidoscope of others and Kali railed against it, lest she blurt out his name. She tried desperately to make her mind go blank but it was a feat she had never been able to master – she wondered if anyone had – because there was always something in there, nagging away, even if it was only the panicked assertion to make her mind go blank, which perversely and inevitably conjured up the very images she wanted to forget. Kali consciously summoned other memories instead, the sights and sounds of previous adventures, but Merrit Moon hovered like a spectre in them all, smiling, advising, telling her when to run. She concentrated as hard as she could and shoved him away, back, into the darkness, and in his stead a cryptographic stone wheel loomed before her, set in a vine-strewn wall. *Three turns to the right and two to the left. No. Oops. Boulder, big boulder. Run!*

She could feel herself slipping, and all the time the question.

"The key, Kali. Where is the key?"

In the end, she fled to the only place she could – home. She surrounded herself with the laughter and the banter of the Flagons, the revelry and rivalry that was her tavern's soul. All her friends were there – Aldrededor, Dolorosa, Red – even Horse, alive once more. She swept away a sudden image of him dying and instead lost herself in memories of exploring the peninsula on his back, the discovery of Thunderlung's Cry, the Rainbow River, the mind-numbing Heights of Low...

"Such a *shame* about the beast," the voice said and, with a vertiginous panic, she realised that it was Munch, and that she must have unwillingly spoken Horse's name aloud. Her panic doubled, for she realised now that in thinking about Horse she was only one step away from thinking about Merrit Moon, and how easy it would be to speak *his* name out loud.

So she left even home behind, going back before the Flagons, before Horse and before Merrit Moon, back to her childhood and beyond – where lay no memory at all. But in doing so she found herself suddenly remembering what she had never fully remembered before, and she was there on a lonely road, during a storm-lashed night, crying like the babe she was, her tears indistinguishable from the rain. She felt herself being handed from one set of hands to another, caught a fleeting glimpse of a hooded man, and then, above her instead, was Red – a younger Red – smiling down.

Then even Red faded away, and she struggled to fill the gap he left behind. It was getting more and more difficult to concentrate now, she realised, and there was nowhere else to go.

But it seemed there was. Suddenly she felt something pull aside, like a curtain in her mind, and for the first time ever she saw, *actually saw*, the place where she'd been found.

Despite her escalating delirium, Kali gasped. It was there before her, clearer and more detailed than the memory of a babe had any right to make it. Clearly some kind of Old Race ruin, its interior was adorned with complex runes and trellised with ornate ironwork as artistic as that of the Spiral, or of anywhere she had ever been. But there was more, here – strange panels of light set into the walls, flights of iron steps leading to machine-filled platforms that *blinked* around the edge, corridors and doors leading away to who knew where. She could feel the whole place *tremble* with power. *Gods* – she wanted to get up, to explore, but she was, after all, only a babe and could not rise from where she lay swaddled and helpless, there, in the middle of it all.

Kali found it didn't matter. For the first time she was seeing what she had never seen or known before – her own origin. It was Munch's drugs, it had to be, and though she would never have believed it, she actually had something to thank the bastard for.

It was a revelation.

But nothing like the revelation that followed.

Because just as she thought it was over, the hooded man entered the room. The same stranger that on that storm-lashed night had taken her from this place and given her into the care of Red.

He bent over her, and she saw his face.

And it was the face of Merrit Moon.

Merrit Moon.

No! she screamed inside her head. The image – *the memory* – was so unexpected, so sudden, so startling, that she couldn't shed herself of it, and as a result couldn't trust herself not to speak his name. The only way – *the only way* – to beat Munch's drugs was to make herself forget the face, but how – *how* – could she possibly forget what she'd just seen?

She had to do something.

She cared too much about Merrit to reveal him.

She had to end Munch's flight of fancy. *Now!*

There was only one thing she could do. Kali rammed her ankles, wrists and neck into the collar's pins, hoping the pain would drop her into a state of oblivion from which even Fitch would be unable to bring her back. Through her agony, she felt him pulling at her, but that only made her the more intent, and instead of simply impaling herself on the pins she began to tug herself to the left and right as much as the collars would allow, letting the pins tear into her flesh, to rip it from her in jagged strips. The pain was excruciating and she felt as if her body was on fire, and her flesh was slick now with her own blood, but still she carried on, roaring not with pain but with unslacking determination. And, at last, she began to feel numb.

She heard distant, echoing curses. And then hands were pulling quickly and roughly at her restraints.

"Damn her," she heard someone say, and realised it had to be Munch. What followed made no sense. "Did you get it? *Did you get it?*"

"I believe so. But I will need time to absorb what I have."

"*Gah*! Make it quick."

Kali sighed, and someone took her, then. The collars released, she found herself being lifted from the chair, the room canting at strange angles around her. The figures of Munch and Querilous Fitch were merely blurs, as ghostly in their appearance as their disembodied voices were haunting. She heard the sound of doors opening, saw dark outlines looming, and realised she was being escorted through the underground of the cathedral. But that couldn't be right, surely, because as she moved she caught glimpses of bright lights, of lots of people, of activity that surely did not belong where she was. Had they taken her somewhere else, then, as she slipped between consciousness and delirium – somewhere where she could hear orders being barked, the sound of factory machines, the bustle of an army at work? Or perhaps she imagined it, because now those things were gone, and she was being led down a stairway that spiralled down before her, where it was quieter and darker and colder than even the chamber had been. Other faces swam before her now, peering at her through hatches in doors, faces that were bearded and straggly and desperate, and one that for a fleeting second she thought she recognised but couldn't possibly have. Some degree of awareness was returning now, and Kali realised she was in a corridor of cells, and even in the state she was in, one thing was clear – these faces she saw, leering out at her, these faces and their owners, they had been here a long time and, if she didn't do something *right now*, so would she be too.

She broke free of her captors and ran, lurching like a drunk, for the end of the cell corridor, to a ventilation shaft set into the wall. As deep and as doomed as they were, the prisoners here still had to breathe, and with a little luck the shaft would reach all the way to the surface. She leapt for a rung that was set just above the hole, and missed. She tried once more and this time found herself slumping down against the wall.

It was no good, the wounds on her ankles and wrists coupled with the loss of blood had left her too weak.

She could do nothing but capitulate as her captors loomed and roughly pulled her up.

Exhaustion overwhelmed her, then. All she remembered was being thrown into a cold, dark cell, and the door being slammed tightly shut behind her. Time passed, and then someone entered her cell and bandaged her wounds.

She slept, without any idea of for how long. And when she awoke, she heard singing.

But it was not the singing she had heard upstairs.

And of all the things that had happened to her in the last few weeks, it was by far the most disturbing.

CHAPTER 7

That voice, Kali thought. *It couldn't be. Not him. Oh gods, please tell me it isn't him!* Tell me it isn't. But the seconds passed and, as had always been the case, the gods didn't tell her anything at all, and she thought: *It is, isn't it?* There couldn't be any doubt. That voice, that tune, those lyrics.

Gods preserve her, those lyrics.

She felt a dizzying swoon that was almost a panic. As the cell seemed to heat up and flex around her, she tried to shut her brain down but it was no good. And as the song concluded, she just couldn't help herself. It was like being some small, furry creature, its ears erect, transfixed by the sound of an oncoming cart, oblivious to the rumbling wheels of doom. She just had to listen.

"... so ever since I've been in a stupor.
Because of that lass named Kali Hoooooper."

A tin cup rattled on the bars of a cell door somewhere down the corridor. "For the sake of everything that's holy, will you *please stop!*" a desperate voice yelled.

"Wait – I think he has. Steaming pits, that was worse than the mangling room," said another.

"Something... I need something to stab my eardrums."

There was a very long, unappreciated sigh that echoed off the stone walls. "Fine," its owner said sulkily. "Just trying to cheer everyone up, that's all."

"We're cheerful, honestly!" someone cried, and then laughed manically, as if to prove it. "Really, really cheerful."

"Is it over? Oh, thank Kerberos... I feel I've been reborn."

Kali ignored the voices. Her heart thudding, she moved beneath the small grille that linked her cell to the next, from where the singing had come. She stretched and curled her fingers over its lip and then pulled herself up with a grunt, her soles skittering on the stonework below. It was something of a strain and her arms trembled with the effort, but as long as she held her grip she could see through the bars.

In the cell next door, there was a man wearing nothing but his undershorts. Just sitting there in the middle of the floor, with his legs folded, picking his teeth with a rockroach leg. Lean and muscular with an unkempt thatch of blond hair, many might have confused him with some debonair lord or playboy type, but she knew that nothing could actually be further from the truth.

Kali dropped back down, shook her head, took a breath, then heaved herself back up, unable to believe it.

The man looked up.

"Hello, Kali," he said.

Kali stared.

"'Liam," she said slowly and dubiously, in response.

"How are you doing?" he said, as casually as if they had bumped into each other on Freiport high street.

Kali's voice quavered with the strain of hanging on. "Ohhhh, you know..."

"Yeah."

"You?"

"Oh, fine, just fine."

There was a pause.

"So..."

"So..."

"Here we are."

"Yep. Here we are."

Kali dropped down again, and blinked. She knew full well what she had just seen but she couldn't shake herself of the conviction that it was impossible. The last time she had seen Killiam Slowhand – she slammed her eyes shut with a cringe, blanking out the details – had been on the Sarcre Islands, and that had been over two years earlier. After that night, he had seemingly vanished off the face of Twilight.

That night, she thought again.

Anger bubbled inside her, and she clambered back up, yelping as she saw Slowhand directly in front of her, working away at the grille to loosen it. "What the hells are you doing here, Slowhand? Come to *rescue* me again?"

"Nope."

"Stop grinning at me inanely."

"Can't help it. But it's still nope."

Kali gestured through the grille, indicating his cell, or rather his imprisonment therein. "Why are you here, then? It *is* me, I know it is – you heard I'd been taken by the Faith so got yourself taken to give me a helping hand!"

"You are unbelievable," Slowhand said, continuing to work at the metal. "Hooper, believe it or not some of the time I don't think about you at all."

"I'm hurt. Also vastly relieved." Kali's eyes narrowed. "So what the hells *are* you doing here? Don't tell me the great Killiam Slowhand was bettered by the Final Faith?"

"I have them where they want me. I mean, they have me where I... Oh hells, never mind."

"You were, weren't you! They caught you!"

"On purpose, all right?"

"What? Why in the gods' names would you want to do that?"

Slowhand sighed heavily. "Because I wanted to look around. See what really goes on behind the scenes with the Final Faith."

"From one of their cells?"

"*Nooooo*, not from one of their cells." He shrugged. "Well, not in the way you mean, anyway. Stand back."

Slowhand punched the grille out of its mounting and Kali instinctively caught it with an oof before it could clang to the floor. *Damn*, she thought, *we still make a great team whether I like it or not.*

But this was still going a little fast for her. She had no idea what was going on.

"Okaaay," she said. "So, what's that achieved? No, wait, don't tell me – you're going to escape from your cell into mine. Brilliant!"

"I see the wit hasn't deserted you," Slowhand said,

wearily. "No, Hooper – it's the other way round. You're going to escape from your cell into mine."

"What?" Kali let the information sink in. "O-hoh, no, no, no," she replied forcefully, looking at herself still in the vest and pants in which she'd awoken upstairs. "If you think you're going to get me in a six foot square cell while we're both wearing nothing but our knickers you've another think coming. This isn't –"

"Because the way out is in my cell."

Kali stopped. She had to admit that had nonplussed her.

"You have a way out?"

Slowhand grinned broadly. "A-ha. Or, to be more accurate, have had a way out for the last week and a half I've been here. I've had to time it with the guard patrols, of course, but, an hour here, an hour there, it's allowed me to have a pretty good look around. Enough, in fact, to make tonight time to go. The escape route's a... little problematic but even in your state you should be able to manage it. So... excellent timing."

Her *state*, Kali thought. The odd thing was, she had already begun to wonder what her state was. She felt much better than she had when she'd first been dumped in the cell, better, in fact, than anyone who'd endured what she had had any right to feel. She had been here – what? – well, the truth was she didn't know – but surely not that long, and she already felt more than well on the road to recovery. She was tempted to look beneath her bandages but now wasn't really the time. Things had turned strange enough already.

"One tiny problem with your master plan," Kali said. "I'll never squeeze through that hole."

"Course you will. From what I've seen you've lost quite a bit of weight lately."

"Excuse me? Are you saying I was fat?"

"No! Great gods and pits of Kerberos, no. It's just that – well, you seem to have lost a bit of the puppy fat you had. You seem a lot more... *lithe.*"

"Lithe?" Kali repeated. She thought again of her recovery. "Yes, well, I do seem to have developed something of a faster metabolism these days..."

"There you go, then," Slowhand said. He winked. "Besides, if nothing else it'll be fun to watch."

"Fun to watch," Kali repeated. "Wait a minute. Killiam Slowhand, have you been watching me in my cell? Lying here in a dungeon, in my underwear?"

Slowhand threw his hands in the air. "Of course I have, woman! Who wouldn't? No, I mean, how else was I to know you were there? And I – I wanted to know you were all ri –" He stopped suddenly, changed the subject. "Hey, if you're worried about getting through the grille, why don't you smear yourself with oil?"

"I don't have any oil."

"Damn! I'll just do my best to imagine it, then."

"Slowhand..."

"Fine, fine. Okay, look. The guards are going to change shift in fifteen minutes so if you're going to do this, Hooper, do it now. Or I leave you here."

Kali let out an exasperated growl and leapt for the opening, pulling herself up and then forwards on her stomach, her hands gripping the lip of the gap on Slowhand's side. It was a tight squeeze, but with a helping hand from Slowhand she made it through, flipping unsteadily into his cell and then, involuntarily, into his arms.

Slowhand grinned broadly. "Been a while."

"Don't even thi –" Kali began, and then stopped. "Whoa, hold on a second here," she said. "Killiam Slowhand, are you wearing make-up?"

Slowhand slid his fingers to that part of his neck which Kali stared at, and they came away smeared with greasepaint he had missed when cleaning himself up. It was amazing how long that stuff stuck around.

"Actually, yes," he admitted. "But it's not what you think."

"Really? And what do I think?"

"Knowing you, gods only knows," Slowhand responded. He took an extravagant bow and added by way of explanation, "Killiam Slowhand's Final Filth – Every Hour On The Hour. *Ta daaaa.*"

"You've got to be kidding me," Kali said. "You've become a *troubadour?*" She couldn't help herself – she started to giggle.

"Hey, a guy's got to earn a crust somehow," Slowhand said, feigning hurt. "Besides, you'd be astounded the places being a travelling player gets you."

"Oh, that's it – it's all to do with getting in here, isn't it?" Kali said.

Suddenly her smile faded and it was Slowhand's turn to study her up close. He whistled, looking concerned. "Pits, they really did a number on you, didn't they?" He stretched out a hand to stroke her cheek, but Kali pulled away, hesitated before speaking.

"'Liam... one of them... some bastard called Munch... he killed Horse."

"What? Oh, hells. Oh, hells, Kal, I'm so sorry." Slowhand's jaw tightened and pulsed, and for a second his eyes went distant, as though remembering – and noting – something. "I know how much the old nag meant to you."

"The old man, he doesn't know yet."

"The old man? Oh, you mean Merrit Moon. You haven't

told him?"

Kali shook her head. "He left for the mountains. To dispose of a key."

Slowhand pushed her to arm's length. "This key. It wouldn't be anything to do with the reason Makennon had you interrogated, would it?"

"The only reason. Whatever the thing is, it's important to her."

Slowhand sighed. "So I've been told. Look, it's going to be a few minutes before we're ready to move, and, in case you hadn't noticed, before then I'm a captive audience. So why don't you tell me all about it?"

Kali did, telling everything, including the find, the old man's reaction to it, everything, including the first and second vision, the one that had resulted in her being here. Slowhand took the news of a clanking army wading through a sea of blood in reasonable stride because, like her, he had seen some things. In turn, he told her about the scrolls Makennon had tried to woo him with – the images of the Old Races and the keys that were somehow meant to be the Faith's destiny – but after both of them were done, they were none the wiser.

Slowhand listened to the activity outside the cell. "Sounds like you have things to do," he said. "So how about we get you out of here?"

Kali looked around the cell, noting that its interior was exactly the same as her own had been, presenting the same obstructions to liberty she had faced. "About that," she enquired. "Just what is it you have in mind?"

Slowhand pointed to the lock in the door, and then, disturbingly, to his shorts, which shimmered slightly. "Krunt scale," he said, proudly. "The humble krunt's greatest weapon in the survival of the fittest." Kali looked blank and he sighed, explaining as he might to a five-year-old. "Krunts are native to the waters of the Stormwall, Hooper – their scales are polarised to repel stormbolts. That means they, themselves, are magnetised."

"They also make good butties, Slowhand. So?"

Slowhand pulled a face. "So," he declared, "they're pitsing uncomfortable to wear but very handy when it comes to manipulating tumblers." He pointed at the lock again, this time with some exaggeration.

Kali couldn't do anything but stare. "Let me get this straight. You've been opening this lock with your... underpants?"

"A-ha," Slowhand said, smiling.

Kali shook her head. "Oh gods," she said. Then the full implications of what he was saying struck her. "Oh gods, Slowhand, don't you dare!"

But it was too late. Slowhand was already pulling them down over his hips, and she spun quickly away.

"Pits – why does everything you do have to involve you somehow getting naked?"

"Don't know. Maybe it's *my* destiny."

"Just get on with it."

"Right," Slowhand said quickly. As he spoke, he stuffed his underwear into the keyhole, forcing it through with his finger, and then stretched an arm through the bars of the door to grab what came through on the other side. He then twisted his shorts into a tight roll and began to pull them back and forth, his face pained by the angle at which he stood, but humming as he worked.

Kali could hear tumblers rolling in their housing. She didn't even want to think about what Slowhand looked like. Definitely, definitely didn't want to loo –

"Are you done yet?" she asked, biting her lip.

"Almost there," Slowhand said, strained. There was a sudden sound of metal falling into place, and then she heard him step away from the door with a sigh of satisfaction.

"Done."

Kali didn't turn. "Put them back on."

"They're a little worn," Slowhand protested.

"Put them back on!"

Kali waited while there was another sigh, a slight shuffling and then a polite cough. These sounds were followed by a creak. She turned to see the door had been opened wide, and the corridor beckoned outside.

"Madam," Slowhand said, with an exaggerated flourish.

The two of them peeped out into the corridor, and saw for the moment that it was empty, the guards, as Slowhand had said, between shifts. But though they weren't there to sound an alarm, there was an immediate clamour from the other prisoners, who stared at them through their bars.

"Oh pits, it's 'im," one said. "No, no, what ah mean is nice bit o' singin', there, Mister. Voice of an angel, you 'ave. Come orrn, let us out."

"Don't say that – he might do an encore."

"It's a calculated risk. Look, do you wanna get yer arse out o' here or not?"

"Can I 'ave five minutes to fink about it?"

"Sorry, boys," Slowhand said. The truth was, he regretted having to leave them here but there was no other choice in the matter. Two might make it out of Scholten Cathedral alive but any more would leave them wide open to detection. He placed his hand on Kali's shoulder and ushered her along the corridor, following close behind. But as they reached its end, they heard footsteps on stone – the new shift descending the stairs.

Kali motioned for Slowhand to freeze and then flattened

herself against the wall. As they passed her unnoticed form and saw Slowhand, they drew their swords, and she stepped out and tapped them both on the shoulder. She flattened the first with an open-palmed punch to the face, and Slowhand handled the second with a blow to the neck from behind.

Kali bent down to one of the crumpled guards and snatched his ring of keys. She tossed it to one of the prisoners they had left behind, who caught them in a hand projecting through the bars. "A half-hour before you make your move," she said, and pointed at Slowhand. "Or he starts to sing."

"Oh, funny," Slowhand said. He punched both guards in the face again to make sure they stayed out cold, then said, indicating the cells: "That's running a risk."

"Hopefully, they'll make it out. But if they don't, they'll provide us with a good diversion."

Slowhand looked at her, surprised. "A little cold and calculating, for you, Hooper."

"Last few days. I'm learning."

Slowhand nodded. As he did, Kali began to strip the tabards and unbuckle the armour from the guards. He placed a hand on hers. "What are you doing?"

"Getting us some clothing. You, in particular."

Slowhand shook his head. "Armour will do us no good where we're going, believe me. And you'd look a bit obvious in just a tabard. Cute, but obvious."

"If this is just a ploy to keep me nearly naked –"

"Trust me."

Kali sighed. "So what's the plan?"

"We head up."

"Up, eh? Here we are in what, some deep cells, and we head up? I'd never have thought of that one."

"Will you shut up and move?"

The two of them began to wind their way up the spiral stairway, staying cautious and keeping low, emerging eventually into the guard room that lay above. There, a guard was slumped in a chair, his feet on his desk, with his back to them, a faint snoring sound coming from the other side of his head. Slowhand seemed to know where he was going, and pointed. Without a sound, the two of them crouch-walked around the edge of the room, coming eventually to a door to a connecting corridor, which Slowhand peered through.

"The hard part," Slowhand whispered. "From here on in it gets a little crowded."

Crowded? Kali thought. And then she remembered being carried down from her interrogation – the sounds she'd heard, the sights she'd seen, or perhaps just imagined. *What was Slowhand saying,* she wondered, *that they had been real? Here, beneath the cathedral?*

"You've told me what you were doing here, Slowhand," she said as they moved into and along the corridor, "but you haven't told me why."

Slowhand hesitated. "The Faith and I have a bit of history. Or I should say they have a bit of history with someone close to me."

"Who are you talking about? Who did they have history with?"

Slowhand was uncharacteristically silent for a second. "That's a story for some other time. Point is, there's a lot more going on with the Final Faith than meets the eye. A *lot* more. And I needed to know what."

"And you found something?"

Slowhand nodded, pointing ahead of where they skulked. "Specifically, this."

Kali turned and, though used to some sights, actually gasped. The corridor ended a few feet ahead of them and, where it did, it opened out into a cavernous chamber carved into the rock and lit by the kind of light cylinders she had only ever seen in the possession of Merrit Moon. But it was *what* they lit that staggered her.

People milled about in what appeared to be some kind of warehouse and distribution centre, though from what Kali could make out very little of what they were storing and distributing consisted of either Final Faith tracts or any other religious baubles, bangles and beads. Instead, crates and packing cases piled high throughout the chamber were marked as containing supplies, both rations and medical, as well as various tools, implements, building materials and virtually anything else that would be needed in establishing Final Faith outposts throughout the land. There was a hint of how they would start to get there, too – iron rails in the floor of the cavern, with carriages upon them – some kind of rail *way*?

From what she had heard of their methodology there was something missing, though, and to satisfy her curiosity Kali crouch-walked into the cavern and forced open a crate that looked to her to be particularly suspect. Sure enough, she found what she had guessed they would contain.

Weapons. A lot of weapons.

She hadn't imagined *anything* when she'd been dragged from the interrogation chambers to the cells, it was all real. And the cavern she saw was not the only one – corridors led off everywhere. The sub-levels of Scholten Cathedral were not so much a religious base as a military complex.

Something else drew her attention.

"Slowhand, wait. What's that?"

Slowhand looked to where Kali pointed. On the other side of the cavern there were two openings in the rock wall, and in each a wooden construction that looked like some kind of lift, one of them rising and terminating at this level and the other, counterbalanced, going down.

Even *further* down.

Kali might not have noticed them at all were it not for the fact that they were heavily guarded, and that alone piqued her interest. What sent it into overdrive was that as she and Slowhand watched, Katherine Makennon emerged from the ascending shaft.

"Now, what do you suppose is down there?" Kali mused, slowly.

"Don't know. Ladies' toilets?"

"Witty. Why are the guards there, and nowhere else?"

"I don't know, but the question's academic. Wherever it is those shafts go, there's no way past those guards, not without alerting the whole of the Enlightened. We have to continue up."

"Slowhand, I thought you wanted the inside story on this place? Don't you want to know what's down there?"

"Of course I do. And I know you do. But not now, Hooper. There'll be another time."

Kali sighed. "Well, at least let's try to see if Makennon gives anything away. She seems to be going our way."

"Fine," Slowhand said, "we follow her. But don't get too close, and whatever you do, stay under cover."

"Stunning tactic. Never would have thought of that one."

"Just move."

"Yes sir."

Keeping behind crates, pillars and whatever else could provide cover, Kali and Slowhand pursued the Anointed Lord, gleaning little but nevertheless coming closer to what must have been an exit. Then, suddenly, Querilous

Fitch appeared. Kali and Slowhand flattened themselves against a wall and listened in.

"I am here to report, Madam, as ordered," Fitch said.

"Sorry not to have been available earlier," Makennon responded, "but we had to seal below."

"More problems?" Fitch asked. "It has been... three days."

Makennon nodded. "We lost another two – including Salome. The defences in this dig are formidable."

Kali looked at Slowhand eagerly, about to speak, but he put his hand to her mouth and shushed her.

"That is unfortunate," Fitch said. "I'll arrange for disposal of the body."

"There *is* no body, Fitch."

"Ah, indeed." He hesitated for a second. "Madam, have you considered using –"

"The girl? No, Fitch, she is far too undisciplined, a loose cannon. Besides, following your recent treatment of her I very much doubt she would be sympathetic to our cause."

"She does not know what happened. And perhaps could be... persuaded?"

"No. I know her kind. You might beat her but you wouldn't break her. There'd come a time when she'd run into a trap rather than trip it for us. No, Fitch, I'll arrange for another. In the meantime, what did you learn from her?"

Again, Kali looked at Slowhand. What *did* Fitch learn? She'd been sure she'd said nothing.

Fitch paused. "The girl was extremely resilient, unexpectedly so for one so young. I suspect hidden depths with this one."

"Depths?"

"Great depths. I... needed to rest after the questioning.

Some of the things she recalled were a strain and I needed to collate what I had gathered."

Makennon stared at him.

"Well?"

"The girl no longer possesses the key, nor is she aware of its exact location," Fitch said, his voice slow and tired. "However, there is a friend. An old friend. A relic-monger named Merrit Moon."

"And you believe that the key lies with him?"

"Yes," Fitch sighed. "But Moon travels."

"Where? Where does he travel?"

"Beyond Pontaine. To the ridge of the world."

Kali saw Makennon swallow. Even for one in such a powerful position as she, the World's Ridge Mountains instilled a sense of awe and unease. It was a place even the Final Faith did not tread lightly.

"Munch has arranged things?" Makennon asked.

"He and his men rode two days ago."

"Good," Makennon said. "Very good." And with that, she dismissed Fitch. Speaking to herself, unaware she was being overheard, she added: "This time, just bring me the key. I do not want an old man cluttering up my dungeons as well."

Kali watched Makennon follow Fitch up the corridor, stunned. She spun to face Slowhand, her expression pained. "How could he know that? I didn't say anything!"

Slowhand looked at her sympathetically. "Pits, you don't know, do you? That man's a psychomancer, Kali. Not so much a mind-reader as someone able to *realise* memories. I'm afraid he's been inside your head."

Kali seethed, knowing there'd been something wrong all along. "Munch told me he was there to stop me blacking out."

"It's a common trick. A dirty trick. While that little

bastard was keeping your conscious mind distracted, his psychomancing friend was poking around in your subconscious and, in there, there's nowhere to hide. You couldn't help what they discovered, Kali, or stop them doing it. You literally weren't to know."

Kali snarled. Munch's abuse of her had gone far beyond the physical and, whatever it might have revealed to her by way of a side-effect, she didn't like that one little bit.

At the moment, though, that wasn't the issue.

"They know where Merrit went, and they know he has the key," she said to Slowhand. Her expression hardened. "As of this moment, the exploring's over. I have to get to the old man. You have to get me out of here now."

"Could prove a *little* difficult," Slowhand said, slowly.

"What?" Kali protested. "But I thought you – "

She stopped – because one of the two guards behind her had just discreetly coughed.

CHAPTER 8

Clearly, the time for stealth was over. Kali informed the guard of the fact by smiling sweetly and punching him hard on the nose. He staggered back against the wall, hands over nostrils pouring with blood, and with a satisfying metallic-cum-fleshy crunch Kali booted him up under his armour, bringing the knee of her other leg up under his chin at the moment he crumpled towards her, howling. The guard flipped onto his back, out cold.

Slowhand, for his part, performed a kind of spin that was half pirouette and half boxer's dodge that took him behind the guard so fast that the man barely had time to register the manoeuvre. As Slowhand came out of the spin, he wrapped his arm around the guard's neck, bent him double and rammed his head straight into the wall. Twice, to be sure he was out. And then, because he was Final Faith, just once more. The guard slumped and Slowhand dropped his unconscious body to the floor like a sack of wet wort.

The pair of them stared at each other, he smiling, she inwardly cursing – dammit, they'd always been good as a team.

Cries of alarm echoed down the corridor and urgent footsteps clattered towards them from all directions. Somewhere far above, they heard the peal of the cathedral's bells changing volume and pitch. The change would mean nothing to pilgrims going about their worshipful business, but to Kali and Slowhand it signalled one disturbing fact – the Final Faith knew they were on the loose.

They ran, not sure in which direction to head in the underground warren but moving with the surety that if they covered enough ground they must eventually come upon the exit. A number of avenues became blocked to them, however, barred gates sliding down from their niches in the rock to block off doorways to rooms and corridors, and to some degree the pair of them felt they were being herded. But herded or not, they were going to be no easy catch. Helpfully, the corridors here were stacked with equipment and supply boxes, and while they presented some impediment to their flight, forcing them to dodge and weave as they ran, they also provided cover and the means to discourage some of the guards from their pursuit. Three who tried to block off a corridor ahead were flattened as Kali forced over one stack, causing a mini avalanche, another two crushed against a wall as Slowhand hefted, without much difficulty, a crate of armour and tossed it towards them for them to catch. There was little room to manoeuvre in the tight confines of the corridors, however, and more confrontations were inevitable. The two of them refused to allow such inconsiderate encounters to slow them down, kicking, punching, léaping and dodging their way past them all, and as the numbers dwindled they started to believe that their escape might be successful. It simply never occurred to them that there would be nowhere to go.

The corridor ahead came to an impassable and totally unexpected end. The rock out of which this entire complex had been carved had, it seemed, provided a starting point in the way of natural caverns, and ahead of them now lay one such chamber. Dropping away from the corridor floor to a depth of about fifty feet, stretching away ahead of them perhaps three times that, the stalagmite-layered area was impossible to traverse around its edge, and even if they had been able to climb down to its floor, it would have been impossible to climb out the other side. The Final Faith had provided a solution to this natural hindrance – a slatted bridge that spanned the gap – but at that very moment, powered by the pumping arms of two of their people on the other side, it was moving away from Kali and Slowhand at a rate that made it impossible to reach.

They skidded to a halt, staring at the bridge as it retracted along guide cables in response to the turning of the large spoked wheel on the other side. An identical wheel on their side was of no help as it was impossible to operate while the other was in use. What was worse, the opposing wheel clearly had visible on it a clamp that could be swung down once the retraction operation was complete, effectively making the device on their side useless.

If they couldn't get across the bridge, they had no way out at all.

Slowhand summed up the predicament succinctly. "Hooper, we're stuffed."

Kali, however, wasn't listening. She stared at the

retracting bridge, weighing up the widening gap, and then without a word to Slowhand ran back along the corridor down which they'd come. The troubadour looked at her dumbfounded, but then his expression turned to alarm as Kali turned and, taking deep breaths, began to pound back towards him. He looked at her, looked at the gap, and then back at her again.

She was going to try to make the jump.

"Hooper, don't be stu –" he began, but Kali had already drawn even with him, then was panting past him, and then she was in the air. Yelling with exertion as she took flight, legs pinwheeling beneath her, she flew forwards, describing a long arc that took her towards the ever-distancing bridge.

Her hands stretched out for a handhold before her – and missed.

But only just. Kali twisted, forcing an extra inch, and slammed into the lip of the retracting edge with an explosive grunt. She dangled there by her elbows as she took a second to recover before heaving herself up onto its walkway. One of the guards was already coming towards her but, as he approached, Kali slid aside, around him, then slapped him in the back with her arm, sending him careering over the lip to the unwelcoming rock floor below. The other guard, seeing what was happening, flung the lock onto the wheel and grabbed a pike from against the corridor wall, charging at Kali and intending to impale her. As he came, she grabbed both rails of the bridge and flipped herself upwards, the guard and his pike passing harmlessly beneath her. Spinning in mid-air, Kali landed behind his back, roared into him and, using his own momentum, rammed the wailing guard into the air to join his friend below.

She took a deep, satisfied breath, walked to the wheel

and flipped off the lock, then began to swing it into reverse.

The bridge began to move towards Slowhand and she watched him fighting off those who caught up while it arrived, echoing her tactic of discarding them one by one into the rocky drop – so many of them, in fact, that with only a few more additions they'd be forming their own bridge across the gap. Kali smiled. He was enjoying himself, she could tell. At last the gap was narrow enough for him to make the jump, and as soon as he leapt for and landed on the walkway she began to retract it again, blocking the path of future waves of guards – perhaps mercifully – from their sweaty but grinning potential despatcher.

Slowhand joined her on the other side. They had escaped the complex but still had a way to go before they were out of danger. Forcing their way up the stairs was a running battle but finally they passed the dungeon level where Kali had been interrogated and reached ground level, bursting forth into the cathedral itself – right in the path of a group of advancing guards.

"This way, move!" Slowhand said urgently.

He raced down a corridor that branched off to the left, and then another to the right, heading towards the heart of the cathedral. Kali glanced more guards moving quickly along adjacent corridors, clearly manoeuvring to block off their route of escape.

"Where the hells are we going?" she shouted. She had to because of the bells and the singing.

"Up," Slowhand responded.

"Further up?"

"Further up."

"And how do we *get* further up?"

Slowhand snapped his head to the left and the right,

then instead pointed ahead. "Through here. I think."

The troubadour burst through a large set of double doors into a transept, and Kali followed.

The pair of them stopped dead, stared.

Approximately two hundred people stared back. And as one they raised their eyebrows.

What else could the Eternal Choir do faced with a heavily sweating man and a panting woman dressed only in their underwear in the heart of Scholten Cathedral?

Kali had to give them their due. They kept on singing.

"Slowhand?" she said, dubiously.

"Okay, that might not have been quite right," he admitted. He listened to the heavy footfalls approaching from behind and bundled Kali into the left rank of choristers before taking up a position on the right. "Sing," he mouthed across the aisle.

"What?" Kali mouthed back.

He gesticulated in front of his mouth. *"Sing!"*

Kali cursed but did as she was bidden, or at least moved her lips in time with the others. Across from her, though, Slowhand went at it with gusto. But though he was apparently oblivious to the guards who clamoured in through the door, Kali wasn't, and she had to remind herself to keep her gaze rigidly forwards as they moved up the aisle, heads turning to study the singers, eyes narrowing in suspicion.

It almost worked. *Would* have worked if the Eternal Choir hadn't chosen that moment to segue from one hymn to another. Because in the fleeting quiet between the two a broken baritone that had become utterly carried away – including from any key – was heard declaring, "...of that lass named Kali Hoooperrr..."

The game was clearly up.

"Idiot!" she hissed at Slowhand as the guards shoved

their way through the choristers towards him. The guards snapped their gaze to her. "Idiot!" she hissed again, but this time to herself.

"Up there!" Slowhand yelled. He pointed to a balcony accessed by stairways sweeping up on either side of an organ positioned at the end of the transept, overlooking the cathedral nave. The curving archway the stairs formed there was lined with the organ's airpipes and draped with Final Faith pennants slung from the balcony's railings, and as Kali's gaze travelled up them she saw that another archway led off the balcony itself, stairs beyond leading upwards again.

"Oh, right," Kali said. "You mean where those *other* guards are?"

"What?"

Slowhand looked again. Four guards had appeared on the balcony, and each had a crossbow aimed directly at their hearts.

"Dammit!" Slowhand cursed. "Where did they –"

"Never mind," Kali sighed, peering at the organ. "You got us into this, I'll get us out."

"What?" Slowhand said. "Hooper, no, they'll –"

As with the bridge, he was too late to stop her. Kali burst from the choristers' ranks and sprinted along the aisle, leaping upwards, towards the organ. She used its keyboard as the first in a flight of makeshift steps – filling the transept with a discordant wail – and the organist's head as the second, eliciting a different kind of wail entirely. From there, she leapt onto the top of the organ, and then into the air, throwing herself forward and stretching to reach one of the pennants that hung from the balcony railing. It tore slightly as she grabbed it but the sudden downward jerk of the cloth granted Kali the extra manoeuvrability she wanted, allowing her to kick off from the balcony wall and use the pennant as a swing to run up and around the inside of the archway's curve. The soles of her feet danced across the organ's airpipes until her increasing speed took her out of the curve and she sailed into the open, first above the organ and then the choristers' heads, gaining height until she began to swing back towards the balcony itself. The guards positioned there tried to target her with their crossbows but the truth was they barely had time to register her coming before the pennant finally tore from its mooring and Kali slammed into them, booting them over the railing in a single yelling and flailing mass.

The organist scarpered as four heavy and heavily armoured bodies crashed like a ton of bricks onto the organ below, making it erupt with dust and buckling its wooden frame. Then one by one, each producing their own prolonged and discordant wail, the bodies slipped down over the keys and thudded to the floor. Their weight being the only thing that held the buckled instrument together, the organ creaked and groaned as each fell away, and as the last joined the pile it emitted a death rattle and gave up the ghost entirely. The organ fell apart.

There was a sharp intake of two hundred breaths, and for the first time in nobody knew how long the Eternal Choir fell silent.

"Er, sorry about that," Kali said in the pregnant pause that followed. "Slowhand, you coming?"

The troubadour ran, dodging the other guards whose mouths still hung open as widely as his had a moment before, and joined Kali on the balcony. They entered the archway and found themselves at the base of a spiral staircase that rose up into a tower, the purpose of which was unknown. But Slowhand again seemed to know where he was going and so Kali followed. And followed. And followed.

It was only as they burst at last through the door at the top of the stairs that she had cause to think her faith might – to say the least – have been a little misguided.

Kali looked down and couldn't believe it. *This was Slowhand's escape route? Bloody great steaming pits of Kerberos, there were birds below!*

Their flight from Makennon's guards had taken them up to the highest accessible point of the cathedral, a rope-and-plank walkway that at some point had been strung around the outside of its main steeple and hung there now as loosely as a whore's belt. Some fifty feet below, where the steeple's tapering spire took over, the narrow, drunkenly undulating and half-rotten platform had perhaps once been used for repairs because as far as any other purpose went it was good for nothing, led nowhere.

Damn Slowhand! She should have known better than to trust him. *What the hells did the idiot expect them to do now – run round and round the thing until the guards following fell off, either through dizziness or exhaustion?*

She stared at Slowhand as he slammed the hatch behind them and barred it. No more than a second passed before there was an insistent hammering on its other side. If the hatch were as neglected as the walkway they balanced upon, it would not be long before they had company.

"So," Slowhand shouted casually above the winds that roared and buffeted here, taking a moment to sweep back his hair, "you're a tomb raider these days?"

Kali steadied herself on the swaying wood, positioning her feet with great care. Through a triangular gap between two planks she could see the toy-like rooftop of a Scholten steam factory belching a tiny plume of white fog in her direction. It was indeed a long way down. "A-ha."

"Like, erm..."

"No! Not like 'erm'."

Slowhand nodded vigorously, swallowed. "Fine. Fine."

Kali jammed her hands on her hips, regretting even that tiniest of movements when the walkway shifted beneath her and slapped against the side of the steeple, creaking loudly. "Look. Do you have a clue what you're doing up here, or not?"

Slowhand took a moment to reply. He was inching away from her along the precarious platform, his palms pressed against the side of the steeple, presumably for stability against the worst gusts of wind. "Hooper," he shouted back, "have I ever let you down?"

"Yes."

"I mean *apart* from the Sarcre Islands."

"Slowhand, those things almost had me *stuffed*. And yes, apart from the Sarcre Islands."

"Okay. Right. But let's get this straight. You have never, have you, actually come to any... *permanent* harm."

Rain suddenly began to hammer the walkway, soaking the two of them instantly. Standing there in her vest and pants, and from beneath dripping, slicked-down hair, Kali stared hard and ground her teeth. "*Nooooo...*"

"And that's because," Slowhand shouted slowly, "I always plan ahead."

He plucked a cloth-wrapped bundle seemingly by magic from the steeple's side, and Kali realised he hadn't been pressing his palms there for stability but searching for a hidey-hole. From the shape of the bundle, it contained one of the weapons that had once been Slowhand's tools of the trade.

"You hid a *longbow* up here? Why on Twilight would you do that?"

Slowhand stripped away the cloth, hefted the impressively sized crescent and pursed his lips. "The amount of anti-Makennon rhetoric I've been spouting of late, I knew it wasn't going to be long before she sent her goons to have a word. I just thought of every eventuality."

"Actually, I meant what *use* is a bow up *here*? What are you planning to do – spear a cloud for us to ride away on?"

"Oh, funny," Slowhand said. Acting quickly, he pulled a coil of thin rope from the same hidey-hole and attached one end to an arrow, the other to one of the more secure parts of the walkway. The coil certainly looked long enough to be able reach a cloud.

Slowhand squinted down at distant buildings, eyeing a trajectory, then aimed the bow high into the air.

"What the hells are you doing?"

Slowhand ignored a louder banging on the hatch. It sounded as if the guards were almost through. "Little idea I came up with. Call it a death slide."

"Nice," Kali said, and then put two and two together. "Hold on – you're going to fire that rope at a building down there and expect us to slide down it?"

"Nope. Building's no good – from this height you'd slam right through the wall. Need to hit somewhere open, target it through a ring."

"A ring?"

"Okay, a big, iron ring," Slowhand admitted. "One I tied between the Whine Rack and Ma Polly's, actually." He pulled back on the bow and winked. "There's a pack of supplies down there and a stables nearby so you should be able to find a horse to get you out of the city. Clever little bugger, eh?"

Kali said nothing. She couldn't even make out the places he talked about. She knew Slowhand was good – *very* good – but to make the shot he planned over such a distance, at such a target, and in *this* weather? Impossible.

Then Slowhand reminded her why he had gained the sobriquet *Slowhand.*

In the space of a second her ex-lover seemed to shut the world away. The wind and the rain and the hammering and the shouts seemed no longer to matter to the man at all, and an aura of great calm enveloped him, as if he lived now in a universe entirely his own. Gone was the happy-go-lucky troubadour he had styled himself as of late, and back was the famed archer who for what had seemed like an eternity had tested the hearts of the men he had fought beside at the Battle of Andon eight years before, during the Great War between Vos and Pontaine. Kali had heard the story told in a hundred of Andon's taverns, how their forces were in danger of being overwhelmed – were *being* overwhelmed – and Slowhand had stayed his hand as his comrades had clamoured at him to loose his arrow and take one more of the invading bastards down. But Slowhand had waited – even as enemy swords and axes had cut and sliced about him, he had waited – because he had chosen his target and would not fire until he knew his aim was true. Finally his arrow flew. Just one arrow across the length of a battlefield that was sheer chaos – through the flailing, bloodied forms of a thousand battling warriors and their dense sprays of blood – unerringly on until it found its home in the forehead of John Garrison, the commanding enemy general. One arrow into one man, but a man on whose survival the morale of the enemy depended. With his death, Slowhand bought Andon's forces the time they needed to gather strength, and the tide of that battle had been turned.

Slowhand let fly. His arrow sang into the sky then arched downwards. He must have calculated its flight perfectly because seconds later the rope it carried with it ran taut.

"After you," Kali said.

Slowhand stared at her, hesitated. "There's just one thing. I'm not going."

"What?"

"There's no time for two runs," he said, looking towards the hatch. "And in this weather it's too dangerous to risk the rope to two."

"I see. But you expect me –"

"*Listen* to me. I saw how you handled yourself during our escape, your reflexes, your speed – what you could *do.* There's something different about you, something changing... something *better.*" He tested the tension in the rope that stretched out into the night sky, wiping the moisture from it on his tunic. "I knew it when I came up here. To be honest, in these conditions I don't know if I *can* make this slide, Hooper. But I know you can."

"I'm not just going to abandon you here."

"Call it payback for the Sarcre Islands."

Kali faltered. Was this Slowhand being serious?

"Use the bow," he said, quickly stripping it of its string then handing it to her, nodding in reassurance. "It'll hold. Go, Kali. Find your friend. Now."

Kali knew there was no other choice, not if she was going to save Merrit Moon. Even if that meant not only abandoning Slowhand, but abandoning him defenceless. She slung the stringless bow over the wire and pulled down until it became a horseshoe, gripping either end as tightly as she could. Then she felt Slowhand's hand in the small of her back, for a second almost tenderly.

"Enjoy the ride," he said. And as he spoke, Kali heard the door to the walkway crash open.

Kali looked down and let her body go loose. "Slowhand, I'll be seeing you again. I'll be –"

Slowhand slapped her off the walkway.

"Bye bye."

Kali gasped, the sky taking her as swiftly and as powerfully as if she had been snatched by a dragon's claw, and though those legendary creatures were now long extinct, she felt for a second what it would have been like to be taken thus. She appreciated also just how powerful they must have been to survive at the heights they had flown, for what she had stepped into was a maelstrom.

Every one of her senses was immediately and utterly overwhelmed as she dropped and the deathslide took her weight, her eyes and ears and flesh battered by the elements, blinding and deafening and, on her skin, as agonising as being slapped by open palms. No one before had been exposed to the heavens at this height – no one had seen Scholten from this unique perspective – but Kali had no opportunity or desire to appreciate the scenery, busy as she was shivering in her underwear and simply clinging on for dear life.

Slowhand's bow slid down the rope with a noise like some large insect, a deep *zuzzz* that made the muscles in Kali's arms flutter as if tickled but at the same pierced them through with pain, making even her teeth ache. The curve of the bow slick with the rain that pelted down, it was difficult enough to hang on without the added hazard of the wind that threatened to dislodge her with every passing second but, roaring with the effort of keeping her grip, she managed. At one point she even managed to twist her neck to look back towards the roof of the cathedral, but when she did wished she hadn't. The guards that had appeared on the rooftop had moved across and reached Slowhand, and as Kali watched the resultant scuffle she thought that she saw the troubadour go down at the point of a knife and tumble screaming from the steeple. And there was nothing she could do about it. *Nothing.*

She continued her inexorable descent, her momentum gaining, and with it the wind resistance against her. Her arms were now corded with the effort of gripping the bow but her increasing speed meant that the length of time before she reached safety was lessening dramatically with every yard she slid. The rooftops of Scholten were coming at her as blurs now, and above the roar of the wind and rain she could actually begin to hear the noises of the city and its people below. Soon she would be on the ground and be able to lose herself in their ranks. Soon she would be safe.

Suddenly, though, something felt different.

There was a lack of tension in the slide.

There could be only one explanation for that, and Kali felt a hard knot of fear in her gut.

Because she was still far from the ground. Far too far to survive the fall she was plummeting into now that the rope had been cut.

CHAPTER 9

Kali estimated she was seventy or so feet from the rooftops, no longer hurtling towards Killiam's ring but dropping back and down, her forward momentum cancelled out by the sudden loss of tension in the slide. Letting go of the bow – a surprise present or a sore head for someone below – her hands flailed for the whipping rope, hoping to use it as a swing to at least get her closer to the ground, but her greater weight had already caused her to fall from its reach, and the lifeline was snatched away into the darkness, signalling its departure by momentarily blinding her with a few heavy drops of rain that had clung to the hemp. There was nothing now that would slow her descent – nothing, of course, but the impact that would inevitably come – and she plummeted towards Scholten like a rejected soul from Kerberos, spat back to Twilight on this dark and stormy night.

It was the Spiral of Kos all over again, only a hells of

a lot worse. There, at least, the bones of the brackan had softened her landing, but here there was nothing between her and the hard stone streets except a packed and undulant layer of the city's jagged and sharply angular rooftops, all bedecked with a collection of chimneystacks, guttering and assorted pointy protrusions that from Kali's unique perspective seemed to have been cruelly designed to bounce her back and forth and shatter all of her bones *before* the ultimate pleasure she had to come.

She was, as Slowhand might have put it, stuffed. Actually going to die. The realisation brought with it a peculiar calm, and as time seemed to slow around her – prolonging her fall until it became almost dreamlike, *relaxing* even – Kali reflected that at least for *this* imminent demise no blame could be attached to the archer, for he had done all that he possibly could do to help her. Fine, she was still having problems getting her head around the fact that the bloody man could actually *be* so selfless, but the one thing she could not deny was that on the walkway he had bought her a little more time, by the look of things sacrificing his own life to give her a few more seconds on the slide. She wished – though very much doubted – that she was wrong about what she had seen, hoping for a second that even Katherine Makennon would not sanction cold-blooded murder on her holy premises, but then she remembered the way Makennon had left her to Munch, and immediately thought otherwise.

Munch. A memory of the courtyard outside the Flagons again flashed into her mind, the blood-soaked picture turning even redder with suddenly returned rage. Horse and now Slowhand, she thought – with Merrit Moon, a man who had never harmed and would never dream of harming anyone in his life, hunted down as well. Makennon and her murderous damned lackey seemed intent not only on ruining her life but of stripping it of everything she held dear.

Well, she wasn't going to let them do that.

No more, damn them both.

No pitsing more!

Kali's awareness of her immediate predicament returned to her, suddenly and vitally, but also differently than before, as if every one of her senses had burst into greater life. Though she still fell in the same slow and almost dreamlike way, every facet of what was around her and, more importantly, rapidly looming beneath her, seemed more distinct, the wind, rain and approaching rooftops separate parts of a jigsaw that she suddenly thought she could piece together in order to survive.

There was just one problem. There didn't seem to be time to open the box the jigsaw came in.

Time returned to normal and Kali dropped, the air above Scholten buffeting her as it whistled past at an ever-increasing rate. But then, instinctively, she turned in the updraught, angling and stiffening her body so that it sliced rather than fell through the firmament, causing her to nosedive towards – and at the same sloping angle as – the nearest and highest roof. The manoeuvre felt like suicide, and she herself figured that it very probably was, but some newly awakened part of her also figured that as reaching the ground was an inevitable given, why not do it in her own way, and in whatever style she could muster?

Hells. What did she have to lose?

The first roof came at her a split-second later, granted the honour of being the first to welcome her to town by the fact it appeared to cover the home of someone rich, building upwards rather than outwards in the cramped streets until the property was five storeys high. The tiles that coated it were a further sign of the owner's affluence, expensive redslate, and recently replaced or repaired. Sadly, whoever lived beneath them would have to give the slate quarry another visit.

Kali relaxed her body as she slammed into the roof, but the impact still sent jarring waves of agony through her and winded her severely, her loud explosion of breath drowning out the sound of shattering tiles as well as splintering timbers as the roof beneath them buckled to accommodate her form. From below came a screech of alarm and the sound of a shattering pot – perhaps some servant in the attic – but Kali could only apologise in passing as it soon became obvious she wasn't staying there for long. Loose tiles skittered down the roof before her, and she with them, sliding forwards on her front, hands clawing at gaps in an attempt to slow her descent towards the lip of the roof, but one that was to little avail. Her momentum uncontrollable, she skidded down, tiles snagging at her vest and pants and scraping her skin so that she felt as if she'd been thrown onto some giant cheese grater, the rough surface threatening to do her more damage than the impact itself. Grunting, she rolled onto her back as she slid but then realised she was heading towards the edge of the roof backwards and upside down, which was no good at all. She quickly flung her legs around at the hips, performing a kind of half-turn, half-roll manoeuvre that righted her so that she now slid feet first and on her behind, but with only a second to spare before she reached the roof's edge.

A hazardous rain of broken tiles and mortaring preceded her over the lip and tumbled towards the street below, soliciting another cry of alarm, and then Kali felt the soles of her feet slam into the iron guttering that lined the lip of the roof, the bolts holding it there loosening from the stonework with her impact. She didn't attempt to halt her descent as she was still sliding far too fast and the impact would have flipped her over and sent her flailing towards the street herself, so instead she used the disintegrating guttering to her advantage. She quickly scanned the buildings opposite, their roofs perhaps fifteen feet away and a storey or so below and, calculating the way the guttering was breaking, chose her target, the chimneystack-crowded roof of a seedy-looking boarding house called Dorweazle's. As the bolts on the guttering sheared Kali dug in her heels and – arms outstretched for balance – stood and rode it as it came away from the roof, using it and the drainpipe it served as a giant stilt to stride the gap between buildings.

It wasn't going to take her all the way, she knew.

The precarious assemblage of metal buckled beneath her when she was halfway across, and more evidence of her passage rained into the street below with a series of resounding clangs. Again, cries of alarm drifted up to her, but again she could only apologise in passing as she really had little choice but to keep moving, flailing and running through the air now as if she were some heavenly messenger who'd lost the power of flight but remained intent on delivering a missive to Dorweazle.

With a loud cry of exertion Kali made it – *just* – thudding down onto the roof of the boarding house in a crouch, though she knew her problems weren't yet over. The steep, badly maintained and rain-slicked roof offered little purchase and she found herself skidding backwards amongst streams of rainwater towards its lip, one still too far from the ground for her liking. She instinctively assessed her situation once more then quickly grabbed the edge of a passing chimneystack to brake her sliding form. The brickwork crumbled in her hands but she didn't stay around long enough for that to matter, instead throwing herself away from the chimneystack and increasing her downward momentum while at the same time skewing herself diagonally across the roof to where another stack jinked crookedly from the tiles. As bricks from the first clattered past her and down, Kali grabbed onto the second, used it as a pivot to spin around, and then flung herself away from it as she had done with the first. The second stack collapsed behind her completely, its bulk rumbling down the roof in her wake, but though Kali suspected Dorweazle might be less than pleased with her fleeting visit she was beyond apologising now – because for the first time she was starting to think that her suicidal manoeuvres just might work.

She was now sliding upright and face first towards the lip of the roof, in exactly the position she wanted to be. Only a couple of storeys separated her from the ground, the last leg as it were, and with luck she'd make it without breaking her own. For the final time she scanned the buildings ahead of her, decided on the way to go and then skied right off the roof of Dorweazle's.

She angled forwards, turning her ski-jump into a dive, and then curled into a ball. Tracing a perfect arc downwards, she fell for two seconds and then impacted with a shop's awning positioned between storeys, breaking her fall halfway. As she hit, and bounced, she uncurled herself from the ball and allowed herself to bounce again, flipping head over heels off the edge of the awning and laughing out loud as she saw her feet approach the ground. By all the gods, she'd made it. She was dow –

Something snagged and she jerked to a halt, toes a foot above the street. She dangled there for a second and then there was an ominous tearing sound. Suddenly, she dropped, the remains of her underwear remaining behind, fluttering from the awning like a flag.

Kali stared. She couldn't believe it. After all she'd just been through!

The second chimneystack, caught until now on guttering, smashed into the ground right behind her and exploded into a cloud of debris and dust. For a second she couldn't see a thing, and then the cloud cleared, and she could.

A small crowd of people stared, murmuring and pointing at her. The naked, ashen-white woman who'd just fallen from the sky. *Oh, this is just great,* she thought. *It was the Curse of Slowhand, come to get her from beyond the grave. Damn him.*

"What?" she yelled, holding her arms out. "They kicked me off Kerberos, all right?"

Bootfalls echoed suddenly, seemingly from everywhere, and Kali realised that the bells of Scholten Cathedral were still ringing, alerting everyone in the know to the fact there was a fugitive in their midst. Shadows loomed on the walls along the street, and she dashed for the nearest alleyway, double jinking and jinking again so that she emerged from another as the owners of the shadows passed it by. They could have been cathedral guard or they could have been city watch, she wasn't sure, because it was no small measure of the Final Faith's influence in the city that the livery they wore was almost exactly the same. But crossed circles or not, you never knew where you stood with the watch, because while some were indeed good men, others – sadly, an increasing number of others, along with a good percentage of the population – were in the expansive pocket of Makennon and her people, bribed to be their eyes and ears throughout Scholten by a regular pouch of full silvers or the promise of divine favour. It would be just her luck to run smack into the wrong ones.

The point was, she could trust no one, and that fact became all the more disturbing when she realised that she didn't have the faintest clue where in the city she was. She knew Scholten passably well but no one could possibly know all of its backstreets, and the rather unorthodox route she had taken to arrive here hadn't given her much chance to look for familiar landmarks, which had left her totally disorientated.

The only thing she did know was that she needed to find Slowhand's stash and the stables near to it. Where had he said it was – between the Whine Rack and Ma Polly's? Okay, the fetish house, as far as she knew, was near the eastern gate, so she'd make her way there.

Kali glanced at the stars to orientate herself and began to move, and it was then that it hit her. She ached like the hells. More, as the chimney's dust streaked off her in the rain so that she could see beneath, she was completely black and blue. Not to mention that she was limping like a trigon, her shoulder felt dislocated and a little finger throbbed like the pits, as if broken. One thing was clear, however. If she was somehow changing, then she was far from superhuman, and she'd been lucky that fall hadn't killed her. It was a handy lesson to bear in mind for the future.

Despite the night hour, the city streets still had traffic, and, regardless of the fact she was naked, Kali was forced to keep to the alleyways, take liberties sneaking through the occasional house and even return to the rooftops once or twice to avoid patrols or civilian spies. Even so, her route was not without danger, and she moved cautiously and stealthily through Gizzard Yards, Red Square and Thumper's Cross. Here and there she spotted the conical helmets, tower shields and red tabards of the watch engaged in less than official business but, in doing so, bided her time until they were done, and then moved slowly on. At last she came upon her destination, a muddy gap between the Whine Rack and Ma Polly's, confirmed where she was by looking up to see a rope dangling limply through a ring, and then searched in nearby bushes for the stash that Slowhand had told her would be there. She found it and, somewhat chilled by now and hoping for warm garb, pulled forth a filigree shirt and pair of stripy tights. She cursed. Slowhand might have been wishing to stay in his troubadour disguise but, sometimes, she worried about him.

There was, at least, a decent pair of boots and a considerable amount of coin also contained therein, and Kali took both. All she needed to do now was find the stables. That task – as it turned out – was relatively easy, because she would have been able to smell them a league away.

Kali followed her nose, slipping along more alleyways, keeping to the walls and in the shadows. The area through which she now moved was less than salubrious and she had to pick her way over collapsed drunks and weave through bins overflowing with rubbish, from which the head of an occasional scavenging polerat poked out. Cries and laughter and the louder sounds of disagreement and argument coupled with the odd smashing plate or bottle leaked from the houses all around her, echoing in the night air. At last, though, she came upon a fence, a slight whinnying and clopping of hooves from beyond leaving her in no doubt that she had found that which she sought. She scrambled up and peered over, and her heart sank. She had either found the wrong stables or Slowhand's requirement of what a horse was or could do was considerably less than hers.

There was some kind of junkyard jammed between the backs of four surrounding tenements, accessed through a covered passage between two of them. A tilting, half-chained sign declared it to be the business premises of one Poombar Blossom, Importer and Exporter of Exotica. And sure enough, the yard was piled high with exotica – if, that was, one considered rusted hunks of metal, old beds and broken cartwheels to be the mysterious produce of distant lands.

A ramshackle bank of three stables suggested that Poombar ran a little sideline in horse trading but, it seemed, his definition of what constituted a horse was about as accurate as his definition of the exotic. Only two of the stables were filled and then just barely, two emaciated nags who looked as if they'd snap in two if mounted chewing half-heartedly on carrots that were, themselves, thin and knackered. One of the horses – Flash, according to a sign on his stable – wheezed so badly that Kali suspected he'd drop dead at the merest mention of the word gallop. *Dammit*, she thought, *this has been a complete waste of time.*

She was about to drop back down from the fence when three things happened. Firstly, two men exited a shed that she presumed served as some kind of office and walked towards what looked like a tackroom near the stables themselves, apparently doing business. Secondly, something in the tackroom didn't like the sound of their approach, and suddenly the ramshackle structure all but exploded, every panel, including the roof, crashing outwards and upwards, shook by violent impacts from within. Thirdly, Flash and his mate reared in panic, snorting so badly that they hyperventilated and, with two loud thuds, fainted to the stable floors.

Kali guessed that, whatever was being kept in the tackroom, it was not a fellow horse. And when a moment later its door was opened and she heard a rattling rumble from within, she knew it for sure. She smiled, because if she was right about what she'd heard then these stables might indeed provide her with a mount, as it appeared that Poombar Blossom dealt in exotica after all.

She leapt the fence and crept into the yard, hiding behind a pile of junk opposite where the men now stood. Through the open door of the tackroom she could now see its inhabitant as well as hear the exchange of the two men attempting to calm it.

"Easy, easy," the rotund thing that must have been Blossom said, and somewhat surprisingly the beast quietened. "There – ya see what I mean?"

"Bloody 'ells, you wasn't kiddin'. Where'dya find this fing?"

"Drakengrat Mountains. Came out o' nowhere an' got caught in the sweepnets o' the roob 'erders. Crippled five of 'em afore they managed to rope it. Me bro' didn't know what else to do so brought it to me."

"Bloody 'ell, Blossom. You know what it is?"

"Not a clue. You?"

"I've never seen anything like it in my life."

"You've never seen anything like it?"

"Never seen anything like it in my life."

"Make a nice addition to your menagerie, eh? Fifty full silver an' it's yours."

"You're 'aving a larf. Twenty."

"Forty."

The two men might never have seen anything like it, but Kali had. Seen and heard, once, and from a distance. And she would, in fact, be doing the man who was currently offering thirty full silver a very big favour by taking it off his hands. Slowhand, unfortunately, had left her nowhere near enough money to join in the bidding and that left her only one way of acquiring it. She debated some distraction to draw the two men away – even contemplated clobbering them both with a rusty horseshoe that lay on the muddy ground – but Blossom was clearly eager to sell the only sellable thing he had and the bartering was over before she knew it. Conveniently for her, part of the price was a tankard in the local tavern and, as the men departed wiping spit-slimed hands, she suddenly found that she had the now quiet junkyard to herself.

At least briefly. One second she could hear Flash's comatose wheezing and the next it seemed that she had somehow timeslipped back to the Great War and Scholten was again being blitzed by elemental bombs. The noise and the thudding made her pause for a moment, until she realised its cause. The tavern nearby – the one where Blossom had taken his punter to seal the deal – was the Knotted Noose, and the Knotted Noose was the home of the Hells' Bellies. Kali imagined the scene and cringed – the only tavern that sober people avoided bursting to life as *customers* entered its doors, its resident dance troupe dropping their pies and pounding gleefully to the stage to entertain the audience they never had. Great gods, she could hear the cannon-like snapping of their garters now...

The horror that was within the Knotted Noose would, however, work to her advantage, as Kali suspected that in the next few minutes she would be making rather a lot of noise of her own. Because breaking in a bamfcat was going to be far from easy.

A real live bamfcat, she thought. No one had ever got near one before, and whatever turn of events had led to this specimen being caught in the herders' nets was a fluke indeed. Bamfcats were found nowhere on the peninsula other than around the higher slopes of the Drakengrat Mountains, but the sheer incongruity of their presence there, together with their utter *difference* to the other indigenous species, had before now led her to wonder whether they were native to those mountains at all. Had someone or something brought them from elsewhere at some point in the past? Or had they, for some reason, migrated themselves? And if so, from where?

Wherever it was, they had evidently needed protection there. Approximately one and a half times the size of a normal horse, the bamfcat resembled such a beast in all but one very important respect – it was heavily armoured. It didn't *wear* armour, it was just the way it was built. Great plates of a glistening black shell-like material curved around its flanks, haunches, back and shoulders, and where the plates did not cover, on its legs and those parts of its body that needed flexibility, its hide was composed of a shiny, hard and knobbly substance that Kali could only equate to dried and bubbled tar. But as its defences went, that was not all. On the rear of its legs, all the way up the crest of its neck and down along its nose, the bamfcat grew sharp protrusions that were and were not quite horns, by the look of their slightly layered appearance retractable or extendable as a situation might demand. One thing was sure, it would win no beauty contests, despite its big green eyes.

"Easy, boy," Kali said as she eased into the shed to undo the beast's tethers. "Or should that be girl?"

There was a low, rattling rumble of indeterminate response. It would have to do as an answer because there was no way Kali was going to check. Slowly – very slowly – she eased it out of the tackroom into the yard, whispering in its ear, "Tell you what, why don't I call you boygirl? And boygirl, guess what? We're going for a little ride..."

Her statement was a little premature she knew because, before she could ride anywhere, she had two practicalities to overcome. The first was that there was no way any ordinary saddle was going to fit this thing, but she solved that by plucking two from the tackroom wall, slinging one above and below and using both sets of straps to circle the bamfcat's girth before cutting the main parts of the lower saddle away. The second was a matter of height – it would take a ladder to climb on the bamfcat's back – but that solved itself when she realised that she already had a ladder – the bamfcat itself.

Kali took a deep breath, muttered more soothing words to the beast and then ran up the horns on its legs. Throwing herself onto its back, she immediately grabbed another horn on its neck – the closest thing she had to reins.

As she'd suspected, it was the wisest thing she could do. All the accoutrements necessary for a ride might have been in place, but there was no telling that to the bamfcat. The sensation of being mounted obviously a novel one to the beast, for a second it stood there simply stunned, and then decided that it didn't like the development at all. And then all hells broke loose.

The bamfcat ceased its rattling rumble and instead roared a roar that drowned out the thudding of the Hells' Bellies, beginning to leap around the junkyard and spinning round and round in an attempt to throw its unwanted passenger from its back. Kali could do nothing but hang on for dear life, her hands clenched around the bamfcat's neck horn, thighs jammed against its flanks. At first she didn't find it too much of a challenge – the places she'd been, she was used to clinging to things – but what concerned her was how long she could maintain her grip – and how long, if at all, it would be before she succeeded in calming the beast. The bamfcat certainly didn't make things easy, deciding, when Kali refused to budge, that if it couldn't dislodge her with leaps and bounds, then it would do so with the aid of whatever lay around the junkyard, first impacting with and demolishing the tackroom and then having a go at the stables, where at that very moment Flash was just coming round. The emaciated nag sprang up, wheezing with terror, and began to run around the junkyard in hopeless circles, searching for an exit, before collapsing again. Kali, meanwhile, did the best impression of a circus performer she could, avoiding the bamfcat's protestations by dodging anything that threatened to crush her, throwing her legs over one side of the beast then another, at one point slipping under and over its girth, and at another lying flat on her back without a grip to pass beneath an overhanging beam that would otherwise have decapitated her. It seemed, for what felt like an eternity, that the bamfcat was never going to surrender its independence, but then, unexpectedly, it began to slow. A few more feeble bucks and leaps followed, together with a half-hearted brush against the collapsed ruins of the tackroom walls, but finally the beast was reduced to a few spasms that were little more than afterthought, and then to a begrudging standstill.

The thing stank overpoweringly of the sweat that oozed thickly from between its plates, but Kali knew that after what she'd just endured she was hardly in a state to win any floral competitions herself. This appeared to be no bad thing. The bamfcat turned its head towards her, eyes dolefully taking in the rider that had beaten it and, with a long and disgusting snort, sucked in the scent of its new owner.

"Good boygirl," Kali said, patting it heavily. She smiled as the bamfcat rattle-rumbled, because this time it sounded more like a purr. "Good, good boygirl."

It was time to go. Kali manoeuvred the bamfcat towards the passage out of the yard but then reined it back. On the other side of the gate she could hear the voices of two patrolling guards, who, despite the continuing thudding of the Bellies, were bemoaning the fact that it was too quiet in the backstreets, and how they'd each give coin for a little piece of the action. *Especially* if they could lay their eyes – and other parts of their anatomy – on the girl who was meant to have scarpered from the cathedral. She was a tasty little piece by all accounts. Running around in her drawers, too. A bit of all right. Worth a stuffing.

Really.

Be careful what you wish for, boys, Kali thought. She smiled and patted the bamfcat soothingly, prompting a rolling of its neck. If it was a piece of the action the guards wanted, then a piece of the action they would get.

"Yah!" she shouted, at the same time ramming her heels into its flanks and pushing its neckhorn forwards. With a snort, the bamfcat responded, galloping forwards and through the junkyard gate.

Through, because there was no need for Kali to bother opening it. Or rather, the bamfcat didn't need her to – because as it galloped forwards it demolished the entranceway in much the same way it had demolished the yard, ramming the gates with its armoured head and ripping them clean away from their hinges. As a result, twin sheets of wood arced through the air of the alleyway, flipping and spinning into the path of the patrolling guards.

"Wha – ? Oh, bloody *huuurk!*" one of them cried as half the gate smacked him in the face, flooring him, while the other, ducking to avoid the second half, swiftly drew his sword and advanced. But then he saw the bamfcat, and stopped. The bamfcat saw him, too, and roared into his face so strongly that his hair streamed back from his scalp. It was difficult to describe the colours the guard's face went, and the only change in colour about his person that could be pinpointed with any accuracy was that of his trousers. He slopped away.

Kali galloped the bamfcat down the alley and out, emerging onto Anclas Way, Scholten's main thoroughfare to its eastern gate. It, too, remained busy despite the night hour – was thronged, in fact, with revellers, tradesmen and, most of all, pilgrims returning from their visits to the cathedral. But as the bamfcat galloped forth, skidding into a turn on its wet cobbles, the area did its best to empty itself as fast as it could.

Kali ignored the screams and cries of alarm, the bodies falling through windows, the collapsed stalls and the rolling trinkets and fruit, and the bamfcat ignored the various objects thrown by some braver members of the crowd that bounced off its armour. Both of them ignored – completely – the cries of a number of startled guards that they should immediately halt.

A moment later, scattering those same guards in their path like ninepins, they exited the closing city gate.

Free at last of Scholten, Kali reined the bamfcat forwards. Towards a horizon that was tinged white and red from the glow of ice and volcanoes. Towards the mountains that formed the ridge of the world. Towards Merrit Moon.

CHAPTER 10

It took Kali two days to reach the World's Ridge Mountains, but even without rest and at the sustained and full gallop to which she subjected her seemingly inexhaustible mount, the journey should have taken longer. The bamfcat, it seemed, was something more than just an armoured horse.

She couldn't put her finger on how it happened, where it happened or even precisely when it happened, but now and again in their journey, the world about them seemed suddenly to blur. This was not simple acceleration on the bamfcat's part – had it been she would have at least felt greater wind resistance – but a rather disorientating case of simply being in one place one second, another the next, as if unbeknownst to herself she had actually nodded off for part of the ride. The biggest hint that something unusual was happening was when they reached the town of Fayence, where, after such a blur, the startled faces of the locals were tantamount to what they might have been had mount and rider appeared right in front of their noses, out of thin air. Odd, that, because as far as Kali knew that was precisely what they'd just done.

Those faces were nothing, though, compared to the looks that followed when, during the brief hiatus, the bamfcat decided to feed. One moment the worgle was happily rolling along the main street in front of them, and the next the rodent was snapped up by a lizard-like tongue the length of two men, the furry ball hooting in panic as it was sucked in and devoured in a single swallow. A dozen of its startled brethren flared like toothbrushes and bounced away, trying to avoid its fate, but the bamfcat's lengthy tongue slipped into every nook and cranny and snapped them up in rapid succession, Fayence's worgle population suffering a devastating blow in seconds.

Kali didn't question how the bamfcat did what it did or how it fuelled itself, however, because it got her where she needed to be and faster than she would have dreamt possible. But with Munch having had such a head start, they still had a lot of ground to make up. Thankfully, the journey so far had been the easy part, and the hard part was yet to come – and with some luck it would slow the bastard down. Kali looked up as they began to near the mountains, and felt the same sense of awe and insignificance that she always did when she came within riding distance of the range. Yes, if anything was going to slow Munch down, the mountains would.

Accessible only at the southern tip of the Sardenne Forest, the World's Ridge Mountains loomed massively ahead and above of her, a forbidding wall of rock that in places seemed to reach higher than the sky. Not just rock, either – the lower peaks of the range were dotted with live volcanic craters that belched lava onto their tortuous slopes, while the upper peaks were sheer faces of ice, glistening white in stark contrast to the orangey-reds of the fires below. Where the two met, and clashed, great steaming geysers blasted upwards, periodically disintegrating the ice and causing it and the rock behind to crumble and fall, the avalanches creating a roar that seemed to be that of the mountains themselves. No one knew what lay beyond the World's Ridge, and if anyone had ever attempted to traverse it, they had not returned. Like the Sardenne Forest, it was a barrier to the inhabitants of the peninsula, but in this case one that daunted even Kali, and she wondered, on occasion, whether there was anything to be made of the fact that the barrier was composed of earth, air, fire and water – the four elements themselves.

They reached the lower slopes, and the bamfcat slowed as it began to climb. It sniffed at her and then at the air, apparently picking up a human scent, and so Kali allowed the animal to lead her, negotiating gorges, precarious trails and natural rock bridges over bubbling streams and billowing pools, hot from the mountains' insides.

At least for part of the way. During the past few days, the bamfcat, apart from being inexhaustible, had manifested an absolute absence of reluctance to do anything it was asked, but after almost a day and a half climbing beyond the foothills there came a point which even the bamfcat would not go further. As she watched the beast's nostrils flaring, Kali suspected why. Wafted down to them from the higher slopes on the occasional blast of bitter, whistling wind, came a stench that could only belong to whatever denizens called these mountains home. The stench was utterly feral, bestial, so strong it was almost sickening. Of all the sights, sounds and smells that they had encountered on their journey, Kali didn't know why this, of all things, should unnerve the bamfcat, but perhaps the inhabitants it sensed were its racial enemy, or perhaps even its natural predator in the place from where it had originally come. She wondered whether the beast that had become her new companion hailed originally not from the Drakengrats but from these mountains – or even beyond.

But that was a question for another time. For now it didn't really matter because the animal had served her well – had got her here when no other beast possibly could – and she had no right to push it any further against its will, even if such an act would be physically possible.

Kali found a suitable spot and dismounted, stripped the bamfcat of its saddle and then slapped the beast on its flanks.

It didn't go anywhere.

"What?" Kali said. "Don't tell me you're going to wait for me?"

The bamfcat flipped out its tongue, perhaps searching in vain for worgles, then hung its head, saying nothing.

"You're not going to be here when I get back, and we both know it. So go."

The bamfcat snorted and lifted its head to stare dolefully at her. There was a certain insanity its eyes that she found disturbingly familiar – and quite comforting.

"Okay, fine!" Kali relented. "Stay there – but something further up has obviously given you the spooks so don't try to follow me, okay?"

Kali left the saddle but flung the saddlebags over her shoulder. She started to climb, hesitated, then turned and patted the beast three times on its neck. "I'll... see you when I get back," she said.

She continued on alone, the foothills behind her, the

true slopes of the World's Ridge rising precipitously before her. Snow covered the ground at her feet in increasingly larger and thicker patches, but here and there pools and rivulets of lava broke through the rocks and stained the whiteness, making it seem as if the jagged landscape was slowly haemorrhaging. She climbed higher and, despite the lava, the temperature dropped considerably, and while she had been too intent on getting here to feel the cold until now, Kali was forced to dig into Blossom's saddlebag for an extra layer of clothing, pulling out a ragged fur coat that looked as if it had seen too many trapping expeditions. That, or its donor had been trapped on a particularly bad hair day. She slung it on. The thing stank to the high heavens but did the job.

In the absence of the bamfcat, Kali had to rely on her own tracking skills to keep on Merrit Moon's trail, secure in the knowledge that as no one dared venture far up into these mountains the signs of passage indicated by dislodged rocks, broken branches and disturbed patches of scree – eliminating those caused by whichever wild animals lived on the mid-slopes – were most likely his. It was possible that as humans were such rare visitors to these heights, those same wild animals were wary of approaching for fear of their place in the food chain, and for the most part Kali managed to avoid encounters with local predators, driving off the odd pack of shnarls or curious bugbear with a wave of her knife and suitable warning noises. Only once did she pause warily, when from far above she heard the haunting echo of what sounded like prolonged screams. They, though, could equally have been the carrion calls of the strange birds that circled high above. In this place, it was difficult to tell.

Birds or not, Kali picked up her pace. Thankfully,

tracking the old man became even easier when, after a further three hours' climb, she came across convergent tracks coming in by a different route, vaguely to the west. Seven people, six men and the smaller, slightly lighter tread of a woman – and horses – heavily equipped. It did not take her long to work out who they might be. Munch was probably using one or more shadowmages to track Merrit Moon, and, despite her fears for him, for once she was grateful for the presence of threadweavers as from there on in their talents resulted in the old man's trail being overlaid by the footprints of his pursuers, making it as obvious to follow as a flaming torch in the dark.

A flaming torch would have been something she'd have been very grateful for at that moment, because Kali was approaching the ice-slopes now, the snow that had become thick beneath her tread taking on the greater solidity of permafrost. A blizzard had begun to howl about her, too, and she huddled inside her furs as she tramped ever upwards, squinting to see past the needle-like flurries that threatened to white-out everything before her. Then, suddenly, she spotted something in a rockface ahead – the dark and variously shaped outlines of what could only be cave mouths. What was more, the trails of the old man and his pursuers – plain on the slight plateau that led to the caves – vanished right into one of them.

Kali's heart thudded and she hurried forwards, relief that she had at last caught up with the old man tempered by the worry that Munch's trail appeared to be only minutes behind his, and she hoped to the gods that she wasn't too late. But she had only taken a couple of paces when her foot crunched on something on the ground, and what she saw when she looked down made her momentarily pause.

The icescape about her was dotted with bones, human and animal, mainly old but some not so, seemingly torn from their respective bodies and stripped utterly clean, some lying in small piles, others resting alone where they had been dragged by... something. What was the most disturbing was that the something had precisely the same odour about it that had stopped the bamfcat in its tracks far below.

Here, the air was redolent with it, its strength almost overpowering. Kali trod cautiously in the direction of the cave, without doubt the source of the stench. She entered slowly, eyes alert for any movement or sound in the darkness. But she saw nothing, and the only sounds were those of her own feet crunching on the tinier deposits on the bone-strewn floor, along with a languid and incessant *drip-plop-drip* from the moisture-laden ceiling that echoed hollowly within the rock.

There should have been no light to see by, but as Kali inched her way inwards, her knife at the ready, she saw that the cave was illuminated by a dull green glow emanating from crystalline formations in the rock. It was hardly daylight but it was bright enough to stop her stumbling blindly over the body that lay mutilated on the cave floor a few yards in.

Merrit! she feared instantly, but quickly realised that it was not. Instead, she looked down at the body – the remains of a body – of what could only have been one of Munch's party, the corpse lying broken and missing an arm and both legs, eyes staring blankly and mouth frozen in a rictal, agonised scream. A black and glistening trail of blood led further back into the cave, and Kali guessed that the poor woman had tried to drag what remained of herself to safety.

Not Merrit. Merrit would not be capable of this.

There was nothing she could do for the woman, so Kali closed her eyelids and moved on. But it wasn't long before she came across another body, and then another, each in an equal or worse state of mutilation. Like the first, they appeared to have been trying to drag themselves to the exit but had never made it, the loss of blood from their amputations too great. Something in this cave had torn them apart like mools in a slaughterhouse, and it was beginning to look like it, not Munch's people, was the biggest danger here.

Kali could feel every fibre of her being warning her to get the hells out of there, but she knew she had no choice but to carry on, to find Merrit Moon, whether he was alive or dead. But as it happened, she did not have to look much further. No more than ten yards on, the cave opened out into a chamber where she found three more bodies heaped together in a small pile, almost indistinguishable from each other, they had been so badly torn. And next to them, covered in their entrails, lay Merrit Moon. The old man was face down on the floor, a staff and opened backpack scattered beside him, a dark pool of blood seeping from beneath his torso. But he was breathing shallowly. He was alive. Just.

"Oh gods," Kali said. She hurried to him and turned him gently over, cradling the back of his head in her palm. The old man sighed and his eyes fluttered open slowly, focusing on her with difficulty. From his complexion he had lost a lot of blood.

It was clear nothing could be done. Merrit Moon was dying.

Kali swallowed.

"Hey... old man," she whispered.

Moon coughed. "You have the smell of Vos about you," he said slowly, having to force the words out. "Have you ridden my faithful friend somewhere less than healthy once again, young lady?"

"No, Merrit, Horse... I mean, yes. But don't worry, Horse is fine... fine. He's waiting for me." She hesitated. "He's waiting for you."

Moon smiled. "You've been looking after him?"

Kali nodded briskly, trying not to let him see her tears. "Of course I have, you old fool. Bacon stew every day." She stared at her mentor, aware that they were both avoiding the issue, and what she really wanted to say erupted out of her. "Pits, old man, I told you not to come here alone!"

Moon shook his head, took her hand. As he spoke, his tongue clicked dryly in his mouth. "Here or elsewhere, it would not have mattered. It wasn't the mountain's cold embrace that finished me, Kali. It was the cold embrace of steel."

He slowly pulled up his tunic, wincing as the cloth tore from drying blood. Kali stared at three distinct puncture wounds in his torso – two in the gut and one near the heart – fury rising. The shape of the blade that had made them was unmistakable – a jagged-edged gutting knife. The worst thing about them was they could so easily have been killing blows but weren't – Moon's soon-to-be murderer had inflicted these mortal wounds and seemingly left him here to die.

"Munch," she hissed.

Moon nodded. "Kali, he took the key. Knew I had it..."

Kali sobbed. "I told Munch about you, old man. Gods help me, I didn't mean to but I told him."

Moon stroked her cheek. "Hush. Whatever you did, I know you couldn't help it. I told you, the Final Faith are zealou –"

"*Damn them!*" Kali shouted, interrupting him.

"Hush," Moon said, again. "Hushhhhh."

"Don't hush me! Damn you, Merrit Moon, stop treating me like a baby!"

Despite his dire state, Moon chuckled, coughed, his breath rattling. "Actually, I'm trying to save your life," he said. His eyes seemed to lose focus on her, stare beyond her. "More outbursts like that one and you'll... arouse them."

"Arouse them? Who?" She pointed at the bodies. "Are you talking about the things that did this? Merrit, for the gods' sake, what happened here? What killed these people?"

Moon sighed heavily, seemingly losing the thread. "The key. I meant to take it deeper... to where they live... but these old muscles are slow and Munch and his men weren't far behind... they found me here before I could..."

He took a shuddering breath, remembering. "Munch didn't even ask for the key. He just pulled me towards him, towards his knife, and then... my blood... the smell of my blood brought them up from below."

Kali's face darkened. "Where's Munch now?"

"I... don't know. I... think he ran from them..."

"Them, again," Kali said. For the first time she thought she could make out a low rumbling in the cave. "I guess we're not talking run-of-the-mill mountain cats here are we?"

Moon shook his head. "Creatures as old as the Old Races, probably much more so. They've lived in these mountains since the world was young, since before even the Sardenne grew – they, and their no-less-legendary cousins." His eyes flicked to the side, and he swallowed. "But I don't have to tell you about them, you can see for yourself."

"They're coming?"

Moon shook his head. "No, Kali. They're already here."

Kali felt the hairs on the back of her neck rise along with an overriding need to hunch down, to make herself small. Because even as the old man had spoken she had sensed the presences all around her, and she raised her eyes slowly and nervously from the old man to the shadows of the chamber. There were six of them, all but naked things, their flesh a green that had nothing to do with the crystalline light. Half as tall again as a human, their thickly muscled bodies and hunched shoulders made them seem shorter, especially while at that moment they squatted in what appeared to be their personal niches in the rock walls, regarding her. Not just regarding her – because as they looked on with their deep-set eyes, their hair lank about their bodies and their mouths protruding teeth, each gnawed droolingly on chunks of meat and bone identifiable as pieces of thigh, an arm, and even a head; meat recently ripped from the corpses around them.

These things. She'd heard tales of them as a child. Tales told in the Flagons meant to scare her but which instead intrigued her. Bogey men. She didn't know what their true name was but she knew what humans called them.

Ogur.

And as she realised she was kneeling in the middle of their dining room, they sure as hells scared her now.

Despite her fear, Kali moved to protect the old man but he held her where she was. "Don't," he told her. "They won't attack." He looked up as one of them took a tentative step towards Kali but then retreated when, much to her surprise, the old man barked at it in some unknown tongue. "At least," he finished wearily, "while I'm alive."

"You can control them?" Kali said, and remembered

his words on his doorstep in Gargas, what seemed an age ago. "Don't tell me – this is your tale for another time."

Moon nodded, winced in pain. "I'd come here in search of Herrick's Passage – a tunnel said to pass under the mountains – but an avalanche meant I never found it. What I found was one of these ogur trapped beneath the ice, and I helped it."

"You're telling me one of these things was *grateful?*"

Moon half-laughed, half-choked. "Grateful? No. Had it not been so weak, it would have torn me apart. Which is why I shared with it the contents of my backpack."

"A quarrel of crossbow bolts, I hope."

"Eight bottles of flummox."

Kali stared at the old man dubiously. "Are you telling me you got an ogur pissed?"

Moon coughed. "Drank him under the table. But he wasn't used to the stuff. The point is, theirs is an alpha society and after that I was treated with a little more respect."

Kali laughed, but it was strained, redolent of a joke shared for the last time. Of all the tales the old man had told her over the years, she was never sure which he exaggerated, but clearly *something* had happened for the ogur to defer to him as they did. Something that had made him feel confident enough to lose the key in the lower depths of their cave, where it could never be reached.

In the odd way that these things did, it suddenly occurred to her to ask him why, now that he'd confessed to drinking flummox, he insisted on serving her that atrocious elven wine. She wanted to ask him many things, actually, but as the old man coughed again she realised there was no more time.

There had to be something she could do!

She dug in her saddlebag for something, *anything* to help, but as she did Moon placed his hand on hers, just as he had in the Warty Witch so long ago. The message now was as clear as it had been then – *put your hand down.*

"It's too late," Moon said, coughing. "What's important is the key. You have to get the key. But you also have to know what it is you're dealing with."

"Merrit, at least let me –" Kali began, but as she spoke thought: *At least let me what?*

"Listen to me, young lady." Moon insisted. "I don't know everything about the key, but I haven't told you everything I know. Snippets from across the years. The key you took is one of four, part of a set that unlocks something that should never see the light of day again. Something *evil* – so evil it is warned against time and time again in Old Race manuscripts written by a hundred different hands."

"What?"

Moon coughed again. "I never found out precisely. If I had I would have done everything in my power to find and destroy it – what the manuscripts refer to repeatedly as an abomination." He paused. "What I do know is that it almost finished the Old Races, wreaked so much death and destruction amongst them that these bitter enemies forged their first alliance in order that they might end its threat."

"But you must have some idea what it is."

Moon nodded. "Oh, yes. Some tales describe it as a kind of giant construct – a supposed marvel of dwarven engineering that became instead a horror – a complex automaton called the Clockwork King of Orl."

"The Clockwork King of Orl?" Kali repeated. "What in the hells do you suppose it does – is meant to do?"

"The important question is what the Final Faith think

it can do for them. If I know those zealots, their intent will be to use the king as a figurehead, a rallying icon for the spread of their church across Twilight. But if the old warnings are even half-truths, the people of Twilight will not be rallied, they will be destroyed."

Kali frowned. "I don't understand. This alliance. If they wanted the king stopped, if it was so dangerous, why not just destroy the thing, or at least destroy the keys?"

Moon sighed. "The king itself, I don't know – perhaps they kept it as a reminder of their folly. The keys, however... in the aftermath, when it came to it, neither side trusted the other in the matter of disposal. Even when both parties were present each suspected that magic might deceive the eye, that secretly one or other party would keep the keys for themselves. They decided instead that they should be sealed away, watched, protected by lethal countermeasures that would ensure no one could get their hands on them again."

"The Spiral of Kos," Kali breathed.

"And three similar containment areas. They each built two sites – two dwarven and two elven – and manned them with mixed representatives of their races." There was no blame in Moon's eyes when he added: "Kali, you have no idea what it is that you've unleashed."

"I'm beginning to get the picture." She bit her lip. "Merrit, please, what can I do?"

"If the Final Faith are going after the keys, you have to find them first, make them inaccessible, hide them, destroy them if you have to. If you cannot, then you must discover the location of Orl, destroy the Clockwork King before the Faith reach it."

"But I've no idea where to start!"

"Go to Andon, to the Three Towers, its Forbidden Archive. There are papers within that will tell you more than I know. They will be difficult to get to, Kali – they are protected – but you must reach them, find out what you can. And when you have, when you know what there is to do, you must do it. Make sure the Clockwork King is not reawoken, any way you can."

Kali felt somewhat daunted by her burgeoning responsibility. "Old man, I'm just a... tomb raider."

Moon slid his hand onto hers, visibly worsening. "No," he said, weakly, "you're not. There's something else you need to know. The night you were found as a baby, by the stranger –"

Kali stroked his hand. "It was you, old man. I know. I saw you when Fitch played with my mind. You and me in the Old Race site..."

Moon raised his eyes, surprised, then coughed, and this time there was blood. "Hells of a time for a reunion."

"Hells of a time," Kali nodded, sniffed. "Merrit, I –"

"Don't you dare hug me when I'm down, young lady," Moon warned, though after a second he, too, smiled. "Kali, please listen. You were my greatest ever discovery, believe that. You should know that I love you like a daughter. But that it was me who found you isn't what I was going to say. You have to know about the site itself."

"What? What about the site?"

Moon didn't answer directly. "There are things happening to you, aren't there? I can feel the changes, see it in the way you move, sense it in your aura. You are more than you were. It's what I always knew, right from the start – that you're somehow different."

"*Different?*"

"The site where I found you wasn't like the others, Kali. It was *uncompromised.*"

"What? What do you mean uncompromised?"

"You know what I mean. Nobody had been in or out in

over a thousand years. It was completely sealed."

Kali stared at him for a moment, speechless.

"It couldn't have been," she said at last. "I mean, how did I get in there? What would that mean?"

"I don't know what it means. Only that it marks you out amongst the people on the peninsula – makes you different from them – and that is something you must remember at all times."

"But what –"

Merrit held up his hand, looked around at the gathered ogur. He was suddenly racked by a spasming cough, and sprayed more blood into his palm. "No more questions," he said. "You have to go – *now*."

"Old man, I'm not just leaving you like thi –"

Moon grabbed her hand, squeezed it tenderly. "Kali, go. I am dying and there is nothing you can do, and as soon as the ogur sense I have passed they will tear you apart. You have to get out of here before I die."

"I can't do that!"

"You *must*, young lady." Moon was struck by another fit of coughing and then laid his head back with a sigh, his hand weak around hers. Kali choked back a sob. Dammit, she had to give him a hug whether he liked it or not.

She leaned in – gently, so as not to hurt him – and, as she did, her hand brushed an amulet resting on his chest. She could have sworn it was glowing slightly. She went to touch it but her hand was unexpectedly swatted away.

"No!" Moon shouted with surprising vehemence for a man on his deathbed. "It's too... near the time."

"Merrit, what – ?"

He actually glared at her. The old man actually *glared*.

"Go, Kali, *now*," Moon shouted. And then, more weakly: "Go now... and don't... look ba –"

Kali knelt there a second longer, stirring only as a series of grunts from the ogur signalled what she wouldn't, *couldn't* believe – that Merrit Moon was gone. Keeping her eyes fixed on the creatures she backed slowly away, settling the old man gently to the ground as she went. Then, with a final look at her mentor's body, she raced towards the cave mouth and safety.

She did not see the blue glow that suddenly suffused the cave behind her.

CHAPTER 11

Kali had seen more than enough death in recent days and had no desire to be reminded of it – but in approaching Andon she had little choice.

It was here that Killiam Slowhand had killed John Garrison, but he had been only one warrior amongst thousands, and the fields around the city still bore the scars of the pivotal battle they had fought. Andon had been besieged for almost two years while Pontaine's army had grown strong enough to repel the enemy, driving them back across the land that had become known as the Killing Ground. Such protracted and bloody engagements were not erased easily from a landscape, and the Killing Ground was littered still with half-buried skeletons uncovered by driving rain, the remains of defensive and offensive trench systems, and rotting and ruined engines of war. It was a ghastly and ghostly place, made all the more haunting by banks of slowly drifting fog.

that alternately concealed and revealed the horrors that remained.

It was before dawn, and Andon's gates were closed to traffic as Kali and the bamfcat appeared in the fog near its defensive walls, suddenly, in a blur. Even at this quiet hour guards patrolled vigilantly, on constant alert as many in the city believed it was only a matter of time before the forces of Vos attacked again, using as their base the forts they had constructed in the once-neutral Anclas Territories, only a few leagues away. Arriving seemingly out of nowhere as she had, some strange phantasm clad still in Slowhand's striped tights and Blossom's mangy furs, Kali had likely spooked the guards, and having no wish to feel the sudden thud of a crossbow bolt in her chest needed to make her business in the city known. She couldn't tell them the whole truth, of course, but a generalisation might do.

Kali got their attention by sticking her fingers in her mouth and whistling. Then she shouted: "Excuse me! I'm trying to save the world. Can I come in, please?"

It was an honest and bafflingly pre-emptive ploy that seemed to work. The guards studied her for a few seconds, shrugged and gave the order for the gates to be opened.

"'Yup, Horse," Kali said.

That she had referred to the bamfcat as Horse was no slip of the tongue. She wasn't sure when, or quite how, the beast had gained her affections but certainly it had started when she'd found it waiting for her on her descent from the ogur's cave – its welcoming and strangely familiar headbutts a display of companionship she'd needed badly when everything else seemed to have gone away. Their bond had grown during the journey to Andon and, after a while, she'd realised she really couldn't go on calling the beast good boygirl because it was just plain daft. Of course, she'd had some hesitation naming it Horse – Horse Too, to be precise – but the bamfcat was hardly a creature that would suit a name like Fluffy or Rex, and in an odd way it was a reminder of the old boy himself.

Horse, however, could not go everywhere, and inside the city it soon became clear that its narrow environs wouldn't take the bamfcat and he'd need to be stabled for the duration. Kali dismounted and walked him into one of a number of stableyards lining the outskirts, manoeuvring his oversized bulk into two stable enclosures, the beast straddling their low, dividing fence.

The stableman appeared and his jaw dropped open. But he did not let surprise interfere with business.

"Two silver tenths," he said.

"I thought the standard rate was one."

"That thing takes up two stables so it's two silver tenths."

Kali was in no mood. "Horse?" she said.

The bamfcat ate the fence and spat a mouthful of splinters at the stableman.

"One silver tenth," Kali said.

"Done," the stableman said, swallowing. "That's one hells of a mount, lady."

Kali patted the bamfcat, smiled. "He sure is. One word of advice – don't feed him anything that hasn't got a face."

"Face?"

"He likes worgles."

"Worgles?"

"Worgles." She pointed across the yard, where one of the furballs could be seen rolling into an overturned bucket. "Just shake 'em out and he'll handle the rest."

Horse's lizardine tongue whiplashed out and back

again, as if to explain. The stableman did a little dance backwards.

"Yew, that's disgusting."

"Yep, that's what I thought, too."

Horse stabled, Kali made her way into Andon proper, working her way through the labyrinth of shadowed streets, alleyways and passages crammed inside its imposing walls. The walls were soon lost to view in the crowded conurbation, and it would have been easy to become disorientated, but as Kali made her way towards the centre of the city she could not have wished for a more obvious guiding beacon. Visible through gaps in the roofline, looming ever larger and more imposing, the beacon had actually been visible from *outside* the city walls – was visible, in fact, from some leagues away – but it was only now as she grew nearer that the sheer impossible scale of the largest building in Andon – indeed, anywhere on the peninsula – truly made its presence felt. The Three Towers made Scholten Cathedral look like a village church.

The twisting, semi-organic looking headquarters of the League of Prestidigitation and Prestige rose above the city fully forty storeys high, a structure that would have confounded the skills of the finest engineers in Pontaine – perhaps even the finest engineers of the Old Races – and its construction had only been made possible with the aid of the more powerful wizards who now studied within. Its rather incongruous presence in the otherwise somewhat seedy city was due to the fact that at one time, on a lesser scale, it had simply been the home of Andon's Magical Guild, housing parlour magicians and entertainers in the service of Pontaine's wealthiest families but, since the Great War, it had gradually transformed itself into something much darker and now housed an organisation dedicated to the study of the effects of powerful sorceries on armies, and to the practice of war itself. Dark secrets were held within its half-built, half-grown heights – within the minds of those who moved there and within the manuscripts, tomes and artefacts that were said to fill its archives – and somewhere amongst those secrets was the information Kali needed to know.

The Three Towers was not a place, however, where one could walk up to the front door and knock. Even the Final Faith did not wield sufficient influence to enter there.

To get inside, Kali needed help. And she knew exactly where she was going to find it.

She continued on, breaking at last from the warren of small streets and out into the centre of Andon, a thronged circular marketplace filled with stalls, vendor carts and street performers surrounding the towers in a hub. Already gearing up for the day's trade, it was where the true hubbub of Andon was to be found and, as a consequence, where those who fed upon that hubbub could also be found. The largest and most successful thieves guild in Andon – the Grey Brigade – were based somewhere here, and it was no small measure of their presence and influence in the area that their playful nickname for it had been adopted by the city's inhabitants, thereafter referring to the place as the Andon Heart.

Kali weaved her way through the milling crowds with no particular destination, at least none she yet knew. Her attention fixed seemingly on the endless array of gaudy stalls and goods, in actuality she had her senses trained on every subtle movement around her. She felt herself *accidentally* jostled or pushed once, twice, three times, and on each occasion felt hands slide gracefully into the pockets of her furs or vest, each of which she had filled with some coin. She had to admit that the dippers working this patch were very good, but when someone knew what to expect – in fact, hoped for it to happen – they had to be *very, very* good indeed if they wanted to go unnoticed.

Kali let the plunder continue until the fifth dipper made his move, and then she made hers. The boy's hand was sliding towards her side when her own lashed out and grabbed it tightly by the wrist.

"That's ten full silver your people have taken from me," she said, smiling. "Even accounting for your share, that's enough to buy me an audience with your boss, don't you think?"

"B-boss, Missus?" the boy said, struggling against her grip. "Don't know what you're talking about."

"Jengo," Kali said. "I'm here to see Jengo."

"Jengo?"

"Jengo Pim."

The boy smiled slyly. "So, you knows his name, eh? That counts for something, I suppose. But who's to say you ain't bringin' him some business old Jengo might not be inclined to undertake?"

"Who says I'm here on business? I'm his sister."

The boy guffawed. "Jengo ain't got no sister. Everyone knows he ain't got no kin and was dumped on the streets like the bastard he is."

Kali leaned closer, looming down on the boy, and tightened her grip. "Then I guess that makes me a bitch."

The boy swallowed. "A-all right, Missus – ah'll take you to him. But I tells you, it ain't no worry of mine if he slits you from ear to ear."

"From where to where?" Kali said, smiling.

"Eh? Oh, never mind. Just follow me."

Kali did, finding that the entrance to the Grey Brigade's

den was hidden almost in plain sight, yards from where she stood. Nevertheless, it would have been impossible to take advantage of without her escort. She was led between two market stalls, the owners of which were obviously guild stationed as sentries, and then along a tight alleyway that jinked away behind them. Kali looked up as she walked, saw that she was being watched from a number of windows above. Clearly, no one who wasn't welcome could approach the guild unseen, and Kali suspected that for any *particularly* unwelcome visitor those who stared at her now, casually crunching fruit, might simply substitute the fruit for a loaded needlereed and the unwanted visitor would be incapacitated before they could take two steps. She guessed the resultant body – unconscious or otherwise – would be spirited away into one of the apparently sealed doorways she passed, there to be stripped, dumped in the river and never seen again.

She reached the end of the alleyway safely, however, and after the boy gave three irregular raps on the solid wooden door that terminated it, found herself inside the den of the Grey Brigade.

Impressive, she thought, as she was led through its busy interior, not only in the number of guild members she passed but also in the facilities provided for them. Everything the Andon thief could desire was provided here, from equipment and training areas to common lounges, dormitories and bar, all of them converted to their present use from the rooms of what looked to have been at one time a large hotel, an enterprise she imagined had been starved of business during the siege.

Grandly enough, Jengo Pim had chosen what had once been the hotel's ballroom for his court, and it was obvious which of those gathered within was he. The thieves guild leader was draped in an ornate, red upholstered chair in the middle of the room, swigging from a bulb of wine and gnawing meat he skewered on a dagger from a serving table beside him. As Kali was brought in, the appropriately roguish-looking man was conferring with two of his lieutenants, but as she approached he dismissed them and turned his attention to her. He jabbed the dagger into the table and wiped his mouth before speaking.

"So – I'm told I have a sister I never knew about," he said, blatantly looking her up and down. "Seems you got the genes I didn't. Nice. Very nice."

"Thanks. But I hear incest makes your bits shrivel and die, so I'd keep your hands off if I were you. The name's Kali Hooper. I'm here on business."

Pim sucked his teeth and spat a piece of gristle across the room. "Figured you might be. But as I have no shortage of business of my own, why should I have an interest in yours? What, in fact, stops me having you killed right here, right now?"

"Because you run a thieves guild, not an assassins guild. You'd need a good reason to bump me off and so far I haven't given you one."

"No," Pim said, lecherously, "more's the pity." He waved a hand at her striped tights and furs. "I could, of course, consider your current outfit a capital crime."

"Yes, well, that's a long story." Without being invited, Kali grabbed Pim's knife, stabbed a piece of meat and bit it off the blade. "Come on, Pim – aren't you just a little bit curious why I risked coming here?"

Pim took a swig of his wine, studied her, smiled. "Let's stick with mildly stimulated. Very well, you have a minute. How can the Grey Brigade be of service to you?"

"I need your help. To break in somewhere."

Pim pulled a face. "Oh, Miss Hooper, after so much promise you disappoint me. Pretty lass like you, what is it? Heard you can recruit some of my people to do an ex-lover's house? Perhaps empty his strongbox of compromising documents?"

"Actually, no, I need to do the job myself. And it's the League of Prestidigitation and Prestige."

Pim spluttered on the wine he'd just consumed, stared at her incredulously. *"The League?"* he repeated. He laughed out loud, and then with a bouncing of his palms invited the others in the room to join him in his jollity, which they duly did. "Bubbling pits of Kerberos, woman, that's impossible."

"Nonetheless –"

"Nonetheless, nothing. It's bloody suicide. Have you any idea what kind of traps are in there? Those sorcerous psychopaths have wired the place with every kind of thread threat you can imagine, and more. There are things that'll fry you, things that'll crush you, things that'll drown you, things that'll make your heart go boom." Pim slumped into his chair and swigged from his wine again. "Listen to me – only three men in the entire history of our guild have tried the towers. The first we found flapping around with his bones gone, the second was last seen ascending to Kerberos *before* he died, and the third came back in a bottle no bigger than this one." Pim shook the wine bulb he held. "No chance. Go home, girl. Go home."

Kali stayed where she was and folded her arms. "Actually, it isn't just the towers I need to gain access to, it's the Forbidden Archive itself."

This time Pim did not splutter. But he did stare and then quaff a mouthful of wine so hard that Kali heard him gulp and swallow it down.

"The Forbidden Archive," he repeated slowly. He turned

to one of his lieutenants. "Kris Jayhinch, please give the lady a razor to slash her throat with – save herself some time."

"What's the matter, Pim? Too much of a challenge for you? Maybe I should take my request down to the Skeleton Quays, tell the guilds there you were too lily-livered to handle it."

The thieves guild leader's eyes flared darkly for a second. The mention of the Grey Brigade's rival guilds had the effect Kali desired, Pim knowing full well that a loss of reputation was what no guild could afford.

"They would likely tell you the same as I," he said, contemplatively, "but then they are desperate enough to take your business." He rubbed his chin, considering. "I must be mad," he sighed before sucking in a deep breath. "Miss Hooper, do you have any experience of our noble art?"

"If by *noble art* you mean taking other people's property without their permission, I guess I do, but not in the way you mean."

Pim rose, handing Kali the bulb of wine. "I'll tell you what – there's a little test I have devised for new recruits, and I want you to take it. If you pass, you'll have my help. If you fail, well... I'll think of something *appropriate*."

Kali took a swig of the wine. "Mister Pim, you've got yourself a deal."

The mention of the test sparked the interest of everyone in the room and, as the thieves guild leader guided Kali through to another chamber, the pair acquired a small entourage of eager spectators. The room into which she was led was larger even than the ballroom – what looked to have been the hotel's reception area – but it had been converted from its original use to function as some kind of obstacle course-cum-training area for the guild. Various vaulthorses, gymnast rings, nets and other paraphernalia had been secured about its edges along with a number of racks containing exotic thieves' tools, but what drew Kali's attention was a small iron cage suspended from the centre of the ceiling, high above the floor. Hanging from a single chain, there was nothing near it and no obvious means to reach it – but Kali guessed that was exactly what Pim's test would require her to do.

"I see you're ahead of me," Pim said, staring up as she did. "The positioning of the cage is an approximation of the high-security containment for Bojangle's Baleful Bells, currently on display in the museum of Scholten. I have stolen them twice, returning them each time so that I might try again – what I like to consider a professional challenge. Said bells are not, of course, present here, merely a personal souvenir of sentimental value, but you should consider it a treasure of equal scarcity. Retrieve it for me and we will talk."

Kali nodded and walked forwards until she stood directly beneath the cage, craning her neck to look up.

"I have to inform you," Pim continued, "that to date not one of my would-be apprentices has managed this feat. Luckily for you, it is not success or failure that I will judge – only the originality of the methods employed in the attempt."

"A-ha," Kali said, not really listening.

"Please feel free to utilise any of the equipment in this room, and any of our tools to be at your disposal. There is a fine selection of gripgloves, pinshoes or spidersocks over here. Some even prefer the jumping jacks..."

"Okay," Kali said. Pim would have regretted turning his back to point out the selection because at that moment she was pulling off her tights.

"There is even a slight possibility of success with

the..."

Tights off, Kali crammed the wine bubble she still carried into the toe of one leg, crouched, took in a few huffing breaths and then leapt, straight up. One arm outstretched above her, teeth gritted, she rose two and a half times her height, straight as an arrow, and then flicked the weighted end of the tights through the bars of the cage, grabbing it as it came out and dropped down the other side. Allowing the elasticity of the tights to drop her back down to the floor, she bounced with them, once, twice, three times, then sailed upwards to grab the base of the cage with a grunt. Swinging her legs up, she flipped herself over so that she was sitting on top of the cage, slid her arm in through the bars to retrieve the souvenir, then dropped it towards the floor. That done, she quickly wrapped the tights about herself, rolled down inside them like some carnival gymnast, flipping herself with a neat twist as she neared the floor, and then settled as lightly as a feather right in front of Pim.

The thieves guild leader stared at her through the dancer's tassel now draped over his head. Kali noticed it was labelled PROPERTY OF HELLS' BELLIES. Meanwhile, someone at the back of the room snickered.

"Original enough for you?" Kali said.

Pim coughed and, after a second, coughed again. "I don't know how you did that but you pass, Miss Hooper." He stared down at her now-bared legs. "By the gods," he breathed, "I could use someone like you on my team."

"Sorry, I work alone," Kali said, smiling. "Now, about your help. The Forbidden Archive. How the hells do I get in?"

Pim stared at her, knowing that, his agreement witnessed, he had no choice but to concede to her request. He nodded and led Kali back to the ballroom, but this time to a large table lain with maps and plans of all kinds. The pile reminded Kali of her captain's chest back home and, as was the case with her own papers regarding places that seemed too much of a challenge, Pim found what he was after buried right at the bottom of the pile. He swept away the less challenging plans to reveal a set of architectural drawings that looked to have been there for years, but that didn't matter because what they showed had not changed.

It was the inner workings of the League of Prestidigitation and Prestige.

Pim slammed a gloopy bottle on the corner of the document to keep it flat, and Kali wondered if it contained the remains of the Three Towers' last victim, perhaps kept as a reminder of the difficulty of the task at hand. He traced the confused patterns of lines on the paper – standard builders' marks and strange swirls that had to denote magical input – with his finger, frowning, remembering. "Big John Sinclair went in here... Hamish the Pumps here, and Nimble Neil Halliwell," his finger made a circle and stabbed down "right here. As I said, none returned. At least, not in their original condition."

"So we can safely assume that whatever traps took them down are still in place in those areas," Kali said. "That could be an advantage – knowing what to expect."

Pim drew in a sharp breath, shook his head. "You might know the what of them, but not the where or when. Whatever did for them did for them quickly, and the trigger could be anything – weight, motion, sweat, breath, noise..."

"Difficult to counter all of those," Kali observed. She studied the plans, the bridges that connected the towers, what appeared to be the location of the Forbidden Archive in the third tower, then lowered her own finger. "What about this conduit here?"

Pim smiled. "You have a good eye for possibility. That was exactly what I was going to suggest to you. Its purpose isn't specified on the plans but from what we can tell it's some kind of alchemical dump shaft that empties into the sewers – dangerous but potentially difficult to trap as any waste potions might have, shall we say, *unforeseen* side effects on the thaumaturgical triggers. But there's a problem – the laboratories dump their waste regularly, every half an hour. The length of that conduit, you'd need to move fast. *Very* fast."

"All those wands, you'd think they'd just make the waste disappear," Kali sighed. "All right, fast I can do. Question is, will it get me safely inside?"

Pim traced the conduit's route. "See for yourself. Once through the conduit you'll be inside their perimeter defences. I don't know what you'll find after that but, with luck, you should be able to reach the stairs to the third tower."

"Any guards to worry about? Patrols?"

"Trust me, this place doesn't need them. It's *deadly*, how many times do I need to tell you that? So I ask you again – are you sure you want to do this?"

"Mister Pim," Kali said seriously, "I really don't have any choice."

For once, Jengo Pim stared nowhere but at her eyes, and, whatever the thieves guild leader saw there, a new note of respect crept into his voice. "Fine," he said, handing her the plans from the table. "Take these in case you need them – it's meant to be a maze in there. Also take whatever equipment and tools you think you'll need for the job. There's just one other thing. Kris Jayhinch goes with you."

Kali stared at Pim's lieutenant. "What? No chance."

"Every chance, Miss Hooper. If you succeed in this suicide mission – which I seriously doubt – then the Grey Brigade gets a share of the loot you find."

"I'm not after loot. I'm after information."

"Then there'll be all the more loot for us." He gestured to Jayhinch. "There is no discussion in this matter – take Kris with you or you do not leave."

Kali sighed heavily. "Fine. But I lead and he follows. And he looks after his own back."

Pim nodded. In truth it was Jayhinch looking after *her* back that for some inexplicable reason had become his greater concern. "Understood." He waved his arm to indicate the equipment racks. "Now, is there anything you need?"

Kali pursed her lips, remembering Orlana Dawn at the Spiral of Kos. "You wouldn't, by any chance, have one of those dark silk bodysuits?" she said.

Kali and Jayhinch left after dark, negotiating alleyways doubly shadowed by the night's azure gloom, until they came to a sewer entrance beneath the looming towers. Jayhinch pulled back a cover with a grating sound, then staggered back coughing as the area was suffused with a cloying and unnatural stench. What materials made up the stench Kali had no idea, but whatever they were they made the hole before them pulsate with an array of colours that looked considerably less than healthy.

There was a flushing sound that began high above them and, giving it a little time to clear, Pim's lieutenant gestured for Kali to drop inside the hole. "Twenty nine and a half minutes," he said. "You did say you wanted to go first?"

Kali did, manoeuvring her landing to avoid a rainbow sludge that was evidently the result of the purge from the towers, then a half-splash from behind her signalled that Jayhinch had joined her not so successfully in the mire. Wiping something that fizzed like acid from his boot, he then moved with her to a grate at the sewer's end – a grate smeared with the thicker contents of discarded experiments from above. Avoiding contact, the pair prised it away with disgust, and then began to climb a conduit that rose upwards, aware that they had just entered the Three Towers' outer wall. The knowledge made them move with increased caution but, however cautious they were, there was no way to prevent what happened next.

Kali wasn't sure what alerted her to the danger, whether it was some slight click or a subtle disturbance in the air, but something did – though unfortunately all she had time to do was shout a warning and then throw herself down. Kris Jayhinch was not as quick.

There was a whooshing crack and Kali kept her head low while whatever threat accompanied the noise passed. She heard an agonised cry and then an odd crackling sound that chilled her to the bone.

She turned to look back. Jayhinch was exactly where he had been a moment before but he would not be accompanying her any further. Arms outstretched towards her, eyes staring blankly and mouth wide in a silent scream, the now grey-coloured lieutenant blocked the conduit as still as a statue.

And with good reason. Pim had evidently been wrong about there being no traps here.

Kris Jayhinch had been turned to solid stone.

CHAPTER 12

Kali blew out a long breath to calm herself, fully aware of how Jayhinch's fate could so easily have been her own. The unwanted thieves guild companion Jengo had thrust upon her had proved himself useful, yes, but in a way she would never have asked for, never have desired.

A gorgon trap was no way for anyone to go. The invidious magic could perhaps be thought merciful if it caused petrification in an instant, but Kali had heard that sometimes it took the internal organs – and most perversely the brain – as long as a day to fully turn to stone.

One minute in, one man dead – or as near as made no difference. That kind of put the Three Towers' quagmire cards on the table. No – it slammed them down with all the arrogant confidence of a winning bogflush, in fact. Suddenly the Three Towers seemed less of an entertaining, professional challenge and more the indiscriminating deathtrap that the thieves guild leader had threatened it would be. From here on in, if she didn't want to share Jayhinch's fate, she was really going to have to watch her step.

"I'm sorry," she said quietly to his immobile form, trying not to notice how a section of his skull – almost scalpless as a result of the lethally traumatic magic – remained as yet unpetrified and glistening, a bloody reminder of the man he'd been only moments before. She stared into his agonised, frozen eyes, wondering if Jayhinch heard her inadequate words, and then turned and continued on alone.

She didn't get far before the next of the defences hit. She experienced a sensation almost like a swoon, and then suddenly the conduit seemed to stretch away endlessly ahead of her, wavering slightly in her vision. Kali craned her neck and looked behind her, seeing that the conduit stretched into the distance that way, too, seemingly without end. But something was clearly wrong with the picture – apart from the fact she *knew* she hadn't crawled that far, the remains of Jayhinch were nowhere to be seen along its yawning length. It was also obvious to her that what she saw could not be real because the Three Towers, individually or as a whole, were simply not that expansive.

The sight that met her eyes, therefore, had to be some kind of illusion. An infinity illusion. But she couldn't see the point of such a trap. Any intruder who made it this far was unlikely to be dissuaded from progressing further as they'd know what they saw wasn't real, so why bother unless –

Unless it was a delaying tactic, meant to confuse while –

Kali's mind raced, wondering which way to go. Her natural inclination in such close confines would be to flatten against the floor as she had not long before, but the mages of the Three Towers clearly liked to play, to twist things, and dropping to the floor seemed wrong – *wrong!* Instead, she slammed her hands and feet against the conduit walls and with a grunt quickly heaved herself up above the floor, hoping to hells she'd made the right choice. At the exact moment she did a wave of ice hurtled towards her from along the conduit, turning the metal beneath her blue-white and sizzling and cracking it with cold. Limbs trembling with the effort it took to keep herself suspended, Kali hung above it, swallowing as she watched her breath condense into crystals over the super-chilled metal only a few inches below. The cold was spreading up the curve of the conduit, too – she could feel it in her palms, and, if she didn't let go soon, she'd be bonded to the metal so badly the only way to break the grip would be to rip the flesh off her palms.

Thankfully, the magically generated ice vanished as quickly as it had appeared, presumably because its job, for those with slower reactions, would have been done. Kali lowered herself back to the conduit floor with a groan, rubbing her palms to restore circulation to the throbbing skin, then did the same to her nose to alleviate a touch of frostbite.

She proceeded upwards, finding that the conduit levelled out some now, and as a result found her feet squelching in patches of alchemical waste that had not been fully flushed away. She avoided the muck as much as she could, stepped lightly and quickly through that which she could not, spurred to such action by the small skeletal remains of floprats who had chanced to crawl here. The remains of the rodents hadn't just been eaten away, their skeletons had been twisted and *changed*.

Her slightly increased pace made Kali no less aware of

the danger around her, and she deftly avoided the triggers for another couple of traps – one apparently designed to release a cloud of living biomagical toxin into the conduit, another – which she purposefully triggered once she'd passed by – to make that section of the conduit momentarily discorporeal, meaning anyone unfortunate enough to be traversing it at the time would become part of the conduit on a permanent basis.

Pits of Kerberos! These guys really are bastards.

She continued on, relieved to find that at last the traps seemed to have stopped. Quite right, too, because anybody who had made it this far bloody well deserved to make it the rest. She couldn't relax until she was out of the conduit, however – the number of delays she'd suffered had eaten into the time she had for safe passage, and she reckoned she had less than a minute left before the alchemical laboratories were purged.

She hurried, the seconds ticking, and spied at last the access hatch marked on the map. The moment she reached it she heard dull, echoing rumblings from above, and grabbed quickly for the hatch wheel to swing it open.

Thread magic coursed through her, a crackling storm of blue energy that paralysed her momentarily before blowing her off her feet and slamming her into the conduit wall. Kali groaned and slipped to the floor, lay there stunned, bucking and spasming involuntarily as small discharges continued to spark off her body.

Dammit, one last trap. They'd lulled her into a false sense of security and caught her unawares.

One thing she couldn't help but be aware of, though, were the noises. The echoing rumblings from above had become a series of metallic clangs, and as she lay there she realised with a dull knot of fear that the drop-hatches from the labs were opening.

Gods! She had to move now! Only she couldn't, not an inch. Not even to thump the conduit in frustration. Annoyingly, all she could do was dribble.

Dammit, Hooper, come on, come on. You've been an idiot, but do you want to die here? Do you want to die and prove Jengo Pim right?

The conduit filled with the sound of sloshing.

Hooper, she screamed inwardly, *do you want to fail the old man?*

Kali roared with exertion and, consciously forcing every movement of her body, lurched forwards, twisted the hatch wheel and heaved the cover open just in time. The last thing she saw before she dived head first through the hatch and it clanged shut behind her was a raging torrent of rainbow sludge.

She plummeted with a yell and thudded onto the floor below as if she had just been birthed by a pregnant mool, embryonic, twitching and covered in splashes of gunk. After a second she thrashed the gunk away, but stayed down while her spasms subsided, coughing and retching loudly. Only then did she perceive where she was – the middle of a corridor in the first tower – and lying there exposed and all but helpless, it occurred to her that her entrance had not exactly been the stealthy one she'd planned. She comforted herself, however, with the fact that the last trap would have killed – or at least hammered the final nail into the coffin of – anyone less bloody-minded than she.

She frowned, wondering. Was it just bloody-mindedness that had got her out of there? Or was it something to do again with the changes happening to her, the things that made her able to do the things she did? One thing was certain – now was not the time to think about it.

Kali groaned and picked herself up. The corridor in

which she'd landed was a shimmering, smooth affair and, thankfully, empty, though it felt oddly not so. The corridor thrummed quietly to itself, as if the power of the Three Towers were contained within its walls, and Kali had the uneasy feeling that, while she saw no one, she was not alone. She felt as if she were being observed from all angles, almost as if she were being watched by the building itself, which, considering the nature of the place, it was just possible she was. Nothing happened as a result of her feeling, though, and she wondered if perhaps it was just a magical suggestion that hung in the air, designed to unnerve anyone who shouldn't be here. Even so, it was pitsing creepy.

Pulling out Jengo's map, she orientated herself and crept slowly forwards, thankful for the fact there'd been no alarms. She'd had more than enough alarms in Scholten. She began to weave her way through a maze of corridors towards the stairs that would lead her upwards and from there, across the bridge, to the third tower and her destination. The Forbidden Archive.

Despite Jengo's concerns, she moved with relative ease. Now that she was within the outer defences, there was little to be wary of in the way of traps, and as most League members were busy blowing up or dissolving things in the labs she passed, they presented little problem. Those mages that she did encounter in her path she simply avoided, a task made easier by the fact that in their flowing and colourful patterned robes it was easy to spot them before they chanced upon her.

Those robes. She found it perverse how these bastards still garbed themselves in the garish showbusiness style of parlour entertainers when their business was no longer entertainment but death. Still, she couldn't help but think that one or two of them were wasted here in the towers and should actually put themselves up for sale as a nice pair of curtains.

As she moved steadily on, only one thing hampered her – here and there certain corridors were blocked by shimmering curtains of different coloured energy and, while the mages moved through them with ease, presumably having protected themselves against whatever the energies did, a stray floprat that attempted to follow ended up as a small puddle of fur and blood. Kali did not want to chance her arm – or any other part of her body – by emulating it. Instead, she found the bottom of the stairs by a different route.

Following echoing, whispering corridors, they appeared before her at last, and Kali looked up their spiralling heights and cursed. According to the map, the connecting bridge to the Forbidden Archive could be found on the thirty-fifth floor. There was no lift. *The hells with a lift*, she thought. *These guys were mages so why hadn't they magicked some kind of... lifty-uppity zoomy tube.* But they hadn't, had they? No. Knowing her luck, they probably just spouted some kind of incantation that stopped them getting absolutely bloody knackered.

She began the long ascent, but it soon became clear that she would never make it all the way up without being detected – the stairs were simply too busy with mages crossing between floors. There was only one alternative. Much as she hated the idea of having to take one on, Kali secreted herself in an alcove near the base of the steps, reasoning that the best way to tackle a mage would be to surprise him from behind. This she did, waiting until she caught one alone then, as he passed cracked him on the head and caught him as he dropped. His robe came off in one.

The body concealed in the alcove, and suitably attired,

Kali continued quickly on. She did not want to be anywhere near him when he woke up.

Thirty-five storeys later she emerged gasping through an exit into the open air, which led directly onto the bridge she wanted. Thirty-five storeys was a dizzying height and Kali expected a worse buffeting than she had received above Scholten, but to her surprise the bridge was totally calm and silent, protected, she assumed, by some invisible magical canopy. *Made sense*, she thought, smiling. After all, if they needed to visit the archive the last thing the League's mages needed was a nasty draught up their robes disturbing their forbidden musings.

Had Makennon got some of her own information from here? Kali wondered. After all, if ever a place needed to be infiltrated by a sender, this was it. The bridge leading to the Forbidden Archive looked harmless enough but Kali had by now seen enough of the things to recognise that the barely visible but variously coloured curtains of shimmering and sparkling energy that separated the bridge into sections promised something nasty the moment she tried to step through them. These were particularly powerful, no doubt about that – she could feel them buzzing in her brain.

She studied the bridge. It had no walls or railings and, naturally enough, no conduits, no side passages and no ledges. None, in other words, of her usual shortcuts. She tentatively touched where she imagined the magical canopy to be, and while her hand moved through it with ease, she guessed that if she passed through it completely there would be no way back in.

Handy enough for suicidal sorcerers but useless as far as she was concerned.

She had to admit, she felt stymied. There was no way across without indulging in some serious lateral thinking.

She was beginning to think she was completely out of laterals when, fortunately, one arrived in the form of a mage coming through the door behind her. As soon as she heard the door open Kali twisted to the side and flattened herself against the wall, watching as a League member came through and began to amble across the bridge, seeming almost to float in his long robe. His relaxed attitude made her presume that he was not about to be frozen, incinerated or generally done to death by any of the traps so, like his brothers below, he had to have some kind of protection about him.

Normally, she would not have welcomed his presence at all, but this, she hoped, was her way through. She had to take the gamble, there was no other choice. She had to stick to him as close as a second skin. Used as she was to sneaking about places, she was about to find out just how stealthy she could be.

As the mage moved past her, Kali moved into step behind him, a living shadow, crouched but moving on tiptoe, matching his every move. As his left leg moved, so did hers, as his right, the same. Every pause, every hesitation and every subtle twist and turn of the mage's body was matched perfectly as he – and she – passed through the first of the defensive curtains and she felt nothing other than a slight fluttering in her muscles. But that she felt even that while she was protected proved her suspicion of how powerful these final traps were.

Two curtains, three curtains, four. Her plan was working – and then it wasn't. She was one curtain away from the end of the bridge when the mage stopped dead in his tracks, causing Kali to wobble and almost bump into him it was so unexpected.

There was what seemed to be an eternal pause. *What are you doing?* she thought. *Come on, come on, tell me what you're doing.*

The mage patted a pocket of his robe, shook his head in self reprimand and tutted loudly.

He's forgotten something, Kali thought. *The bloody idiot's forgotten –*

Oh, cra –

She moved as he did, a hundred and eighty degrees in perfect silence and synchronisation, staying in the same position behind him all the time. She couldn't believe she managed it, but she did, and the mage didn't even have a clue she was there. Though outwardly calm and in control, as Kali watched him walk back the way that he had come, she was surprised he didn't hear her heart threatening to burst out of her chest.

He disappeared through the door and she was left trapped between the last two curtains.

She threw her hands in the air and walked quickly around in a circle. There was no way forwards, no way back – and absolutely nowhere to hide when Mister Duh! Forgot My Head returned.

Idiot!

There had to be a way through – and she had to work out what it was fast. The first step was finding out what kind of trap she was looking at. Kali quickly tore a small patch from her dark silk bodysuit and tossed it at the curtain. There was a *zuzzz*, a puff of smoke and then nothing – the patch was gone. This was some kind of electrical trap and if she tried to step through she'd end up doing a dance that would put the Hells' Bellies to shame.

A very brief dance.

Dammit! She wasn't going to find out the location of the keys this way.

The keys, she thought, something nagging at the

back of her brain. These differently coloured curtains with their different magics – surely the mages couldn't constantly invoke protection against each? What, then, if they instead carried with them some kind of key? She hadn't seen anything actually being used and so what could it – ?

She looked down. The pattern on her stolen robe scintillated slightly, more so when she moved closer to the curtain. *Gods*, she thought, *was that why the mages still wore them – because the robes themselves were the keys?*

Again, it was a gamble, but if she didn't take it she was stuffed anyway. Kali took a deep breath and walked slowly forwards, passing through the energy field with ease.

She cringed. All the effort she'd put into marking Mister Duh! Forgot My Head when she could have passed through any time.

Idiot!

She opened the door ahead of her and she was inside at last. The Forbidden Archive.

Her eyes narrowed.

Or... not.

What in the hells was this? Kali wondered, aghast. There was nothing here. After all her effort, the upper half of the third tower was an empty chamber, completely featureless apart from a solitary, podium-like structure at its centre and a red glow that suffused the place and seemed to emanate from the walls.

Okay – if this had been a guided tour, then she'd have demanded her money back.

She moved towards the podium, her footfalls clattering despite the fact she wore shnarl-hide soles. Of all the things she had encountered so far it was the clattering that made her shiver. This place was *weird*.

Kali mounted the podium and found it inscribed with a number of symbols, none of which she recognised, the symbols being magical not linguistic, and not her area of expertise. She pressed one, then another, and then each in turn, but nothing happened. She tried a different order and, again, nothing. On her fourth unsuccessful attempt she threw up her arms in frustration, then quickly stepped back as the air in front of her seemed suddenly to change. Then, spiralling down seemingly from thin air above came a number of tiny shapes that began to gather before her eyes, and as they did an object began to assemble itself from these tiny building blocks. Some kind of container – elven by the look of it – marked with the familiar circular symbol of their race.

Kali moved her hand forwards to touch the container but found nothing there.

An idea struck her, and she waved her hands again. As rapidly as it had appeared, the container disassembled itself and spiralled back towards the heights of the chamber, replaced by another object spiralling down and assembling itself in its place. This time it was a manuscript containing, by the look of it, some kind of outlawed spell.

Kali's gesticulations became more varied, and she dismissed and summoned more and more objects, each redolent to some degree of evil and possessed of an ominous aura. She had no idea what magics were involved, but it was becoming clear to her what was happening here – the League of Prestidigitation and Prestige obviously considered the collection of the Forbidden Archive too dangerous to keep physically in one location and so had devised this method of *virtually* retrieving each object for study from elsewhere – perhaps some plane that could not be physically reached at all.

It was an indication of their power and it was wondrous, but it did her very little good. How out of all the collection was she meant to find what she needed, because if she had managed to summon the items she had at random then the collection itself had to be immense, with infinite combinations of symbology. And hells – she didn't even really know what it was she was looking for.

There had to be a way of narrowing it down. Kali looked at the symbols on the podium again, reasoning that not even the League's mages could reasonably be expected to remember every combination, and that maybe they were subdivisions – some kind of cataloguing system. Instead of pressing it this time, she replicated the first symbol on the podium with arm movements, feeling what she had missed before, some kind of receptive magical field slightly thickening the air, and a second later a box not dissimilar to the first she had summoned assembled itself. Kali took a gamble and tried waving it on, and to her surprise the gesture worked – another curiosity assembling itself in its place. But she was clearly in the section for artefacts when what she wanted was manuscripts. She replicated the next symbol – spells – and the next – ancient relics. Only on the fourth and last did she find what she was looking for, or at least a place to begin.

Kali's gesticulations increased in pace and she began to summon, study and dismiss manuscript after manuscript, growing more and more adept with the practice until she looked as if she were conducting some complex symphony. She found she was able to pull writings towards her for closer study, turn them around or upside down to seek hidden illuminations and, in the case of actual tomes, flip from page to page with ease. The number of ancient documents stored astounded her, but her joy at discovering such a treasure trove was tempered by the knowledge that she had no time to truly study any but those she sought. Having still not found them and increasingly aware that the forgetful mage could return at any time, her efforts became more urgent, a degree of frustration creeping in as she hurled each document on with a snap of her hand.

Then suddenly, there. Images similar to those Slowhand had described from Makennon's archive in Scholten. There, on the first manuscript she saw, and on more following, diverse and variously decomposed references presumably collected here from different sources and different times.

Kali stopped cycling, hands moving slowly so that she could fold back and forth between the most telling documents, an illuminated manuscript, a map, and what appeared to be some ancient bard's tale of events. It was all there just as Slowhand had said. The hellsfire, the damnation, the vast horde marching under what appeared to be the crossed-circle banner of the Final Faith – not to mention the people kneeling before the horde in apparent worship. Also, looming over them in the background, a figurehead that could have been a representation of the Lord of All – what Makennon believed to be the horde's leader – but to less subjective eyes could equally have been anything else, including, troublingly, a gigantic and stylised version of your typical – how could she put this? – small, warlike person.

In fairness, Kali could see how Makennon had inferred what she had, but there were things here the woman must have been blind not to notice, that leapt off the pages and were simply wrong. For one thing, as had occurred to Slowhand, it seemed to her that the kneeling figures were not human, their physiognomy, though stylised again, more Old Race, elf *and* dwarf. For another, it struck her that they were not kneeling in worship but in supplication, praying to the marching horde and its leader, not for their help in divine ascension but for their mercy.

All of this, of course, was a matter of perception, but as Kali studied the text of the illuminated manuscript and then cycled to the bard's account, it became more a matter of interpretation. She was fluent in neither dwarvish or elvish – hells, who was? – but she had over her explorations picked up enough bits and pieces to recognise key words and put together the bones of a story.

The... middle times? A war between a clan of dwarves and a family of elves... dwarven defeat... no, near-annihilation. Survivors... and a sorcerer. Belatron? Belatron the Black? The Butcher? Anyway... a war machine... a *leader*... built to avenge... no, to *satisfy?*... the dwarven dead. But something wrong. Yes... something gone horribly wrong... a massacre. More death than in the war itself... genocide for both elf and dwarf... and a desperate alliance to stop it...

Kali blew out a breath. That, as far as she was concerned, clinched it – mostly. Everything here tallied with what Merrit Moon had told her, and was, in turn, totally at odds with what Katherine Makennon believed. The only thing she couldn't understand was why the symbol of the Final Faith and its prominence was on not one but two of the manuscripts she studied? Surely this was no representation of the Final Faith's future, it was a warning to everyone on the peninsula from the past.

So much for the history. Merrit Moon had wanted her to stop this thing and what she needed to do was find the information relevant to the here and now, to the threat they faced. She cycled to the map and studied it. The old man had said that between them the elves and the dwarves had built four containment areas for the keys, and there they seemed to be, marked in four widespread locations by two circles and two crosses, each with a representation of a key drawn in above. Why they were not marked by four circles or four crosses, instead of both, Kali wasn't sure, but she supposed the differing symbols were simply elven and dwarven equivalents of X marks the spot. Yes, she thought, remembering the runic circles at the Spiral of Kos, because as one of the circles here lay in the Sardenne Forest at the approximate location where the Spiral had been, that had to be what they were. Knowing that, even though the map was old and parts of the peninsula coastline looked different, she should be able to extrapolate the locations of the other keys from there. Only one thing confused her – the small amount of text on the map made passing reference to five keys not four. Had the old man been wrong and there was actually another, missing location? No, that didn't make sense – the map itself contradicted it. What, then, if there was a fifth key needed to access Orl itself? Yes, that could be it, even though there was no indication of a location for a fifth key on the map. *Dammit*, she thought, looking at the text again, she wasn't that good so maybe she'd just interpreted it wrong.

She had to concentrate on the matter at hand. She possessed the rough locations for the four keys but, for insurance, she needed the location of Orl itself. If this map, for whatever reason, had been meant to be some kind of overall guide, then it had to be here. Somewhere.

Kali took a deep breath and studied the map again, something nagging at her. Suddenly she pulled it towards her for a closer view of the key in the Sardenne. The whorls in the ornate head of the key looked familiar, and with good reason – the drawing was a stylised map of the topography of the area centred on the Spiral of Kos, a more detailed map of its location! But important as that was, there was something else – some of the whorls on the key seemed extraneous, nothing to do with the local topography and seeming to belong somewhere else entirely. Her heart thudded as she realised she was looking at part of a map within a map.

She waved her hand, flipping the document from side to side and slightly up and down, pulling it towards her to zoom in on each key in turn. For the moment she ignored the locations of the containment sites each gave, concentrating instead on the extraneous whorls, overlaying each set in her mind. Together, they formed a topography she recognised, part of the peninsula far to the west.

Kali zoomed to that part of the map. There did appear to be some kind of site marked, but the map was damaged around it, barely legible, and the marking could apply to anywhere within a number of leagues. But what she *could* make out appeared again to be the symbol of the Final Faith.

No, she thought, *that had to be wrong!* Because if it wasn't, what would that mean? That Makennon was right? That she was destined to find Orl?

There was something else that shook her, too – more dwarven text, but text that made no reference to the site being called Orl but... Mor... Mar... no, it was no good, she couldn't make it out.

Pits of Kerberos, she'd come in search of answers and all she'd found were more questions. But at least she had a rough location, and that would do as a start. She zoomed again, searching for landmarks that might help further, but then everything before her eyes suddenly faded. Kali blinked. The Forbidden Archive was a featureless red chamber once more.

"Find anything of interest?" a voice asked.

Kali spun and found herself facing a bearded figure who had to be Mister Duh! Forgot My Head. Only, seeing him from the front, his eyes and expression did not strike her as forgetful at all but instead rather threatening and intense.

Disliking tackling them head on or not, Kali didn't know what else she could do. She rushed the mage, intending to silence him before he could alert others of his kind, but with a sweep of his hand the man did something with the air in front of him and she found herself bouncing back off an invisible field of force that felt like rubbery water. She flung a fist at him instead, hoping that would penetrate, but another sweep of the hand wove a different thread and, this time, she was slammed back and away from him, without any physical contact at all.

Kali yelped as she crashed into the podium and flipped over it, then smashed jarringly and numbingly into the far wall. She picked herself up, wiping blood from her lip.

Again, she ran at the mage, and this time he simply raised an arm and she found herself rising with it, treading air before she could get anywhere near him. The mage smiled, slowly rolled her over in the air and then manoeuvred her helplessly floating body to the side of the chamber. Kali felt herself pressed against the wall and, as she struggled futilely against the invisible grip that held her there, the mage moved his arm again and she found herself being slowly dragged all the way around the circumference of the tower, as if she were dirt to be smeared from his hand.

It was, frankly, embarrassing. But embarrassing was all it seemed to be. Presumably the mage could have flung her around like a doll if he so wished, but he simply continued as he did, smiling, as if this were his way of proving a point.

He even let her down gently, positioning her back on her feet before him.

"Okay, that wasn't fair. You've got me, so what happens now?"

The mage smiled. "Absolutely nothing. I mean you no harm and will defend myself only as and when necessary. I have been employed to provide a client with the same information you now seek, and that employment is now done. It would be churlish of me to censure you for obtaining the same knowledge by your own means, would it not? And I *could* have turned you in the moment you fell through that hatch."

"It was *you* watching me."

"I... sensed you, yes."

"You're the sender," Kali realised. "The Final Faith's source."

The mage bowed. "Poul Sonpear at your service. Trusted archivist for the League of Prestidigitation and Prestige. But the Final Faith are quite generous when it comes to persuading people to bend the rules a little. Tell me," he added with genuine intrigue, "just why is it you and they find this material of such great interest?"

"You've seen it. What the hells do you think?"

"I have no opinion. I have seen many thousands of such manuscripts and these, as are they all, are open to subjective interpretation."

You can say that again, Kali thought. People saw what people wanted to see. Never more so than when they pursued their interest with religious zeal. And that remained exactly the problem here.

"What if I were to tell you these things warn against the end of civilisation as we know it? That unless I recover a key that the Final Faith took from a friend of mine, they're a quarter of the way to unleashing something –"

Kali paused, unsure how to go on.

"Something?" Sonpear urged.

"I don't know yet, okay?" Kali shouted at him, piqued. "But something very, very bad. A clockwork king."

Kali frowned, aware, after the intensity of her search, of how *unthreatening* that sounded.

Sonpear laughed. "Then I would suggest that you will not be able to stop them."

Kali balled her fists. "What are you saying? That this is, after all, where you call your friends to finish me off?"

"Not at all. I wish only to point out to you that the Final Faith's journey along their path of discovery has progressed somewhat further than you think."

"Say again?"

Sonpear sighed heavily. "My... exchanges with the Final Faith's receiver work two ways and, though I do not intend to, it is sometimes hard to avoid absorbing... *peripheral* information. This key that you refer to – the one taken from your friend and that I believe you originally acquired from the Spiral of Kos? – it is not the first to fall into their hands."

Kali swallowed. Suddenly what Munch had said in the Spiral about hazards he'd recently encountered made sense. "They have more?"

"There have been two previous expeditions – to forgotten sites called, I believe, the Shifting City and the Eye of the Storm."

Names that sounded suitably trap-like, Kali thought. And they must have been two of the sites the map referred to, but she – and, presumably, Merrit – had never heard of them. But then they didn't have the resources the Final Faith had – the bastards.

"And they were successful?"

"I gather so." Sonpear stared at her. "Young lady, the Final Faith are already in possession of three of your keys and are about to acquire possession of the fourth."

"What? Where?" Kali said, urgently.

"A site that has so far caused them considerable problems and loss, and by inference therefore the most dangerous of them all. And it is located beneath the most convenient and unexpected place you can imagine – the Final Faith's headquarters at Scholten Cathedral itself."

Kali's mind flashed back to her and Killiam's escape – the curious lift shaft, the place she had wanted to go.

"Slowhand, you fark," she said.

"Excuse me?"

"I have to go," Kali said, knowing she needed to reach the key first. "Listen, you're the spy – is there a back way out of here?"

CHAPTER 13

Much as Kali had negotiated her conduit above Andon, so the man without clothes negotiated his below Scholten – only here the conduit was constructed not of metal but of stone. Dank stone. The dank stone of a sewer, in fact, sheened and slimed by substances worse than those Kali had encountered at the Three Towers – vile, brown, smelly substances that a man as clean and fastidious as he should not even have to think about, let alone drag himself through.

Somewhere beneath the Scholten Cathedral kitchens Killiam Slowhand tried not to think about the sludge that coated him, especially as there was nothing at all between the sludge and him. *Every inch* of him.

The archer shuddered.

It could have been worse, he supposed. For one thing, he could be beneath the Final Faith's privies rather than their kitchens. For another, more importantly, he could be dead. The knife that had been lunged at him on the walkway had been intended to deliver a fatal wound but had instead only grazed his side, something to do with the fact that he had grabbed its wielder and thrown him off the towering building as soon as his arm had come towards him. As the guard's scream faded in Scholten's night sky, his friends would probably have avenged him, finished him off, were it not for the fact that the head guard, just caught up, had ordered him to be taken alive. The order came on the specific instruction of Katherine Makennon, but why she wanted him kept alive, he didn't know – perhaps so she could have her Mister Fitch turn him to her cause, or perhaps merely so that she could revel in his reincarceration. She had certainly seemed to revel as she had had him stripped of what little clothing he had, and he wondered whether something had been going on there, whether perhaps a little of his charm had rubbed off on her after all? Because surely she couldn't have rumbled the old abrasive underpants trick?

Whatever the reason, it had led him to his present unsavoury predicament. Makennon had returned him to a cell but this time somewhere she could keep an eye on him, a small oubliette she just happened to maintain in her private courtyard, which was obviously used only for very special guests. He had felt quite flattered by this and had returned the favour by singing romantic ballads night and day – his very own Eternal Choir. But all good things had to come to an end and, after two weeks, she had ordered his execution at the earliest opportunity.

This was fine by him, as he had never intended hanging around. He'd have been gone the first night had he not needed to lose a little weight first. Not that he was overweight, of course, just – well, a little *big*. A little big for the hole in the oubliette floor, that was.

It was a flaw in security but a necessary one, because with the amount of rain over Scholten, without it he or anyone else kept in the oubliette would have drowned. The hole had probably once been too small for anyone to pass through but it was also long unmaintained – its grate rusted – and, over time, the draining water had worn away its edges, providing a smooth-edged if extremely tight squeezeway through the floor. The fact was, if he had been fully clothed, he'd have had to strip anyway to get through.

Definitely. Yes, without a doubt.

Slowhand shook his head. Hooper would never have believed that he'd done it again. Once – *just once* – he'd like to catch her losing her clothes in the line of duty. Then she'd know that these things just had a way of *happening*. But no – there was no chance of that, was there? Not with little Miss Prissy Knickers.

Slowhand continued crawling forwards, estimating he'd pass beyond the cathedral walls in about ten more minutes. Ahead of him, he could actually see a dim circle of azure night sky that was the sewer's outlet.

Unfortunately, that same light was also partly obscured, silhouetting something coming straight towards him. And down here it could have been anything.

Slowhand cursed. Feeling somewhat vulnerable in his present state, he looked for somewhere to hide. His eyes darted ahead of him, behind him, down and up, but he was in a sewer and there was nowhere to go. He was actually so involved in doing what he did that he failed to notice how quickly the something was coming at him. And the something was so involved in getting where it wanted to be that it didn't notice him.

Heads collided.

"Ow, dammit!"

"Jeeeeshhh!"

A face popped up right in front of his.

"Slowhand?" Kali Hooper said.

He strained to see in the dark. "Hooper? Oh hells, don't tell me – you can see better in the dark, too?"

"Looks like it. *So...* how are you doing?"

"Oh, you know..."

"Mmm."

"Mmm."

The usual exchange went on for a while until Kali suggested they backtrack slightly in her direction, where an access shaft meant the roof of the sewer opened up. They moved to it, and Kali and Slowhand stood.

As he rose, the sewer's detritus slipped off his body, and Kali saw what was beneath. Or rather wasn't.

She turned quickly away. "Oh gods, you're naked again, Slowhand. How in the hells do you manage it?"

"Hey – don't blame me, blame Makennon," he defended himself. "Or maybe even yourself – in case you've forgotten *you're* the reason I got locked up again." He waved at himself. "Like this."

"You told me to go!"

"Of course I did – but I didn't expect you to come back! What the hells are you doing here, Hooper? Did you forget something?"

Kali's expression became serious. "I was too late to save the old man."

Slowhand faltered. "Gods, I'm sorry."

"I know you are. But before he died, he told me what's going on. Sent me to Andon. This whole mess is worse than we thought."

Slowhand bowed his head, sighed. "When is it ever anything else? Tell me."

Kali explained the gist of what she'd learned, omitting

only those parts she was still working out in her own head, and, as she did, the expression in the archer's eyes changed from anticipation to resignation, and he rested his palms on the sewer wall, slowly banging his head against them. "I suppose this means I'm not escaping any more?"

"I... might be grateful for a little help."

Slowhand punched the sewer wall. "I knew it!" He pointed ahead, would have jumped up and down like a petulant brat if he could. "Do you realise I'm only a hundred yards from the exit! A hundred yards, Hooper. I see the light at the end of the tunnel!"

"I know. I came in that way. Slowhand, what can I say? The outside world's not all it's cracked up to be?"

"Aaarrgh!" Slowhand roared in frustration.

"Oh, will you stop it," Kali chided him. "Look, I hardly expected to find you crawling about down here, all right? In fact, I thought you were dead." She paused, quietened, and added softly, "I'm glad you're not, by the way."

Killiam stared at her in her new dark silk bodysuit, and his tone softened. "Yeah, me too. Like the new look, by the way. *Very* nice outfit. Clingy. It, er, shows off your good points."

Kali folded her arms. "It's damp and I'm cold, you pervert. Now, are you with me or not, because I want out of this sewer..."

"Oh, funnily enough, so did I!" Killiam offered, flinging up his arms, though by now it was obvious that he didn't mean it. Nevertheless, the action resulted in something flying off his hands and slapping Kali in the face. Slowhand looked down, apologised.

Kali wiped the article away, shaking her head. "There's an access shaft in the ceiling about two hundred yards back," she said. "Comes out near the Eternal Choir. We can work our way back down to the complex from there."

"Okay, I'll go first," Killiam said, bending back to enter the tunnel.

Kali grabbed him. "O-ho, no. If you think I'm going to crawl along looking at your rear end in all its glory, you've got another think coming." She got down on her hands and knees. "I go first."

"Fine, fine," Killiam said, tiredly. But as Kali moved forwards into the tunnel he smiled at the sight of her bottom, stuck his finger in his mouth to wet it, and drew a tick in the air. It was only a moment later he realised his mistake.

"Guh... uh... ahhhh... pits..."

"Hah!" Kali said. "What was that, by the way? On your – ?"

"Sewerkraut, I think."

"Don't you mean –"

"No, Hooper. I know what I mean."

The pair found the access shaft and up it a ladder that rose to cathedral level, which they climbed, shoving aside a grate. They emerged into a corridor filled with the singing of the Eternal Choir, and the first thing Killiam did was flatten a guard who stood in a doorway mouthing the words as he listened to it. He quickly stripped him of his armour, then donned it himself, bundling the body into a dark niche.

Kali looked him up and down. "Better," she said.

Slowhand shrugged, buckling up his collarpiece. "Yeah, well – this time we're not planning to go flying anywhere, are we?"

"The door's just down there – come on."

"Wait," Slowhand said. "There's something I need to get first. From Makennon's chambers."

"What? Are you nuts?"

"Trust me, Hooper. I've a feeling we're going to need this thing."

Slowhand led Kali to the Anointed Lord's audience chamber – deserted, Kali guessed because Makennon was down at the dig – and opened a compartment in the wall. Kali found herself staring at the most magnificent-looking longbow she had ever seen. She knew where it must have come from – the Battle of Andon, eight years earlier. This was the weapon that had killed John Garrison.

Slowhand weighed it in his hands, ran his palm along its sleek lines. "Suresight," he said. "Never thought I'd see her again."

"Careless of you to lose her."

Slowhand pulled a quiver from the compartment too, lined an arrow against the shaft, pursing his lips and nodding in approval. Then his expression darkened. "Yes, well... After Andon I'd had enough of killing. Everyone had." His tone lightened once more. "But times move on. Let's go."

"Hold on," Kali said, looking around. "If Makennon's in the habit of keeping souvenirs, maybe..."

She rifled through a nearby chest and with a cry of triumph pulled forth her toolbelt, removed from her prior to her interrogation. She also found her torn and tatty old outfit, and as she held it up to examine it, wasn't sure what disturbed her more – the fact that Makennon had felt fit to keep it, or the fact that Dolorosa had been right in her observation that it did indeed *steeenk*.

She left the remains of the garment where it was and they continued on to their original destination, moving down out of the cathedral and into its sub-levels once more. This time, they avoided all the guards they could, having no wish to announce their return to the lower depths.

There was only one problem. The bridge across the cavern had been retracted to the other side, the wheel there locked. What was more, two guards paced back and forth in front of it.

"Dammit," Kali said. "They've battened down the hatches."

"Not a problem," Slowhand said.

He unslung his bow.

Kali stared at the distant wheel and guards. So far they hadn't been spotted but...

"What the hells are you doing?" she whispered. "Take one of them down and the other will sound the alarm before you can hit the second. Oh, and even if you could get the second, then there'll be no one to activate the wheel. We need to think this through."

"No, we don't," Slowhand said. He primed an arrow and hefted the bow. A nerve in his jaw twitched as he waited, but then, at the exact moment the pacing guards crossed paths, he let fly. The single arrow pierced both of their necks, dropping them instantly, then carried on to impact with the wheel clamp with a solid thud, releasing the lock.

"Hells, you're good," Kali said.

Slowhand smiled, patting his bow. "It's good to have the old girl back."

Kali brought the bridge to their side and the two crossed, sneaking their way through the remainder of the complex until they neared the shafts that had so aroused Kali's curiosity what seemed now an age before. This time, they weren't guarded, but with the bridge supposedly retracted they didn't really need to be.

"Hooper, why here?" Slowhand asked. "I mean, an Old Race structure on this site, and then, centuries later, the cathedral built here too, presumably with the Final Faith not then knowing what was beneath it. Can that just be coincidence?"

"Maybe," Kali replied. "Or maybe this has always been a site of some significance, sociologically, historically or religiously. Maybe people, whoever they are – or were – are simply drawn here. Actually I've come across a few old manuscripts that suggest there may even be a number of nodes located across the peninsula, nodes that could be part of a network of –"

"Enough, Hooper," Slowhand said. "What do you expect we'll find down there?"

"Oh, that's easy. Something deadly."

"Something deadly," Slowhand repeated. "Right, fine, thanks for sharing that with me."

"My pleasure." Kali gestured towards the lift. "After you."

"No, no, I insist. After you."

"Slowhand, get on the bloody lift."

"You are getting quite domineering, you know that?"

"And you love every minute of it."

The lift was hardly the engineering marvel that Kali had ridden at the Spiral of Kos but it did the job, creaking on a rope as it descended a shaft that had been roughly cut from rock and felt strangely warm. The marks of modern tooling suggested to Kali that the shaft was the work of the Final Faith, which likely meant that the site to which they were heading had another – original – entrance elsewhere, but what or where that was she didn't know. She had never come across anything resembling an entrance in her explorations of the countryside surrounding Scholten, so maybe it had become blocked over the years by rockfalls or subsidence, or maybe had even been deliberately sealed. It didn't really matter because they were heading where they wanted to go.

The question was, where was that? The lower the lift descended, the less the creaking of its supporting rope could be heard, the sound overwhelmed by a growing hissing and pounding coming from below, as if machines were at work in the rock. As the sounds became so loud that the shaft itself began to vibrate, Slowhand looked to Kali for some kind of explanation, but she could only shrug. It was only when – at last – the lift reached bottom and they negotiated a small tunnel that their source became clear. Staggeringly so.

"My gods," Slowhand said. He, like Kali, was staring into a natural cavern in the bedrock far beneath Scholten that was bigger than the Final Faith's distribution centre, looming above them into shadow and dropping away beneath them to a bubbling lava lake some hundred feet down. The lake surrounded an island of rock that rose out of it to their eye level, and on that island – connected to where they had entered by a narrow and recently suspended bridge – stood a structure that was far from natural and could only be the secure location of the fourth and final key. Looking something like a cross between a kiln and a furnace, its width that of seven men and its height of five, the stone dome sat solidly on the island perch, pistons positioned all around its circumference pumping out great bursts of black smoke while, in the centre of its roof, a round hole, some kind of chimney, belched out thick clouds of steam. If, Kali reflected, the Spiral of Kos had had a distinctly elven feel about it, then this site had dwarf written all over it in letters bigger than the dwarves themselves.

She wondered what kinds of traps dwarves favoured.

As if on cue, a piercing scream emanated from somewhere within the stone dome, and a few moments later Makennon and a bunch of cronies stormed out of the single entrance. Kali and Slowhand hid as the group passed, Makennon clearly cheesed off, and Kali presumed that she had just lost another of the tomb raiders she'd apparently been throwing at this thing.

This was her chance. The trouble was, she couldn't risk using the main entrance because Makennon had likely left guards behind and, as far as she could see, that left her with only one choice.

Slowhand saw her staring at the chimney, timing the gaps between its eruptions of steam.

"Oh, no. No, no, no. No, Hooper, no."

"Don't worry. You aren't coming with me."

"Of course I am. But not that way."

"There is no other way, Slowhand. But no, I need you to stay here. Watch my back in case Makennon returns."

"You think I'm letting you go in there alone?"

"Listen, you *just* said –"

"I *know* what I said –"

"Slowhand, listen. Think back to the night of my escape. Now look at those belches of steam. There's *no time* for us both to go."

Slowhand couldn't argue the point, and sighed. "Fine, I've got your back. But Hooper, this is still suicide."

"Since when did that ever stop me?"

Kali moved across the bridge, clinging to its cabling and staring down at the bubbling red lake below. *Lava*, she thought, *luvverly*. Reaching the dome, she worked her way around the outside rim of the structure until she had moved completely behind it, she wondering idly if this dwarven thing had remained active since the day it was built. That seemed unlikely. It was far more probable that Makennon had either accidentally triggered its mechanisms in her efforts to recover the key or one of the less than capable tomb raiders she'd hired hadn't been able to resist pulling some nice, shiny lever on the wall.

You just couldn't get the staff these days.

Kali wasted no time. She leapt for the side of the dome and scrambled onto its sloping surface, feet scrabbling behind her but maintaining enough purchase to enable her to grab a fingerhold on the rough stone. This done, she pulled herself slowly upwards until she reached the apex of the dome, ducking back as the chimney belched out a cloud of steam. Once it had done so, she peered inside the flue. A shaft dropped away before her, dark, dirty and utterly uninviting – just the way she liked it.

She sat back while another cloud erupted. Two minutes between belches. She was going to have to be very precise in the matter of timing. She would also have to be ready for anything as she would be going in blind, literally plunging into the unknown. But whatever was going on in this fiery hole, it seemed likely that the chimney would take her to the heart of the matter.

She stared across the cavern, found Slowhand and then jabbed her finger downwards, indicating she was going in. The archer's mouth opened, his head shook, and then he was holding it in his hands in disbelief.

Another cloud belched, and Kali scrambled inside.

She anchored herself against the sides of the chimney with her elbows and thighs, shuffling quickly down, estimating it would take her no more than a minute to descend the depth of the dome, more than enough of a safety margin between belches of steam. Quite how she'd exit the chimney near its base she hadn't yet worked out, but that she considered to be one of the challenges of her trade.

Something, though, was wrong – that was already becoming clear. All she could see beneath her was darkness, the perspective of the flue veeing below, and she suddenly realised that the shaft went deeper than she'd anticipated, the heart of the site not within the dome but the pitsing rock itself.

In other words, she'd never make it in time. Already she could hear booms coming out of the darkness below, what she presumed to be precursors of the next release of steam. There was only one thing for it – and that was to let herself freefall as far as she could.

Kali released her grip and immediately plummeted down the flue. She yelped as she slid down, down and down, her body thudding painfully into the sides of the shaft. More than once she crashed against unexpected ridges or bars, and the impacts bounced her sideways and around until she was in danger of becoming utterly disorientated in the dark. She couldn't allow that, however, or she'd be encountering the origin of the steam first-hand, something that just might spoil her day and the rest of her life.

She had to risk it. She jammed herself against the sides of the shaft once more, careering a further ten feet before she came to a jarring halt, and then looked down to see just where in the general scheme of things she'd ended up.

As it turned out, she'd made her move *just* in time. Not far below her the shaft widened and then branched off in a number of directions, splitting to envelop some central core. Had Kali continued down any one of them she would have been dead, because in each a lapping red glow was reflected from what could only have been the lava lake itself.

Kali didn't want to go there. But she did want to get inside the central core.

She eased herself down what remained of the shaft before it split, aware of the limited time she had but also that one slip would bring the same instant death as being consumed in a belch of steam. She dropped onto the roof of the central core and quickly heaved open a metal panel she found there. Dropping into a shaft of about her own height, she slammed the panel shut just as a final boom heralded a release of steam that made the metal above her rumble with the force of its release. Kali sighed with relief, but it was a short sigh, because as much of a challenge as getting this far had been, she suspected the hard part was yet to come. This was, after all, the site that Makennon had been trying to access since last she'd been in Scholten – and it was whatever lay below the *second* panel – the one she now found under her feet – that was going to be the true test of her mettle.

Kali pulled a rope from her toolbelt and secured it to the side of the shaft, dangling from it as she booted the panel open. Then she moved herself around until her head peeked through a hole on one side of a curving ceiling.

Well, she thought, *this is interesting.*

She was looking down into what appeared to be a dwarven forge, a circular chamber whose floor and walls were plated with metal panels decorated with the same repetitive runic shapes as had been at the Spiral of Kos, except here they were crosses instead of circles. The design of the walls made them look as if they might rotate, allowing access in and out, but for now they were tightly shut. Beyond this, the chamber was featureless apart from the forge itself, a raised and central metal mould carved with a complex coil design, in which lay the fourth of the keys. The parallel was obvious – other than for the fact this chamber was claustrophobic rather than vast, it was a dwarven version of the Spiral of Kos, right down to the presence of an observation area built into a curve of the wall behind a window of what appeared to be reinforced glass.

It was also, quite clearly, designed to be equally deadly. What Kali had ignored until now was the fact that the floor of the forge was blackened here and there by the twisted and charred remains of Makennon's unsuccessful tomb raiders, all of whom appeared to have been roasted alive, and one of whom still smoked where he or she had recently fallen.

It hadn't been too hard to work out that the trap here was going to be heat-based, but now it was time for her to find out exactly what she was up against. And if she was right...

Kali dug in her toolbelt and pulled out a small, polished stone she kept for such occasions, then dropped it towards the forge's floor. It struck one of the metal panels and bounced onto another, then another, and, with a moment's gap between them, the first and third panels sank slightly into the floor with a grating sound.

Kali smiled. She knew it. The panels were weight-sensitive, probably rotating at random to provide a false sense of security but in actuality trapping anyone who thought they'd found a safe path to the forge. All she had to do now was find out what they did.

On the subject of which...

She felt the heat before she saw it, the carved coils on the side of the mould turning first a dull red, then brighter, and then brighter still until they were almost white-hot. Kali knew now the reason for the dome's pistons and steam chimney – they had to be part of some elaborate mechanism that pumped lava into the dome from the lake surrounding the island, probably pressurising and concentrating its flow before delivering it here, to the forge itself. The carvings on the mould were not simple decorative patterns, they were sophisticated heating coils.

And what heat! Kali had to draw back into the shaft as the mould itself began to glow, gradually matching the intensity of the coils, and as it heated up, so too did the key inside. And after perhaps half a minute, watched through a heat haze, the key seemed to start receding away in her vision.

Only it wasn't receding, she realised, it was melting.

A few seconds later she stared down at a key that had become completely molten.

It wasn't what Kali had been expecting, but she had to admit it was ingenious. This place hadn't been built so much as a trap as a preventative, the mechanisms involved designed not to stop anyone stealing the key but to stop them *leaving* with it. The fact that that same anyone would die horribly, roasted alive by the heating coils, was simply a side effect.

The weight-sensitive panels reset themselves with a metallic chuk and the key started to cool again. Fitting exactly into the mould as it did, it started to regain its form in no time.

Kali knew now what she had to do. There was no way she could reach the key with her rope so instead she was going to have to play a game. And it was going to be exactly the same game she used to play as a girl, disturbing the regulars in the Flagons. Its aim was to get all the way around the bar using only furniture – okay, and the occasional head – and *without* touching the floor.

Exactly like that game. Only deadlier. So much so that every one of her movements had to be precise.

Kali took a steadying breath, and then slowly lowered and then removed her hands from the rope so that she was suspended only by the waist, then turning face downwards let her body find its own level as the rope took her weight. It was a delicate balancing act but, when stabilised, she was able to raise her arms and legs so that she hung horizontally spread-eagled, her limbs outstretched.

She gave a small kick, and turned, examining the chamber about her. There was a ledge there she could use, a ridge in the wall over there, and – *whoah, difficult one* – a slight rib between panels there. But then she'd be next to the key. *Okay*, she thought, running it through her head again – *One, ledge, two, ridge, three, rib... four, key.*

Oh, the hells with it, just go!

Kali swung forwards on the rope, building enough momentum to carry her over the first gap, then cut her rope cleanly with her knife. She sailed away, arcing forwards, hit the ledge and twisted, at the same time kicking herself away with her foot. Flipping forwards, somersaulting smoothly in mid-air, she felt her toes touch the ridge and lunged forwards, spinning this time slightly to her right, correcting her balance with a flap of her arms as her hip grazed the wall. There wasn't enough width in the ridge to keep that balance for long so she hopped quickly along it, only at the last second batting the wall with her hand so that she flew sideways out into the room. She let herself fall, inclining head first, then landed on the ridge with the palms of her hands, immediately cartwheeling once, twice, then three times, and coming upright at the exact point the ridge came to an end. Flexing her legs and bouncing as she returned to vertical, she leapt upwards and forwards, yelling with the exertion it took, and crossed the final gap between herself and the key. Landing on the edge of the mould on the balls of her feet, she windmilled her arms once more for balance, then stood upright, looking down at the object she sought.

Piece of pits, Kali thought. She only wished she could have done that sort of thing as a kid. It would have earned her a drink or two.

Kali bent and extracted the key from the mould – *oh, ooh, ow, ow, ow* – a little prematurely as it happened. She juggled it from hand to hand, her heart lurching as she almost dropped it on the third pass, then sighed with relief as it cooled. The key firmly in her grip, all she had to do now was get out of the place. She was about to start examining the walls for an escape route when a long rumbling signalled the rotation she'd suspected they were capable of. A number of doors were revealed, which then opened – a spiral stairway visible beyond them – and in each stood one of Makennon's people, aiming a crossbow directly at her. If that wasn't bad enough, framed in the last to open was Makennon herself – and beside her was Killiam Slowhand.

He didn't speak. But Makennon did.

"Miss Hooper, we meet again," she said. "Pray, tell me, what brings you here today?"

Kali smiled. "Oh, you know, out for a walk, fell down a hole..."

"And there was I thinking you'd taken up a career as a chimney sweep. You should, you know – as an occupation it's much less hazardous."

"But not as rewarding," Kali said, holding up the key.

"Give me that key, Miss Hooper."

"No." Kali looked down at the panelled floor. "Want to come get it, Anointed Lord?"

"I'd rather you just threw it to me."

"Not going to happen."

Slowhand spoke for the first time. "Hooper, just do it.

The lady has you outgunned."

"Nice backwatching, Slowhand."

"They had us marked as soon as we entered the cavern. Took me as soon as you disappeared inside. I guess they wanted you to do the job for them. Give her the key, Kali."

"She's not getting the final key!" Kali shouted. She hovered on the edge of the mould, her intention clear. "It melts with me, if need be."

Makennon sighed loudly. "I gather that since our last talk you have been doing some research into the keys and what they are?"

"I've seen and heard a few things."

"And I imagine this *behaviour* is because you veer to the... darker interpretations of the facts to hand."

"That's right. End of the world, and all that. But hey, I'm not the one blinded by holy light."

Makennon smiled coldly. "I understand your concerns, I do. But I have seen insufficient darkness to dim that light, and perhaps the opposite is true of you. So, as I once said to Mister Slowhand – what if I could prove to you that it were otherwise?"

Kali faltered momentarily, remembering what she had seen on the map. But she dismissed the concerns quickly. This was, after all, *still* the Final Faith.

"Makennon, you're not getting your hands on this key."

"Hooper..." Slowhand urged again.

"Slowhand, no! This thing is dangerou –"

Kali never even saw it happen. One second Slowhand had no bow in his hand, and then he did – and an arrow knocked the key from her grip, its trajectory perfectly aligned to bounce the key to Makennon's feet. The Anointed Lord bent to pick it up.

"Thank you... *Lieutenant*," she said.

Kali stared at the archer. She didn't know what to say.

"Hooper, they'd have –" Slowhand began, but broke off as a sudden push from Makennon sent him sprawling into the centre of the chamber. At the same time, Makennon and her guards retreated, and the walls began to rotate back to their closed position.

The last thing Kali heard from the Anointed Lord was, "Gentlemen, we have an appointment in Orl."

The wall sealed itself with a jarring thud. And the floor beneath Slowhand sank slightly with a grating sound.

The coils in the mould began to glow.

Slowhand took a look at the charred bodies and the reddening mould. "Oh, pits," he said.

"Pits?" Kali repeated. Now that the mechanism was activated there was no reason to stay perched where she was, and she jumped down, trying to find a way to reopen the wall. There was none. "That's all you can say after betraying me?"

"They would have killed you, Hooper, you know that. I was saving your life."

"Maybe," Kali said. Now she was pulling at the panelling, trying – desperately – to find some kind of off switch. Again, none, and sweat was already breaking out thickly on her body. "Dammit!"

She stared at the mould, at the window of the observation area and back again. That done, she moved with Slowhand to the rim of the chamber, but the heat was still intense – as intense as it would need to be to make the key molten in a matter of seconds.

And seconds was all they had, because her hair had begun to smoke. Her double take on the mould and the windows had given her an idea of how to get out of there, though, even if it would take split-second timing. But first she needed to deal with Slowhand. She needed him but his breathing was becoming increasingly laboured – he was having a much harder time of it than her.

Kali dug into her toolbelt and pulled out what appeared to be a small conch. The shape of it was something that could be bitten down on in the mouth, and Kali did this, testing the thing with a couple of inhalations before handing it to Slowhand.

"Use this," she said. "It'll be easier."

Slowhand took the conch, bemused. What, she thought he'd feel better if he could listen to the sea? He looked inside, and then recoiled. There were things inside – horrible, little, pulsing, slimy things.

"Don't ask me," Kali said. "But they produce oxygen. The supply's limited but it does gradually refill. Go ahead, chomp down, it'll make a difference."

Slowhand did so, reluctantly. And his eyes widened as the *things* did what they did, filling his lungs with cool air. "Fwer joo ged theef fings?"

Kali shrugged. "That one? That one I bought from a pirate in a little place called Crablogger Beach." She dug in her belt again. "*This* one, however, I found in an elven ruin – and I've had it for a long, long time."

Slowhand stared at her questioningly as Kali rolled the icebomb in her hand, remembering her encounter with Merrit Moon all those years ago. "Keep it because one day you might need it," he'd said. *Well, old man, guess what...*

"If this thing still works, things in this room are about to go from very, very hot to very, very cold very, very quickly. You know what happens when things do that?"

"They blow up in your face?"

"A-ha. So find somewhere to use as cover."

"Hooper, there *is* no cover."

Kali looked upwards. "Then Killiam Slowhand is going to have to be a little bit faster for once."

Slowhand followed her gaze. "Understood."

"Right, then," Kali said. She pressed the stud on the globe and threw it towards the forge. For a second nothing happened, and then everything before their eyes exploded and turned white.

The old man had not been exaggerating about the power of these things. It might have been tragically effective when he'd used one outside, but in these close confines it was almost elemental in its impact.

The forge frosted, and they waited. The floor cracked beneath their feet. The very air they breathed seemed to be crystals, and still the pair of them waited. The timing had to be perfect.

The two of them were covered in a thin sheen of ice now, and shivering violently. Their breath froze as it left their mouths.

There was a crackling sound from above, perversely sounding as though the forge were on fire.

The glass of the observation chamber frosted from left to right, as if something invisible had painted it white.

"Now, Slowhand!" Kali shouted.

The archer struggled to steady his grip. Kali could hardly blame him. She, too, was shaking like a leaf.

"Slowhand..."

Slowhand let fly three arrows in quick succession, the first spidering the frozen glass, the second cracking it and the third shattering it completely.

The glass blew out at the same time the forge exploded. Sharp slices of death – glass and metal – rained and hurtled at them from above and below.

They didn't hang around to feel their touch. As soon as his final arrow impacted with the wall of the observation chamber behind the glass, Slowhand grabbed Kali about the waist, circling her so his hand could still grab the rope, and then launched the pair of them up towards the broken window, frozen hand alternating with frozen hand as they climbed.

Behind and below them the forge didn't know what to do with itself, the chunks of the mould that had landed on its floor again triggering the heating coils at the same time as they crackled with intense cold. And as Kali and Slowhand reached window level, the stark contrast between temperatures caused a renewed series of explosions, and the whole chamber blew.

Kali and Slowhand were sent hurtling towards the observation area wall, thudded into it and landed on the floor, stunned. But as its floor subsided beneath them, they knew there was no time to waste.

The whole place was going up.

They ran, exiting first the observation area and then the dome itself, the whole place quaking beneath them. Makennon and her party had already left but some guards remained. They were not concerned with Kali and Slowhand, however, as they were too busy screaming and running for their lives.

The reason for this was that the lava lake surrounding the dome had ceased its gentle bubbling and become now a seething, broiling mass that lurched and spat at the rock that contained it. Thick, liquid fire had even begun to spit above its lip and, as Kali and Slowhand looked on one last, unfortunate woman was engulfed in a burning tongue that fried her screeching form to a skeleton in less than a second.

Those same lava spurts hitting them wasn't their main problem, however.

It was the lava spurts that had hit the suspension

bridge.

Because as they watched, their only way off the central island warped and twisted in the intense heat, and then its cabling snapped away with a sound like a whiplash.

Almost instantly, the bridge was gone.

"Hooper?" Slowhand said, worriedly.

Kali looked down, her brow beetling. "We're stuffed," she said, succinctly.

What she neglected to mention was what Slowhand had not yet noticed. Because she didn't want to worry him more.

The lava lake was rising.

CHAPTER 14

Resurrection was a second coming. Somewhat more than a second, actually, but in the circumstances Merrit Moon thought it would be churlish to complain about the delay.

The sharp intake of breath with which he returned to life echoed around the cave of the ogur, empty now apart from the ogur themselves, gathered in a tribal huddle where, by the look of the cleanly gnawed bones around them – *all* of the bones of Munch's people – they had been sitting for some time. They stared at him in silence, their expressions a mix of fascination and fear caused by what was likely the strangest occurrence they had ever seen.

The occurrence was no less strange to Moon himself, this being the first time he had died.

Or not – as the case seemed to be.

That the artefact had worked – albeit in a way and on

a subject he would never have anticipated – renewed his faith in the Old Races and the wonders, rather than the horrors, they had once achieved. He doubted, however, that the ogur that had triggered the amulet had found its effects wondrous in any way, and he sighed. Perhaps it was a horror after all.

The poor creature knelt before him, hand outstretched and touching the amulet, but it was not what it had been. Where moments before it had been indistinguishable from the rest of its tribe – solid and formidable, awesome – it was now a shadow of its brothers, wasted and drained. The same ogur that had attempted to approach Kali – likely the alpha – it had obviously been the first to approach his body and it had paid the price.

The creature still breathed, haltingly and raspingly, and stared at him in utter helplessness and confusion, but there was nothing Moon could do to help it, and he felt deeply sorry. It had not, after all, been greed that had motivated the ogur to touch the amulet, just primitive curiosity. It had yet to learn – and he hoped it would have the chance to do so – that all that glistened was not gloob.

Therein lay the simple beauty – and horror – of what the amulet was. Moon thought back to his hidden room in his cellar in Gargas, and the mixed emotions the sight of it had engendered in him. Sitting there on the shelves amidst other acquisitions he had deemed too dangerous for even someone such as Kali to see, its physical beauty was undeniable – a scintillating, perfectly faceted gem inlaid in gloob that could have been used to pay the ransom of a king. It was for that reason that he kept the amulet locked away, because if the wrong eyes were ever to see the gem it would be impossible to resist, taken from his possession with no knowledge of what it truly was and what it truly did. Not that he didn't trust Kali implicitly on that level, of course. It was just that by the amulet's very nature – the fact that in the absence of the direst circumstances it could not be tested – it was unpredictable and therefore potentially very, very dangerous.

He had found the amulet in an elven site many years before, certain as soon as he had that it was more than it seemed, because if there was one thing he had learned in his long career it was that Old Race artefacts generally were. It had taken two years of research following the find to identify what it was, cross-referencing a dozen Old Race manuscripts, until he finally knew that what he had acquired was an example of a battlefield boobytrap that the elves called scythe-stones. Products of their science or their sorcery – or both, he still wasn't sure – they masqueraded as spoils of war, prime to be plucked from the fallen body of an elven victim, but in actuality what they did was transfer the life essence from a victorious warrior to the defeated at the moment of death, reversing their roles and effectively turning the tide of many a battle. The psychological effect on the surrounding enemy was not to be underestimated either, because the host body fleetingly absorbed some of the features of the victim, looking almost as if its soul were being stolen from the body. In a way it was, Moon supposed, and to the enemy – the superstitious dwarves – the supernatural aspect was often far more disturbing than the truth of what had actually happened.

Moon looked at the ogur again, and frowned. The efficacy of the amulet couldn't be denied – he was, after all, alive – but nevertheless something seemed to be wrong. For one thing, the process was meant to be almost instantaneous, and for another he... didn't feel quite right. Whatever was happening here wasn't happening the way it was meant to, and apart from his own discomfort it was evidently prolonging the agony of the poor creature before him. As Moon watched, the ogur's body and features seemed to shrink in on themselves even more than they already had, the blue wisps that were still being drawn from it by the amulet seemingly extracting its essence still. Moon was, as yet, still too weak to move, and so he had no choice but to witness the process continuing for another few minutes, at the end of which time he turned his eyes away. For the amulet had taken everything from the ogur, and now, in the end, the beast all but disintegrated before him, collapsing into a desiccated heap on the cave floor.

The amulet snatched what wisps of it remained in the air with a sigh.

Wrong, Moon thought. *That was wrong.* And the other ogur in the cave obviously thought so, too, because now they were stirring from their prone positions, grunting with what sounded like growing confusion and agitation. What was happening? Now that their alpha was dead, had their deferment to him ceased? Was he now as exposed to their primal hunger as Kali would have been had she remained in the cave?

No, Moon thought, *it wasn't that* – but it made his situation no less dangerous. Something had to have changed about him during the revitalisation process – perhaps something as simple as his scent – and the reason that the ogur were no longer deferring to him was because to their senses he was no longer the man they had deferred to before. The end result, however, was the same. He was no longer welcome here amongst the ogur – not as anything but food, that was – and he had to get out of their cave before their slowly revising opinion of him resulted in his being ripped apart.

Moon rose from the cave floor, slowly and cautiously, noting as he did that his resurrection seemed to have booned his old and tired limbs with a renewed resilience and strength that he had not felt for a good many years. This was hardly the time to celebrate the fact, however, because while the ogur's state of confusion seemed to have passed, their agitation had grown markedly. Their grunts were becoming more frequent now, their mannerisms more threatening – and their gaze more hungry.

Slowly, Moon bent to retrieve his staff and backpack, and then with equal slowness he eased towards the tunnel that led out of the cave. The ogur gathered about him as he moved, sniffing at him, clawing curiously at his clothes, and Moon realised that it was probably only a matter of seconds before one of them actually lunged. He was having to push his way between them now, and could feel their clawings becoming heavier, more insistent. And then one of them did what he'd been expecting and grabbed him roughly by the arm, attempting to rip the limb away.

Moon batted the ogur off and *roared*.

What? he thought. What had that just been? What had he just *done?* That he'd actually been able to physically repel the ogur? That he'd made that *noise?*

Oh, this wasn't good. This wasn't good at all.

It was not, however, the ideal circumstance to dwell on the matter, and for now all he could do – what he *needed* to do – was take advantage of it. The remaining ogur, it seemed, had been as disturbed by his unexpected actions as he had himself, and their clawings had become more hesitant, in some cases even ceased. And the ogur that had lunged for him was actually retreating submissively back into the cave.

What is happening? Moon wondered. Were the ogur,

after all, deferring to him? Or were they perhaps sensing some of the alpha whose life essence he had stolen away? Whichever of the two it was, he knew that he needed to press the issue before they changed their minds again.

Instinctively, he roared for a second time. And this time, without even thinking about doing it, he repeatedly thumped the rock of the cave walls in warning.

By all the gods, what was happening?

The ogur – all of them, now – backed off into the cave, and, free from their threat, Moon turned towards the exit. A second later he emerged onto the ice plateau and, again before he knew what he was doing, began inhaling deeply of the air.

No, he realised, he wasn't inhaling it, he was *sniffing* it.

And on it, he could smell Kali Hooper.

Impossible. It was just impossible. He had no idea how long he had spent in the cave but it was not an inconsiderable amount of time, and yet Kali was *there* on the air, as if she had left him only a moment before, her scent traceable despite the stench of the ogur cave and the blizzard that still numbingly blew outside it. She was as clear as day to him, as vital as if she had remained nearby – but she hadn't, he knew and he realised he was smelling a scent that should long ago have become undetectable to the human nose. A *human* nose but not that of a creature that survived by...

Moon remembered the resilience and strength he had felt as he had risen from the cave floor, remembered the batting away of the ogur and his roar, remembered his hammering of the cave walls. Most of all, he remembered that he had not felt... *quite right*. Gods, he knew there was meant to be a fleeting transference from a victim but was it possible the amulet had somehow – ?

He lifted his palms to his face, feeling the features there. He half-expected to feel those of an ogur bulging beneath his fingers but, no, his face still felt like his own. He looked down at his body, and it too seemed to be the same. Only...

He gazed at one of his own footprints, frozen in the plateau ice. The footprint was from before he had entered the ogur cave and he turned to place his foot beside it. And the footprint was smaller.

Merrit Moon's heart sank. So, he had changed, then. Perhaps was still changing. The only question was, to what degree and at what pace? The artefact that he had brought with him into these mountains in the hope that it – if it became necessary – would buy him more time to complete his mission had, instead, infused him with not only the ogur's life essence but part of the ogur itself. How and why that should happen, he didn't know – perhaps it was something to do with the ogur's body chemistry, or perhaps the fact that their species were so different that it was the only way the amulet could cope with the transference – but whatever the cause it left him with but a single thought: *Oh gods, Kali, what have I done?*

Thinking of his protégée made Moon's heart sink even further. He had taken no pleasure in not telling her about the amulet, in fact it had pained him greatly, but how could he have told her when even he was not sure whether the artefact would work? As she had knelt over his dying form, what right had he had to build up her hopes by telling her he might yet live if there was a danger those hopes would be shattered if the artefact failed to work? No, he couldn't have done that to her, any more than he could have let her touch the amulet at the moment of his passing. *Damn Munch*, he thought, because if that little thug had finished the job instead of leaving him to suffer then it would be him who would now be lying on the cave floor, as dried and as drained and as dead as he deserved to be.

Moon caught Kali's scent on the air once more, and he wondered where she now was. Had she succeeded in finding the information she needed, and was she on her way to protect the other keys? One thing he did know, he needed to find her, not only to help, if he could, but to let her know that he lived, even if it was not in quite the same fashion as he had lived before.

He began to trudge down the mountain, his legs feeling strangely powerful beneath him, and he drew a deep breath into his lungs so that they expanded as he had never known them to do before. There were obviously some advantages to his changing form, and if he could use his apothecarial skills to prevent any further changes – if they were to come – then he had to admit that he might not be too discomforted by his strange fate, after all. If he was going to find Kali, however, he would need to seek medicines or potions in Andon or Fayence, because there would be no time to sweep north to...

Merrit Moon faltered. He suddenly realised that he couldn't remember where he lived. Gar – ? Garg – ? *Oh, this was ridiculous. Damn the hells, where was it that Thrutt lived?*

Thrutt? he thought. *No, his name wasn't Thrutt, it was –*

Ah. So that was how it was going to be. Clearly, he was still changing, and the changes to him were not going to be merely physical, they were going to be mental as well. However much of this creature – this *Thrutt* – now resided within him, he was possibly faced with a battle for dominance that only one of them might win.

Far from fearing that possibility, the idea intrigued him. The ogur obviously had the advantage on the physical side, but on the mental he would equally obviously be the victor. This thing was a creature of instinct and sensation, a hunter and a cannibal, but nothing more. In other words, for such a big head, there was remarkably little going on upstairs. It had no rationality, no logic, no intelligence with which it would be able to hold its own, and so...

Again, Moon faltered. *Did that make sense?* he wondered. A situation such as this had no precedent after all. He wasn't talking about a possession here, and this was no mere battle of body and wills, this was something completely different, a process forged in the minds of beings who... of beings who...

Moon suddenly found himself confused by his own chain of thought, and then a wave of blackness washed through his brain that left him momentarily dizzy and blank. He tried to pull the thoughts back but suddenly realised that he no longer knew what they were. He'd been thinking about... thinking about...

The sound of Thrutt's roar echoed through the mountains.

No! Moon thought. He had to get a grip on this, on himself, at least until he could find those medicines or potions that might help. But if he was going to do that then he had to hurry, hurry, hurry, because Andon and Fayence were both so very far away and he had never been there before.

But wait – of course he had. So many, many times.

Hadn't he?

Moon began to pound down the slopes below him, passing a place where tracks intersected, forcing himself to think about anything and everything that made him what he was. He thought of his shop, he thought of Horse, he thought of his adventures and, inevitably, he thought of Kali. He was glad that he had been able to tell her how much she meant to him because he had never been able to do that before, as he had never been able to share with her the secret of how he had found –

There was a sudden stinging sensation in his right side, and he paused, rumbling curiously. Another such sensation stung him on his left, and this time he slapped at the part of his body where it had occurred. The sting transferred itself to his hand, and he lifted it – bigger than he remembered, and tinged slightly green – to see what had stuck there. It was a tiny dart that had caught in the soft flesh of the palm. And it looked like a piece of reed. *Needlereed.*

Moon's low rumble turned into a growl, and he sniffed the air around him, his nose jerking roughly as he did. There were men nearby. Men in hiding, at least four of them, and one of them smelled strangely familiar to him. Yes, he had the smell of one of the oomans who had invaded his cave...

No! Merrit Moon thought. Not his cave, the ogur's cave – but the smell of the man remained familiar all the same. And it made anger grow inside him – dark, uncontrollable, feral anger. He tried to stop it but he was losing his grip, could feel it, his thoughts running together, and the things that had stung him in his side, he saw that some substance dribbled from their ends, that it was on his skin and in it and...

Gods, no, what was happening, and why now – why?

As Merrit Moon roared more loudly, more primally, than ever before, the men with the needlereed darts came from behind the rocks and at him, but the toxins that had been fired into his system – the ones he had dimly thought had been meant to subdue him – had instead the opposite effect and stripped him of any fear of their coming. Primitive survival instincts taking over completely, Moon felt himself subsumed – drowned – by the primal reactions of a wounded beast and, dropping down into the depths of the dual consciousness he now seemed to possess, he found himself experiencing what happened next only as a kind of semi-aware observer. The observer was dully conscious of the fact, however, that it was not he who met the unexpected ambush but Thrutt the ogur.

Unfortunately, even he was not capable of defending himself against the ambush for long as the toxins were indeed working, albeit slightly more slowly than they might have done before, and as Thrutt batted away first one attacker and then another, the adrenalin – and strength – that had flooded his veins was slowly sapped by their effects until, by the time he had batted a man away for the seventh time, he was slowly sinking to his knees. As he did, three of the men picked themselves up from where they had fallen, examined the one who had been shattered against a rock and then cautiously moved forwards to loom above him.

Orders were given. And then he found himself being bundled into a wagon whose sides had been built as a makeshift cage. And as Thrutt stared out between the thick wooden bars, from somewhere within him Merrit Moon stared, too – right into the eyes of the man who had killed him.

"Make sure the wagon is secured and prepare to return to Scholten," Konstantin Munch ordered, slapping its sides. He stared at the ogur in captivity and himself growled. He did not like plans that did not go *according* to plan, especially when the plan was his own.

He thought back to the moment it had formed in his mind, the moment when, from his hiding place in a narrow crevice, he had observed the Hooper girl running from the ogur cave. That she had apparently somehow escaped Scholten's deep cells had come as little surprise – she was *extremely* resourceful, after all – but that she had seemingly recovered from her interrogation to such a degree *had* surprised him, though not as much as what had occurred after she had gone. The strange blue glow that had suffused the cave had drawn him from his hiding place with an overwhelming curiosity, and despite the danger he had eased himself painfully back down the cave, ignoring his own injuries from the ogur attack, to discover its source. What he had witnessed there, again from hiding, he knew of, but had never thought he would see. Perversely, though, the miracle of elven magetech was less important to him than the fact that the old man would live again – because now that he knew Kali Hooper was on the loose once more, it struck him that he might come in very useful as a hostage-cum-bargaining chip should the girl try to thwart his plans in the future. He would have taken the old man there and then, if he could, but the presence of the ogur and the fact that Moon seemed to have drawn a little more than life essence from his victim, stayed his hand. Instead, he had returned to his base camp and ordered his men there to construct the holding wagon in readiness for what would be the old man's inevitable descent from the hills. He knew he would be wanting to find his irritating pupil after all.

That, though, was when it had all gone wrong. Moon *had* descended from the hills, certainly, but the man he had caught in his ambush had borne scant resemblance to the man he had been when he had inserted his blade in his chest and guts and, in fact, had borne less resemblance as the ambush had progressed. Clearly, something had gone wrong with the scythe-stone process, which was tragic for the old man but even more so for him – for how was he meant to use Moon as a hostage when Hooper would be unable to recognise her mentor at all? No, unless this strange transformation reversed itself – which of course it *might*, which made it unwise to slaughter the beast – all he was stuck with was a sideshow freak, good only for the circus when it came to Ramblas Square.

Munch growled again and turned away from the holding wagon, wincing with pain. His injuries from the ogur attack were... troublesome and he ought to get them seen to. He turned to the mage he had left with the base party, intending to solicit some relief, but then saw that the woman was concentrating hard and staring into the distance in the way that those blessed – or cursed, he thought – with telescrying abilities did. Still, they did make life in the field somewhat easier.

Munch waited until she had finished, returning to reality hollow-faced, and with a shiver and a sigh.

"Well?" he asked.

"News from Scholten, sir. From the Anointed Lord. She wishes to inform you that she is in possession of the fourth and final key."

Munch drew in a deep breath. *At last.*

"There is something else, sir. A location where she wishes you to rendezvous with her party – the site known as Orl."

Munch laughed. *Yes, Orl,* he thought. *Orl indeed.*

He ordered his remaining people to break camp, and mounting the holding wagon instructed its driver to move out.

Towards the Final Faith's destiny.

Towards his own.

CHAPTER 15

Everyone seemed intent on hot-footing it to Orl, and that included Kali Hooper. It was just that for the moment – oddly self-defeatingly – she was telling Slowhand not to move. Not an inch. In fact, she would have preferred it if he didn't even breathe.

It was nothing personal. Granted, it might have been *very* personal at one time but, since his recent reappearance, Slowhand had been somewhat helpful so the least that she could do was try to save his life.

The lava lake had calmed somewhat and was no longer belching out angry plumes of fire, but it was continuing to rise. It had almost reached them now and, any second, threatened to bubble over the lip of the rock on which they stood, at which time they would be hot-footing it whether they had escaped or not.

Thankfully, all was not lost – and, in a manner of speaking, Orl was not lost, either. The pair of them stood no longer on the island but on a small shelf of rock behind and across from the dome, on the opposite side to the incinerated bridge. They had managed to reach it through a combination of her gymnastics and Slowhand's ropes and arrows, an exercise in teamwork that had resulted in a couple of embarrassing tangles but had got them there in the end, she with a sprained thigh and he with a smile on his face.

The shelf, though, was a precarious perch, only a few inches wide and crumbling in an ever-increasing number of spots beneath their feet. But it did lead to a way out. Possibly.

Kali's reasoning that there had to have been an original entrance to the dome had, in their time of need, led her to seek it out as an escape route and, while successful in doing so, the tunnel she had found was blocked as she'd suspected it might be, manifesting itself now as a vague tracery of rocks beyond the remains of a long-collapsed stone bridge, some of the component parts of which had been visible as tiny islands in the lava before they had been consumed by the bubbling mire. Kali wasn't sure that the tunnel behind the tracery of rock was going to be passable and the only way she could find out was by removing the rocks from the tunnel mouth. The problem was, she had to do it very, very slowly and very, very carefully, otherwise the resultant rockslide would sweep them both into the hottest – and last – bath of their lives.

"You have to think of it like a jigsaw," she said slowly and quietly to Slowhand. She gently removed a rock with an archaeologist's hands, dropping it into the burgeoning lava with a plop. "Each piece dependent on the other to construct – or, in this case, deconstruct – the whole picture without forcing any one piece."

"Really?" Slowhand said, nodding, his arms folded tightly against his chest. He would have smiled at the way her tongue stuck out between her lips as she worked, other than for the fact the lava had reached the soles of his boots and they had begun to sizzle slightly. "Is this an easy jigsaw?"

"Urrm... somewhere between medium and challenging?"

"Right. Like a bowl of fruit with a binyano, an apple and a pear?"

"I guess so," Kali said. She removed another rock and dropped it away, freezing as the collapsed rocks left behind in the fall settled slightly. "If they've all been tipped on the floor and trampled by a betwattled cyclops."

"Fine. You are good at jigsaws aren't you?"

Kali's hand hovered over another rock before changing her mind and extracting the one next to it. Again, she dropped it away. "Nope. Never could stand the things."

"Oh, that's great. Hooper, look, how about that one there? No, that one. That one looks –"

"Will you stop waving your hands about and stand still?"

Slowhand hopped from foot to foot, his soles sticking and stringing whenever they made contact with the rock.

"Getting – a – little – difficult – to – do – that. Could you *please* get a move on?"

"I'm trying, all right!" Kali snapped. The sweat running off her now had as much to do with pressure as the heat of the lava. She bent and dropped a heavier rock, regretting snapping when Slowhand took the opportunity to wipe her brow.

"Just one more..." she said through clenched teeth. "Easy... easy..."

There was a sudden shift in the rockface, and then a low rumble, and Kali spun herself away from the front of the fall to flatten herself against the wall to its left. Slowhand needed no urging to do the same and, at the very second he spun to the right, the whole pile of rubble collapsed away from the tunnel mouth, avalanching down into the rising lake.

Behind the fall, the tunnel was clear.

"Go, go, go!" Kali shouted, and just in time. The sudden and dramatic fall of rocks into the lava had disturbed its recently calm rise and it began again to spurt and belch. Unnoticed by Slowhand as he darted into the shadowy tunnel mouth, a patch of the molten fire spattered onto his trouser leg, burning into the cloth, but before it could reach his skin Kali followed him in and tore the offending patch away.

"Don't get excited," she said. "That's all that's coming off."

"Hey, flesh happens," Slowhand retorted, and stared at her heavily perspiring form. "Hot stuff."

Kali shook her head – the man could never resist. She followed him into the dark, making out a winding tunnel that curved away into the rock. She hesitated to think when last it had been used, but for a second thought that she caught a stale whiff of whatever had been the last thing to tread the passage, something overtly male – the smell, perhaps, of dwarf? Her eyes adjusted further to the dark and all her instincts cried out for the time to examine her surroundings – especially as she could now see this was no mere cave but a constructed tunnel complete with those X-shaped dwarven runics – but that was simply not to be. The avalanche that had stirred the lava back into angry life had, it seemed, disturbed more than just the lake, perhaps ruptured another vent beneath the dome and, as she watched, the lava began to bubble into and then sweep with increasing acceleration up the tunnel behind them.

"Hooper," Slowhand said. "I strongly suggest that we run."

"Ohhh, running as we speak," Kali said, passing him.

Slowhand put on his own spurt and the two of them raced up the tunnel as fast as they could, but the collapsed rock at the dome entrance was not the only place where the integrity of their dark confines had been compromised, and every few feet or so they found their progress slowed by roof-falls which they had to clamber over. Thankfully, these same roof-falls acted also as makeshift dams – albeit briefly as it didn't take long for the lava to engulf them – and they managed to stay ahead of the flow. *Just.*

"Hooper, how far to the exit?" Slowhand asked, vaulting over another blockage in front of them.

Kali leapt in his wake, a spray of pebbles from her heel vanishing into the lava that was now immediately behind her. She slammed a palm onto the wall. "Not sure. But the temperature of the rock suggests we've still a way to go – maybe a tenth of a league?"

"Pits of Kerberos – *a tenth of a league?*"

"Excuse me! You *did* ask."

"I know but, hells, Hooper, sometimes I wish you didn't know as much as you do."

Kali stopped, slammed her hands on her hips and nodded back where they'd come from. "I got us out of there, didn't I?"

Slowhand sighed and grabbed her as the lava plopped over where they had vaulted, catching up with her heels. They ran on. "Maybe," he said, nodding ahead, though Kali was still so busied staring daggers at him that she hadn't noticed what he had.

"Fark."

"What?"

"The tunnel dips. Deeply. Some kind of U-bend."

"What?" Kali said again. "Why in the hells would it do that?"

Slowhand pointed towards the roof of the tunnel. "Maybe because of that."

Still moving, Kali looked up, then skidded to a halt. A few yards in front of them, the roof of the tunnel nosed downwards and changed in texture, no longer composed of rock but something else, some kind of fossilised remains, a dark and chitinous substance that reminded her of the brackan in the Sardenne. But these remains were not those of any brackan, because they were bigger – much, much bigger – and as well as nosing down they folded themselves through the walls on either side of the tunnel and into its floor, immortalised as an organic archway in the rock.

"The speed of this stuff, we'll never make it out the other side," Slowhand said.

Kali studied the dip, saw that the tunnel levelled out again beyond it and then turned her eyes on the fossil. These remains had to be hardy, considering it was clear to her that the dwarves had had no choice but to tunnel under them rather than through.

"Help me," she said, picking up a rock.

"Throwing stones at the lava won't make it go away."

"The fossil!" Kali shouted. "There, where it's been cracked by the tunnel subsidence! We can bring that part down!"

Slowhand looked exasperated. "Why?"

Kali leapt onto a slight rise of rocks at the tunnel's edge, avoiding the lava that had now caught up with them. Slowhand did the same on the opposite side, looking down warily as the red river overtook them and began to flow into the dip.

Kali smashed at the section of the fossilised remains with the rock. "'Liam, just help me!" she pleaded.

The urgency of her tone persuaded him and – though he still didn't have a clue what she hoped to achieve – Slowhand joined in. It took a fair number of strikes but finally the dark mass came loose from its resting place of ages and crashed down into the lava-filling dip, flipped over to become a bowl shape floating on the surface.

Some kind of carapace, it could just as easily have been a boat.

Kali began to hop from rock to rock at the side of the tunnel, towards it. "Move," she shouted.

Slowhand did as he was bidden, mirroring Kali, and it did not take him long to realise what she had in mind. And it was just a little bit frightening.

Kali reached the rim of the dip and hurled herself forwards, crashing into the bowl with an explosion of air and a grunt. Slowhand was half a second behind and almost didn't make it, but, as he threatened to shortfall into the roaring red river, Kali stood, balancing unsteadily, and grabbed his flying form by the scruff of the neck. She yanked him to safety and Slowhand crashed down next to her, winded.

The makeshift boat rose on the lava until it rode above the opposite side of the dip. And there, sailing the lava with its speed building slightly, it continued along the tunnel.

Slowhand stared at the passing rock walls, and down at the lava river, thinking it was a little like being on some carnival ride, only hotter. Like that new thing they'd had at Scholten Fair, the Tunnel of Luurrvv. The blupping of the lava even sounded quite romantic.

"Hooper..." he said, sweeping back his hair.

"Get your head down," Kali said.

Slowhand raised his eyebrows, looking surprised. "Don't you want to take things a little more slowly?"

"Down, you idiot!" Kali repeated and, as she spoke and Slowhand obeyed, the carapace slammed into a thick stalactite dropping from the tunnel roof. The impact sent the makeshift boat into a spin and it began to career along the tunnel, crashing into its walls and generally out of control. As the pair of them clung to the carapace's sides, lava splashing all about them, it seemed to Slowhand that his Tunnel of Luurrvv had suddenly become a tunnel of soon to suffer very painful death.

Kali, though, didn't seem too perturbed.

"You get up to this kind of thing every day?" Slowhand asked, swallowing.

"Course not. Maybe once a week. Not enjoying the ride?"

Enjoying was not perhaps quite the word but Slowhand had to admit it was exhilarating, but only after the carapace had taken enough knocks without splitting open to reassure him that it might, after all, be safe enough to survive the trip. The flow of lava had sped up again beneath them, and now the carapace moved through the tunnel at dizzying speed, impacting and spinning with each new twist and turn as it made its inexorable way towards the tunnel's end. Then, suddenly, the tunnel began to slope downwards, its exit visible ahead. But the exit, too, was blocked.

"Hooper?" Slowhand said.

Kali smiled. "We'll be fine... fine."

Slowhand did not look convinced as they hurtled towards the pile of rocks blocking their only way out of the lava. He imagined the carapace shattering on impact, spilling them both into the lethal surge that would inevitably envelop them.

"You're saying you think this thing's strong enough?"

"Definitely," Kali said.

"How can you know?"

"Because," Kali began as the carapace slammed into the rock fall and broke through it. "This thing we're on," she continued as they sailed out into daylight, "has been down here a long, long time."

The carapace plummeted down some unknown hillside, the wind roaring past them, skimming the erupting lava flow as it went.

"Meaning?" Slowhand shouted.

"It belonged to something you don't see around any more!" Kali shouted back.

"What, for hell's sake –"

The carapace impacted with the hillside, bounced and flew. It bounced again, this time more violently, throwing them both into the air.

Kali flailed towards a landing and yelled, "*A drraaaggggonn!*"

Slowhand stared at her and, while staring, thudded into the ground. He tumbled down the hillside, rolling, bouncing and cursing until, like Kali, he at last came to a bruised and aching stop. "A dragon?" he repeated.

"Oh, yeah," Kali said with exhilaration. She stood and stared at the carapace as it screed past them and then stopped further down the hill. Kali hadn't felt like it for quite some time but she whooped.

Slowhand stood and stared at the aftermath of their flight from the dome. The lava on which they had ridden was still gushing from the tunnel mouth above them, but the majority of it that had spilled forth was thickening in the outside air, turning grey and mottled on the slopes, smoke and steam rising from its curdling surface.

Kali stared into the distance. There, she could see that smoke also rose above the city of Scholten, and on the air she could just make out the distant ringing of the cathedral's alarm bells. She smiled. Makennon actually had something to be grateful to her for. If she hadn't opened the tunnel, giving the lava an escape route rather than letting it build as if in some huge pressure cooker, then there would be little left of the underground complex, and perhaps even her cathedral itself might now be reduced to rubble.

It was quite ironic. Kali Hooper – saviour of the Final Faith. Ah well, they could thank her later.

In the meantime, there was the small matter of a key to pursue. Four keys, actually.

"There's just one problem," Slowhand said. "We're stuck in the middle of nowhere and, in case you haven't noticed, we don't have any transport."

"Actually, we do," Kali said, and to Slowhand's surprise stuck two fingers in her mouth and whistled. "Little thing I've been teaching him," she said.

Slowhand looked baffled. "Teaching him. Teaching who?"

"Horse."

"Horse?"

"A-ha. Horse Too, to be precise."

"And where is this Horse Too?"

"Stabled in Scholten, where I left him."

"And you expect him to hear you whistle from here?"

"Horse is not your normal kind of horse."

"I see. Okay. Then just how is he going to get out of the stable, exactly?"

"Oh, he'll find a way."

Slowhand shook his head. Maybe the heat in the tunnel had got to Hooper after all. He was about to say something else when there was a sudden blur accompanied by the sound of heavy hoofbeats, and where there had been empty space between him and Kali a moment before he now found himself staring at something that resembled a Vossian siege machine. A large chunk of stable fencepost attached to a rope dangled from its neck.

"Slowhand, meet Horse. Horse, this is Slowhand."

The mysterious creature stared at him balefully, and snorted.

"What in the pits is that?" he heard himself asking.

"Bamfcat," Kali said simply.

Horse's tongue suddenly lashed out and wrapped itself around Slowhand's face.

Kali smiled. "I think he likes you."

"Mmmmrrrrumfff."

"Definitely."

"Grruuurrkk."

"Okay, Horse, that's enough. Let him go."

Seconds later, Slowhand found himself sitting behind Kali on the beast's back, Hooper leading him back to Scholten, a move he wasn't entirely sure was wise given the circumstances of their last visit. But Kali, as it turned out, only wanted to speak to the gate guard – and did so from a distance so she wouldn't be recognised.

"The Anointed Lord?" she shouted. "Has she left the city?"

"Three hours ago, Ma'am."

"Dammit," Kali said, looking to the west. Makennon now had the four keys – and therefore the location of the site – but she *still* only had a rough idea of where it was. "She could be taking any one of the three roads. If we lose her..."

Slowhand dismounted from Horse and examined the ground. It was thick with tracks heading into and out of the city, but he seemed confident as he pointed ahead and said, "Actually, she took that one."

"Slowhand, there's no way you could know."

"Take a look," the archer said.

Kali did, and laughed. "That woman's too full of herself for her own good," she said. She stared again at what could only be Makennon's tracks, because the horseshoes of her mount had been carved with the symbol of the Final Faith.

On her trail, they headed west, crossing Vos, and came within sight of Makennon's party as they travelled on towards the coast. Kali longed to pass the Anointed Lord, to reach Orl first, but she knew that without the exact location of the site, she and Slowhand could be seeking it out for weeks. The journey was long, Makennon and her party proceeding with the surety of something within their grasp that negated the need for haste, but their progress worked to Kali and Slowhand's advantage, allowing them to stop off in the coastal town of Malmkrug to acquire rations and essential supplies, including squallcoats for the worsening weather. Beyond Malmkrug, they passed along the southern rim of the Drakengrat Mountains, and there Horse sniffed the air, recognising the place where it had been found. The beast hung its head wistfully, though, because perhaps it did not recognise it as home.

The Drakengrats faded into the background as the party and their pursuers neared Oweilau, and here the coastline took a turn to the north-east, where eventually it would swing fully east once more, towards Dellendorf and, eventually, Freiport.

Kali did not think they would turn that far, however, as the location of the site had been towards the end of the peninsula, so they would likely stick to the western paths as far as they could go. This they did, and eventually came to point where they could be no more than an hour or two's travel from the Sarcrean Sea. Kali itched to continue ahead now that they were so close – was certain now that she would be able to find the site herself – but as Makennon's party made camp for the night it soon became clear that they could go no further for the time being. Camped bang in the middle of a gorge, there was no way they could get past them without being detected, and no way around without attracting the attentions of the shnarls who at night roamed the coastal rocks in vicious packs. No – all they could do was make camp for the night themselves, then get ahead of Makennon's party in the morning when they'd moved once more onto open ground.

The pair of them watched from a ridge as the Final Faith bedded down, their assorted wagons circled in protection. There was little to see, and Kali and Killiam were about to call it a night when, from the east behind them, more wagons made their way towards the camp. They had to have been behind them all the time and Kali and Slowhand hid as they passed, she snarling at the unexpected yet somehow inevitable arrival of the leader of the group.

"Munch," Kali said. "Pits, I should have known."

Slowhand frowned. "Munch, maybe. But what the hells is that?"

Kali looked at the caged wagon towards which Slowhand pointed, and immediately recognised the creature held therein.

"That," she said, "is one of the ogur from the World's Ridge Mountains."

"*They exist?*" Slowhand said.

"Oh yes."

"Care to tell me why Munch has brought it here?"

"Holiday by the sea?" Kali said. "No, seriously, I haven't a clue."

She yawned.

"Time for bed, eh?" Slowhand said. "Just you and me and a seductively crackling fire?"

"You and me, maybe, but no fire, crackling or otherwise. This stage of the game, we can't risk them spotting us."

Slowhand sighed. There she went again, treating him like an idiot. "Actually, I already knew that. No matter," he added, winking, "instead we can get up close and personal, share some body heat."

Kali stared at him. "There's another possibility," she said. "In the Drakengrats, when bad weather hits and they can't get off the mountains, the high shepherds slice open the stomach of one of their flock and crawl inside for the night, using the intestines for warmth..."

Slowhand looked shocked. "You wouldn't – not Horse?"

"Who said anything about Horse?"

There was a moment's silence.

"I'll get some blankets from the saddlebags," Killiam said.

"Yes, you do that."

Minutes later, they had bedded down for the night, blankets a few feet apart. Lying in the azure darkness, each sipping on a bottle of flummox, Kali stared up at the night sky and its coming eclipse while Slowhand kept an uneasy eye on Horse, watching as the beast's tongue lashed out into the shadows surrounding the camp, snapping back every now and then with something dark, furry and squealing in its grip. The thing didn't *seem* to be interested in him any more, and so he turned his attention to Kali. The expression in her eyes as she stared at the stars troubled him.

"Hooper, how long have I known you?" he asked.

"Too pitsing long."

"I'm serious. I've known you long enough to know when something's bothering you. What is it?"

"What do you think, Slowhand? I lost two of my oldest friends."

"I know that. But I know there's something else." He paused. "The old man told you something in the World's Ridge Mountains, didn't he? Something about you, about the things you can do?"

Kali hesitated, and then told him about the old man's parting words, about how and in what circumstances he had found her, inside the sealed site.

Slowhand stared.

"How in the hells could it have been sealed?" he said. And after a delay, added, "Who are you, Hooper?"

"Slowhand, I wish I knew."

The archer saw Kali's expression grow reflective, and changed tack slightly in the hope he could cheer her up. "There's one thing I don't get. You came out of nowhere, an orphan with no family at all – so, why Kali Hooper? Where did you get the name?"

The question seemed to have the desired effect, and Kali smiled.

"Until I was about five, everybody just called me half-pint, but when I started to grow it didn't seem appropriate any more, so someone suggested I take Red's name instead. He wanted to call me after his mum, Dora. Dora Deadnettle, can you believe it? Needless to say, I vetoed that."

"Wise move."

"A-ha. So they suggested a number of other names but

none of them worked, and I went back to being half-pint. Then, one night, Pete Two-Ties started staring at the beers and writing their names down, playing with the letters he got..."

"The letters?"

"The letters. And out of all of them, Pete found that one beer, in particular, worked."

"Which was?"

Kali took a swig of flummox. "Orki Hop Ale."

Slowhand couldn't help himself. He spat his flummox out.

"Wait a minute. Are you telling me that's all your name is – an anagram?"

"That's right. I'm named after a beer. Got a problem with that?"

Slowhand shook his head, swallowing hard. "No, no, no... no. Absolutely appropriate, really."

"I thought so."

Slowhand concentrated, mouthed letters. "Could have been worse, given what Two-Ties had to work with. Kira Pohole..."

"I don't think so."

"Erika Phool."

"No..."

"Karlie Pooh."

"All right, Slowhand, that's enough!"

They drank some more.

"Now it's my turn. You never told me – what is it between you and the Final Faith? Why the vendetta?"

Slowhand's expression darkened, and he stared off into the night. "That question's in a whole different league, Hooper."

Kali shifted onto her side, cradling her head in her palm. "I know. And if you don't want to tell me, that's fine. But

I think you need to share with someone, Slowhand, and after what we've been through in the past few days..."

Slowhand sighed, and his eyes flickered as if viewing some distant memory. "I have a sister," he admitted, eventually. "A twin sister."

Kali had to admit she was gobsmacked. Somehow she had never thought of Slowhand as being, well, human. Not in the way of his having family, at least. She'd never really imagined him being a child, growing up – always seen him as he was now, having arrived in the world fully formed, grinning, winking and stroking back his hair. That there had been a sister that he had grown with was a double revelation to her.

"I never knew."

"There's no reason why you should have. Jenna was... taken before we met."

"Jenna," Kali said. "Hold on. What do you mean – taken?"

"The Final Faith," Slowhand said. "In their early days, and maybe still now – to build up their numbers – they had an indoctrination programme... actually, more like forced assimilation. Jenna was working in Freiport when the Faith's *recruiters* paid her a visit."

"She went willingly?"

Slowhand shook his head, took a long swig from his flummox. "Jenna didn't have a religious bone in her body. Before that day."

"What are you saying? That they brainwashed her?"

Slowhand stared at her. "You've experienced Querilous Fitch's manipulations first-hand. Yes, I believe they turned her, somehow – her and others."

Kali swallowed. "But why Jenna? And where is she now?"

"Jenna was a battlefield tactician for the Freiport

Independents – I guess they had a use for her talents. As for where she is, I don't know – but not for want of looking. She could be garrisoned somewhere remote, maybe even a member of the Order of Dawn. But I'll find her, Hooper – if I have to tear the Final Faith apart, eventually I'll find her."

"I know," Kali said.

Slowhand lapsed into silence after that, and after a few minutes turned in his bedroll, settling himself down for sleep.

Kali lay there staring at him for a moment, deciding.

Maybe it was the flummox, but more likely it was the fact that Slowhand had just revealed a side of himself that she'd never suspected before.

She stroked his cheek.

"In the meantime..." she said.

And agony hit. Another vision. Only this time she was outside of herself, looking at her own body as it lay slung in the arms of an ogur. Her flesh was grey, her clothing thick with blood, and worst of all, she did not appear to be breathing.

The ogur pounded through the night, carrying her body and, as it went, it roared and roared and roared.

Kali heard herself scream.

"Hey, hey, hey!" Killiam Slowhand said urgently, soothingly, and as quickly as it had come, the vision was gone. Kali realised that she had screamed out loud and was wrapped in his arms and he was rocking her back and forth. "Bad dream, bad dream," he said. "Shush, shush."

The night had not turned out quite as she expected, but Kali did not move from Slowhand's arms. She continued to lie there and he continued to rock her back and forth, and she stared up at the stars.

So much had happened to her since this whole thing

had begun – so much she didn't understand – but now at least she knew how it was all going to end.

She knew she was going to die.

Here. Soon.

And she knew what was going to kill her.

CHAPTER 16

Dawn came – and at the same time, didn't. The eclipse that had been on the cards for weeks was now finally coming to fruition, and instead of daylight replacing the azure twilight that had bathed them during a fitful sleep, a different kind of halflight made it seem as if the night simply continued on, imbuing the air with a languor that seemed to depress and slow the morning down. It was an atmosphere that failed to make Kali feel any better about her vision.

The languor did not last for long, however. The imminent cosmic conjunction also brought with it one of the worst storms Kali or Slowhand could remember, beginning with heavy and warm drops of rain that soon became splatters and then a downfall, this whipped by an increasingly tumultuous wind that Kali reckoned would be a full-blown hurricane within the hour.

The light and the weather worked to their advantage,

though. Both of them donned squallcoats and, from the ridge that had sheltered their camp, watched and waited as Makennon and her expedition broke their own, ready to move out as soon as they did. Guiding Horse by a horn, they walked him through the gorge perhaps a hundred yards behind the Final Faith, their presence so close to the enemy group obscured and obfuscated by the driving storm. As soon as their party had passed through the gorge, Kali and Slowhand veered to the east, and when they were a sufficient distance away both of them mounted the bamfcat and rode him on. They could not spur Horse on to full gallop – the terrain near the edge of the peninsula was simply too treacherous, unpredictable and prone to landslip even in good weather – but that didn't really matter because, even at the rate they travelled, they had soon drawn ahead of Makennon and Munch.

They were going to find the site and they were going to beat the Final Faith to it. The only thing they had to do was work out what to do when they got there.

They continued on for another hour, checking occasionally that Makennon's party remained behind them and that they hadn't missed something obvious – unlikely but still possible in the continuing storm. The sky darkened more and more as each minute passed, until it was a deep purple verging on black. It seemed logical that the worsening light would make finding Orl more difficult but, in fact, it was becoming an increasingly more simple task because they were running out of land. They could hear the Sarcrean Sea breaking violently on the far western edge of the peninsula now, and ahead of them Kali was just able to make out the looming and jutting stone of the coastal feature she had heard about but to this point never travelled this far west to see – the so-called Dragonwing Cliffs. The peculiar rock formations did sweep up on the horizon almost like wings, reminding them both of the fossilised remains in Scholten, but these were merely inanimate rock, carved over the years into their current shapes by the rather unique weather patterns of the nearby Stormwall. A meteorological anomaly that defied all natural explanation, the Stormwall wrapped the end of the peninsula about a league offshore, like a giant hand formed out of cloud, thunder, lightning and rain. No one had ever passed through it, only around it, and all shipping – what shipping dared this roughest part of Twilight's already tempestuous seas – avoided it by as much wheelage as they could. Why it was there – and why it maintained its roiling, booming and flashing presence in all weathers – no one knew, only that what lay beyond it – the Sarcre Islands – basked in a tropical weather system that was unknown anywhere else in the known world, and that, strictly speaking, should not exist.

The Stormwall and the Sarcre Islands, Kali thought. If she were to believe all normal accounts of this desolate part of the peninsula, there was nothing beyond them and nothing else here. But according to other accounts, there had to be.

Kali decided to tether Horse before they went any further, the terrain becoming too dangerous for his large and heavy form to negotiate. And, as it turned out, she did so just in time. Kali and Slowhand were making their way forwards, their long squallcoats flapping about them, when Twilight's distant sun moved fully behind Kerberos and its eclipse became full, plunging the Dragonwing Cliffs into almost total darkness. The pair could still see where they were going, by starlight, and just, but for the most part now the only guide they had to how close to the edge they were was the increasingly deafening roar of the waves crashing onto the rocks below. Even this, though, was only an intermittent guide, and they had to pause quite frequently when the sound of the sea was obliterated by the whistling and insanely howling wind.

Able to communicate only by gestures, they at last reached the edge, expecting to look down and see only the wild turmoil of the Sarcrean Sea. For a moment their expectations were met but, then, glimpsed between squalls, they spotted what they might least expect to see in the presence of so much raging water – fire. Both faltered momentarily but, yes, fire it was – flickering and fluttering plumes floating on the surface of the water. No, Kali realised, after a second, not on the water but leading across the water, twin lines of wind-blasted and mounted torches, to be precise, forming a wide avenue that narrowed with perspective as it led out into the sea.

Kali followed the fiery avenue back with her eyes, able to distinguish more now that she knew what it was. The torches seemed to climb the cliff face, disappearing only the higher they came, where they were obscured by the very edge she overlooked. Swallowing slowly, she beckoned Slowhand to follow her, moving slightly along the cliff, and there the two of them found themselves standing at the top of a part of the Dragonwings that veered diagonally rather than vertically, an age-old projection down and beyond the cliff wall that was less precipitous than its bordering sides. The feature at first seemed natural but then revealed itself to be distinctly and unnaturally shaped. In fact, it appeared as if at some time long in its past the projection had been deliberately and laboriously carved into deep and broad increments that looked suspiciously like risers.

The hells with suspiciously, Kali thought. *They couldn't be anything else.* At the same time as Slowhand lowered his jaw in surprise, she realised she was looking down a mammoth flight of steps.

This was the site, Orl, it had to be, she'd found it. Her elation at the fact was, however, marred by the knowledge that, while the steps were clearly old, the torches were not. She might have beaten Makennon herself here but the Anointed Lord had obviously sent in advance troops, probably during the night, to prepare the place for her arrival. Gods, what was it with that woman – did she want everywhere she went freshly painted too? Would she only use a privy where people couldn't hear her tinkle?

Advance troops or not, she was still going in. The question was, into what? She hadn't until now known what to expect of Orl, but if she had pictured anything it wouldn't have been this. She stared at the avenue of torches again, leading into the sea. What exactly, she wondered, was Orl doing *out there?*

Kali patted Slowhand on the shoulder, pointing down, and the two of them moved onto the steps, but Slowhand halted her almost immediately, pointing out two sentries illuminated by the flare of the torches a good way below and away from where they stood. Both Final Faith thugs were positioned beyond what would have been the shoreline but on what, they could now see, was actually a rock jetty thrusting out between the waves. While their presence was a hindrance to Kali and Slowhand's immediate plan, what was more disturbing was what lay at the end of the jetty itself. For there, half-obscured by the lashing rain and battered by the thrashing waters, was an ominous-looking grey structure shaped something like a cowl. Enshrouding the end of the jetty, it sat solidly amidst the maelstrom, a great shadowed maw offering entry into whatever the cowl enclosed, what appeared to be gigantic black pipes arching from its roof and down into the sea – or from the sea into its roof – that from this distance appeared to thrust from it like an insect's legs. Whatever the hells it was, both Kali and Slowhand knew what it looked like. A giant, heavy spider, just sitting there, waiting.

Kali knew she had to get closer, find out what it was. But with the presence of the sentries, there were only two ways they were going to be able to do that.

Slowhand had already thought of one. He was already raising his bow and lining up twin arrows, but Kali stayed his hand, shook her head.

"Take them down and Makennon will know we're here!" she shouted. "We have to get around them!"

"There is no way around them!" the archer shouted back.

Kali nodded. "Yes, there is!" She pointed down the steps to the side of the stone jetty. "We swim around!"

"No chance, Hooper. If the cold doesn't get you, then the currents around the Dragonwings will. You'll be smashed and dead on some Sarcre Island beach before you know it!"

Kali stared at him. "No, I won't!"

Slowhand sighed. The trouble was, he knew Kali was right and that, really, they had no other choice. "Remind me again – why didn't I escape the sewers when I had the chance?"

Crouching and keeping low, using alternate torch supports for cover, the pair began to clamber down the weatherworn rock steps, each of which was half as high as themselves. As they did, they noticed that the tops of the risers were fractured and cracked in places, as if they had once been trodden by some immense and sustained weight, something *formidable* that had at some point in the past ascended these cliffs. They couldn't concern themselves with what, though, as their immediate priority was to reach the jetty unseen. Thankfully, the sentries appeared to be more concerned with what lay behind them than in front, and they managed the long descent without discovery. Once down, they crab-walked to the edge of the jetty and, other than a moaning hiss from Slowhand, slid silently into the water.

As Slowhand had no hesitation in pointing out, the water was farking freezing, and even right next to the shore Kali could feel strong, swirling undercurrents tug at her and try to pull her away into the darker depths, but she fought against them, keeping to the jetty's side and clinging to it with cold, wet hands. As Slowhand followed, she inched her way along the stone, and the further she went, the more uneasy she began to feel – a feeling that was difficult to explain, almost as if they were sharing the water with... something. But she saw nothing.

At last they drew even with the two sentries, waiting for a particularly strong gust of wind before continuing, lest the smallest ripple give them away. They pulled themselves perhaps another twenty yards along the jetty before deeming it sufficiently out of view to climb out, but just as they were about to do so, a series of clatters and rumbles from the shoreline made them plunge back into the water.

"Dammit, Makennon!" Kali hissed.

"Too late to make a run for it," Slowhand advised. "Stay down."

They did so, heads bobbing as if decapitated on the surface of the water, and watched as Makennon and her retinue rumbled slowly along the jetty towards their position. The woman had brought everything with her down the steps, including the wagons on strangely articulated wheels, and staring up from the water at the torchlit procession of horses, mages and soldiers – not to mention Munch and his cage containing the ogur – both Kali and Slowhand felt like small children watching the arrival in town of some bizarre carnival. The trouble was, it looked as if this particular carnival would be pitching tents just ahead of them, blocking the path to the cowl.

Or would they? As Kali and Slowhand watched, the procession reached the far end of the jetty and then continued on into the cowl-shaped structure, each of the wagons disappearing into the maw until the rear of the last seemed to tip and was gone. Slowhand stared at the front of the cowl, craned his neck to stare at its rear, and worked out that there was no way it was deep enough to take them all.

"Now there's a turn-up for the books," he said. "Like that magic trick where you pull worgle after worgle out of a hat." He paused. "Only in reverse." He paused again. "And with wagons instead of worgles."

"Make more sense if it just continued down, eh?" Kali said. She looked at Slowhand's bemused expression and found she had to explain by waggling her fingers. "More steps," she said. "It must be underwater. Orl must be underwater."

The concept was clearly difficult for Slowhand to grasp, and she couldn't blame him – she had never seen anything like it either. "Underwater? Hooper, you *are* sure this is Orl, aren't you? Not some forgotten tunnel under the Stormwall? Maybe they are taking the ogur on holiday, after all."

His question was half-rhetorical and, in truth, he expected an answer like: "Of course I'm sure," but what Kali actually said was: "No."

"No?" he repeated.

"No," Kali echoed. "The scrolls in Andon were... a little contradictory in places. Oh, don't get me wrong, this is Orl all right, I'm just not sure that it's called that. But now that we're actually here there may be a way to find out. Come on."

Kali heaved herself from the water and a confused Slowhand followed, shaking his leg to rid his pants of water. Kali had already reached the cowl and was examining it when he caught up.

"Old Race sites sometimes have identifying runics," she said, "particularly if they're of dwarven origin. I think it was a clan thing."

Slowhand smiled. "You mean they gave their houses names? Like Dunhammerin'?"

"Something like that. Should be one just about – *ah*."

Kali knelt by a rough inscription, brushed away seasalt and grime with her hand, concentrated and frowned. These carved runics were never completely decipherable – there were far too many cryptographic elements she simply didn't have knowledge of – but in general she was able to get the gist of what they were saying. And the gist of this one confirmed what she thought. This place wasn't called Orl, it was called Martak.

No, wait, she thought. The runic contained too many characters, there were gaps where they shouldn't be, and the emphasis was *wrong*...

Hells, Martak wasn't a word, it was a –

Kali's mind filled again with the images and accounts from the manuscripts in the Three Towers. Yes, what she read fitted with them, made sense. But if that was the case – if this place *wasn't* called Orl – then why the reference to the Clockwork King of Orl, a phrase that even the old man himself had used? Could it be he was mistaken

– that Makennon and her people were *also* mistaken – and it was again a reflection of how difficult it was to decipher the Old Race language? That, or perhaps even some of the old manuscripts *themselves* were wrong, that somehow, over the long years, the phrase had become misinterpreted, corrupted? What she would need to do in that case was put the phrase in context, think about it in the overall terms of the accounts she'd read...

Unbidden, her second vision leapt once more into her mind, the desolate landscape, the pounding, the figures rising over the horizon.

My gods, she thought, *what had happened here at Martak? What had driven the dwarves here, to this lonely place at the edge of the world? What had become of them?*

Exactly what was the Clockwork King?

Questions, again. And only one way to find out the answers.

Kali peered into the cowl, making sure their way was clear. They were going in.

"Well, this is a new one," Slowhand said, gazing uneasily up at the shadows that enveloped them. He felt as if he were indeed entering some giant maw.

"What are you talking about?" Kali said, her voice echoing slightly in the dark.

"You – actually going in through a front door."

"Hey, there's a first time for everything."

They might have been going in through the front door but that didn't make them welcome guests – just the opposite, in fact. While there was little danger of their being confronted by the original inhabitants of Martak, there was no way to tell if Makennon had stationed any men on the steps down. They could also hear the clattering of her convoy further below – sound travelled easily inside the cowl – and they took care to move slowly, making no sudden moves whose echoes might alert the Faith to their presence behind them.

Thankfully, as they proceeded down more of the huge steps, the sea baffled most of the sound for them. While they could still make out the crashing of the waves outside, the sound was for the most part overlaid by the noise of the great black pipes that curved into the cowl from under the sea. Actually, they weren't strictly pipes any more, but tubes, each the thickness of two men, their casing after they entered the cowl changing from rough and barnacled metal to smooth, if age-grimed, glass. What could be seen inside was a murky detritus and seaweed-filled brine that glowed slightly and, agitated by the outside motion of the waves, slopped back and forth within. Bladed fans also stirred lazily along their length at regular intervals, their purpose, for the moment, unknown.

The steps that had led the way down the cliff continued down and down, and in the light from the betubed sea – caused by algae, Kali guessed – they could be seen in more detail than had been possible above. They were less weatherworn, too, and this extra factor drew Kali's gaze to their risers.

"Look at this," she said, kneeling and brushing away grime.

"Erm, what exactly?" Slowhand queried.

"There are more runics here. Carved into the fronts of the steps."

"So?"

"So..." Kali said. She frowned as she studied them. For once, the runics were easy enough to understand, common words in the dwarven language. "I don't like what they say."

"And what do they say?"

Kali pointed at each of the runics in turn. "Death. Kill. Destroy."

"Oh, that's nice. So I take it the people who lived here weren't very pleasant?"

Kali frowned. "I'm beginning to think no one lived here at all."

"What?"

"I don't think this was any kind of settlement, Slowhand. I think this was some kind of military outpost. An army barracks."

"An army?" Slowhand said in mock surprise. "Should have seen that coming the first time you mentioned the word 'dwarf.'"

"Maybe, but –" She paused and stared at the steps again, at the same weight-induced cracks in them that she'd seen above. "I think this one was a very unique army."

"Oh?"

This time, Kali stared down the stairs. "What's more – I think it might still be down there."

Slowhand stared. "Okaaaay, now you're starting to worry me. Hooper, this place has got to be how old? A thousand years?"

Kali rose. "I know," she said in a tone which despite the circumstances was clearly excited. And with no further explanation she began to skip down the stairs. "You coming, or what?"

Slowhand stood where he was for a second. *Why does she never tell me anything? he thought. What am I? Lackey? Hired hand? Someone to just stand guard and shoot things? Hells – am I a sidekick?*

He sighed. *Yep, that's about the longbow and the shortbow of it. Gods, what was it about this bloody woman?*

He followed.

It was obvious now that the steps were continuing far under the sea – actually under the seabed, unless Kali missed her guess – and it was a feat of engineering that only dwarves could ever dream they could achieve. But the steps were only the half of it, and as they came to the bottom of their present flight, the true scale of what they had achieved here became awesomely clear. A long corridor stretched away before them, and one after another in rows against both walls, there were statues of dwarves. Each the height of five men, the bearded, behammered likenesses, posed in various battle-ready, grimacing positions, were clearly meant to be warriors, and despite being awed by the fact that she was for the first time looking upon faces from another age, Kali also shivered at the impression they gave. The runic messages on the stair risers, and now this – it seemed as if the entire exit from Martak had been designed to provoke bloodlust, to incite a hunger for violence and war.

Kali and Slowhand proceeded, coming eventually to another, shallower set of steps, and Kali sensed they were near now to the main area of the complex. The first sign of it was when they came up the rear of Makennon's carnival, her people having reached the base of the steps but having had their progress halted there by the largest pair of doors Kali or Slowhand had ever seen. Sighting them, Kali flung out a blocking arm, slapping Slowhand in the face.

"Ow! Hey!"

"Shush!"

Both of them crouched on the steps, observing what was going on. The reason that Makennon and her people could not get the doors open was clear, and seeing what it was Slowhand stared at Kali, his expression questioning and concerned. But the expression on Kali's face told him that exactly the same concerns were running through her mind.

The huge doors had been sealed shut with a massive, glowing rune. A rune in the shape of a crossed circle.

"Hooper, isn't that – ?"

Kali swallowed. Pulsating slowly with a red fire, the giant rune was the symbol of the Final Faith, all right, but she could not believe that she was seeing it. There had to be another reason for its presence here, because otherwise all of Makennon's babblings about the Final Faith's destiny threatened to prove right. No, there had to another reason. *Had* to be!

One thing was clear. If it was the symbol of the Final Faith then Makennon was nevertheless having problems bending it to her will – and it was obviously not going to be wiped away with a wave of the Anointed Lord's hand. As they continued to watch, Makennon gestured to the mages in her party and the men and women congregated in front of the rune, beginning to weave their magical threads that would dispel it.

Makennon and company had clearly reached a temporary impasse and, as they worked out how to get the doors open, Kali realised it was her and Slowhand's chance to get ahead of their party. She looked around for a way to do so, certain with the knowledge of experience that there was always a way past these things, if you looked beyond the obvious. Her gaze fastened on one of the higher seawater tubes that ran along the corridor close to the ceiling. Where the tube met the wall in which the door was set, there was a small crawlspace around it. She nudged the archer, indicated it.

Slowhand knew what she had in mind. Quietly, he

unslung his bow and took a roped arrow from his quiver, aiming upwards. The arrow flew and arced perfectly over the tube, taking the rope with it and wrapping it round and round until it was fixed firmly. Slowhand tested its grip and then indicated for Kali to climb.

She did, and he followed, and the two of them moved silently along the top of the tube in a crouched position, high above the oblivious Makennon and her people. There, they ducked into the crawlspace and through the wall. They passed through about twenty feet of darkness carved from the rock beneath the seabed and emerged finally into a space that was detectable only by their sudden freedom of movement as it was almost totally devoid of light.

Then their eyes adjusted slowly to the darkness, and they both gasped out loud.

Because the scale of the statues in the corridor outside was nothing compared to the scale of this room.

The first people to do so in over a thousand years, they had just entered what they, and Makennon, had journeyed to the edge of their world to find.

The throne room of the Clockwork King.

CHAPTER 17

The throne room was vast. That such an excavation could exist here, hewn from rock beneath the waves, was mind-boggling enough, but made even more so by the fact that as they stared around it in wonder the sea hung above them like a sky.

This – a bit to Kali's disappointment but to Slowhand's huge relief – turned out to be an illusion, the huge, stone buttresses of the throne room walls reflecting and magnifying the glowing seawater in the tubes, so that it seemed to ripple and shift in kind. But Kali's disappointment was mollified by the fact that the glow served a useful purpose, providing an effective, if haunting, illumination, bathing in a blue-green light this marvel of dwarven engineering that had been lost from sight and mind since before her own civilisation was born. What their eyes beheld as they further adjusted to the light was no illusion, however – but they could have been forgiven for thinking that it was.

The throne room stretched out ahead of them, bigger even than the inside of Scholten Cathedral, an immense rectangular chamber that could once have welcomed titans and giants as courtiers, and which, for all they knew, perhaps once had. A central aisle that was as wide as a road, inlaid with dwarven mosaics, led forwards, and at its end – distant but nonetheless still dominating the room – a huge and shadowed, seated figure loomed high in the dark. As compelling as it was, though, it was not the only figure in the room, and as Kali dropped from the pipe and began to wander slowly up the aisle, her head turned from left to right, staring up at three raised galleries, accessed by broad interconnecting stairways, that ran the entire length of the throne room on either side. As the corridor outside had been lined with dwarven statues, so were these, but in this case with many, many more, each and every one of them draped in cobwebs but otherwise identical and separated from the next only by their own width again. Kali swallowed as she studied one statue after another, the unease she had started to feel on the surface growing with each frozen visage she passed.

But uneasy as she was, Kali could barely control her other feelings. On the one hand, the sheer scale of this place and its contents made her feel like a starving mouse beneath a feast-laden table, and she longed to explore, to investigate, to catalogue the things she'd found – to *touch them*, the first person to do so for literally ages. On the other hand, however, she knew that was not why she was here, and the feeling of elation she felt at her greatest find to date was marred by the fact not only that – strictly speaking – *she* hadn't found it, but that, incidentally, she had to destroy it, too. Or, at the very least, stop it doing what it did.

Whatever it was that was.

Doubts resurfaced once more – that what the old man had told her was partly wrong, that perhaps Makennon's destiny did lie where she said – but the doubts were fleeting. She knew what she had seen and read in the Three Towers, knew what ideas of her own were forming, and most of all, she knew how this place felt – and it felt wrong. No, more than wrong. Troubled. Tainted. Bad. Something truly awful had happened within these walls, a long, long time ago, and its aura remained and resonated still.

She jumped as a hand touched her shoulder. "Nice place they've got here," Slowhand said. "Cosy."

Kali nodded, only half-listening, and walked further up the aisle until she came close enough to study the giant, seated figure at its end. No, not seated, *bethroned*. The idea that the Clockwork King might have been some kind of giant walking automaton had always verged on the edge of preposterous in her mind, but even so she'd been ready for anything. But looking at it now it was clear that the King was not designed as a giant that would arise from its throne, have a quick stretch, and pound across the peninsula sweeping all in its path aside. No, in actual fact, it seemed to be just a statue – a towering and staggering and very pitsing imposing statue, it had to be said, but a statue nonetheless.

Kali craned her neck, staring up to study it, and found herself being stared back at by a pair of giant stone eyes set in a gnarled, bearded and cruel dwarven face. Though the eyes were only stone, their stare was distinctly unsettling, made all the more so by the fact the face was draped in the same lengthy cobwebs as the statues against the walls, and Kali pulled her own gaze away, examining the rest of the statue instead. The giant figure wore – or had been *sculpted* wearing – the kind of studded leather armour she recognised as being from dwarven middle history, and in one hand held a like-period battle hammer, in the other a spiked dwarven shield. Again, cobwebs dangled from the shield's spikes, so long that Kali found she could walk through them like a curtain. It was only as she did that she noticed one of the less obvious features of the statue – one around the side.

Around the side and, then, to the rear, actually. For there the same kind of seawater tubes that ran into the cowl ran around and into the back of the Clockwork King. No, she realised, tracing the tubes back, they weren't the same kind of tubes – they *were* the same tubes, splitting and terminating here and in other places throughout the throne room as they ran around its walls like arteries.

Now that, Kali thought, *was odd.* And there was something else that was odd – now that she had seen that the statue was just a statue, why was it called the *Clockwork* King?

She sighed, moving to the part of the massive construction that she had purposefully saved for last. Directly in front of the throne was a large stone plinth inlaid with what looked like templates for the four keys, a complex-looking mechanism that seemed, in parts, to rotate and, presumably, lock into place.

There was a sound like a prolonged roll of thunder, and distracted as she was Kali had difficulty placing its source until Slowhand tapped her gently on the shoulder and, when he had her attention, pointed back the way they had come. It seemed that Makennon and her mages had managed to release the runelock, and the vast doors were opening. They were about to have company.

Makennon's soldiers came first, and then the Anointed Lord herself, sweeping into the throne room with a regal stride that suggested she had already claimed the place as her own. Nevertheless, for a few seconds she displayed the same reactions to the scale and content of the place as Kali and Killiam had, nodding to herself in approval. But then she spotted their distant figures standing before the king, and her brow furrowed in disbelief and annoyance. She gestured to the front members of her entourage, despatching them to various tasks around the chamber, and then strode up through the wide aisle towards the throne.

Kali's heart thudded, though not because the Anointed Lord approached. The reason for her sudden burst of adrenalin was the doors through which Makennon had passed – or rather what was now revealed upon them. Opened towards her and showing their outside face, Kali could see the remains of the fire runic that Makennon's mages had dismissed to gain entry, an embery half-circle that as she watched slowly extinguished and faded away into nothing. Suddenly everything became clear, and all the confused pieces fell into place. Gods – how could she have been so blind!

She turned to Slowhand, saw that he too stared and wondered if he had realised the same thing. But he hadn't. In actual fact, Slowhand was fighting a potentially embarrassing twitch of excitement. *Hells, Katherine looked good in her tight and shiny battle armour*, he thought. *That walk, the way those hips swivelled when she moved...*

He swept back his hair, waiting.

And Makennon walked right past him without even a glance.

"Kali Hooper," she declared with a long sigh. "The Spiral of Kos, Scholten, the World's Ridge Mountains, Andon, Scholten again, and now, finally, here in Orl. Tell me – for the record – just how many of you are there?"

Kali remembered her first encounter with Makennon, and her *questioning*. "Oh, just the one – but enough to mess with your head."

"She does that a lot," Slowhand said, leaning in with a grin.

"And I'm about to do it again," Kali said, silencing him with a glance. "Makennon, listen to me, this place isn't what you think. It hasn't got anything to do with the Final Faith, and never has had, I know that now. Coming here was a big mistake."

"For you, perhaps, Miss Hooper," another voice said as its owner approached, boots thudding on stone. Kali scowled. "The girl does not know what she is talking about," Munch continued. "Like anyone young she adopts an overfamiliarity with things older than herself that is, at best, arrogant and, at worst, offensive in the extreme."

"Speaking of offensive..." Slowhand said.

"Makennon, listen to me," Kali went on, ignoring both. "This place isn't called Orl, it's called Martak. And Martak isn't a dwarven word, it's a dwarven phrase – M'Ar'Tak. You know what it means, Katherine? An eye for an eye."

"The girl spouts nonsense," Munch interrupted. "You have seen the evidence with your own eyes. Anointed Lord, we have worked hard for this moment – please, order the activation of the keys."

"Katherine, no –"

Makennon held her gaze for a few seconds. "The signs are clear," she said after some consideration. She turned and signalled for the remainder of her entourage to enter the throne room, prompting a smile from Munch. "Bring them forwards."

Kali spun in frustration. "Dammit, Makennon, you want to know about signs? Then let me tell you about the one on those doors, the one that was so difficult to break because it was so obviously there to keep you – to keep everyone – *out*. That runic wasn't the symbol of the Final Faith because it's actually *two* runics, one overlaid on the other. A circle and a cross, Katherine, different symbols but ones used by the elves and the dwarves to mean the same thing. *That's* why there were two of each on the map showing the sites of the four keys, because the elves and the dwarves built two sites each. They're *warning* symbols, woman! They mean stay away, danger. They mean *death*."

"Oh, now you tell me." Slowhand muttered.

"And the one on those doors?" Kali went on, pointing back along the throne room. "That was the elves and the dwarves combining their symbols to shout the meaning to the world. Because when together they'd finally managed to stop whatever evil came out of this place, they sealed it with the biggest warning sign of all."

For the first time Makennon seemed to waver, and Kali was about to press her advantage when the wagon containing the keys trundled into the throne room. What gave Kali pause, however, was what followed it – the wagon containing the ogur. The ogur spotted her, too, and began to pound against the bars of its cage, its roars clearly audible even across the distance that separated them.

Munch saw what was happening and frowned. The old man's... *changes* had not lessened and there was surely no way the girl could recognise him, so this reaction made him curious. But, he thought, what did it matter if it had thrown her off guard?

"Is there a problem, Miss Hooper?" he asked.

"No. No, I –"

"Then I suggest we do what we came here to do."

Munch turned to Makennon. The Anointed Lord took her gaze off Kali and looked at him and, after a second, nodded.

"Destiny awaits," Munch said, smiling.

He signalled to some of the soldiers and they unloaded four crates from the first wagon, then carried them forwards to the plinth, breaking the seals and revealing the keys packed safely in straw inside. Munch ran a hand over each with a reverence that made Kali frown. "With your permission, Madam?" he said to Makennon.

The Anointed Lord inhaled, drawing herself up to her full, imposing height. "Go ahead," she said.

Munch lifted the first key from its crate and placed it in its matching template, pressing it home with a sound like a shifting stone slab, then rotated the plinth until it locked into place with a grating thud. It struck Kali that he looked far too much like he knew what he was doing, and she frowned as he expertly did the same with the second, and then the third key, until only the last remained. As he lifted it from its crate she moved to stop him, but with a click of her fingers Makennon had her restrained by the soldiers, along with Slowhand.

"Please – you don't know what you're doing!" Kali hissed.

"On the contrary, Miss Hooper," Munch said, in a tone which made her feel suddenly very cold, "I do."

He inserted the fourth key, repeating the same procedure as before, and then stood back as the plinth took on a life of its own. Each of the keys now turned of its own accord, first clockwise or anti-clockwise, and then back again, and then in a seemingly random pattern that Kali realised had, in fact, to be some kind of combination.

Her theory was proven correct when, after a further four or five turns – it varied with the keys – each again locked, but into a different position from which it had started, and then sank further into the plinth with more resounding thuds. A panel opened in its centre and from it rose a patch of what looked to be spikes arranged in the shape of a hand.

"Yes," Munch said. "At last, yes."

He placed his hand gently on the spikes.

Everyone in the chamber looked down as the floor trembled beneath their feet, then up and around as the seawater in the glowing tubes began to bubble and stir, the strange arterial system coming to life. The fans that punctuated their length began to slowly rotate and the detritus that had so long ago been sucked in with the seawater began to flop and toss in the glass tubes, and then began to circulate around the system with greater and greater speed. Bubbles began to bounce in the water now, a sign that more was being sucked in from the sea above, and the mounting speed of the fans increased its circulation and pressure, churning the murky water until it turned opaque and then a milky white. There was no sign of the seaweed or detritus any more, only a seething rush of pressurised liquid that raced through the tubes all around the throne room, heading towards what appeared to be each of the statues against the walls and, ultimately, the Clockwork King.

The roar of it was deafening. The whole of Martak shook.

But it was nothing compared to the shaking to come.

Kali swallowed as the water thundered into the pipes that fed the enormous statue, and as it did, the Clockwork King proved itself to be far more than a statue after all. As Kali and the others watched in amazement, great plates of stone detached themselves from various parts of its body, separating along hairline cracks for the first time in a thousand years. Dust poured from the edges of the rising plates and from the edges of the holes in the statue that remained, and as the dust fell away, the interior of the Clockwork King was revealed. There, powered by the inrushing seawater, great metal cogs and wheels turned and rotated, and pistons thumped, their movements extending the thick metal rams on which all could now see the plates were rising away from the component parts of the statue they had once been. As they did, the cogs and the wheels inside the king began to twist and turn, and then so did the rams, and as each plate followed suit, they slowly moved in different directions towards the walls and ceiling of the throne room. Kali looked up and around and saw that indentations in the stone matched each of the giant plates exactly.

It was at that moment that Kali realised there had been no confusion about the number of keys described in the scrolls in the Three Towers. The mention of a fifth key hadn't made any sense to her back then, but it sure as hells did now. And there was a fifth key, no doubt about it.

The fifth key was the Clockwork King.

And she suspected she knew what it opened.

She looked up again as a series of deep booms signalled that each of the stone plates had locked into their corresponding positions, and then she looked left and right towards the galleries, swallowing. Despite wanting to know all about the wonders of this place earlier, all she could think now was: *Let me be wrong. Please, let me be wrong.*

But she wasn't. That became clear as soon as the pipes that seemed to feed the statues in the galleries began to churn even more than before, and then a series of deep and prolonged rumblings drew everyone's glances towards the sides of the throne room. One after another, all along the walls, the dwarven statues were sliding upwards, the dust of ages pouring from them, their cobwebs tearing away. Moving slowly, each rose its own height and eventually came to rest with a thud, and revealed behind where each had stood was a space as dark as a tomb. And out of each space came a whiff of something foul.

Makennon's people had begun to scatter as soon as the statues had started to move, but now the Anointed Lord shouted for them to stand their ground. Kali glanced urgently at her and saw, despite the order, that she was looking increasingly uneasy, as if the soldier's part of her mind was weighing up the tactical advantages and disadvantages of what this place might offer, finding them at odds with that part of her that had been driven here by religious zeal. She might have brought a little too much of the warrior to her role of Anointed Lord, but it was highly unlikely she wished to further the Final Faith's cause by endangering all life on the peninsula, including her own.

"Makennon, stop this," Kali said. "I can see in your eyes you suspect what I said is true – or at least worth considering. Look at this place and think. How can anything in this graveyard fulfil the destiny of your church? I don't know what you expected to find but I'd guess this isn't it. This can't be anything good."

She grabbed Makennon by the shoulders, shook her and forced her to look at the tomb-like entrances. More cobwebs shifted slightly where they dangled in front of the darkness, disturbed, perhaps, by a breath of something from within.

"That monstrosity on the throne isn't the Clockwork

King of Orl, Katherine," Kali persisted, shaking her once more, "it's the Clockwork King of *All*. Ask yourself, woman – *all what?*"

Makennon hesitated for what seemed to be an age, regarding Kali with unwavering eyes. Then finally she nodded, flicking her finger at Munch to stand him down. But he didn't move. Makennon instead flicked her finger at the soldiers to stand him down. They didn't move, either.

Munch laughed. "The problem with giving me autonomy to choose people for these missions, Anointed Lord, is that I chose carefully. And the people I chose on your behalf for this mission I did so because I knew you might have second thoughts." He sighed. "Second thoughts I cannot allow."

Makennon looked furious but knew better than to move. The soldiers already had their crossbows trained on her.

"What is this, Konstantin?"

"Destiny. But not, as I led you to believe, the destiny of the Final Faith. No, I simply needed its resources to find my way home."

"Home?"

"Home." Munch looked almost sad as he added, "It was my destiny to come here, Katherine – not yours. I am sorry."

"Pff, I'll bet," Kali said. "You know what, Stan – I had you pegged right from the start. Well, almost."

"Munch, what are you saying?" Makennon asked again.

"He's saying that he's a dwarf," Kali explained. "Or at least as much of a dwarf that the one million millionth drop of dwarvishness he'll have left in his blood after all this time qualifies him to be. And unless I miss my guess, that blood's from the clan responsible for what happened here."

"Quite correct, Miss Hooper. I am the last of Clan Trang – what became Clan M'Ar'Tak."

"Listen, pal," Slowhand interjected. "If I know my history, the dwarves were a noble, advanced race of miners, engineers and warriors, not homicidal bearded shortarses with faces like a mool's arse."

Munch glared at him, but his voice remained calm. "You wish proof of my claim, Mister Slowhand? Then I shall give you proof." He glanced up at the gallery tombs, which as yet remained as they had been. "The last part of the process to activate the Clockwork King of All."

Slowhand winced as, without flinching, Munch suddenly rammed his palm onto the patch of spikes in the centre of the plinth, smiling as his blood formed a pool beneath them.

"That had to hurt."

"Know this," Munch said. "The Clockwork King responds only to those whose veins still flow with the blood of Belatron the Butcher."

Slowhand shot a glance at Kali. "Who in the hells is Belatron the Butcher?"

"Bad guy," Kali answered. "I think."

"With a name like that I'd guess it's a pretty safe bet. Gods, you couldn't make this up," Slowhand added to himself in a whisper.

Neither could he have made up what happened next. Munch's blood seeped away into the plinth, and as it did the Clockwork King began to move again. Only this time, instead of sending out rams, its lower half reconstructed itself into the form of another throne on a circular platform. Except this throne was man-sized – more accurately, dwarf-sized. There was something else, too

– it was surrounded by strange cylinder-shaped crystals.

"Oh, look," Slowhand said light-heartedly, though with tension in his voice. "He's built himself a chair."

Munch settled himself into it and the Clockwork King remade itself once more, smaller components from within assembling themselves into some kind of metal ring that moved forwards to encircle Munch's head. More spikes shot out of it and embedded themselves straight into his skull, and as they did the cylindrical crystals began to glow. Munch jolted and spasmed in the throne for a few seconds and then smiled. "Yes, Mister Slowhand, that hurt, too. But not, I am pleased to say, as much as my warriors are going to hurt you."

"Warriors?" Slowhand queried, dubiously.

"Not nice," Kali said. "I've seen them before..."

Munch closed his eyes and concentrated. A deep and rhythmic pounding suddenly reverberated throughout the throne room, and then from each of the spaces behind the statues figures marched before halting, more than one from each, and each of which thrice the size of a man. Standing there with their arms and heads slumped like those of ogur, they filled the galleries now and, like the interior of the Clockwork King itself, they were things of metal, of cogs and pulleys and gears, though they had been assembled in such a way that, like the king, they also superficially resembled dwarves, although grotesquely so. Each wielded a dwarven war hammer in one hand and a double-bladed axe in the other, but while the axe was of relatively normal size the hammer was as grotesquely enlarged as each warrior itself – a vicious-looking slab of iron-ribbed stone that was actually part of the ogur-like arm and would likely shatter walls, let alone bones, with a single blow. The only thing the warriors did not carry was a shield, but the giant hammer made such armour unnecessary, its bulk, used defensively, protection enough.

These were the things of which the manuscripts and all the tales had warned. Let slip once on Twilight, it had taken the combined technologies and sorceries of the elves and the dwarves to stop them. Let slip again, onto a Twilight where such abilities were as yet in their infancy, they would be formidable and unstoppable.

"By all the gods..." Katherine Makennon breathed.

"Don't you mean – ?"

"Slip of the tongue. What *are* these things?"

"They are M'Ar'Tak," Kali said. "Clan Trang's vengeance for the bloody carnage the elves reaped upon them. Isn't that right, Stan?"

Munch smiled on his throne. And then his face darkened. "History paints the dwarven races as the merciless ones, the warmongers, the roaring, blood-lusted, cold-blooded killers, but in our war with Family Ur'Raney it was they who proved to be merciless. Our war had raged for months, our forces driven back across the western territories we contested, the Ur'Raney seemingly able to summon endless reinforcements and our people falling before them – many to their blasted scythe-stones before they learned better. Before we knew it, our army was devastated, pushed back here, to the edge of the world. We thought they would stop, allow us to lick our wounds and leave, but they did not, instead driving us over the Dragonwing Cliffs, slaughtering us even as we fell, and forcing those who survived that slaughter into the sea. For the first time in the history of our race, dwarves were forced to hide, because there was nothing else they could do. They hid in the caves that permeate these cliffs like floprats because otherwise they – and Clan Trang – would have been exterminated."

"One of those who hid was Belatron, wasn't it?" Kali said. "He's what started all this?"

Munch nodded. "Belatron, our greatest wielder of magics. And within him a simmering hatred of the elves, a thirst for revenge that grew over the months – and then the years – into what you now see before you."

Slowhand spoke up. "You're saying that a small bunch of bloodied survivors burrowed into the sea and built an army of clockwork men to do their fighting for them. Apart from being a little unrealistic, that's not a very dwarven battle ethic, is it?"

"No, not to do their fighting for them," Munch said.

The archer gestured up at the warriors. "Then what do you call –"

"To do their *own* fighting," Kali said, cutting Slowhand off. "Because they're not clockwork men – at least, not wholly." She peered at the massed ranks and made out what the others had apparently yet not, that within the skeletal structure of each warrior were brains riveted into metal skulls, hearts suspended within metal ribs and, most grotesquely of all, eyeballs set deep within metal sockets. These things were not simply mechanical, they were vessels for the remains of warriors who had been slaughtered by the Ur'Raney.

And the most disturbing aspect about them was that, whatever mix of technology and dark magics had been used to create them, the organs remained fresh. Kali could tell that because each had a smaller version of the ring that encircled Munch's skull embedded in a still-pulsing brain.

"They called them the Thousand," Munch explained. "Dwarven warriors partly resurrected from where they had fallen to the elves and restored to fight again."

"Belatron harvested their bodies," Kali realised with

disgust. "Returned to the battlefields and ripped their remains apart when they should have reached their final rest. That's why they called him Belatron the Butcher."

"They were *warriors!*" Munch exclaimed. "Each and every one of them would have given their right arm for the chance to fight for their clan once more!"

"Seems they did," Slowhand said. "Amongst other things."

Munch slammed his fist onto the side of his throne. "Clan Trang had to rise again! M'Ar'Tak had to march!"

"*Wo-hoah.* Steady, shorty."

"It all went wrong, though, didn't it, Stan?" Kali said. "This throne you're sitting in – this skullring you're wearing – is what Belatron used to control them. Only he couldn't, could he? Because by the time he'd done with them, by the time their brains had realised what they now were, and by the time he had forced them up those steps and indoctrinated them with his messages of death and killing and war, they had, all of them, become completely insane."

"They turned on their own," Makennon said. "And then they turned on everything else. A marching horde, but nothing to do with the Lord of All. How could I have been so blind, so stupid, so wrong?"

"You weren't wrong, Makennon," Slowhand said, looking at Kali. "Like Hooper, here, you just didn't have access to all the information. Something, in your case, I'm sure a certain short bastard had a lot to do with."

Makennon swung on Munch. "Why do you do this, Konstantin? Do you want to use your army to bring down the Final Faith?"

Munch laughed. "The *Faith?* The Faith is fleeting. My army is to be used to bring about a resurgence of the dwarven race, by giving them the freedom to emerge from their underground enclosures by annihilating anything that stands in their way."

"I've got some news for you," Slowhand said. "Your lot died out a long time ago. There *are* no more dwarven enclosures."

"Actually, there might be," Kali said, hesitantly.

"What?"

"Tale for another time."

"Oh."

Kali turned back to Munch. "Munch, listen to me. Belatron couldn't control these things, and neither will you. They won't wipe out *anything* that stands in your way, they'll wipe out *everything*, including yoursel –"

"Enough!" Munch barked. He inhaled deeply and his blood-stained brow furrowed with concentration. "It is time."

All along the galleries, the heads of the clockwork warriors rose from their slumped positions and stared ahead, ruptured vessels in their unnatural eyes making them appear to flare red. Then, in military step, they began to march forwards and pound down the steps from the three levels – an army on the move. Munch blinked and four separated from the horde, coming to stand around him as bodyguards, but the rest, assembling in ordered ranks of five abreast, stood ready to march towards the exit.

"No!" Kali shouted, pulling free of her captors. Determined to halt their progress, to prise Munch from his seat of power, she ran forwards, eliciting a warning cry from Slowhand. Munch looked at his clockwork bodyguards but then sniffed, as if using them was hardly worth the effort, and instead signalled to his people to turn their crossbows on Kali instead of Makennon – and fire. Their bolts slammed into her from every direction, the impacts forcing a series of grunts as she attempted to stagger on, and, though her reserves must have been considerable and she almost made it, she found herself faltering and staring at Munch with a look of pained surprise in her eyes. Munch sighed and drew his gutting knife from his belt, aiming it provocatively and directly at her.

"No further, Miss Hooper."

"Damn you, you bas –" Kali began. But she never finished her curse. The knife flew with as much force as Munch could muster and embedded itself solidly in her chest. It stopped Kali quite literally dead in her tracks and, her breath whistling strangely, she looked dully down at the protruding blade – what little of it she could see – then, stunned and confused, dropped to her knees and, slowly, onto her face. A small groan escaped her, and, as a pool of blood began to spread ever more largely beneath her, one thought overrode all others.

This wasn't how she was meant to die.

"Hooper?" Slowhand said.

"Should you be thinking of trying the same, *minstrel*," Munch advised, staring at the still and bloodied body, "there are plenty more bolts in my people's possession."

Slowhand stared. The throne room was utterly silent apart from the roaring of the ogur as it battered at the bars of its cage with as much fury as the archer had in his eyes. No words were necessary, though, as Slowhand's expression said it all. He was going to kill Munch – and very soon.

The standoff was broken by Makennon.

"Munch, this is insane! What if Hooper was right? If Belatron the Butcher – their creator – couldn't control these things, what chance do you have?"

Munch smiled, looked at his bodyguards and blinked.

The four clockwork men stamped their feet as one, quaking the floor of the throne room.

"He's doing it," Makennon said quietly to Slowhand. "He's actually *controlling* them."

"Probably something to do with the fact that he's as insane as they are. The question is, how long will it last?"

Makennon tried to reason with Munch one last time.

"Konstantin, he's right. These things might obey you now but what about when you've razed Andon, Freiport, Scholten? Because that is what you want to do, isn't it? But how strong will you be, then? What's to stop your army going on to kill the very dwarves whose resurgence you desire? This is *fantasy!*"

Munch glared. "You call me a fantasist? You, a religious zealot who clutches at any straw and follows any carrot that is dangled before her eyes? You pathetic woman – your whole reason for existence is a fantasy!"

Makennon drew herself up to her full height. "I was a general, Konstantin Munch. It is my job to know when an army stands unfit to march."

"On the contrary," Munch said. "It is my job to tell them when to."

He closed his eyes and concentrated, and the massed ranks of clockwork warriors began to pound slowly towards the door. Their orders received, Munch opened his eyes, stared around at everyone in the throne room and then looked to his bodyguards. "Kill them all," he ordered.

All hells broke loose. Slowhand and Makennon staggered back as the four mechanical warriors began to systematically attack everyone who had been in the Anointed Lord's party, their axes and hammers slicing and crushing, chopping and pounding, beating and tearing their bodies apart. Those that were armed tried to defend themselves with their crossbows and blades, and those that were not – the mages – with their fireballs and storms, desperately weaving cones of protection as they fought to keep their attackers back. Screams of agony echoed around the stone chamber, and its walls were splattered and sprayed with blood, and there was nothing anyone could do to stop themselves dying. Nothing at all.

In his caged wagon, the ogur raged.

"You little bastard!" Slowhand shouted, and, without thinking, began to run towards Munch, but Makennon pulled him back.

"You'll never get near him," she said. "We have to get out of here."

Slowhand glared at her, knowing she was right. But still he shrugged her off, staring at Kali's body.

"I'm not leaving her down here."

"You won't get near her, either, you fool – those things will tear you apart."

"I'll find a way."

Again, Makennon grabbed him, but this time by both arms and more forcefully, spinning him to face her. Her gaze – her intense gaze – was for a second no longer that of the Anointed Lord, aloof and ruthless, but that of a professional warrior, the general she used to be. In it was the sadness of one who had lost one of their own together with the harsh pragmatism that acknowledged that in what they did someone had to fall in battle. It was inevitable.

"She's dead, Lieutenant. The battle is lost. Anything else is suicide. Retreat with me. *Now.*"

Slowhand was suddenly furious. "And where the hells do you suggest we retreat *to*, General? Have you any idea what your religious scheming has unleashed here? How many people on the peninsula are going to die?"

"I don't know! But there must be something that can be done to stop this. But first we need to *retreat*, regroup. You know that."

Slowhand swallowed. "There is something we can do," he said, suddenly. He unslung his bow, quickly strung an arrow and aimed it at Munch's head, squinting to get a bead through the clockwork warriors. "I might not be able to get near him but I can finish that bastard from right here."

But he didn't loose the arrow. Because what he had just noticed was that in all the confusion the ogur had escaped its cage.

And it, and Kali's body, were gone.

CHAPTER 18

The storm outside Martak had worsened dramatically since Kali and the others had entered the sub-aquatic complex, and was now in stark contrast to its shelter, making it seem almost welcoming despite the nightmare the place had been. Forks of lightning split a night sky blackened by the eclipse, the flashes of light so severe it seemed the universe was, with homicidal slashes, slicing itself apart. A freezing wind caught and flung back to the cliffs by the Stormwall chilled and cut straight to the bone. The wind did not prevent the heavy rain from hammering straight down, however, and it was the wet, cold crashes of the raindrops on her flesh that kept Kali from fading into the oblivion she knew was very close.

She wasn't dead, that much was clear, but neither did she have long to live – she could feel it in every fibre of her fading being. Her body had been battered too much, pierced too many times, and she had lost too much blood to hope – even with her newly discovered powers of recovery – to survive. The fact made her feel immensely sad. She had hoped to live long enough to make a difference, but she hadn't. She had come so far, done so much, and yet she had failed.

Failed herself. Failed Slowhand. Failed Twilight.

Most of all, she had failed Merrit Moon.

Her regret and diminishing consciousness was so debilitating that for a while it did not occur to her to question where she was. But then even she couldn't ignore the violent shaking of her head any longer.

She groaned, eyes attempting to take in her situation, but her view bouncing everywhere. Then, what vestige of fear of death remained in her already dying form cut through her much more sharply than any bolt or knife, including Munch's, could ever have done. Because she saw that she was slung in the massive, green-tinted arms of a beast that was pounding up the cliff steps outside Martak, a beast that she dimly recognised – but mainly smelled – to be an ogur. What was more, the ogur was roaring, again and again and again.

This was it, then. The moment.

Her vision come true.

It was too much for her. Finally, too much. She hadn't asked for any of this, and she was no longer strong enough to fight the inevitable. With a great weariness and a long, drawn-out sigh that became hopelessly lost in the stormy night, Kali Hooper felt her body relax and then felt herself die.

I'm sorry, old man...

"There!" Killiam Slowhand shouted as he saw her slump

in the ogur's grip. "She's there!"

"Slowhand, keep back!" Makennon warned.

Not a chance, Slowhand thought. The disappearance of Kali's body had been the catalyst he'd needed to flee Martak, his desire to rid Twilight of Konstantin Munch overwhelmed by his concern for his ex. He and Makennon had made for the exit just before Munch's army had begun their slow march through it and, frankly, he had all but forgotten about the dwarf and didn't much care. But if there was *anything* he could do to stop Kali suffering at the hands of this thing that, for whatever reason, had taken her, then he would do it.

He flung himself over riser after riser, pursuing the ogur all the way to the top of the cliffs, and there stood panting heavily, watching in disbelief as the ogur laid Kali's body gently down onto the rocky ground. Nevertheless, he ran forwards, attempting to shield her from whatever was the beast's intent, but the hulking creature batted him away like some buzzing insect, sending him smashing into nearby rocks. Slowhand picked himself up, wiped blood from his mouth and, roaring, went for the ogur a second time, but a loud roar from the beast that was much, much louder than his own – not to mention a steely grip on his arm from the now caught-up Makennon – held him back.

Panting even more heavily, Slowhand unslung his bow and aimed an arrow directly between the ogur's eyes, impossible to miss even though his grip wavered uncharacteristically with grief and fury. The pouring rain slicking down his hair, running in rivulets down his face and reminding him so much of the walkway on Scholten Cathedral. He addressed the beast through clenched teeth.

"Leave – her – alone."

The ogur stared directly at him, an unexpectedly sad and thoughtful expression in its eyes making him falter in his intent. And then, while the still-wavering Slowhand shook his head to shake the water from his eyes, the ogur did something he hadn't expected at all. It pulled the crossbow bolts and the gutting knife from Kali's body, tossed them aside and then removed a strange blue amulet from around its neck and instead strung it about hers. It deliberately let go of the amulet – almost as if it were *giving* it to her – and then, after a few seconds, touched it again.

Again, the ogur stared at him, and somehow Slowhand knew it was asking him to *wait*.

Somewhere behind those primal eyes, Merrit Moon saw the desperate figure of Killiam Slowhand, continued to struggle for dominance of his transformed body and prayed the archer would give him time. He had no idea whether what he was about to try would work – as far as he knew scythe-stones had never been used twice, or in such a way – but if it did then Kali Hooper would live again.

His action would come at a price, though. The transference of his own life essence to Kali would likely kill him in turn, but even if it did not – if Thrutt had made him strong enough – then it would leave him so weak that he would no longer be able to fight the assertion of the ogur within, and he could be trapped within its form for the rest of his life. But it seemed a fair and just trade – after all, it was he who was responsible for her being here in the first place, was it not? Besides, she was his Kali – the closest thing to a daughter he had – so what choice was there, really?

He actually *willed* his life away.

A blue wisp appeared between ogur and corpse, and,

feeling its hungry tug like a meathook through his heart, Merrit Moon had to struggle against his own instinct to survive, forcing himself to remain where he was as the process continued. The wisp became a snake, and then a cloud that filled the air between them, and then Kali's body took on a blue glow as it became suffused with the stuff of himself. Moon felt suddenly as if he had been folded inside out and pulled away, and then the cloud was snatched into Kali, and then it became a snake and a wisp once more, and then it was gone. The sound of the amulet doing what it did – a long sigh – was echoed by one of his own, and then his body slumped to the ground with a thud, breathing shallowly.

Kali Hooper's eyes snapped open. She coughed. And then she sat up, abruptly, ramrod straight.

"Great gods," Slowhand whispered.

"Lord of All," Makennon said.

"Slowhand?" Kali asked.

The archer scurried to her side. His voice trembled, partly in wonder at what he had just witnessed, partly in thanks that – somehow – he had Kali back. "H-hey, how you doing?"

"Ohhhh, you know..." Kali said weakly. "You?"

"Ohhhh, you know. Fled certain death, watched you come back from it, now starting to wonder once again whether we have a chance of stopping an invincible clockwork army intent on destroying the world – in other words, your usual." He hesitated, looked doubtful. "You up to speed with this?"

"*Unnh.* A-ha." Kali coughed again and held her chest, from where she found her fatal wound had gone. And as she did, she caught sight of the figure beside her, and scrambled back on the ground.

"It's all right... I think," Slowhand said. "I don't know

how or why but... the ogur helped you."

"Helped?" Kali said, puzzled. She picked herself up, her own metabolism aiding the effects of the amulet, and studied the creature. It was weak but conscious, and its face seemed almost to ripple before her eyes, caught somewhere between the beast she thought it was and something heart-thuddingly familiar. She touched the amulet around her neck, remembered seeing it on the old man, then moved to touch the ogur's face. And as she did, the ogur's hand moved over hers and moved it gently down, much as another had in the Warty Witch a long, long time ago.

Kali swallowed. There was something familiar there – *and the eyes.*

"My gods," she said. "Merrit?"

"What?" Slowhand exclaimed.

"It's the old man," Kali said, excitedly. "I don't know how or why but he's here, inside this, this... *thing*. The cave in the World's Ridge, where I last saw him – he didn't die!"

"Oh, Hooper, come on –"

"Your friend is correct," Makennon said. "Munch told me how this happened, about an artefact. Its effects are meant to be temporary but..."

Kali looked at the ogur, concerned. What had, a moment before, seemed so familiar in its eyes was fading, as if Moon were going away, and as she watched the spark in them faded to something feral – the eyes that she remembered from the beasts in the cave. The ogur emitted a dull growl, then, and as if afraid something worse might follow, roughly shoved her away, rose and stomped along the cliff.

"We have to do something to help him," Kali said.

"Hooper, I'm not sure we can," Slowhand cautioned.

"It seems to me that in doing what he did he's sacrificed something."

"Like what?" Kali said.

Slowhand looked grave. "Like himself."

"Then let us hope his sacrifice has not been in vain," Makennon said. Her attention had been drawn by a series of quaking thuds from far below. "Because they're coming."

The three of them turned to look down the steps leading to Martak, and at their base saw that the first units of mechanical warriors had completed their slow march from the throne room and emerged from the cowl. They marched in the same organised lines of five, in rank after rank after rank, filling the jetty with their broad bodies, metal feet pounding into the stone, and, as they gradually drew closer to the steps, rocks at the top of the cliffs began to tremble and shed scree that bounced and skittered below.

Their assault on the peninsula would soon begin.

"We have to stop them," Slowhand said.

"Oh brilliant. Just bloody brilliant."

"I see the old Hooper is indeed back."

"Well, honestly..."

"If you two are finished," Makennon said, "I think someone's already ahead of us on that one." She pointed a little way along the clifftop, where the ogur was pushing its shoulder into a boulder that balanced there, clearly trying to dislodge it and send it crashing below.

"I think it knows what it's doing," Makennon said.

"Damn right," Kali said, smiling. "The old man's still in there somewhere."

"Well, are we just going to stand here or are we going to help it?" Slowhand enquired.

"*Him*," Kali corrected.

"Fine, him. Come on!"

The three of them joined the ogur behind the boulder and leant their weight to pushing it, and with a dull rumble the giant piece of rock dislodged from its perch and went tumbling away, bouncing first off rocks and then onto the stone steps. With a series of crashes that were audible even over the storm, it continued down, bouncing two then three steps at a time, then more, gathering momentum as it went.

The mechanical warriors did not even react to its approach, their minds – Munch's mind – intent on their single imperative of reaching the surface and the humans who dwelled there. The boulder smashed into their front rank and sent five warriors staggering back, causing a knock-on effect behind them, and as the giant rock continued to roll through the second and third ranks their relentless march was momentarily thrown into confusion, the affected warriors trying to recover from the impact, those behind attempting to march on around them. Then, in unison, five of the giant dwarven battle hammers were swung at the boulder and it was shattered first to rubble and then, to dust. The warriors' march continued, the damage to them insignificant.

"We need more boulders," Slowhand declared. He repeated the statement more loudly to the ogur as if, somehow, being an ogur made it deaf. He then pointed at more boulders, just to make himself extra clear, but the ogur had already stomped towards them of his own volition. "Yes, more boulders!" Slowhand agreed needlessly.

Makennon assessed the *ammunition* available to them. Short of attempting to smash away the Dragonwings themselves, most of the rocks available to them were smaller than the first. "This isn't going to work," she said.

"The last one barely scratched them."

"Maybe not," Slowhand responded, heaving. "But we can at least slow them down."

"And what will that achieve? There are no reinforcements coming."

"I don't know, okay? But I, for one, am not going to just stand here."

He and the ogur sent another boulder tumbling.

Kali, meanwhile, stared down the steps, and then inland, back along the peninsula. She bit her lip. "Slowhand, carry on with what you're doing because it just might help, but Makennon has a point. There's only one way to stop those warriors and that's to destroy what Munch used to animate them – destroy the Clockwork King. But that means first having to finish their general – finish Munch."

Slowhand and the ogur made another rock roll, and the archer nodded. "Finish Munch," he repeated, breathlessly. "Hooper, you have to be kidding. Even if you had a chance against his bodyguards, how in the hells would you get back down to him? Those things would mince you before you got halfway down the steps."

"There's one way," Kali said.

She swept up Munch's gutting knife from the ground and jammed it in her belt. Then, she stuck two fingers in her mouth and whistled. A second later, Horse stood next to her, braying, his broken tether dangling around his neck.

Kali mounted him and slapped his flank, welcoming his help.

Now it was Slowhand's turn to stare down the steps, Kali's intention dawning. "Oh, no," he said. "No, no, no. No..."

"*Hyyahh!*" Kali shouted.

She reined Horse around and galloped him towards the top of the steps, kicking his flanks to spur him on. Horse reached them and jumped, soaring in a determined arc over four of the risers before his hooves thudded back onto stone with an impact that made them spark and jarred Kali to the bones.

"*Hyyahh!*" she shouted again.

Horse thundered down the steps before them, Kali keeping her gaze straight ahead in the bouncing, rushing diagonal the world had become, and again kicked his flanks, spurring the bamfcat to greater speed.

"*Hyyahh!*"

They hit the jetty, and the world levelled, and still she kicked, bringing Horse to full gallop, the front ranks of the marching warriors now no more than ten yards ahead. As she'd hoped she would, she heard a distinctive shnak as the horns on Horse's body snapped fully from their housings, the bamfcat reacting instinctively to the danger to come.

Good boygirl, she thought, *good, good boygirl.*

And then they rammed straight into the army of the Clockwork King.

Kali was aware of little more than a sudden and rapid series of thuds and jarring impacts as Horse ploughed into and then through the advancing warriors, her world skewing this time into a seemingly endless number of fractured tableaux, flashes of hammers and axes and swinging arms, and of red, glaring eyes. There was nothing she could do but ride Horse as a helpless passenger, nothing she could do to affect their progress – all she could do was hope it continued, and that Horse's armour was strong enough to keep him from harm. The great beast ploughed onwards through the warriors, cutting a swathe through their middle, sending them staggering aside, and then, glimpsed through them at last, jarringly and shakingly, was the maw of the cowl. There were still far too many of the warriors between them and it, though, and within it, many, many more, still working their way up from the throne room, and the constant wall of metal and corrupted flesh was beginning to take its toll on Horse, not only in terms of slowing his momentum but in the amount of damage his armour was now taking. She couldn't – and wouldn't – push him any further, but that didn't really matter because it had never been her intention to reach the cowl, anyway. All she'd needed Horse to do was get her close to the water.

And now she needed to make sure Horse was safe.

Kali rose high in the saddle so that she touched only his stirrups, and then patted the bamfcat's neck. "It's time to do that thing you do," she said quickly, and hoped to the gods that he understood. "You know, the thing. Do it, Horse. Do it now!"

The bamfcat roared, and for a second Kali thought that perhaps he hadn't understood, but then she realised it wasn't that at all.

"Yes, you great lump, I'm fond of you, too, but you need to do the thing! Pits, Horse, do the thing and do it n – "

Horse reared, and the air cracked, and then the bamfcat vanished from under her, and suddenly Kali was flying over the heads of the marching warriors, all alone. She knew exactly what she was doing, however, and immediately turned what could have been a flailing tumble into an arched dive, taking her over the edge of the jetty. And then, like Horse, she, too, vanished – head first into the churning sea.

Kali hit smoothly, slicing beneath the surface like a knife. There, however, her smoothness came to an end, the churning maelstrom that was battering the side of the jetty flinging her around like a worgle in a whirlpool. It took her some time to orientate herself, arms and legs slapping and kicking against the currents, but finally she swam in the direction she wished. But she did not head for the surface, as might be expected. Instead, she swam towards the dark foundations of the entrance cowl to Martak. Slowhand had been right – there was no way to reach Munch through the warriors – but there *was* a way to reach him.

And there it was. Or, rather, they were.

The intakes for the water pipes loomed before her in the murky depths, the churning water around them exacerbated by the pumps somewhere inside Martak that drew it in. Kali had to fight against the pull so that she was not sucked against the grilles she saw protecting the pipes' mouths, and, thrashing and kicking again, manoeuvred herself so that she was able to grab both sides of one of the pipes, and there, amidst a cloud of bubbles as blinding as fog, tugged and wrenched at the grille until it came away. She let it fall to the seabed and then – her breath short – dug in her belt for her breathing conch before she thrust herself upwards and in.

It was almost peaceful inside the tube, the distant thudding of the pumps like a heartbeat, the rotation of the fans – slower now that their job in releasing the king and his army was done – a relaxing thrum. This was the first chance she'd had to appreciate the complex network of pipes that seemed to power the mechanics of the place, and, while she found it an achievement, she also found it rather odd because it was so distinctly *un-dwarven*. But then, she supposed, they hadn't had much lava to drive their engines here at the edge of the sea.

There was nothing peaceful about what was occurring

beneath her, however, and as Kali wiped away the grime on the inner surface of the tube, and looked out, she saw the vaguely distorted forms of the advancing army of clockwork warriors marching in rank after rank along Martak's exit corridor. But she had no interest in them. They were the responsibility of Slowhand and the others now, and her concern was in reaching the man who controlled them and what he, in turn, controlled.

Kali swam along the tube, timing her strokes through the slowly rotating fanblades, heading horizontally and then downwards, rubbing the glass occasionally to determine how far into the complex she was. Eventually the light outside became shadowed and she realised she was passing through the section of tubing that ran through the surroundings of the first door, which meant there was only one short section of corridor remaining. There was, however, a problem. Her breathing was becoming laboured, and she realised the conch symbiotes had almost exhausted their current supply of oxygen. She would need to pick up her pace, get out of the tube quickly, or she'd become part of the flotsam floating around this hellhole for the rest of time.

She swam faster, ignoring her surroundings until a second batch of shadow told her she had at last returned to the throne room of the Clockwork King. But her breathing was becoming desperate now, and she could taste the toxic taint of her own used breath. She'd poison herself if she didn't get out of there right away.

Bubbles exploding from the sides of her mouth, Kali felt desperately around on the base of the tube, searching for some weakness in its length. She found a seal that linked sections and then pulled Munch's gutting knife from her belt, working at the strange, almost organic seal. It was more difficult than she expected, and her movements became increasingly jerky, imprecise, but at last a downwards spiral of bubbles indicated the seal was coming apart, water leaking into the throne room below.

She wondered if Munch would notice – notice that she was coming for him.

She stabbed his knife into the weakened seal, and a sudden lurch in the base of the tube warned her that it was about to give. Just in time she jammed herself inside the tube as the whole section dropped away from the rest of the network and hung down at an angle, water slamming into and over her back as it poured down into the throne room.

Kali released herself and went with the flow which, quite conveniently, washed her right in front of Munch, sitting there, on his throne.

"Miss Hooper," the dwarf resurgent said. "Even I have to confess this is something of a surprise."

"Hi, Stan," Kali said. "Have to say, you look a little rough."

He did, too. Munch was almost slumped in the throne he had so arrogantly adopted, looking drained and fevered. His eyes seemed unable to focus on her – or were, perhaps, focusing on a thousand things – and he involuntarily spasmed every few seconds. The blood that had leaked from where the spikes had stabbed into his skull had not dried, because the sweat that ran from his every pore wouldn't let it.

"Controlling the Thousand is proving to be something of a challenge," he said, wearily. "But one that I will master."

"Can't let you do that."

Munch paused. "Ah. You have returned to kill me."

"Not here to see if you've grown any higher."

"I am afraid," Munch said haltingly, almost as a gasp,

"you are an inconvenience I cannot afford."

"Now, where have I heard that before? I suppose this is the part where you set your dogs on me?"

"Indeed." He blinked, and his four bodyguards snapped to face her, their feet thudding down as they adopted an attack stance.

Kali was ready for them. She'd been ready the moment she'd dropped from the tube to the floor. She only hoped that, in trying to do what she wanted to do, she was as capable as the events of recent days had suggested she could be.

Because if she wasn't, she was dead.

Again.

Four hammers slammed down from her left and from her right, impacting hard with the stone floor of the throne room and cracking it wide. They were clearly only warning blows but nevertheless Kali was already gone, backflipping away and feeling the heavy whoosh of the hammers' mass as she went. She straightened, turned and ran, inviting them to follow, which they duly did, their feet pounding on the damaged floor behind her.

Kali ran almost to the end of the throne room, seemingly intent on fleeing from their pursuit but planning nothing of the kind. For one thing, there was nowhere to go – the gallery steps and corridor were still filled with the mechanical warriors' slowly deploying ranks – but for another she knew exactly where in the throne room she wanted herself, and her would-be butchers, to be.

What she wanted to do, in fact, was let them drive her into a corner.

The mechanical warriors came on, hammers raised and axe blades swinging, while a somewhat weak cackling from Munch echoed in the distance. Kali stood her ground, waiting for her moment. As the four approached, she bounced on the balls of her feet, watching their axes, but, particularly, their hammers, not only for which of the warriors would swing the first blow but how they would swing it. She had, after all, learned a new trick in the Spiral of Kos.

The first two disappointed, and she dodged their downward swings by deftly rolling between them, but the third, swinging its hammer horizontally, was exactly what she'd been hoping for. As the hammer swung towards her, momentum guaranteed to carry it onwards and upwards, she ducked beneath and then instantly sprang onto its upper face from behind, letting it carry her into and then propel her through the air. She landed exactly where she wanted to be, on top of the very water tube she and Slowhand had first used to enter the throne room, but she did not use it to leave, instead simply standing there until her attackers swung at her again. This they did, and Kali glanced over at Munch as the hammers smashed towards her, watching to see if he'd realised his mistake. For at her current height, the deadly bludgeons of the bodyguards could not quite reach her, and instead they smashed into the tube itself. Glass shattered and water exploded, sending the bodyguards staggering back beneath its deluge.

Kali had leapt away at the moment of impact, and now ran further up the tube, in the direction of Munch, where she heard him roar in anger. Yes, he'd realised his mistake but, as was the way of these things, it did not stop him repeating it. The bodyguards pounded after her, hammers and axes swinging all the way, and as they swung they shattered more and more of the tube, so that entire sections of it fell away to the throne room floor. They didn't crash down, however, but splashed and sank, the increasing deluge of water from the ruptured system beginning to flood the throne room, the still rotating fans pulling more and more of it in from the sea. Kali continued her flight along the tubes and the warriors followed, almost berserk now, though their rage – Munch's rage – could do little to help them in what had become a forced wade through the rising waters. Again they swung, though more sluggishly now, their giant hammers slowed as they ploughed through the flood and, again, more sections of the tubes disintegrated before them. The water was deep enough for Kali's purpose now, and she stopped her flight, instead diving into the water herself, and there she clenched her gutting knife as she swam beneath the surface in the direction of her mechanical pursuers. There was always a way, she thought, not only to get into places but to defeat things, and swimming into the midst of the pack of bodyguards she slashed the wiry tendons on the ankles of all four, the water preventing them being able to manoeuvre fast enough to stop her. With a series of mechanical groans they collapsed beneath the ever-rising flood to the throne room floor.

Kali swam, and then waded from the water onto the base of the Clockwork King.

Munch, more feverish and manic-looking than ever now, seemed almost to shrink back before her.

"I knew that you were resourceful," he declared wearily. "I never realised quite how much."

As he spoke, an entire run of the water tubing collapsed from the throne room walls, weakened by the loss of the rest of its network, and beyond it, even more began to buckle. A crack appeared in the throne room wall.

"Yeah, well," Kali said, darkly. She was thinking back to the Flagons. "That slashing the ankle thing? Someone gave me the idea."

"Miss Hooper..."

"Stand up and face me, you bastard."

Blood ran slowly down Munch's forehead. "You know as well as I that I cannot – I will not – leave this seat. I am helpless before you. So, go ahead – what are you waiting for?"

"*Aaargh!*" Kali roared, plunging the gutting knife downwards. But at the last moment she froze, the tip of the knife shuddering in her grip an inch from Munch's heart.

The dwarf chuckled deeply, and Kali regarded him with a hatred that could not manifest itself.

"You may have become some kind of fighting machine," Munch said, "but you will never be a true warrior. Not so long as you cannot finish your opponent. That is what differentiates the victor from the defeated on the battlefield."

"I can't let you continue this..."

"Then do what you came to do, girl. Stop me. Kill me. *Go on – do it!*"

Munch sounded almost as if he wanted her to. Kali pulled back her arm, ready to plunge the knife downwards once more, but again desire and conscience clashed, leaving the blade suspended and trembling, her whole body doing the same in furious frustration.

"Do it or all that you know will be gone, girl. Pontaine, Anclas, Vos, Gargas. Everything you know."

"You've already taken enough away from me."

"Soon there will be others who do what you do now – only they will be of the dwarven race. And it will be your bones they will pick over. *Your* bones, Kali Hooper. The bones of a fleeting and inconsequential speck in history."

"Not if I have anything to do with it."

Munch chuckled again. "Then do what must be done.

Only you can't, can you? You have let down all those who trusted you, brought about the end of everyth –"

"No."

"The end of everything. You've lost, girl. You have los –"

There was a dull crunch and Munch's eyes widened suddenly in shock and disbelief, and for a moment Kali simply stared at him, wondering what had happened. Munch was staring back, directly into her eyes, but it took her a few seconds, during which a small tendril of blood ran from his left nostril, to realise that his eyes had already fogged and he was seeing nothing.

The arrow quivered slightly where it was embedded in the centre of his forehead.

Kali turned. How he had managed to get past the clockwork warriors she had no idea, but from the far end of the throne room a battered and bedraggled-looking Killiam Slowhand waded towards her through the rising and increasingly tumultuous water. He lowered Suresight to his side, its job done.

"In future, why don't you leave it to the sidekick to do the killing?" he said. He suddenly stretched his arms out and looked surprised. "What? You thought I'd let you do this alone?"

Kali inhaled a deep, trembling breath. There was no time for thanks or celebration, however, because there was still the problem of destroying the Clockwork King. But as Kali began to contemplate the problem, it was solved for her. The cracks that had begun to appear in the throne room walls widened suddenly, and as they did the ceiling itself began to crack and subside. Suddenly a wide gash appeared in what was effectively the sea bed and, along with chunks of rock, water began to pour down on the very spot where she and Slowhand stood.

Kali and the archer staggered back, watching the deluge pour onto the Clockwork King, and as the rocks crashed onto and shattered its cogs and pistons and gears, water poured thunderously onto the crystals that had brought its army to life. There was a series of sparks and then small explosions, and, at the opposite end of the throne room, the warriors that continued to march towards the exit suddenly stopped. Just like that.

Kali and Slowhand stared at them, watching to see if they moved again. But they didn't.

"Okaaaay..." Kali said.

Slowhand suddenly pulled her to the side as a chunk of rock hurtled down and smashed into the deluge next to where they stood.

"The whole place is coming down," he said. "Time to go."

"No argument there."

"After you."

"No, no, after you."

"Hooper, just –"

"Move. I know."

They swam towards the exit, manoeuvring themselves around the frozen forms of those clockwork warriors that had ground to a halt before it, and preparing to do the same with those in the corridor itself. Their red eyes stared as dully as those of Munch now, and they seemed strangely at peace.

The sea can have them, Kali thought.

Slowhand swam through the doors before her, and she was only an arm's length behind him when a sudden surge in the water caught her from behind and sucked her away in its backwash, returning her to the heart of the collapsing and flooding chamber. And, unbelievably, she saw that the doors to the throne room were closing.

"Slowhand!" she yelled.

The archer had already noticed her absence and had turned around, attempting to swim back to her aid. But it was almost as if the water was consciously trying to keep him back, one small surge after another catching him and holding him where he was so that he did little more than tread water. He stared up at the closing doors and roared with anger and frustration.

"Hooper!"

Dammit, Kali thought. *Dammit, dammit, dammit!* But as much as she tried to reach the closing gap, similar surges to those that frustrated Slowhand held her back. The rumbling of the doors could be heard even over the roaring of the inrushing sea, and the last thing she saw of Slowhand was his anguished face as they closed finally with a resounding boom.

Kali splashed around. The seawater continued to rush in with a roar and she rose slowly towards the throne room ceiling. Then, suddenly, the roaring stopped and she realised she was fully underwater, the throne room completely flooded.

As rocks fell about her in slow motion, an eerie silence descended. Kali fumbled in her equipment belt and withdrew her breathing conch, jamming it in her mouth, then floated there and stared into the murk. She might have been cut off from Slowhand but she was not alone, and below her the lifeless body of Munch drifted from its seat and rose up, ascending above the still forms of his warriors. Kali let the corpse float past her face without reaction, but then another shadowy shape in the water caught her eye and she almost spat out her conch in shock.

Because the seawater that had poured in from above had brought something with it.

Kali back-pedalled in a sea of bubbles. There, hovering before her in the water, was a humanoid figure – but humanoid was as close as it came to anything human-looking she had ever seen on Twilight.

Some kind of... fishman. She'd heard reports that similar creatures had been sighted in Turnitia but she'd dismissed them as the ramblings, perhaps even the ravings, of thieves too gone on flummox to be grounded in reality. But here one was, right in front of her – and it was staring at her.

Communicating with her.

Not talking, though. The thieves she had spoken with had described the fishmen as black-eyed, green-scaled, razor-toothed and bespined, but this one was different, its scales silver, face smooth and mouth toothless, with glowing nodules that hung from either side of its jaw. But neither mouth nor jaw moved as it spoke. Instead, Kali heard its words inside her head.

And, what was even more disturbing, it knew her name.

Kali Hooper. I am pleased that your path has brought you where you should be. That you have achieved what you must.

Kali found herself responding without even knowing how. And finding herself doing so without the need to speak, she found herself asking everything in her head at once.

Where I should be? What are you? Just what the hells is going on?

The creature floated where it was, regarding her, a paper-thin tail moving lazily behind it, and Kali felt a kind of smile – a very cold one.

Questions. Questions all the time, since when you were a child. Even then we could hear you – here, beneath the sea.

What? Are you saying you've been spying on me?

Spying? No. Watching. You, and the others. The Four.

The Four?

Four known to us. Four unknown to each other. Four who will be known to all.

Oh, gods help me, you're one of those who talks in riddles. I've come across your kind before. Statues, mainly, but –

Riddles? No. Only answers not yet formed.

Listen! You're doing it again! Hey, it's been a long day – how about some simple answers to some simple questions?

The creature floated before her, saying nothing. Kali took it as an invitation to continue.

Who are you?

Our name would mean nothing. We are the Before. The After. Those who have always been and will be again.

Will you stop it!

I... we... they... apologise.

Kali scowled, then frowned. *The Before?* she thought. *The After?*

My visions? she asked. *Were you responsible for them?*

Yes.

How? Why?

The first, to offer a solution. The second, to drive you. The third – the third to remind you of your own mortality... and, more importantly, that everything is not as it seems. The creature paused. *We know you but... we were uncertain of your resolve.*

What? You thought I'd give up? Back off because what I faced was too much? Then, Mister – you are a Mister? – however much you think you know me, you don't know me at all.

From this moment, no. Your path is what it has become. It was important to us only that you were here – at Martak.

Kali trod water. Martak. The way the creature spoke of it – spoke of her – it was almost as if they both had a place in some unknown scheme of things. It suddenly occurred to her once more how un-dwarven the water network had felt.

You were here when all this began, weren't you? You helped the dwarves to build this place – to build the Clockwork King?

They were dying. They had no resources. The balance had to be maintained.

The balance?

Too many of the elven ones, too few of the dwarves. The ferocity of the Ur'Raney was unanticipated, and their numbers after their victory had to be... curtailed.

Curtailed? You're saying you did what you did to give the dwarves an advantage? By all the gods, you wanted the Ur'Raney culled, didn't you? Only it all went wrong – the warriors you helped the dwarves create turned on their own as well – and then on everyone and everything else...

The creature remained silent for a second. *We chose our agent badly... everyone makes mistakes.*

But why would you do that?

The balance had to be –

Maintained? Kali shouted in her head. *What balance – why the hells are you talking abou –*

She suddenly choked and realised that, once more, her breathing conch was near to exhausted, something that her conversational partner had also spotted.

I would suggest that you have time for one more

question.

One more question, Kali thought, and despite the fact she had a thousand in her head – about the balance, about this undersea creature, about the Old Races – she knew exactly what it had to be. Because, somehow, she knew it was relevant.

Do you know where I come from?

The creature laughed – not laughed in her mind but actually, physically laughed – and was suddenly obscured in a cloud of bubbles that came either from whatever orifice it used to breathe or simply from the stirring of the water created by its thrashing reaction. Wherever the bubbles had come from, when they went away the creature was gone.

Damn you, Kali thought. Whoever or whatever you are, damn you.

More rock fell about her from above, and with her last lungful of air she began to swim upwards, kicking and kicking until at last she passed through a fissure in the ceiling of the throne room and up, out into the sea. She broke its broiling surface and began to swim towards the shore. Slowly, wearily, she ascended the steps, glancing down at the jetty and the stilled warriors that would remain there now, until the weather of the area simply wore them away.

Slowhand, Horse and the ogur were assembled above. There was, however, one member of the party missing.

"Where's Makennon?"

"She skedaddled when the army stopped. Probably halfway back to Scholten Cathedral already, licking her wounds. Glad to see you made it, Hooper. But then, I should have known you would."

Kali waved him away, too knackered to speak. Her

banter with Slowhand would, she knew, resume some time soon. There were, after all, things to do, among them find his sister and a cure for Merrit Moon.

Before that, however...

Kali patted Horse and took a bottle of flummox from his saddlebag. She drank deeply, and burped.

And then she stared down at Martak. At the sea. And she thought of what she had just encountered in it.

There were more questions to be answered than ever before. It was good, then, that she liked a challenge. In fact, she felt a renewed determination to discover the secrets of Twilight and the ultimate fate of the Old Races. And in doing so, she knew, she would leave nothing unexplored, nothing undiscovered, nothing untouched.

THE END

MIKE WILD

Mike Wild is much older than he has a right to be, considering the kebabs, the booze and the fags. Maybe it's because he still thinks he's 15. Apart from dabbling occasionally in publishing and editing, he's been a freelance writer for ever, clawing his way up to his current dizzy heights by way of work as diverse as *Doctor Who*, *Masters of the Universe*, *Starblazer*, *'Allo 'Allo!* and – erm – *My Little Pony*. Counting one *Teen Romance*, one *ABC Warriors* and two *Caballistics Inc.*, *The Clockwork King of Orl* is his fifth novel. However, only his beloved wife and tuna-scoffing cat give him the recognition he deserves.

Abaddon Books

COMING FEBRUARY 2009...

Now read the first chapter from the third book in
the thrilling *Twighlight Of Kerberos* collection...

TWILIGHT of KERBEROS

THE LIGHT OF HEAVEN

DAVID A. MCINTEE

A GABRIELLA DEZANTEZ ADVENTURE

COMING FEBRUARY 2009

ISBN: 978-1-905437-87-0

£6.99 (UK)/ $7.99 (US)

WWW.ABADDONBOOKS.COM

CHAPTER 2

The shooting cell was cramped, but it was well hidden, and that was the most important thing to the man inside. You could stand right outside and look straight at it, and see nothing. Just the way he needed it to be.

The shooting position itself was a bare two feet high, forcing him to lie flat, with a small loophole giving a good field of vision. Thankfully there was a small cubbyhole behind it, just large enough to stand up in and stretch. He made sure to do this at least once an hour during wakefulness. He knew better than to let himself become cramped or numb and so miss the only shot he knew he would have.

He had placed a covered chamber pot and a knapsack of provisions in opposite corners. He also had a bucket of earth next to the chamber pot, to hide the smell with. It would be embarrassing, as well as fatal, to be discovered because of an out-of-place stink. He had spent one night sleeping in the cell already, and there would be another before his chance would come. He had known that when he first entered the cell, and the timing had felt right. It was better to already be in position, waiting, than to try to slip in when the target was already on the way.

The cell granted a good view of the esplanade that fronted the castle, a blank white expanse with a cliff face to the right, and tradesmen's stalls and shops in a descending terrace to the left. Despite the chill weather, there were people on the street below. Most were tradesmen going from one piece of work to another, or hawkers selling their wares to sailors and fishermen. A dog stood out stark black against the snows at the edge of the park. Elsewhere, a cart rumbled out of the castle.

The assassin had a keen eye, and was confident that he could put an iron-tipped bolt through the chest of anyone he could see in the esplanade below. But he was after one target, and one only. Besides, some of the people down there were there to confuse and confound any pursuers while he escaped and he didn't know who they were. They didn't know him, he didn't know them; it was safer for all of them that way.

The man in the cell smiled and aimed his crossbow at a couple standing near the dog. The woman was pretty enough, the man not sufficiently handsome for her, in the shooter's opinion. The man looked on his woman proudly, as if he wanted any observer to see what a catch he had made. Then, for an instant, he looked up at the clouds, and his throat was an inviting target. He would never see his death coming. However, the man in the shooting cell settled for cocking a finger at him.

A madman – a role in which he was certain the aristocracy, if not the Final Faith, would cast him, until they knew better – could create great terror and confusion from this position. A few seemingly random bolts from the blue piercing heads and hearts would create outrage across the nation. Shoot the dog too, and the populace would really get into a frenzy. There were people who would get a thrill of pleasure from that. He wasn't one of them, but for a moment he could understand them. He shivered, thinking that this was a sort of understanding he could do without.

In any case, he reflected, he wouldn't settle for so small a reaction. He slid out of the narrow shooting position feet-first, and made use of the chamber pot and the earth. By touch alone – he daren't light a candle and give away his position to the outside world – he then retrieved a small water skin from a knapsack and warmed himself up with some stinging liquor.

Dim yellow spots of light hovered at regular intervals along the road outside. The gas lamps were steady enough, but not very bright. He was glad he wouldn't have to rely on them for his work.

Getting the right balance of simplicity and forward planning had been at the forefront of his thoughts for many months. The best way to kill someone with the least chance of getting caught was always – and would always be – to hit them over the head with a piece of street debris in a dark alley one night. The more one planned and set conditions, the more likely it was that some element would become a stumbling block that would get you hanged. With that in mind he didn't wonder that he had nightmares of being trapped in a coffin, so long as he was here. He almost regretted the decision to take up his position two days in advance of the duty he had been hired to undertake. Almost, but not quite. It was better to be part of the scenery, invisible, than to skulk his way to a good position when the streets were thronged.

He squinted up at Kerberos. It looked the colour of a bruise tonight, like blood purpling under dead skin. He looked away, half imagining that it was a bilious, sickly eye, watching him. It felt like a spotlight, picking him out for all to see, and that, any moment now, he would hear the cries of alarm and anger. Then the soldiers would come, hunting him.

He turned away with a grimace, but could still feel its diseased light on him. He curled up and closed his eyes, as he often did when he felt troubled. He always hoped that he would sleep, and find the thing that troubled him gone in the morning.

Erak Brand was awake and alert as soon as he stepped out onto the esplanade in front of Castle Kalten. An army of servants from the castle had swarmed around the open space overnight, putting the finishing touches to the banner-draped enclosures that now housed the various groups who had come to view the wedding of Freihurr vom Kalten's eldest son, Motte, to Undina of Ohnen.

He was lucky to have seen any of it, of course, since he'd been on duty in the castle itself, but a wedding always gave him a cheerful buzz. It wasn't so much the dancing or the food as the idea that two people were so committed to each other, and to showing that to the Lord of All.

Well, maybe it was the dancing and the food as well.

He walked around the edge of the esplanade, watching the people who were beginning to fill it up, ready for the happy couple to be presented to them when the private ceremony was completed. Weddings had always been a time for a celebratory drink, and carousing, and if people were going to flaunt the Anointed Lord's temperance laws, it would be at an occasion like this.

He glanced through the crowd in search of Gabriella DeZantez, but didn't see her. She too would be patrolling the town and making sure that the celebration didn't lead to lapses in morality.

Ducal soldiers of Kalten lined the castle walls, their dress armour glinting even in the overcast light of the winter's day. Their weapons were as deadly as always, but they wore scarlet surcoats over their mail. Erak himself, like the other knights of the Order of the Swords of Dawn who were in Kalten, wore his normal armour and pastel blue Final Faith surplice. In the Lord of All's eyes, it was a day for vigilance, like any other.

That buzz was still there, though, and he was determined to enjoy it just enough to be glad of it but not enough to be distracted by it.

As the morning wore on, more people gathered around the esplanade. The smells of hot foods and fish became stronger, and Erak wondered how much of it was masking the smell of grain spirits. The wedding ceremony was taking place in the castle's main hall, of course, but it was the tradition that the bride and groom be presented to the people afterwards, for their approval as well as the approval of the Lord of All.

Everybody loved to see a happy couple, especially if it meant a chance to take an hour's break from hard labour, or to taste a delicate sweetmeat from foreign parts, not usually served to a fisherman on the west coast.

Finally, an honour guard of Ducal soldiers marched out of the castle gates and formed up on the esplanade. The wedding ceremony in the great hall was obviously complete, and the main participants would come to take their bows before the crowd.

Eight members of the Swords emerged, their raised swords forming an archway through which Motte and Undina walked. Freihurr vom Kalten and Undina's father followed, as did an Eminence of the Final Faith. From the white hair, Erak knew he was being honoured to see Ludwig Rhodon. Three more Eminences were approaching the gate behind him, blessing the crowd.

And that was when the buzz of pleasure stopped.

Finally, this morning had come. Watery dawn light woke the man in the shooting cell. There was no more claustrophobia, since he could see where he was. He knew that he wouldn't have to spend another night crammed into that wooden trap.

Outside, a normal day in Kalten was beginning. Flatbed carts pulled by teams of two or four horses were moving to and fro along North Cliff, fetching and carrying goods around the city from the various docks and markets.

The crossbow the assassin picked up was particularly powerful, to get good distance, and needed a windlass to draw. The man unrolled an oilskin, which had half a dozen quarrels nestled in its slim pockets, and slid one bolt out. Its tip was diamond-shaped and it weighed two ounces. It was surprisingly short for something intended to be shot by such a large bow, only eight inches instead of the usual fifteen or so. The assassin had chosen this bolt for its balance of range versus stopping power. Shorter, it would go further than an average bolt, but hopefully the weight meant it would still pack at least as much punch when it hit flesh.

He rolled the oilskin back up, five quarrels still inside. He wouldn't like to be arrogant enough to insist that he only needed one, but nor would he like to be stupid enough to think that he would be granted time to reload and shoot again.

The man that had just emerged onto the esplanade didn't look that remarkable. He was almost albino, and wore simple robes that were carefully tailored to give the impression of piety. Only the small crossed circle of the Final Faith on his cloak-pin indicated how important he was.

There were only eight members of the Order of the Swords Of Dawn visible as an honour guard, and they all carried swords, but none had crossbows. A few more Swords were meandering through the growing crowd, and one of them stopped to cuff a man who was surreptitiously drinking from a small skin. The knight sent the man on his way, and poured the contents of the skin over the cobbles.

The assassin smiled to himself. If the Swords were more concerned with enforcing the Anointed Lord's crazed temperance laws than with security, so much the better.

Trying to put the scale of what he was doing out of his mind, he loaded the quarrel into the crossbow and wound it. When it was cocked, he lay flat, putting the business end of the bow to the loophole overlooking the esplanade.

He nestled the stock into his shoulder. Snow was still falling, but he was confident that he still had a clear shot.

The bowman wished he could take the time to wait, and enjoy his first sight of an Enlightened Eminence of the Final Faith. But he could not waste the time. He squeezed the trigger bar gently, the taut cable snapped forward, and the quarrel was launched spinning through the air. It was a beautiful shot, and he wished there was some way for people to admire his skill. The quarrel soared in a long, shallow arc, spinning slightly, and passed between the bride and groom.

If his estimate was correct, it hit the Eminence Ludwig Rhodon just to the right of the sternum. At least four inches of it would have gone through his robes, underclothes, and ribcage, and ruptured his heart.

People had always said that aristocrats and Eminences had blue blood, but it was the red kind that was spilling loose from the ruptured Faithful heart, and red blood that the Eminence was drowning in.

The assassin felt a momentary disgust but pushed the emotion away. The death was quick, merciful. Not entirely painless, but less painful than it might otherwise have been, had it been at the hands of some amateur extremist with a dagger dipped in poison.

His next order of business was simple survival. He left the crossbow where it was, and slid out of the shooting cell. He opened the trapdoor, dropping into a dark passageway. He slid down a ladder at the end, and exited from the thirty foot high beacon tower. The beacon dominated the eastern edge of North Cliff, and a staircase wound its way up the outside, to allow a constant stream of wood to be taken up to the beacon itself, but the man doubted that even the Order of the Swords of Dawn knew that the interior still retained the ladders and scaffolding of the builders who had constructed it. Not looking back, he darted across the road to the drovers' road and began to walk briskly but calmly. He knew better than to run, as running would attract attention.

Up to the left, the knights from the Swords were barging around, harried by one of their own Eminences as they set up a perimeter around the victim. The screech of Ducal soldiers' whistles began to be taken up.

The assassin kept walking.

Erak rushed towards the falling Eminence, as did every knight of the Swords in the esplanade. The Ducal soldiers rushed forward, shoving the crowd back, while the honour guard ushered the bride and groom, and their fathers, back into the castle.

Erak saw the green robe of a Healer hesitating near the castle gate, clearly unsure whether to risk entering the line of fire for a patient. Erak grabbed him and shoved him towards Eminence Rhodon. "See to the Eminence!"

The Swords of Dawn were swarming out of every nook and cranny, but no-one seemed to know what had happened. Questions and counter-questions flew across the esplanade and within the castle courtyard.

In the meantime, the assassin was walking further away. It had all gone perfectly, as far as he was concerned. Every man-at-arms he passed was rushing towards the castle, while the bowman, drab in his charcoal-coloured cloak and grey tunic and trews, walked slowly in the opposite direction.

He kept up this slow pace though every fibre of his body wanted to run as fast as he could. This way he looked like an over-fed celebrant who had left before anything untoward happened. Nothing could get in the way of his simple ruse now. Feeling genuinely in need of a touch of the celebration he deserved, he helped himself to a shot from a silver hip-flask. It was the good stuff, smuggled in from Freiport. It burned smoothly on the way down – and exploded more roughly into his front teeth when a fist smashed into them. The fist belonged to an athletic-looking knight from the Order of the Swords of Dawn.

The knight was a shade shorter than himself, wearing a tunic, gambeson, and warm trews bound tightly to what looked to be shapely legs. Greaves were strapped to the shins, and bracers to the forearms. Iron caressed the shoulders and torso, under a surplice bearing the crossed circle of the Final Faith. Staring out from under the helmet was a finely-chiselled face with high cheekbones and cropped copper hair. The assassin couldn't help hesitating as he saw her eyes. One was clear sapphire blue, the other a striking almond flecked with gold.

The assassin froze for a moment, startled out of his confident walk. "What the –" Instinctively, he pushed past her and started to run. How could they have found him? Divination sorcery? Had he left a clue?

Gabriella DeZantez started to run, bolting after the fleeing man. Why was he reacting so strongly when he had only been breaking the prohibition on drinking spirits? He wouldn't have gone to a gibbet for that. On the day of a Ducal wedding he'd have got away with having his booze poured away.

Her heart pounded, every other beat feeling as if it was being given a kick by the slam of her foot onto the cobbles. Gabriella found herself wishing that she had the breath to swear with. If nothing else, she decided, she wanted to give this man a good kicking just for making her angry by making her run.

The street ahead sloped down to a shallow grey estuary. Boats bobbed up and down there, making a fence between the slope and the water. Falling snow curtained off the warehouses and docks on the southern side. The clunking of woodwork and distant calls of working men floated, muffled, across to Gabriella, under the dark segments of a wooden pontoon bridge which loomed up close, before stretching into the grey void. Ahead, the fleeing man darted left, into an alley with Gabriella running furiously after.

Behind her, she heard horses' hooves booming thunderously. Gabriella was baffled. Who were they chasing? She looked around, seeing several mounted Knights of the Swords. The horses heeled around, Preceptor DeBarres waving to Gabriella. She couldn't read his expression under his helmet, but the tone of his hoarse shout was convincing enough that something major was afoot. "Sister DeZantez! Have you seen anyone?"

"Just the man I'm chasing. Who are you chasing?"

"Someone put a quarrel through Eminence Rhodon!"

She had no reason to assume her fleeing drinker was the same man, but some sense told her that it was a good reason for him to run. "My man went down Three-Tun Alley! You'll never get those horses through there!"

"Keep after him, and we'll set up a catchment area. Drive him towards us." Gabriella grimaced, forcing herself to run faster, and wishing she had a bow. It didn't have to be one of those Volonne-designed repeaters either. Abruptly, her quarry hesitated, and she heard the shouts of men from the other side of him. Several soldiers and members of the Swords were cutting him off. He darted left, towards another street opening, and Gabriella followed without missing a beat. They skidded down a near-vertical unpaved alley that was as much a sewer as a passageway, and out onto a promenade fronted with food stalls.

A ruffian suddenly lunged out from the shadow of a hay-wain, slashing at her with a tulwar. Gabriella pivoted aside, drawing her swords and catching his wrist between them. His hand, still gripping the tulwar, arced to one side, while the rest of him crashed back against the wagon under a heavy kick from her boot.

She didn't spare him another glance. A few travellers and labourers ducked aside as the pursuit passed, much to Gabriella's relief. As her legs and feet began to ache, and the cold gulps of air burned her lungs, she thought about dropping back and letting the other members of the Order catch him. It was only a brief thought, however, and one quickly overridden by her desire to avenge herself for having to run.

The fugitive had now sprinted for the base of the cliff. Gabriella wouldn't be surprised if he started making for the Jolly Sailors, as most criminals seemed to these days. The Jollies was a veritable thieves' quarter, though none in Kalten called it such by name.

She stopped trying to work out his course; the Jollies was all she needed to know. He could disappear into that rat-warren of rotgut tap-houses and flophouses. It would take half the Order to comb the place, and by the time they did, everyone who had legs would have fled the area.

Gabriella wasn't sure whether to care much whether she or another caught the man. The important thing in the Lord of All's eyes was just that he was caught. She mentally spat at the thought. The bastard was hers!

Though everyone else in pursuit, both members of the Order and the Duke's soldiers, had all gone different ways to get ahead of the fugitive and ambush him, Gabriella had kept following her ears. His footfalls were audible enough for her to keep track of them, and she had followed him through an alley barely wide enough for her shoulders to fit through. She burst out into an old yard filled with cluttered little workshops. The yard stank like the privy that people clearly used it as, and was surrounded on three sides by the old brickwork of some kind of warehouse, three storeys high. The fourth side was a row of plastered walls with narrow back doors to the shops. None of them looked open or disturbed.

The assassin ran, not slowing to look back. His lungs burned with the cold air, almost as much as his muscles burned with the strain of over-use. No doubt there would be another pursuit in addition to that one girl by now – Kalten's Imperial soldiery and the Swords of Dawn – but he also knew that others were tasked with getting in their way. He didn't know who, or how many, but there were those who would have been told to attack and obstruct anyone giving chase to a fleeing man on this day.

Gabriella skidded to a halt and looked around. There was no sign of the man, but she could still hear footsteps. Something clattered above her, drawing her gaze to the roof. She couldn't see anyone there, but there was a decaying zigzag of steps up the side of the warehouse, so he could have gone that way.

As soon as she stepped towards them, two scruffy-looking beggars bounded down the stairs from above. "Stop her," one of them said to the other. "She mustn't catch up." This one leapt at her from half-way up, slashing wildly with a wickedly curved dagger. She spun, letting his attack slide off the blade in her left hand, and slashed with the right. The man fell, screaming. The second man almost tripped over him as he ran at her, and that gave Gabriella the moment she needed to step forward with a stopping kick, planting her boot in his chest to halt his advance before smashing his nose with a pommel.

She jinked past them, not wanting to waste the time to either see how wounded they were or finish them off; they'd been put in her way to delay her, and she wasn't going to let that happen.

She ran up the steps. If nothing else, she would get a better view of the surrounding area and might be able to spot her quarry. The wood was discoloured, and the dampness that tainted it was slick. Gabriella had to pull herself up by the wooden frame as much as run up the steps.

At the far end of the roof, the man in charcoal was just dropping out of sight. Gabriella sprinted across the tiles in pursuit, as the man ran across the next roof.

The pitch-covered planking was wet from the new snow, but at least the heat rising from inside the building meant it hadn't frozen over.

Gabriella dropped off the edge without thinking, the landing on the lower roof jarring her from heels to hips. She stumbled, but kept running. Ahead, the man scrambled up a wooden ladder, pausing halfway to look over his shoulder. He redoubled his speed, and disappeared up on to a higher roof. Gabriella reached the foot of the ladder and hesitated. If he was waiting for her up there, he could easily push her off to her death. On the other hand, if he was afraid of getting caught, hopefully he had kept running, and she would lose him if she didn't climb. So she climbed.

He was almost at the opposite edge, where there seemed to be a gap before a boathouse. A narrow street must run between the buildings there, probably with a slipway from the next boatyard. Gabriella kept going, but suddenly the tile under her leading foot gave way with a crack.

Panicked, her heart in her throat, she flung herself forward, grabbing at the roof as the rotted beam under the tiles collapsed. Gabriella rolled and was off again as a shower of wreckage clattered an awfully long way down inside the building.

The man had extended his lead, so she had to really push herself to keep up. She was running so hard that she barely had enough energy left to smile, as she saw the wide gap between the buildings ahead. At the end of the boathouse roof there was a full street before the next building. There was no way the fleeing man could jump across that the way he had jumped the narrow cuttings so far.

Nobody seemed to have told him about the physical impossibility of such a leap, as, incredibly, he accelerated off the edge of the roof. She darted forward, careful to slow and not repeat his suicidal error. Before she reached the edge, she saw the man's left hand reach out even though he was still yards from the other side of the road. Too late Gabriella realised that he wasn't jumping for the gable opposite. He was jumping for the block and tackle that jutted out from the wall halfway down, his left hand catching the rope just below the block.

He swung around the rope as it began to carry him the rest of the way across the street, his right hand coming up. At the last instant, she saw the saw the glint of the crossbow's iron lath, just as his fingers clenched on the trigger bar. Arcing backwards up towards the gable, he loosed a quarrel at her.

Gabriella was already diving before the bolt was launched, flying headlong towards the shelter of a chimney. There was no sudden pain beyond that in her elbows and knees as they hit the tiles, so she knew the bolt had missed.

Looking up, she saw the man let go of the rope at the high point of its arc, and fall backwards towards the opposite roof. He hit with a crack she could almost feel, let alone hear, and rolled, coming up into a run.

Free of his weight, the block hanging from the yardarm swung back towards her and Gabriella leapt. Something felt as if it jerked her arms with the intent of pulling them out of their sockets. Screaming in pain, she was forced to let go, and then the other roof was rising to slam into her.

She rolled onto her back, tasting blood, and staggered to her feet. She stumbled off after the fugitive, drawing her sword. She held no illusions that it would be any use against his crossbow, but the feel of having anything with which to defend herself made her feel a little better.

The fugitive was ahead, but hadn't looked round. He held the crossbow in one hand, and dashed for a wooden scaffold that looked uncomfortably like a gallows. There, he wrapped his hands and knees around a rope dangling off the far end of the building. Gabriella started running for it, and peered over the edge. The man was just disappearing inside the building. Gabriella took hold of the rope, and got herself onto it.

She slid down to a pair of large double doors belonging to a warehouse. A smaller door set into one of them was ajar. Gabriella pushed through. The warehouse was half empty, the remaining crates bearing rough scrawls identifying their ownership. Bare wooden scaffolds and stairs led up to a catwalk halfway up the wall. The vast space was dark and gloomy, filled with enough pools of shadow to hide an army of ambushers. It also stank of mould and dampness.

There was plenty of dust on the floor, so it was easy to make out the fugitive's tracks. Trying her best to stick to the shadows herself, so as not to make an easy target, Gabriella crept along after the footprints.

The tracks led to a trapdoor near the rear of the warehouse. Gabriella listened for any sign of the man. There was none. If the cellar was just a bolt-hole, well even a cornered rat will fight, and the man she was chasing had already showed willing to shoot at her. On the other hand, if there was a tunnel to a neighbouring building, or to Kalten's poor excuse for a sewer system, he could be long gone.

She looked around, and spotted a piece of wood broken off from a crate. She picked it up, opened the trapdoor and tossed it down into the hole, listening for any reaction. There was none, but the wood sounded as if it had hit something very softly and quietly just before hitting the sewer floor. Taking a chance, Gabriella leapt into the hole rather than climbing down the ladder.

He was waiting for her ten feet down. If she had taken the ladder down she would have got his knives in her back. As it was, he got both her boots in the head, and they tumbled and rolled. The knives clattered into the ink-black darkness of the sewer, but Gabriella kept hold of his tunic so she knew where he was. She punched him repeatedly before he could recover, then hauled him to his knees and smacked his head against the slick walls until he stopped moving.

Shaking as she recovered her breath, she leaned against the wall. Was this the man who had shot Rhodon, or just a random sinner? Three people had attacked her as she pursued him, and at least two of them had done so specifically to end that pursuit. That fact suggested that he was more than a man taking an illicit drink.

Now her problem was going to be hauling him back up the ladder to the warehouse.

For more information on this
and other titles visit...

Abaddon
Books

Price: £6.99 ★ ISBN: 978-1-905437-54-2

Price: $7.99 ★ ISBN: 978-1-905437-54-2

Price: £6.99 ★ ISBN: 978-1-905437-87-0

Price: $7.99 ★ ISBN: 978-1-905437-87-0

PAX BRITANNIA

UNNATURAL HISTORY

Jonathan Green

Price: £6.99 ★ ISBN: 978-1-905437-10-8

Price: $7.99 ★ ISBN: 978-1-905437-10-8

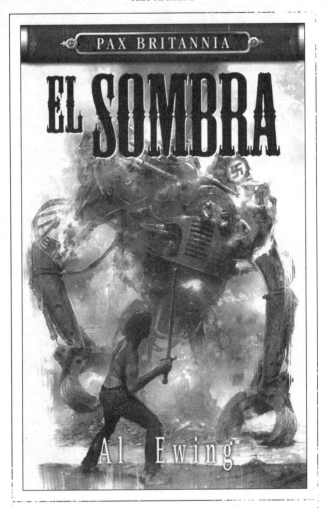

PAX BRITANNIA

EL SOMBRA

Al Ewing

Price: £6.99 ★ ISBN: 978-1-905437-34-4

Price: $7.99 ★ ISBN: 978-1-905437-34-4

PAX BRITANNIA

LEVIATHAN RISING

JONATHAN GREEN

Price: £6.99 ★ ISBN: 978-1-905437-60-3

Price: $7.99 ★ ISBN: 978-1-905437-60-3

Coming Soon

Price: £6.99 ★ ISBN: 978-1-905437-86-3

Price: $7.99 ★ ISBN: 978-1-905437-86-3